MY MAN BOVANNE
Toni Cade Bambara's feisty woman shows the younger generation that love—and sex— don't stop at sixty.

SHILOH
Bobbie Ann Mason reveals the unbridgeable gap between husband and wife.

BEG, SL TOG, INC, CONT, REP
Amy Hempel portrays a woman desperately trying to knit together her torn emotions and tangled life.

HOW TO BECOME A WRITER
Lorrie Moore takes a wry look at the agony (mostly) and ecstasy (sometimes) of choosing to write.

IT'S JUST ANOTHER DAY IN BIG BEAR CITY, CALIFORNIA
Ann Beattie combines a recalcitrant Coke machine and flying saucers in an outrageous West Coast slice of life.

Witty and wise, these stories are just a sample of what you will find in this wonderful anthology.

NEW WOMEN AND
NEW FICTION

SUSAN CAHILL has taught literature at various colleges in New York City and has edited a number of anthologies, incl… *Women & Fiction*, al… She is co-author (wi… *Guide to Ireland* and… appears yearly. Her …

New Women
and
New Fiction

Short Stories
Since the Sixties

Edited and with an Introduction by
Susan Cahill

A MENTOR BOOK

NEW AMERICAN LIBRARY

NEW YORK AND SCARBOROUGH, ONTARIO

ACKNOWLEDGMENTS

"The Shawl" by Cynthia Ozick. This story first appeared in *The New Yorker*. Copyright © 1984 by Cynthia Ozick. Reprinted by permission of Cynthia Ozick and her agents, Raines & Raines.

"Last Courtesies" by Ella Leffland. From LAST COURTESIES AND OTHER STORIES by Ella Leffland. Copyright © 1980 by Ella Leffland. Reprinted by permission of Harper & Row, Publishers, Inc.

"Days of Awe" by Joanne Greenberg. This story first appeared in *Ploughshares*. Copyright © 1980 by Joanne Greenberg. Reprinted by permission of Wallace & Sheil Agency, Inc.

"A Walker's Manual" by Bette Pesetsky. From STORIES UP TO A POINT by Bette Pesetsky. Copyright © 1982 by Bette Pesetsky. Reprinted by permission of Alfred A. Knopf, Inc.

"Grow Old Along With Me, The Best Is Yet To Be" by Penelope Lively. From CORRUPTION, published by William Heinemann Ltd. Reprinted by permission of Murray Pollinger.

"Alopecia" by Fay Weldon. From BEST FOR WINTER: *Selections from 25 Years of WINTER'S TALES*, edited by A.D. Maclean. Reprinted by permission of Wallace & Sheil Agency, Inc.

"Victory Over Japan" by Ellen Gilchrist. From VICTORY OVER JAPAN. Copyright © 1983, 1984 by Ellen Gilchrist. Reprinted by permission of Little, Brown and Company.

"Fear" by Sallie Bingham. From THE WAY IT IS NOW by Sallie Bingham. Copyright © 1971 by Sallie Bingham. Reprinted by permission of Viking Penguin Inc.

"Games At Twilight" by Anita Desai. From GAMES AT TWILIGHT AND OTHER STORIES by Anita Desai. Copyright © 1978 by Anita Desai. Reprinted by permission of Harper & Row, Publishers, Inc.

"My Man Bovanne" by Toni Cade Bambara. From GORILLA, MY LOVE by Toni Cade Bambara. Copyright © 1971 by Toni Cade Bambara. Reprinted by permission of Random House, Inc.

(The following page constitutes an extension of this copyright page.)

MENTOR TRADEMARK REG. U.S. PAT. OFF. AND FOREIGN COUNTRIES
REGISTERED TRADEMARK—MARCA REGISTRADA
HECHO EN CHICAGO, U.S.A.

SIGNET, SIGNET CLASSIC, MENTOR, PLUME, MERIDIAN
and NAL BOOKS are published *in the United States* by
New American Library, 1633 Broadway, New York, New York 10019,
in Canada by The New American Library of Canada Limited,
81 Mack Avenue, Scarborough, Ontario M1I 1M8

First Printing, June, 1986

2 3 4 5 6 7 8 9

PRINTED IN THE UNITED STATES OF AMERICA

For
Renée Wiener

Contents

Introduction

Genius tends to take your breath away. Prepare, reader, for breathlessness.

The contents of this book may at first take you by surprise simply because the names of some of the writers are not well known. Ellen Wilbur and her beautiful story "Faith" come to mind. But most of all it is the talent of these twenty-one writers, its rock-like strength, that astounds. The qualities of their art are originality, a brave, hard irony, and a liberating comic sense that is solidly based, like all good comedy must be, on a serious understanding of life.

Where, you might ask, have these writers been hiding themselves? The question is off-target. What we must ask is why have these writers been hidden away, like so many difficult daughters in a medieval fortress? With few exceptions, their books are not available in most bookstores, they are neither advertised nor kept in print by their publishers, their fiction seldom appears in the so-called "women's magazines," and it is rarely included in the syllabi or anthologies used in college English courses.

Somehow, artists keep faith, as do their disciples. The conspiracy of neglect does not reach all corners, the joke is finally on the difficult daughters' captors. For among working writers and diligent readers of fiction, names such as Bobbie Ann Mason, Ella Leffland, Toni Cade Bambara and Mary Robison are not forgotten even long after the rave reviews of their first books, after the prestigious literary awards and nominations for awards, after their first books have been let go out of print. The serious reading public, that vast intelligent audience for good fiction so ignored by the dungeon-keepers, the shredders, and the accountants, remembers. This book is for us, in honor of our good memories, which are nourished along the way by magazines such as *Ploughshares*, publishing programs such as Vintage's Contemporary Fiction series, and bookstores like Womanbooks in New York City.

This book is also for the many readers who have enjoyed the first two volumes of *Women & Fiction* to which the present volume is a worthy sequel. The time is perfect for a new collection of women writers. By now the short story renaissance is common knowledge. What is more apparent every year is the abundance of first-rate women writers at the center of this movement within contemporary literary history. *New Women & New Fiction: Short Stories Since The Sixties* includes those writers who have been published and acclaimed for the most part since the sixties, though a few wrote earlier, for example, Cynthia Ozick; it includes those writers who, in most cases, were born or were growing up during and just after the second world war; there are a few here who, born in the fifties, were children during the years of the Vietnam War (Jayne Anne Phillips, Lorrie Moore, Amy Hempel). All of these women, whether they are pushing thirty or forty, or are past fifty, have a strong and persevering history as writers. Many of them (Joy Williams, Cynthia Ozick, Anne Tyler, Fay Weldon, Mary Robison) have been called (by first-rate male writers and editors such as Richard Yates, John Updike, Gordon Lish, William Abrahams) the finest writers being published in America and England today. Their praise is clearly a result of the artist's unfailing taste for the strong voice and clear vision: for a passionate moral force.

The writers and the stories you are about to read deserve their reputation. Like their predecessors in *Women & Fiction* 1 and 2, they are quite simply extraordinary. Unlike their predecessors their style is sometimes minimalist, their humor deadpan; but their sympathy, their love for their characters, covers a range that transcends anyone's time or generation. What these women writers have to say about the ways men and women live together now, about our births and deaths and rebirths, about our various and diverse paths to a down-to-earth wisdom, is, in this collection, always fresh, sometimes radiant, always true. The stories have been chosen not because they illustrate any ideology, whether that of women as victims or vanquishers or a little bit of both. The only editorial bias these selections reveal is toward the exceptionally well-made, the luminous and moving work of art. Other standards of selection, creating a wide range of plots, have been variety of setting (New England, the New South, the Midwest, New York City, California, Florida, London, India) and diversity of character (married women, divorced women, young mothers, disaffected couples, Joy Williams' magnificent grandfather, lonely single women, mothers and daughters and teen-aged sons, happy lovers and hilarious pessimists.)

The choices have not been easy. Including some writers means, of necessity, excluding others. Except in the obvious case of Anne Tyler, a case of editorial self-indulgence, I have, in general, included the writer whose best or most ongoing and prolific work has been done in the short story rather than the novel. This criterion explains why a novelist such as Gail Godwin is not here, nor Rosellen Brown, Louise Erdrich, Renata Adler, Robb Forman Dew, Carolyn Chute, Susan Kenney, Elizabeth Taylor, Elizabeth Jolley, and Mary Gordon. Then, too, other writers whose dates make them eligible for inclusion in the present volume (for example, Alice Walker, Edna O'Brien, Tillie Olsen, Margaret Drabble, Elizabeth Cullinan, Grace Paley) have already appeared in either the first or second volume of *Women & Fiction*. (To this editor, the three separate volumes of *Women & Fiction*—the first one was published in 1975—comprise one large and rich assembly of writers who are women, whose writing is a source of joy and freedom.) Perhaps the hardest choice has been to select the one story by a given writer that best demonstrates her talent and best contributes to the range of experience and tone one tries to represent in any collection. The very pleasant but difficult truth is that I liked all the stories in Lorrie Moore's first collection, *Self-Help*, all of Joy Williams' *Taking Care*, all of Bobbie Ann Mason's *Shiloh*, every word put to paper by Mary Robison. In the end, playing favorites, picking the one story that still after three or more readings takes your breath away, haunts you for at least a few months or a year after you first read it, is what anthology-making is about.

As in *Women & Fiction* 1 & 2, I have preceded each story in this collection with a brief introduction containing a few biographical details, the titles of the writer's books, and a small sampling of commentary on that writer's work by other professional writers of fiction and criticism. Usually, working writers have a finer sense of what a writer is about than many of the standard reviewers one reads in the daily newspaper. From some reviewers, for instance, we often get put-downs or sociological labels placed on young writers such as Ann Beattie, Lorrie Moore, or Mary Robison, who are dubbed Spokeswomen for the Bored Generation, their fiction dismissed on the grounds of its so-called nihilism. Writers of fiction, however, make sharper readers in many cases than reviewers. Because of who they are and how they spend their time, they perceive the charity that inspires another writer's attention and commitment to the concrete, to the everyday and intimate, to the ordinary moment, to this thing, to that person, to all that is seemingly insignificant. They know that less is often honest, more is often a sign of the big lie. That is why, in quite a few cases, I have quoted the comments of working novelists and professional critics, male and female, on the women writers included in this book: they can recognize the actual triumphs that are so often brought to life in our contemporary, so-called nihilistic fiction. In the face of a writer's deliberate compression, they are not so quick to shout "Despair, again, and in one so young!" Such readers and writers understand the implications for all fiction writers of what Elias Canetti, winner of the 1981 Nobel Prize for Literature, has written in *The Conscience of Words:*

Among the most sinister phenomena in intellectual history is the avoidance of the concrete. People have had a conspicuous tendency to go first after the most remote things, ignoring everything that they stumble over close by. The elan of outgoing gestures, the boldness and adventure of expeditions to faraway places camouflage their motives. The not infrequent goal is to avoid what lies near because we are not up to it. We sense danger and prefer other and unknown perils. . . . The situation of mankind today, as we all know, is so serious that we have to turn to what is closest and most concrete. We don't even have an inkling of how much time is left for us to focus on the most painful things. And yet, it could very well be that our fate is contingent on certain hard knowledge that we do not yet have.

The best writers, especially the best women writers, have always been up to what lies nearest, have always had the courage of the concrete. The twenty-one writers represented in this collection are not afraid of what is smallest or closest, and they are not afraid to tell us how they feel.

CYNTHIA OZICK was born in the Bronx, New York, in 1928. A graduate of New York University, she has lived for many years in New Rochelle, New York. She is married and is the mother of a daughter who is now in college. She is the author of two novels, *Trust* and *The Cannibal Galaxy*; three volumes of short stories, *The Pagan Rabbi*, *Bloodshed*, and *Levitation*; and *Art & Ardor*, a collection of essays. She has received many honors and awards and the highest critical praise. In 1984, when her short story "Rosa" won first prize in the O. Henry Prize Story Awards, the editor of that series, William Abrahams, wrote, "I would not hesitate to name Cynthia Ozick as one of the three greatest living American writers of short fiction." Writing in *The New York Times Book Review*, Edmund White extolled Miss Ozick's fiction in a similar vein: "Miss Ozick strikes me as the best American writer to have emerged in recent years. Her artistic strength derives from her moral energy, for Miss Ozick is not an esthete. Judaism has given to her what Catholicism gave to Flannery O'Connor—authority, penetration and indignation."

Cynthia Ozick

THE SHAWL

Stella, cold, cold, the coldness of hell. How they walked on the roads together, Rosa with Magda curled up between sore breasts, Magda wound up in the shawl. Sometimes Stella carried Magda. But she was jealous of Magda. A thin girl of fourteen, too small, with thin breasts of her own, Stella wanted to be wrapped in a shawl, hidden away, asleep, rocked by the march, a baby, a round infant in arms. Magda took Rosa's nipple, and Rosa never stopped walking, a walking cradle. There was not enough milk; sometimes Magda sucked air; then she screamed. Stella was ravenous. Her knees were tumors on sticks, her elbows chicken bones.

Rosa did not feel hunger; she felt light, not like someone walking but like someone in a faint, in trance, arrested in a fit, someone who is already a floating angel, alert and seeing everything, but in the air, not there, not touching the road. As if teetering on the tips of her fingernails. She looked into Magda's face through a gap in the shawl: a squirrel in a nest, safe, no one could reach her inside the little house of a shawl's windings. The face, very round, a pocket mirror of a face: but it was not Rosa's bleak complexion, dark like cholera, it was another kind of face altogether, eyes blue as air, smooth feathers of hair nearly as yellow as the Star sewn into Rosa's coat. You could think she was one of *their* babies.

Rosa, floating, dreamed of giving Magda away in one of the villages. She could leave the line for a minute and push Magda into the hands of any woman on the side of the road. But if she moved out of line they might shoot. And even if she fled the line for half a second and pushed the shawl-bundle at a stranger, would the woman take it? She might be surprised, or afraid; she might drop the shawl, and Magda would fall out and strike her head and die. The little round head. Such a good child, she gave up screaming, and sucked now only for the taste of the drying nipple itself. The neat grip of the tiny gums. One mite of a tooth tip sticking up in the bottom gum, how shining, an elfin tombstone of white marble gleaming there. Without complaining, Magda relinquished Rosa's teats, first the left, then the right; both were cracked, not a sniff of milk. The duct-crevice extinct, a dead volcano, blind eye, chill hole, so Magda took the corner of the shawl and milked it instead. She sucked and sucked, flooding the threads with wetness. The shawl's good flavor, milk of linen.

It was a magic shawl, it could nourish an infant for three days and three nights. Magda did not die, she stayed alive, although very quiet. A peculiar smell, of cinnamon and almonds, lifted out of her mouth. She held her eyes open every moment, forgetting how to blink or nap, and Rosa and sometimes Stella studied their blueness. On the road they raised one burden of a leg after another and studied Magda's face. "Aryan," Stella said, in a voice grown as thin as a string; and Rosa thought how Stella gazed at Magda like a young cannibal. And the time that Stella said "Aryan," it sounded to Rosa as if Stella had really said "Let us devour her."

But Magda lived to walk. She lived that long, but she did not walk very well, partly because she was only fifteen months old, and partly because the spindles of her legs could not hold up her fat belly. It was fat with air, full and round. Rosa gave almost all her food to Magda, Stella gave nothing; Stella was ravenous, a growing child herself, but not growing much. Stella did not menstruate. Rosa did not menstruate. Rosa was ravenous, but also not; she learned from Magda how to drink the taste of a finger in one's mouth. They were in a place without pity, all pity was annihilated in Rosa, she looked at Stella's bones without pity. She was sure that Stella was waiting for Magda to die so she could put her teeth into the little thighs.

Rosa knew Magda was going to die very soon; she should have been dead already, but she had been buried away deep inside the magic shawl, mistaken there for the shivering mound of Rosa's breasts; Rosa clung to the shawl as if it covered only herself. No one took it away from her. Magda was mute. She never cried. Rosa hid her in the barracks, under the shawl, but she knew that one day someone would inform; or one day someone, not even Stella, would steal Magda to eat her. When Magda began to walk, Rosa knew that Magda was going to die very soon, something would happen. She was afraid to fall asleep; she slept with the weight of her thigh on Magda's body; she was afraid she would smother Magda under her thigh. The weight of Rosa was becoming less and less; Rosa and Stella were slowly turning into air.

Magda was quiet, but her eyes were horribly alive, like blue tigers. She watched. Sometimes she laughed—it seemed a laugh, but how could it be? Magda had never seen anyone laugh. Still, Magda laughed at her shawl when the wind blew its corners, the bad wind with pieces of black in it, that made Stella's and Rosa's eyes tear. Magda's eyes were always clear and tearless. She watched like a tiger. She guarded her shawl. No one could touch it; only Rosa could touch it. Stella was not allowed. The shawl was Magda's own baby, her pet, her little sister. She tangled herself up in it and sucked on one of the corners when she wanted to be very still.

Then Stella took the shawl away and made Magda die.

Afterward Stella said: "I was cold."

And afterward she was always cold, always. The cold went into her heart: Rosa saw that Stella's heart was cold. Magda flopped onward with her little pencil legs scribbling this way and that, in search of the shawl; the pencils faltered at the barracks opening, where the light began. Rosa saw and pursued. But already Magda was in the square outside the barracks, in the jolly light. It was the roll-call arena. Every morning Rosa had to conceal Magda under the shawl against a wall of the barracks and go out and stand in the arena with Stella and hundreds of others, sometimes for hours, and Magda, deserted, was quiet under the shawl, sucking on her corner. Every day Magda was silent, and so she did not die. Rosa saw that today Magda was going to die, and at the same time a fearful joy ran in Rosa's two palms, her fingers were on fire, she was astonished, febrile: Magda, in the sunlight, swaying on her pencil legs, was howling. Ever since the drying up of Rosa's nipples, ever since Magda's last scream on the road, Magda had been devoid of any syllable; Magda was a mute. Rosa believed that something had gone wrong with her vocal cords, with her windpipe, with the cave of her larynx; Magda was defective, without a voice; perhaps she was deaf; there might be something amiss with her intelligence; Magda was dumb. Even the laugh that came when the ash-stippled wind made a clown out of Magda's shawl was only the air-blown showing of her teeth. Even when the lice, head lice and body lice, crazed her so that she became as wild as one of the big rats that plundered the barracks at daybreak looking for carrion, she rubbed and scratched and kicked and bit and rolled without a whimper. But now Magda's mouth was spilling a long viscous rope of clamor.

"Maaaa—"

It was the first noise Magda had ever sent out from her throat since the drying up of Rosa's nipples.

"Maaaa . . . aaa!"

Again! Magda was wavering in the perilous sunlight of the arena, scribbling on such pitiful little bent shins. Rosa saw. She saw that Magda was grieving for the loss of her shawl, she saw that Magda was going to die. A tide of commands hammered in Rosa's nipples: Fetch, get, bring! But she did not know which to go after first, Magda or the shawl. If she jumped out into the arena to snatch Magda up, the howling would not stop, because Magda would still not have the shawl; but if she ran back into the barracks to find the shawl, and if she found it, and if she came after Magda holding it and shaking it, then she would get Magda back, Magda would put the shawl in her mouth and turn dumb again.

Rosa entered the dark. It was easy to discover the shawl. Stella was heaped under it, asleep in her thin bones. Rosa tore the shawl free and flew—she could fly, she was only air—into the arena. The sunheat murmured of another life, of butterflies in summer. The light was placid, mellow. On the other side of the steel fence, far away, there were green meadows speckled with dandelions and deep-colored violets; beyond them, even farther, inno- cent tiger lilies, tall, lifting their orange bonnets. In the barracks they spoke of "flowers," of "rain": excrement, thick turd-braids, and the slow stinking maroon waterfall that slunk down from the upper bunks, the stink mixed with a bitter fatty floating smoke that greased Rosa's skin. She stood for an instant at the margin of the arena. Some- times the electricity inside the fence would seem to hum; even Stella said it was only an imagining, but Rosa heard real sounds in the wire: grainy sad voices. The farther she was from the fence, the more clearly the voices crowded at her. The lamenting voices strummed so convincingly, so passionately, it was impossible to suspect them of being phantoms. The voice told her to hold up the shawl, high; the voices told her to shake it, to whip with it, to unfurl it like a flag. Rosa lifted, shook, whipped, unfurled. Far off, very far, Magda leaned across her air-fed belly, reaching out with the rods of her arms. She was high up, elevated, riding someone's shoulder. But the shoulder that carried Magda was not coming toward Rosa and the shawl, it was drifting away, the speck of Magda was moving more and more into the smoky distance. Above the shoulder a hel- met glinted. The light tapped the helmet and sparkled it into a goblet. Below the helmet a black body like a domino and a pair of black boots hurled themselves in the direction of the electrified fence. The electric voices began to chatter wildly. "Maamaa, maaamaaa," they all hummed together. How far Magda was from Rosa now, across the whole square, past a dozen barracks, all the way on the other side! She was no bigger than a moth.

All at once Magda was swimming through the air. The whole of Magda traveled through loftiness. She looked like a butterfly touching a silver vine. And the moment Magda's feathered round head and her pencil legs and balloonish belly and zigzag arms splashed against the fence, the steel voices went mad in their growling, urging Rosa to run and run to the spot where Magda had fallen from her flight against the electrified fence; but of course Rosa did not obey them. She only stood, because if she ran they would shoot, and if she tried to pick up the sticks of Magda's body they would shoot, and if she let the wolf's screech ascending now through the ladder of her skeleton break out, they would shoot; so she took Magda's shawl and filled her own mouth with it, stuffed it in and stuffed it in, until she was swallowing up the wolf's screech and tasting the cinnamon and almond depth of Magda's saliva; and Rosa drank Magda's shawl until it dried.

ELLA LEFFLAND was born in 1932 in Martinez, California, the hometown she brought to life in her third novel, *Rumors of Peace*. After graduating from San Jose State where she studied painting and creative writing, she worked as a mess girl on a Norwegian tramp steamer, a door-to-door salesperson, a Kelly Girl, and a researcher for *Encyclopaedia Brittanica*. Since the publication and strong reception of her first novel, *Mrs. Munck* (1970), she has been able to support herself on her writing alone. (Of the writing life Ella Leffland has commented, "It's harder than digging a ditch and as necessary as opium.") If there were a listing of the ten best fictions of the seventies, Miss Leffland's third novel would, in the opinion of this editor, surely be included. The time is 1941, just after Pearl Harbor; the heroine is eleven-year-old Suse Hansen, as appealing a junior-high school girl as may be found in current fiction. Suse expects her hometown on the West Coast to be bombed at any minute. Despite her terror and fear of the Enemy, she comes to know a compassion for all the victims of war that is profoundly affecting. This novel has been compared to John Knowles' *A Separate Peace* and Carson McCullers' *A Member of the Wedding*. Miss Leffland's short stories have appeared in *The New Yorker*, *Harper's* magazine, *Cosmopolitan*, *The Atlantic Monthly*, and *Mademoiselle*. One of her stories appeared in *The Best Short Stories of 1970* and she shared first prize in the 1977 *O. Henry Prize Stories* collection for "Last Courtesies," the story included here. Of her collection *Last Courtesies*, the critic John Romano wrote, "There is not a contemporary writer of short stories from whom truth of feeling, splendidness of insight, and a human beauty both aching and real can more confidently be expected."

Ella Leffland

LAST COURTESIES

"Lillian, you're too polite," Vladimir kept telling her.

She did not think so. Perhaps she was not one to return shoves in the bus line, but she did fire off censorious glares; and, true, she never yelled at the paper boy who daily flung her *Chronicle* to a rainsoaked fate, but she did beckon him to her door and remind him of his responsibilities. If she was always the last to board the bus, if she continued to dry out the paper on the stove, that was the price she must pay for observing the minimal courtesy the world owed itself if it was not to go under. Civilized she was. Excessively polite, no.

In any case, even if she had wanted to, she could not change at this stage of life. Nor had Aunt Bedelia ever changed in any manner. Not that she really compared herself to her phenomenal aunt, who, when she had died four months ago at the age of ninety-one, was still a captivating woman; no faded great beauty (the family ran to horse faces), but elegant, serenely vivid. Any other old lady who dressed herself in long gowns circa 1910 would have appeared a mere oddity; but under Bedelia's antiquated hairdo sat a brain; in her gnarled, almond-scented fingers lay direction. She spoke of Bach, of the Russian novelists, of her garden and the consolations of nature; never of her arthritis, the fallen ranks of her friends, or the metamorphosis of the neighborhood, which now featured motorcycles roaring alongside tin cans and blackened banana peels. At rare moments a sigh escaped her lips, but who knew if it was for her crippled fingers (she had been a consummate pianist) or a repercussion from the street? It was bad form, ungallant, to put too fine a point on life's discomfitures.

Since Bedelia's death the flat was lonely; lonely yet no longer private, since a supremely kinetic young woman, herself a music lover, had moved in upstairs. With no one to talk to, with thuds and acid rock resounding from above, Lillian drifted (too often, she knew) into the past, fingering its high points. The day, for instance, that Vladimir had entered their lives by way of the Steinway grand (great gleaming relic of better times) which he came to tune. He had burst in, dressed not in a customary suit but in garage mechanic's overalls and rubber thong sandals, a short square man with the large disheveled head of a furious gnome, who embellished his labors with glorious run-throughs of Bach and Scarlatti, but whose speech, though a dark bog of Slavic intonations, was distinctly, undeniably obscene. Aunt Bedelia promptly invited him to dinner the following week. Lillian stood astonished, but reminded herself that her aunt was a sheltered soul unfamiliar with scabrous language, whereas she, Lillian, lived more in the great world, riding the bus every day to the Opera House, where she held the position of switchboard operator (Italian and German required). The following morning at work, in fact, she inquired about Vladimir. Several people there knew of him. A White Russian, he had fled to Prague with his parents in 1917, then fled again twenty years later, eventually settling in San Francisco, where he quickly earned the reputation of an excellent craftsman and a violent crackpot. He abused clients who had no knowledge of their pianos' intestines, and had once been taken to court by an acquaintance whom he had knocked down during a conversation about Wagner. He wrote scorching letters of general advice to the newspapers; with arms like a windmill he confronted mothers who allowed their children to drop potato chips on the sidewalk; he kept a bucket of accumulated urine to throw on dog-walkers who were unwary enough to linger with their squatting beasts beneath his window. He had been institutionalized several times.

That night Lillian informed her aunt that Vladimir was brilliant but unsound.

The old woman raised an eyebrow at this.

"For instance," Lillian pursued, "he is actually known to have struck someone down."

"Why?" Her aunt's voice was clear and melodious, with a faint ring of iron.

"It was during a conversation about Wagner. Apparently he disapproves of Wagner."

Her aunt gave a nod of endorsement.

"The man has even had himself committed, aunt. Several times, when he felt he was getting out of hand."

The old woman pondered this. "It shows foresight," she said at length, "and a sense of social responsibility."

Lillian was silent for a moment. Then she pointed out: "He said unspeakable things here."

"They were mutually exclusive terms."

"Let us call them obscenities, then. You may not have caught them."

The old woman rose from her chair and arranged the long skirt of her dove-gray ensemble. "Lillian, one must know when to turn a deaf ear."

"I am apparently not in the know," Lillian said dryly.

"Perhaps it is an instinct." And suddenly she gave her unique smile, which was quite yellow (for she retained her own ancient teeth) but completely beguiling, and added: "In any case, he is of my own generation, Lillian. That counts for a great deal."

"He can't be more than sixty, aunt."

"It is close enough. Anyway, he is quite wrinkled. Also, he is a man of integrity."

"How can you possibly know that?"

"It is my instinct." And gently touching her niece's cheek, she said goodnight and went to her room, which peacefully overlooked the back garden, away from the street noises.

Undressing in her own smaller room, Lillian reflected, not for the first time, that though it was Bedelia who had remained unwed—Lillian herself having been married and widowed during the war—it was she, Lillian, who felt more the old maid, who seemed more dated, in a stale, fusty way, with her tight 1950s hairdo, her plain wool suits and practical support stockings . . . but then, she led a practical life . . . it was she who was trampled in the bus queue and who sat down to a hectic switchboard, who swept the increasingly filthy sidewalk and dealt with the sullen butcher and careless paper boy—or tried to . . . it seemed she was a middlewoman, a hybrid, too worldly to partake of aunt's immense calm, too seclusive to sharpen herself on the changing ways . . . aunt had sealed herself off in a lofty, gracious world; she lived for it, she would have died for it if it came to that . . . but what could she, Lillian, die for? . . . she fit in nowhere, she thought, climbing into bed, and thirty years from now she would not have aged into the rare creature aunt was—last survivor of a fair, legendary breed, her own crimped hairdo as original as the Edwardian pouf, her boxy suits as awesome as the floor-sweeping gowns—no, she would just be a peculiar old leftover in a room somewhere. For aunt was grande dame, bluestocking, and virgin in one, and they didn't make that kind anymore; they didn't make those eyes anymore, large, hooded, a deep glowing violet. It was a hue that had passed. . . . And she closed her own eyes, of candid, serviceable gray, said the Lord's Prayer, and prepared to act as buffer between her elite relative and the foul-mouthed old refugee.

Aunt Bedelia prepared the dinner herself, taking great pains; then she creaked into her wet garden with an umbrella and picked her finest blooms for a centerpiece; and finally, over the knobbed, arthritic joint of her ring finger, she twisted a magnificent amethyst usually reserved for Christmas, Easter, and Bach's birthday. These touches Lillian expected to be lost on their wild-eyed guest, but Vladimir kissed the festive hand with a cavalier click of his sandals, acknowledged the flowers with a noisy inhalation of his large, hairy nostrils, and ate his food with admirable if strained refinement. During coffee he capsized his cup, but this was only because he and Bedelia were flying from Bavarian spas and Italian sea resorts to music theory, Turgenev, and God knows what else—Lillian could hardly follow—and then, urged by aunt, he jumped from the table, rolled up the sleeves of his overalls, and flung himself into Bach, while aunt, her fingers stiffly moving up and down on her knee, threw back her head and entered some region of flawless joy. At eleven o'clock Vladimir wrestled into his red lumber jacket, expressed his delight with the evening, and slapped down the steps to his infirm 1938 Buick. Not one vulgar word had escaped his lips.

Nor in the seven following years of his friendship with Bedelia was this precedent ever broken. Even the night when some drunk sent an empty pint of muscatel crashing through the window, Vladimir's respect for his hostess was so great that all scurrility was plucked from his wrath. However, when he and Lillian happened to be alone together he slipped right back into the belching, offensive mannerisms for which he was known. She did not mention this to her aunt, who cherished the idea that he was very fond of Lillian.

"You know how he detests opera," the old lady would assure her, "and yet he has never alluded to the fact that you work at the Opera House and hold the form in esteem."

"A magnanimous gesture," Lillian said, smiling.

"For Vladimir, yes."

And after a moment's thought, Lillian had to agree. Her aunt apparently understood Vladimir perfectly, and he her. She wondered if this insight was due to their shared social origins, their bond of elevated interests, or their more baroque twinhood of eccentricity. Whatever it was, the couple thrived, sometimes sitting up till midnight with their sherry and sheet music, sometimes, when the Buick was well, motoring (Bedelia's term) into the countryside and then winding homeward along the darkening sea, in a union of perfect silence, as the old lady put it.

Bedelia died suddenly, with aplomb, under Toscanini's direction. Beethoven's Ninth was on the phonograph; the chorus had just scaled the great peak before its heart-bursting cascade into the finale; aunt threw her head back to savor the moment, and was gone.

The next morning Lillian called Vladimir. He shrieked,

he wept, he banged the receiver on the table; and for ten days, helpless and broken, he spent every evening at the home of his departed love while Lillian, herself desolated, tried to soothe him. She felt certain he would never regain the strength to insult his clients again, much less strike anyone to the ground, but gradually he mended, and the coarseness, the irascibility flooded back, much worse than in the past.

For Bedelia's sake—of that Lillian was sure—he forced himself to take an interest in her welfare, which he would express in eruptions of advice whenever he telephoned. "You want to lead a decent life, Lillian, you give them hell! They sell you a bad cut of meat, throw it in the butcher's face! You get shortchanged, make a stink! You're too soft! Give them the finger, Lillian!"

"Yes, of course," she would murmur.

"For your aunt I was a gentleman, but now she's gone, who appreciates? A gentleman is a fool, a gentleman's balls are cut off! I know how to take care of myself, I am in an armored tank! And you should be too. Or find a protector. Get married!"

"Pardon?" she asked.

"Marry!"

"I have no desire to marry, Vladimir."

"Desire! Desire! It's a world for your desires? Think of your scalp! You need a protector, now Bedelia's gone!"

"Aunt was not my protector," she said patiently.

"Of course she was! And mine too!"

Lillian shifted her weight from one foot to the other and hoped he would soon run down.

"You want to get off the phone, don't you? Why don't you say, Vladimir get the shit off the phone, I'm busy! Don't be a doormat! Practice on me or you'll come to grief! What about that sow upstairs, have you given her hell yet? No, no, of course not! Jesus bleeding Christ, I give up!" And he slammed the receiver down.

Lillian had in fact complained. Allowing her new neighbor time to settle in, she had at first endured—through apparently rugless floorboards—the girl's music, her door slams, her crashing footfall which was a strange combination of scurry and thud, her deep hollow brays of laughter and shrieks of "You're *kidding!*" and "Fan*tas*tic!"—all this usually accompanied by a masculine voice and tread (varying from night to night, Lillian could not help but notice) until finally, in the small hours, directly above Bedelia's room, where Lillian now slept, ears stuffed with cotton, the night was crowned by a wild creaking of bedsprings and the racketing of the headboard against the wall. At last, chancing to meet her tormentor on the front steps (she was not the Amazon her noise indicated, but a small, thin creature nervously chewing gum with staccato snaps), Lillian decided to speak; but before she could, the girl cried: "Hi! I'm Jody—from upstairs?" with a quick, radiant smile that heartened the older woman in a way that the hair and hemline did not. Clad in a tiny, childish dress that barely reached her hip sockets, she might have been a prematurely worn twenty or an adolescent thirty—dark circles hung beneath the eyes and a deep line was etched between them, but the mouth was babyish, sweet, and the cheeks a glowing pink against the unfortunate mane of brassy hair, dark along its uneven part.

Having responded with her own name (the formal first *and* last) Lillian paused a courteous moment, then began: "I'm glad to have this opportunity of meeting you; I've lived in this flat for twenty-four years, you see . . ." But the eyes opposite, heavily outlined with blue pencil, were already wandering under this gratuitous information. Brevity was clearly the password. "The point is"—restoring attention—"I would appreciate it if you turned down your music after ten P.M. There is a ruling."

"It bugs you?" the girl asked, beginning to dig turbulently through a fringed bag, her gum snaps accelerating with the search.

"Well, it's an old building, and of course if you don't have carpets . . ." She waited to be corroborated in this assumption, but now the girl pulled out her house key with fingers whose nails, bitten to the quick, were painted jet black. Fascinated, Lillian tried not to stare. "Not to worry," the girl assured her with the brief, brilliant smile, plunging the key into the door and bounding inside, "I'll cool it."

"There's something else, I'm afraid. When that door is slammed—"

But the finely arched brows rose with preoccupation; the phone was ringing down from the top of the stairs. "I dig, I dig. Look, hon, my phone's ringing." And closing the door softly, she thundered up the stairs.

After that the phonograph was lowered a little before midnight, but nothing else was changed. Lillian finally called the landlord, a paunchy, sweating man whom she rarely saw, and though she subsequently observed him disappearing into his unruly tenant's flat several evenings a week, the visits were apparently useless. And every time she met the girl, she was greeted with an insufferable "Hi! Have a nice day!"

Unfortunately, Lillian had shared some of her vexation with Vladimir, and whenever he dropped by—less to see her, she knew, than to replenish his memories of Bedelia—his wrath grew terrible under the commotion. On his last visit his behavior had frightened her. "Shut up!" he had screamed, shaking his fist at the ceiling. "Shut up, bitch! Whore!"

"Vladimir, please—this language, just because Bedelia's not here."

"Ah, Bedelia, Bedelia," he groaned.

"She wouldn't have tolerated it."

"She wouldn't have tolerated *that!* Hear the laugh—hee haw, hee haw! Braying ass! Bedelia would have pulverized her with a glance! None of this farting around you go in for!" His large head had suffused with red, his hands were shaking at his sides. "Your aunt was a genius at judging people—they should have lined up the whole fucking rotten city for her to judge!"

"It seems to me that you have always appointed yourself as judge," Lillian said, forcing a smile.

"Yah, but Vladimir is demented, you don't forget? He has it down in black and white! Ah, you think I'm unique, Lillian, but I am one of the many! I am in the swim!" He

came over to her side and put his flushed head close, his small intense eyes piercing hers.

"You read yesterday about the girl they found in an alley not far from here, cut to small bits? Slash! Rip! Finito! And you ask why? Because the world, it is demented! A murder of such blood not even in the headlines and you ask why? Because it is commonplace! Who walks safe on his own street? It is why you need a husband!"

Lillian dropped her eyes, wondering for an embarrassed moment if Vladimir of all people could possibly be hinting at a marital alliance. Suddenly silent, he pulled a wadded handkerchief from his pocket with trembling fingers and wiped his brow. He flicked her a suspicious glance. "Don't look so coy. I'm not in the running. I loathe women—sticky! Full of rubbishy talk!" And once more he threw his head back and began bellowing obscenities at the ceiling.

"It's too much, Vladimir—please! You're not yourself!"

"I *am* myself!"

"Well then, I'm not. I'm tired, I have a splitting headache—"

"You want me to go! Be rude, good! I have better things to do anyway!" And his face still aflame, he struggled into his lumber jacket and flung out the door.

That night her sleep was not only disturbed by the noise, but by her worry over the violence of Vladimir's emotions. At work the next day she reluctantly inquired about her friend, whose antics were usually circulated around the staff but seldom reached her cubicle. For the first time in years, she learned, the weird little Russian had gone right over the edge, flapping newspapers in strangers' faces and ranting about the end of civilization; storming out on tuning jobs and leaving his tools behind, then furiously accusing his clients of stealing them. The opinion was that if he did not commit himself soon, someone else would do it for him.

On the clamorous bus home that night, shoved as usual into the rear, Lillian felt an overwhelming need for Bedelia, for the sound of that clear, well-modulated voice that had always set the world to rights. But she opened her door on silence. She removed her raincoat and sat down in the living room with the damp newspaper. People at work told her she should buy a television set—such a good companion when you lived alone—but she had too long scorned that philistine invention to change now. For that matter, she seldom turned on the radio, and even the newspaper—she ran her eyes over the soggy turmoil of the front page—even the newspaper distressed her. Vladimir was extreme, but he was right: everything was coming apart. Sitting there, she thought she could hear the world's madness—its rudeness, its litter, its murders—beat against the house with the rain. And suddenly she closed her eyes under an intolerable longing for the past: for the peaceful years she had spent in these rooms with Bedelia; and before that, for the face of her young husband, thirty years gone now; and for even earlier days . . . odd, but it never seemed to rain in her youth, the green campus filled the air with dizzying sweetness, she remembered running across the lawns for no reason but that she was twenty and the sun would shine forever. . . .

She gave way to two large tears. Shaken, yet somehow consoled, and at the same time ashamed of her self-indulgence, she went into the kitchen to make dinner. But as she cooked her chop she knew that even this small measure of comfort would be destroyed as soon as her neighbor came banging through the door. Already her neck was tightening against the sound.

But there was no noise at all that night, not until 1 A.M. when the steady ring of the telephone pulled her groggily from bed.

"Listen, you'll kill me—it's Jody, I'm across the bay, and I just flashed on maybe I left the stove burners going."

"Who?" Lillian said, rubbing her eyes, "Jody? How did you get my number?"

"The phone book, why? Listen, the whole dump could catch fire, be a doll and check it out? The back door's unlocked."

Lillian felt a strange little rush of gratitude—that her name given to such seemingly indifferent ears on the steps that day, had been remembered. Then the feeling was replaced by anger; but before she could speak, the girl said, "Listen, hon, thanks a million," and hung up.

Clutching her raincoat around her shoulders, beaming a flashlight before her, Lillian nervously climbed the dark back stairs to her neighbor's door and let herself into the kitchen. Turning on the light, she stood aghast at what she saw: not flames licking the wall, for the burners were off, but grimed linoleum, spilled garbage, a sink of stagnant water. On the puddled table, decorated with a jar of blackened, long-dead daisies, sat a greasy portable television set and a pile of dirty laundry in a litter of cigarette butts, sodden pieces of paper, and the congealed remains of spare ribs. Hesitating, ashamed of her snoopiness, she peered down at the pieces of paper; bills from department stores, including Saks and Magnin's; scattered food stamps; handwritten notes on binder paper, one of which read "Jamie hony theres a piza in the frezzer I love U"—then several big hearts—"Jody." A long brown bug—a cockroach? was crawling across the note, and now she noticed another one climbing over a spare rib. As she stood cringing, she heard rain blowing through an open window somewhere, lashing a shade into frenzies. Going to the bedroom door, which stood ajar, she beamed her flashlight in and switched on the light. Under the window a large puddle was forming on the floor, which was rugless as she had suspected, though half carpeted by strewn clothes. The room was furnished only with a bed whose convulsed, mummy-brown sheets put her in mind of a pesthouse, and a deluxe television set in a rosewood cabinet; but the built-in bookcase was well stocked, and, having shut the window, she ran her eyes over the spines, curious. Many were cheap paperback thrillers, but there was an abundance of great authors: Dostoevski, Dickens, Balzac, Melville. It was odd, she puzzled, that the girl had this taste in literature, yet could not spell the simplest word and had never heard of a comma. As she turned away, her eardrums were shattered by her own scream. A man stood in the doorway.

A boy, actually, she realized through her fright; one of

Jody's more outstanding visitors, always dressed in one of those Mexican shawl affairs and a battered derby hat, from under which butter-yellow locks flowed in profusion, everything at the moment dripping with rain. More embarrassed now than frightened—she had never screamed in her life, or stood before a stranger in her nightgown, and neither had Bedelia—she began pulsating with dignity. "I didn't hear anyone come up the stairs," she indicted him.

"Little cat feet, man," he said with a cavernous yawn. "Where's Jody? Who're you?"

She explained her presence, pulling the raincoat more firmly together across her bosom, but unable to do anything about the expanse of flowered flannel below.

"Jody, she'd forget her ass if it wasn't screwed on," the boy said with a second yawn. His eyes were watery and red, and his nose ran. "If you'll excuse me," she said, going past him. He followed her back into the kitchen and suddenly, with a hostlike warmth that greatly surprised her, he asked, "You want some coffee?"

She declined, saying that she must be going.

At this he heaved a deep, disappointed sigh, which again surprised her, and sank like an invalid into a chair. He was a slight youth with neat little features crowded into the center of his face, giving him, despite his woebegone expression, a pert, fledgling look. In Lillian's day he would have been called a "pretty boy." He would not have been her type at all; she had always preferred the lean profile.

"My name's Jamie," he announced suddenly, with a childlike spontaneity beneath the film of languor; and he proffered his hand.

Gingerly, she took the cold small fingers.

"Hey, really," he entreated. "Stay and rap awhile."

"Rap?"

"Talk, man. Talk to me." And he looked, all at once, so lonely, so forlorn, that even though she was very tired, she felt she must stay a moment longer. Pulling out a chair, she took a temporary, edge-of-the-seat position across the hideous table from him.

He seemed to be gathering his thoughts together. "So what's your bag?" he asked.

She looked at him hopelessly. "My bag?"

"You a housewife? You work?"

"Oh—yes, I work," she said, offended by his bold curiosity, yet grateful against her will to have inspired it.

"What's your name?" he asked.

He was speaking to her as a contemporary; and again, she was both pleased by this and offended by his lack of deference. "Lillian . . . Cronin," she said uncertainly.

"I'm Jamie," he laughed.

"So you mentioned." And thought—Jamie, Jody, the kinds of names you would give pet rabbits. Where were the solid, straightforward names of yesteryear—the Georges and Harolds, the Dorothys and Margarets? What did she have to say to a Jamie in a Mexican shawl and threadbare derby who was now scratching himself all over with little fidgety movements? But she said, breaking the long silence, which he seemed not to notice: "And what is *your* bag, if I may ask?"

He took several moments to answer. "I don't know, man . . . I'm a student of human nature."

"Oh? And where do you study?"

"Not me, man, that's Jody's scene . . . into yoga, alpha waves, the whole bit . . . even studies macrame and World Lit at jay cee . . ."

"Indeed? How interesting. I noticed her books."

"She's a towering intellect." He yawned, his eyes glassy with fatigue. He was scratching himself more slowly now.

"And does she work, as well?" Lillian asked, once more ashamed of her nosiness.

"Work?" he smiled. "Maybe you could call it that. . . ." But his attention was drifting away like smoke. Fumbling with a breadknife, he picked it up and languidly, distantly, speared a cockroach with the point. Then, with the side of the knife, he slowly, methodically, squashed the other one.

Averting her eyes from the massacre, Lillian leaned forward. "I don't mean to sound familiar, but you seem a quiet person. Do you think you might ask Jody to be a little

less noisy up here? I've spoken to the landlord, but—''
She saw the boy smile again, an odd, rueful smile that
made her feel, for some reason, much younger than he.
''You see—'' she continued, but he was fading from her
presence, slowly mashing his bugs to pulp and now dropping the knife to reach over and click on the food-spattered
television. Slouched, his eyes bored by what the screen
offered, he nevertheless began following an old movie.
The conversation appeared to be over.

Lillian rose. She was not accustomed, nor would Bedelia
have been, to a chat ending without some mutual amenity.
She felt awkward, dismissed. With a cool nod she left him
and descended the splashing stairs to her own flat. Such a
contrast the youth was of warmth and rudeness . . . and
Jody, an illiterate studying Dostoevski at college . . . food
stamps lying hugger-mugger with bills from Saks . . . it
was impossible to bring it all into focus; she felt rudder-
less, malfunctioning . . . how peculiar life had become
. . . everything mixed up . . . a generation of fragments. . . .

Climbing heavily back into bed, she wondered what
Bedelia would have thought of Jody and Jamie. And she
remembered how unkempt and disconcerting Vladimir had
been, yet how her aunt had quickly penetrated to the
valuable core while she, Lillian, fussed on about his bad
language. No doubt Bedelia would have been scandalized
by the filth upstairs, but she would not have been so
narrow-souled as to find fault with spelling mistakes, first
names, taste in clothing. . . . Bedelia might not have pulverized Jody with a glance, as Vladimir suggested, but
instead seen some delicate tragedy in the worn cherubic
features, or been charmed by the girl's invincible buoy-
ancy . . . it was hard to tell with Bedelia, which facet she
might consider the significant one . . . she often surprised
you . . . it had to do with largeness of spirit. . . .

Whereas she, Lillian, had always to guard against stuffi-
ness. . . . Still, she tried to hold high the torch of goodwill
. . . too pompous a simile, of course, but she knew clearly
and deeply what she meant . . . so *let* Vladimir rave on at
her for refusing to shrink into a knot of hostility; what was
Vladimir, after all? Insane. Her eyes opened in the dark as

she faced what she had tried to avoid all day: that Vladimir had been wrenched off the tracks by Bedelia's death, and that this time he felt no need to commit himself. Without question it was Lillian's duty to enlighten him. But she winced at the thought . . . such a terrible thing to have to tell someone . . . if only she could turn to Bedelia . . . how sorely she missed her . . . how sorely she missed George's lean young face under his Army cap . . . youth . . . sunlight . . . outside the rain still fell . . . she had only herself, and the dark, unending rain. . . .

"Stop this brooding," she said aloud; if she had only herself, she had better be decent company. And closing her eyes she tried to sleep. But not until a gray watery dawn was breaking did she drop off.

The Opera House telephoned at three minutes past nine. Leaden, taut-nerved, sourly questioning the rewards of her long, exquisite punctuality, she pulled on her clothes, and, with burning eyes and empty stomach, hurried out of the house. At work, though the board was busy, the hours moved with monumental torpor. She felt increasingly unlike herself, hotly brimming over with impatience for all this switchboard blather: calls from New York, Milan; Sutherland with her sore throat, Pavarotti with his tight schedule—did they really think that, if another *Rigoletto* were never given, anyone would notice? She felt an urge to slur this fact into the headphone, as befitted a truant traipsing in at a quarter to ten, as befitted someone with minimally combed hair and crooked seams and, even worse, with the same underwear on that she had worn the day before. As if a slatternly, cynical Lillian whom she didn't recognize had squeezed slyly into prominence, a Lillian who half-considered walking out on the whole tiresome business and indulging in a lavish two-hour lunch downtown—let someone else serve, let someone else be polite.

Sandwiched into the bus aisle that night, she almost smacked an old gentleman who crunched her right instep under his groping heel; and as she creaked into the house with her wet newspaper and saw that a motorcyclist had been picked off on the freeway by a sniper, she had to fight down a lip curl of satisfaction. Then, reflectively, still in her raincoat, she walked to the end of the hall where an oval mirror hung, and studied her face. It was haggard, flinty, stripped of faith, scraped down to the cold, atavistic bones of retaliation. She had almost walked off her job, almost struck an old man, almost smiled at murder. A feeling of panic shot through her; what were values if they could collapse at the touch of a sleepless night? And she sank the terrible face into her hands; but a ray of rational thought lifted it again. "Almost." Never mind the querulous inner tremble, at each decisive moment her principles had stood fast. Wasn't a person entitled to an occasional fit of petulance? There is such a thing as perspective, she told herself, and in the meantime a great lust for steam and soap had spread through her. She would scrub out the day in a hot bath and in perfect silence, for apparently Jody had not yet returned from across the bay. God willing, the creature would remain away a week.

Afterward, boiled pink, wrapped in her quilted robe, she felt restored to grace. A fine appetite raced through her, along with visions of a tuna casserole which she hurried into the kitchen to prepare, hurrying out again at the summons of the telephone. It was Vladimir, very excited, wanting to drop by. Her first response was one of blushing discomfort: entertain Vladimir in her quilted bathrobe? Her second she articulated: she was bone-tired, she was going to bed right after dinner. But even as she spoke she heard the remorseless door slam of Jody's return, and a violent spasm twisted her features. "Please—next week," she told Vladimir and hung up, clutching her head as tears of rage and exhaustion burst from her eyes. Weeping, she made a tuna sandwich, chewed it without heart, and sank onto her unmade bed. The next morning, still exhausted, she made an emergency appointment with her doctor, and came home that night with a bottle of sleeping pills.

By the end of the week she was sick with artificial sleep, there was an ugly rubber taste in her mouth, her eye sockets felt caked with rust. And it was not only the noise and pills that plagued her: a second neighborhood woman had been slashed to death by the rain man (the newspapers, in their cozy fashion, had thus baptized the slayer). She had taken to beaming her flashlight under the bed before saying the Lord's Prayer; her medicinal sleep crackled with surreal visions; at the sullen butcher's her eyes were morbidly drawn to the meat cleaver; and at work not only had she upset coffee all over her lap, but she disconnected Rudolf Bing himself in the middle of a sentence.

And never any respite from above. She had called the landlord again, without audible results, and informed the Board of Health about the cockroaches; their reply was that they had no jurisdiction over cockroaches. She had stuck several notes under Jody's door pleading with her to quiet down, and had stopped her twice on the steps, receiving the first time some capricious remark, and the second a sigh of "Christ, Lilly, I'm trying. What d'you want?" Lilly! The gall! But she was gratified to see that the gum-snapping face was almost as sallow as her own, the circles under the eyes darker than ever, new lines around the mouth. So youth could crumble, too. Good! Perhaps the girl's insanely late hours were boomeranging, and would soon mash her down in a heap of deathlike stillness (would that Lillian could implement this vision). Or perhaps it was her affair with Jamie that was running her ragged. Ah, the costly trauma of love! Jealousy, misunderstanding—so damaging to the poor nervous system! Or so she had heard . . . she and George had been blessed with rapport . . . but try not to dwell on the past . . . yes, possibly it was Jamie who was lining the girl's face . . . Lillian has seen him a few times since their first meeting, once on the steps—he smiled, was pleasant, remembered her, but had not remembered to zip his fly, and she had hurried on, embarrassed—and twice in the back garden, where on the less drenching days she tended Bedelia's flowers, but without her aunt's emerald-green thumb . . . a rare sunny afternoon, she had been breaking off geraniums: Jody and Jamie lay on the grass in skimpy bathing suits, their thin bodies white, somehow poignant in their delicacy . . . she felt like a great stuffed mattress in her sleeveless dress, soiled hands masculine with age, a stevedore's drop of sweat hanging from her nose . . .

could they imagine her once young and tender on her own bed of love? or now, with a man friend? As if everything closed down at fifty-seven, like a bankrupt hotel!—tearing off the head of a geranium—brash presumption of youth! But she saw that they weren't even aware of her, no, they were kissing and rolling about . . . in Bedelia's garden! "Here, what are you doing!" she cried, but in the space of a moment a hostile little flurry had taken place, and now they broke away and lay separately in charged silence, still taking no notice of her as she stood there, heart thumping, fist clenched. She might have been air. Suddenly, sick from the heat, she had plodded inside.

The next time she saw Jamie in the garden was this afternoon when, arriving home from work and changing into a fresh dress for Vladimir's visit, she happened to glance out her bedroom window. Rain sifted down, but the boy was standing still, a melancholy sight, wrapped in a theatrical black cloak, the derby and Mexican shawl apparently having outlived their effectiveness as eyecatchers . . . youth's eternal and imbecile need to shock . . . Jody with her ebony fingernails and silly prepubescent hemlines; and this little would-be Dracula with his golden sausage curls, tragically posed in the fragile mist, though she noticed his hands were untragically busy under the cloak, scratching as usual . . . or . . . the thought was so monstrous that she clutched the curtain . . . he could not be standing in the garden abusing himself; she must be deranged, suffering prurient delusions—she, Lillian Cronin, a decent, clean-minded woman . . . ah God, what was happening, what was happening? It was her raw nerves, her drugged and hanging head, the perpetual din . . . even as she stood there, her persecutor was trying on clothes, dropping shoes, pounding from closet to mirror (for Lillian could by now divine the activity behind each noise) while simultaneously braying into the telephone receiver stuck between chin and shoulder, and sketchily attending the deluxe television set, which blared a hysterical melodrama . . .

Outside, the youth sank onto a tree stump, from which he cast the upstairs window a long bleak look . . . they

must have had a lovers' quarrel, and the girl had shut him
out; now he brooded in the rain, an exile; or rather a
kicked puppy, shivering and staring up with ponderous
woe . . . then, eyes dropping, he caught sight of Lillian,
and a broad, sunny, candid smile flashed from the dismal
countenance . . . odd, jarring, she thought, giving a polite
nod and dropping the curtain, especially after his rude
imperviousness that hot day on the grass . . . a generation
of fragments, she had said so before, though God knew
she never objected to a smile (with the exception of Jody's
grimace) . . . and walking down the hall away from the
noise, she was stopped woodenly by the sound of the girl's
doorbell. It was one of the gentlemen callers, who tore up
the stairs booming felicitations which were returned with the
inevitable shrieks, this commingled din moving into the
front room and turning Lillian around in her tracks.
With the door closed, the kitchen was comparatively bear-
able, and it was time to eat anyway. She bought television
dinners now, lacking the vigor to cook. She had lost seven
pounds, but was not growing svelte, only drawn. Even to
turn on the waiting oven was a chore. But slowly she got
herself into motion, and at length, pouring out a glass of
burgundy to brace herself for Vladimir's visit, she sat
down to the steaming, neatly sectioned pap. Afterward,
dutifully washing her glass and fork in the sink, she glanced
out the window into the rain, falling in sheets now; the
garden was dark and she could not be sure, but she thought
she saw the youth still sitting on the stump. It was beyond
her, why anyone would sit still in a downpour . . . but
everything was beyond her, insurmountable . . . and soon
Vladimir would arrive . . . the thought was more than she
could bear, but she could not defer his visit again, it would
be too rude. . . .

He burst in like a cannonball, tearing off his wet lumber
jacket, an acrid smell of sweat blooming from his armpits;
his jaws were stubbled with white, great bushes sprouted
from his nostrils.

"You look terrible!" he roared.

Even though she had at the last moment rubbed lipstick

into her pallid cheeks. She gave a deflated nod and gestured toward the relatively quiet kitchen, but he wanted the
Bedelia-redolent front room, where he rushed over to the
Steinway and lovingly dashed off an arpeggio, only to
stagger back with his finger knifed up at the ceiling. "Still
the chaos!" he cried.

"Please—" she said raggedly. "No advice, I beg of
you."

"No advice? Into your grave they'll drive you, Lillian!"
And she watched his finger drop, compassionately it seemed,
to point at her slumped bosom with its heart beating so
wearily inside. It was a small hand, yet blunt, virile, its
back covered with coarse dark hair . . . what if it reached
farther, touched her? . . . But spittle already flying, Vladimir was plunging into a maelstrom of words, obviously
saved up for a week. "I wanted to come sooner, why
didn't you let me? Look at you, a wreck! Vladimir knew a
second one would be cut—he smells blood on the wind!
He wants to come and pound on your door, to be with
you, but no, he respects your wish for privacy, so he sits
every night out front in his auto, watching!" Here he
broke off to wipe his lips, while Lillian, pressing hard the
swollen, rusty lids of her eyes, accepted the immense duty
of guiding him to confinement. "And every night," he
roared on, "while Vladimir sits, Bedelia plays 'Komm,
Jesu, Komm,' it floats into the street, it is beautiful,
beautiful—"

"Ah, Vladimir," broke pityingly from her lips.

Silence. With a clap of restored lucidity his fist struck
his forehead. It remained tightly glued there for some
time. When it fell away he seemed quite composed.

"I have always regretted," he said crisply, "that you
resemble the wrong side of your family. All you have of
Bedelia is a most vague hint of her cheekbones." Which
he was scrutinizing with his small glittering eyes. Again,
nervously, she sensed that he would touch her; but instead,
a look of revulsion passed over his features as he stared
first at one cheek, then the other. "You've got fucking
gunk on! Rouge!"

With effort, she produced a neutral tone. "I'm not used to being stared at, Vladimir."

"Hah, I should think not," he snapped abstractedly, eyes still riveted.

Beast! Vile wretch! But at once she was ashamed by her viciousness. From where inside her did it come? And she remembered that terrible day at work when a malign and foreign Lillian had pressed into ascendancy, almost as frightening a character change as the one she was seeing before her now, for Vladimir's peering eyes seemed actually black with hatred. "Stinking whore-rouge," he breathed; then with real pain, he cried: "Have you no thought for Bedelia? You have the blessing of her cheekbones! Respect them! Don't drag them through the gutter! My God, Lillian! My God!"

She said nothing. It seemed the only thing to do.

But now he burst forth again, cheerfully, rubbing his hands together. "Listen to Vladimir. You want a husband, forget the war paint, use what you have. Some intelligence. A good bearing—straighten the shoulders—and cooking talent. Not like Bedelia's, but not bad. Now, Vladimir has been looking around for you—"

"Vladimir," she said through her teeth.

"—and he has found a strong, healthy widower of fifty-two, a great enjoyer of the opera. He has been advised of your virtues—"

"Vladimir!"

"Of course you understand Vladimir himself is out, Vladimir is a monolith—" A particularly loud thump shuddered the ceiling, and he jumped back yelling, "Shove it, you swine! Lice!"

"Vladimir, I do not want a man!" Lillian snapped.

"Not so! I sense sex boiling around in you!"

Her lips parted; blood rushed into her cheeks to darken the artificial blush. For certain, with the short, potent word, *sex*, his hands would leap on her.

"But you look a thousand years old," he went on. "It hangs in folds, your face. You must get rid of this madhouse upstairs! What have you done so far—not even told the landlord!"

"I *have!*" she cried; and suddenly the thought of confiding in someone loosened a stinging flood of tears from her eyes, and she sank into a chair. "He has come to speak to her . . . time and time again . . . he seems always to be there . . . but nothing changes. . . ."

"Ah, so," said Vladimir, pulling out his gray handkerchief and handing it to her. "The sow screws him."

She grimaced both at the words and the reprehensible cloth, with which she nevertheless dabbed her eyes. "I don't believe that," she said nasally.

"Why not? She's a prostitute. Only to look at her."

"You've seen her?" she asked, slowly raising her eyes. But of course, if he sat outside in his car every night . . .

"I have seen her," he said, revulsion hardening his eyes. "I have seen much. Even a bat-man with the face of a sorrowful kewpie doll. He pines this minute on the front steps."

"That's her boyfriend," Lillian murmured, increasingly chilled by the thought of Vladimir sitting outside all night, spying.

"Boyfriend! A hundred boyfriends she has, each with a roll of bills in his pocket!"

Tensely, she smoothed the hair at her temples. "Forgive me, Vladimir," she said gently, "but you exaggerate. You exaggerate everything, I'm afraid. I must point this out to you, because I think it does you no good. I really—"

"Don't change the subject! We're talking about her, upstairs!"

She was silent for a moment. "The girl is—too free, I suppose, in our eyes. But I'm certain that she isn't what you call her."

"And how do you come to this idiot conclusion?" he asked scornfully.

She lifted her hands in explanation, but they hung helplessly suspended. "Well," she said at last, "I know she reads Dostoevski . . . she takes courses . . . and she cares for that boy in the cape, even if they do have their quarrels . . . and there's a quality of anguish in her face . . . ."

"Anguish! I call it the knocked-out look of a female cretin who uses her ass every night to pay the rent. And that pea-brain boyfriend outside, in his secondhand ghoul costume to show how interesting he is! Probably he pops pills and lives off his washer-woman mother, if he hasn't slit her throat in a fit of irritation! It's the type, Lillian! Weak, no vision, no guts! The sewers are vomiting them up by the thousands to mix with us! They surround us! Slop! Shit! Chaos! Listen to that up there! Hee-haw! Call that anguish! Even pleasure? No, I tell you what it is. Empty, hollow noise—like a wheel spun into motion and never stopped again! It's madness! The madness of our times!''

But as he whipped himself on, Lillian felt herself growing diametrically clear and calm, as if the outburst were guiding her blurred character back into focus. When he stopped, she said firmly, ''Yes, I understand what you mean about the wheel spinning. There is something pointless about them, something pitiful. But they're not from a sewer. They're people, Vladimir, human beings like ourselves . . .''

''Ah, blanket democracy! What else would you practice but this piss-fart abomination?''

''I practice what Bedelia herself practiced,'' she replied tartly.

''Ah,'' he sighed, ''the difference between instinct and application. Between a state of grace and a condition of effort. Dear friend Lillian, tolerance is dangerous without insight. And the last generation with insight has passed, with the things it understood. Like the last generation of cobblers and glass stainers. It is fatal to try to carry on a dead art—the world has no use for it! The world will trample you down! Don't think of the past, think of your scalp!''

''No,'' she stated, rising and swaying with the light-headedness that so frequently visited her now. ''To live each moment as if you were in danger—it's demeaning. I will not creep around snarling like some four-legged beast. I am a civilized human being. Your attitude shows a lack of proportion, Vladimir; I feel that you really—''

A flash of sinewy hands; her wrists were seized and crushed together with a stab of pain through whose shock she felt a marginal heat of embarrassment, a tingling dismay of abrupt intimacy. Then the very center of her skull was pierced by his shriek. "You *are* in danger! Can't you *see!*" and he thrust his face at hers, disclosing the red veins of his eyes, bits of sleep matted in the lashes, and the immobile, overwhelmed look of someone who has seen the abyss and is seeing it again. Her heart gave the chop of an axe; with a wail she strained back.

His fixed look broke; his eyes grew flaring, kinetic. "One minute the blood is nice and cozy in its veins—the next, slice! and slice! and slice! Red fountains go up—a festival! Worthy of Handel! Oh marvelous, marvelous! The rain man—" Here he broke off to renew his grip as she struggled frantically to pull away. "The rain man, he's in ecstasies! Such founts and spouts, such excitement! Then at last it's all played out, nothing but puddles, and off he trots, he's big success! And it's big city—many many fountains to be had, all red as—as—red as—"

Her laboring wrists were flung aside: her hands slammed against her face and pressed fiercely into the cheeks.

"Vladimir!" she screamed. "It's Lillian—Lillian!"

The flared eyes contracted. He stepped back and stood immobile. Then a self-admonishing hand rose shakily to his face, which had gone the color of pewter. After a long moment he turned and walked out of the house.

She blundered to the door and locked it behind him, then ran heavily back into the front room where she came to a blank stop, both hands pressed to her chest. Hearing the sound of an engine starting, she wheeled around to the window and pinched back the edge of the shade. Through the rain she saw the big square car jerk and shudder, while its motor rose to a crescendo of whines and abruptly stopped. Vladimir climbed out and started back across the pavement. Her brain finally clicked: the telephone, the police.

With long strides she gained the hall where the telephone stood, and where she now heard the anticipated knock—but mild, rueful, a diminished sound that soon fell away. She moved on haltingly; she would call the police, yes—or a friend from work—or her doctor—someone, anyone, she must talk to someone, and suddenly she stumbled with a cry: it was Vladimir's lumber jacket she had tripped over, still lying on the floor where he had dropped it, his wallet sticking out from the pocket. Outside, the Buick began coughing once more, then it fell silent. A few moments later the shallow, timid knock began again. Without his wallet he could not call a garage, a taxi. It was a fifteen-block walk to his house in the rain. If only she could feel Bedelia's presence beside her, look to the expression in the intelligent eyes. Gradually, concentrating on those eyes, she felt an unclenching inside her. She gazed at the door. Behind it Vladimir was Vladimir still. He had spoken with horrifying morbidity, and even hurt her wrists and face, but he was not the rain man. Bedelia would have seen such seeds. He had been trying to warn her tonight of the world's dangers, and in his passion had set off one of his numerous obsessions—with her fingertip she touched the rouged and aching oval of her cheek. Strange, tortured soul who had stationed himself out in the cold, night after night, to keep her from harm. Bending down, she gathered up the rough, homely jacket; but the knocking had stopped. She went back to the front room and again tweaked aside the shade. He was going away, a small decelerated figure, already drenched. Now he turned the corner and was lost from sight. Depleted, she leaned against the wall.

It might have been a long while that she stood there, that the noise from above masked the sound, but by degrees she became aware of knocking. He must have turned around in the deluge and was now, with what small hope, tapping on the door again. She hesitated, once more summoning the fine violet eyes, the tall brow under its archaic coiffure, which dipped in an affirmative nod. The jacket under her arm, Lillian went into the hall, turned on the porch light, and unlocked the door.

It was not Vladimir who stood there, but Jamie, as wet as if he had crawled from the ocean, his long curls limply clinging to the foolish cape, his neat little features stamped with despair, yet warmed, saved, by the light of greeting in his eyes. Weary, unequal to any visit, she shook her head.

"Jody?" she thought she heard him say, or more likely it was something else—the rain muffled his voice; though she caught an eerie, unnatural tone she now sensed was reflected in the luminous stare. With a sudden feeling of panic she started to slam the door in his face. But she braked herself, knowing that she was overwrought; it was unseemly to use such brusqueness on this lost creature because of her jangled nerves.

So she paused for one haggard, courteous moment to say, "I'm sorry, Jamie, it's late—some other time." And in that moment the shrouded figure crouched, and instantaneously, spasmlike, rushed up against her. She felt a huge but painless blow, followed by a dullness, a stillness deep inside her, and staggering back as he kicked the door shut behind them, she clung to the jamb of the front-room entrance and slowly sank to her knees.

She dimly comprehended the wet cloak brushing her side, but it was the room that held her attention, that filled her whole being. It had grown immense, lofty, and was suffused with violet, overwhelmingly beautiful. But even as she watched, it underwent a rapid wasting, paled to the faint, dead-leaf hue of an old tintype; and now it vanished behind a sheet of black as the knife was wrenched from her body.

JOANNE GREENBERG (pseudonym Hannah Green) was born in Brooklyn, New York, in 1932. She was graduated from American University and the University of London. She is the mother of two sons and now lives with her husband in a mountaintop home in Colorado. She writes daily, teaches sign language and works with a firefighting and emergency rescue squad. Her highly acclaimed novel, *I Never Promised You a Rose Garden*, was published under her pseudonym of Hannah Green. Under her own name she has published six other novels, including *The King's Persons, The Monday Voices, In This Sign, Founder's Praise, A Season of Delight*, and *The Far Side of Victory*; her three collections of short stories are *Summering, Rites of Passage*, and *High Crimes and Misdemeanors*. Of *Rites of Passage* Joyce Carol Oates wrote, "This group of twelve excellent short stories is all the more remarkable for its being not only artistically 'beautiful' but morally and spiritually beautiful as well." In much of her work Mrs. Greenberg demonstrates a mature awareness of the power and importance of the human family's spiritual traditions. The story that follows here, "Days of Awe," like her novel *A Season of Delight*, tells with the greatest dignity of a Jewish mother whose children have rejected their spiritual tradition.

Joanne Greenberg

DAYS OF AWE

I used to dislike shopping, the rushing to too many stores, all the details to remember. Now it's almost pleasant. I shop in the morning when the stores are uncrowded and the early light gleams off the beige brick and glass of the storefronts. Since Joshua and Miriam are grown and gone, there's less to do and I can see the young mothers, some of them harried and embattled, with a sympathy that will soon, very soon, become nostalgia. I like the silence and order of the house now that I'm used to it. Adam and I sit close together at his end of the table. We thought we would have less to talk about when the children were gone, but it turned out not to be so. The daily happenings still happen and the greater events also.

Rosh Hashanah, the Jewish New Year, has just passed; these are the Days of Awe, the days between the New Year and Yom Kippur, the Day of Atonement. In the old days, people faced this week in terror. They cried aloud in the synagogues, they ran weeping to their neighbors, pressing unpaid debts upon them before it should be too late and their measuring by the Lord be over and the mark against them made and blotted. We don't weep now. Debt is fashionable and we are decorous, rational, and fearless, but it's still possible to dream old-fashioned nightmares during the week of Awe. I am forty-seven and the freedom and wealth of my life here are shadowed during this week with smoke whispering from the chimneys of camps I have never seen. My grandparents' villages are gone. This Gilboa is in Pennsylvania and it is autumn here, a blue and golden day, with the mellow warmth of late summer still in it. I go in to my shopping.

The stores are in a covered mall but the mall is pleasant, lit by skylights. Down the long center gallery are places to sit; there are trees and shrubbery planted under the skylights. The people on the squad know that Thursday I'm out of service until noon, so my pace is leisurely but not idle. Store to store, steadily. I have my list. I'm a good housewife.

But when I come out of the grocery store, instead of going directly to the car and home, I go to one of the mall's benches and sit down. It's not so I can remember before I leave the one or two things I've forgotten on my list. I want to think about the holiday a little more—about chimneys and villages I have never seen—to give it its time.

There's a young man approaching the bench. I smile a little, in acknowledgment, and move over. To my surprise, he comes up to me and I see that the basket he is carrying is not for shopping but has flowers and leaflets in it. He takes one of these leaflets and hands it to me. There's a picture of a boy and a girl on it.

"Excuse me, ma'am," he says politely, "but did you know that millions of our children are hooked on drugs?"

My hand almost starts for my purse and the donation I think he wants, but then I remember and my heart sinks.

"You're not the Salvation Army or a drug program," I say, and the words come tired and sad. "You're the Unification Church."

"We do a lot of good," he says. "We have programs in all the major cities for drug addicts and runaways."

"You steal Jews," I say.

He has been taught to answer such things, but he misgauges me.

"We're not anti-Semitic," he says. "I myself had a Jewish background. My parents are Jewish."

We are both surprised and he is mortified when I begin to cry. The tears are so sudden and so overwhelming that they have come up into my eyes and flowed over before I know it, as though they had been waiting in ambush for this boy's arrival. But my voice is still steady, and while I have it, I have him.

"Hitler killed one-third of us. A language, a culture, a way of life. Only our dispersion saved us from complete extinction. Now through that—that wound in our People, more blood is flowing away. You and all the others, to the cults that promise heaven which, if they get the power they hunger for, will revenge their parents with hell."

"We don't seek—"

"*You* don't, you poor sap," I cry, "but *they* do. Somewhere in Illinois my son is dressed in yellow and is chanting someone else's ancestral language. His head is shaved. He and you eat, and don't eat for what you call ritual reasons. You're burlesque artists, parodists!"

"Judaism is a bankrupt faith."

I am suddenly, overwhelmingly tired. "When did you invest a moment of yourself in it?" I say.

It's no good and I see it. He can't see my visions, understand my pain. Free and equal. I know, I know. I am I and you are you. My voice is compromised. I'm crying outright.

Blushing wildly, he leaves me. Like any good American, he is unnerved by the public demonstration of emotion. Except in groups. A Jewish mother weeping is his metaphor for hell, a banality he cannot endure. And I, too, am American. I can't sit blubbering in a shopping center mall at eleven in the morning for no visible reason. I'm back on call at eleven. I blow my nose and dry my eyes and drive home.

No more about the Illinois renunciate, I tell myself. But my mind drifts as I drive. Joshua has given over his name, an ordinary Jewish name by which other Jews can know him and other Christians, too, as one of a people, a line, a tradition, a curse, a sorrow, a glory, a law. His new names are Sanskirt. He doesn't realize it but he comes two generations too late. How popular he might have been in Munich in 1934. He is that one most enviable of forebears, an Aryan. It is an irony I cannot share with him. It occurs to me that it has been three days since I last thought of Joshua-Sanjit. Three days without anguish and now the anguish returns.

Miriam also has gone into a world where Jews disappear. She is liberated from her husband and works at a Women's Center in California. I admire her commitments to battered wives and rape victims and the exploited of the Third World. Sadly for me, none of her commitments involves the continued existence of her own people. The blacks and Chicanos with whom she castigates me multiply in all their variety and rich profusion. The poor of the world are not an endangered species. Her former husband was not Jewish and she laughed at me when I begged her to consider raising Kimberley, who is legally so, as a Jew. It wasn't for me, I said, but for our people, so that Hitler would lose again, would lose forever.

"Everything has to change," she said, "some things have to die out, I guess."

Did I tell her that about Biafra, about the American Indians, that she should say it was about *my* minority? *My* people? I wonder: Is there anyone more lonely than the champion of an unfashionable cause?

Unaccountably, as I ride, the day opens outward. The autumn smells its briny apple-smell, but the sun is still in summer. I have the windows open and though I was angry and sobbing twenty minutes ago, there was a relief in the tears and I feel better for them, close to the day and the center of my life. Adam and I didn't die when Miriam met a man and moved in and married without our presence. I made apologies to the family, to my mother who blames me for the loss, to all the aunts and uncles, and went on living. Joshua quit college and found the tide that carried him so far away, and we didn't die then, either. We only spoke a little more quietly when we sat together at dinner. In our ancestral castle we live like modern nobility. There are rooms shut, to save on heat. We remember those rooms, every inch of them, and everything with which they were furnished, but we don't often unlock them and we try to live warmly in the rest of the house.

When I get home, I back into the driveway so that the car faces out. I go into the house and before I unload my groceries, I check the call box. No red light. I call Rita Neri, our dispatcher. I am home.

"O.K.," she says, and we hang up. I'm in the fire and rescue service of this district. There's a dispatch box in the stairwell, and a red gumball light on the roof of my car. If there's an auto wreck or a fire or a heart attack or a serious fall or a sudden illness in Gilboa or the farms or suburbs around it any time of the day or night, I'll hear about it on the call box and I'll go and help deal with it. I've been on the squad for five years, and the whole district including "The Loop" of the Interstate is heavy with anecdote for me.

I unpack my groceries then and put them away. There's no class today, nothing special for me to do, and although I know I should study or do the windows or write letters, I do none of these things. I sit down at the kitchen table and let the day wash over me.

Last year, our student rabbi spoke about the High Holidays and gave examples of Galut—exile. The harvest festival of Succos, soon to come, would find our evenings too cold to sit, as the celebration decrees, under the stars in magical booths hung with bunches of grapes. It is balmy in this season in Jerusalem, but one does not stay dreaming starward, somnolent and peaceful in these latitudes. Half an hour in a *succah* in this Gilboa and hypothermia would set in. To be unable to celebrate the feast correctly, seasonably, is exile, he said, be we ever so wealthy and at peace, be our neighbors ever so warmly disposed to us.

It was a good sermon and must have been partly true or I wouldn't have remembered it. But God is everywhere and He has arranged recompenses for His exiles. The wine-crisp tang of autumn does not blow through Jerusalem. Halleluiah the hills, but not in Haifa. Haifa has hills enough, but they never blaze with a thousand fires in a hundred tones of rose-gold, flame and orange, yellow, purple, umber. My exile lies in fragrant piles on my doorstep and breaks beneath my feet in the snap-twig woodsmoke mornings of my father's chosen land.

Now, I think, would be a suitable time to cry. The house is clean and in order. Adam isn't due home for hours. I could get the old pictures of Joshua and Miriam out of the boxes in the attic and set them around me and remember the hope and the work and the planning, the new starts, the books we read, the pangs of conscience we suffered. It's too late. I have cried my cry already in front of another woman's fool and it's over. The phone rings. I smile. Had I been crying, whoever it was would have caught me at it.

It's Riva, my mother-in-law. Poor woman; she was never very religious but because she's Adam's mother she feels she owes it to her position to uphold the values of her generation. "Grace, Yom Kippur is tomorrow and I still haven't settled things in my mind. What are we planning to do?"

"I think it will all go pretty much as it did last year," I say. "The service will start at nine-thirty, with one break. Afternoon is one-thirty with one break and four-thirty to sundown. Some people will want to go home and break the fast with their families. For those who want to stay there will be a light meal, dairy. What do you want to do? If you want to stay, we will too. If not, we'll all come back here and eat. In any case, I'm down for a potato pudding and a salad. What do you think?"

"When Elia was alive it was so much nicer. We all stayed then. Now . . . And I wish we didn't have services at the town hall. It's so . . ."

"I know," I say. "But right now there is no other place. We've gotten too big for Bert and Joan's basement."

"It was nice there."

I know what she means. Five years ago, the Jews of Gilboa, Russian Grove, and Tarrant numbered no more than twenty families, and of these only half were obser-vant. For years we met in the Finegolds' rumpus room. "The Sisterhood" was four women, the "Hebrew School" eight kids and a teacher; then a new housing development came in between Tarrant and Gilboa and Jews from the suburbs west of Midlothian found it pleasant to come west on the Interstate to us instead of going to the city. Two years ago we found we had to look for another place. Since then we've been meeting in a corner of the town hall basement. There are cooking facilities there and lots of chairs; there are no religious reminders to distract us, but we are dwarfed in the large hall. The sound we make, even praying all together, doesn't fill half the space. We are conscious as never before of ourselves as a minority, a decimated minority.

"I know, Riva, but what can we do? I'm grateful the town fathers let us meet down there. They could have gotten stuffy and talked about separation of church and state. I wish there were a bigger house or a smaller hall that would have us." She sighs into the phone. My signals go up. "What's the matter—is something wrong?"

"No—no. I suppose it's the end of summer. Whenever I have to put on a heavy sweater in the morning, I remember I'm an old lady. Elia used to say, 'One foot in the grave and the other on a banana peel.' " We talk for a while longer—something she isn't saying, isn't ready to say—and when we hang up I find I'm tense and tired. I put up a cup of tea and have a piece of the cake Adam brought home last night. Food, the Jewish tranquilizer. I should be grateful; it could have been booze. Leaving the kitchen door open, I go out to the little porch in back and sit down.

Adam grew up in Gilboa. It was a small Pennsylvania farm town before Midlothian got big with the heavy industry of World War II. Elia Dowben came here in 1912 and set up a dry goods and clothing store. Over the years, the dry goods business was taken over by chains, but the old man, a Russian Jewish peasant from Shedletz, turned out to have a designer's eye for style and an intuitive sense of the wants of his customers. The clothing store flourished. Three years later, he contacted a marriage broker in New York who supplied him with a wife, Riva, from a village near Shedletz. They and their children were the only Jews in Gilboa until the mid-forties. I was raised in Chicago. I met Adam in college and came to Gilboa, to what my family still considers an exile worse than Babylonian. I like the town and the sense of community that, although changed and diluted by the new populations, still speaks in an older voice, in the fire department and the church and between neighbors. It roots Adam, centers him. Although a Jew, he's less an exile than the people I grew up with.

The Caetanos' teen-age daughter is entertaining her friends and the music drifts across to me mellowed, sweetened by distance. I have a book on trauma that I am studying for a class and I dip into it desultorily. It's more important just now to study exactly how the golden field gets its shadows and how the shadows pull long and then how the sun will go behind the hills on the way to Midlothian. When the sun goes, the shadows are destroyed. Then everything stands in equal light, a glow in which each visible thing is made real, complete, itself. And because the year has turned, there will be a little haunting coolness when the light goes. Because we are a little higher than the town we get the light later, so I sit and wait for the first lights to be lit down there. The District. My Chicago relatives are aghast at my doing fire and rescue work. It seems bizarre to them, although there are middle-aged women doing it all over the country. I like the work for many reasons, one of them being that I am able, by virtue of what we do, to look out over Gilboa and on to the great loop of the Interstate exit by exit and know that all of it is, at this moment, within the widest limits possible, at rest.

I think that I should get myself ready for the holiday, stop thinking about classes or cleaning or rescue, take what advantages there are in the serenity of an empty house, and slow down so that I can overtake the holiday at its pace, walking. Adam will be home at five-thirty. We'll eat and be ready for the evening service, and this time we should leave early and walk slowly. We could even go down over the field while it's still light, the short cut that our kids and the ones who live on these streets take to school.

The alarm, two ululant wails and the sheriff's man: "Attention Gilboa Fire and Rescue. You have a first aid at the Methodist Church, Federal and Larch." The call is repeated. I am in my red rescue coat and out the door before the end of the second call. It's six blocks to the church, but there are as many turns, and even with red light and siren, dangerous at this time of day. When I get to the church, Geri Pines, the squad captain, and some of the others are there. Geri radios to the rest of the squad to stand down; we will not need any more people.

We go inside and a woman motions us down to the basement. Then I remember the day, yes, Wednesday, Altar Guild day, and there they are, around the table at their newest project, the raffle quilt for the repair of the leak on the south wall. We stop for a moment. Who is it? Who among all these old women that we know is the one in pain, the one who is short of breath—I think *no*, but it is. They stand aside, away from her as they never would do for one of their living friends in pain. It's Violet, my friend Violet Cleve, my first friend in Gilboa. She's sitting at her place at rest in her chair. Her hands are on the quilt the women are making. She looks no different from her usual self. I go over and feel for a pulse. None. She's cold. Her legs have stiffened. I know we could not resuscitate her. I know what it would take to try. I shake my head. Geri comes over and listens, then feels at the legs. "How old a woman was she?" Geri asks. I open my mouth to say "seventy," but Addie Arvis says, "Ninety-five. She was ninety-five." Of course. The years, the years have gone by.

"She's been sitting here quietly dead for half an hour at least," Geri says. It's a statement that tells the squad we will not start work on her. It's something on which we all must agree and we all do. The ladies haven't wanted to move her. They are standing back, murmuring at the suddenness. Geri goes out to call the coroner from Midlothian. Someone must stay until he comes and I ask to let it be me. We ease Violet over on to a bench, and cover her. Since the death was unexpected, state law takes over. There's nothing more to do.

I sit and wait, thinking how satisfying rescue is except when there is nothing to be done—except when the pain and death are those of a friend.

Adam is home. I hear the mailbox slam shut because he knows I sometimes forget the mail. I haven't this time. I smile. There's a silence as he comes up the walk and then there is the sound of his step on the front porch and then the door opening. He's early. This past year he's been taking off for a couple of hours on the days when the store is open until nine. I want him to come out here where I'm sitting. I want to tell him about the young man with the flowers and the Jewish parents. We've been through twenty-five years together: a war, death and birth, hopes blossoming, hopes in blight. I want to tell him this, too, but I'm worried that he'll take it the wrong way. Men have strange ideas about the fragility of women. I don't want him to see my weeping as more than it was. But what it was I don't know myself. Now I hear him moving through the house. It makes me smile again. He'll glance at the mail on the hall table, then come into the kitchen and take the cracked mug, the big one with his name on it that the children gave him one birthday long ago, and he'll pour himself a cup of coffee and soon he'll be out here to sit in his butt-sprung old chair and look out over the field and down the long hill to where Gilboa's main streets, hidden by trees, lift their few spires and building tops. Beyond Gilboa, the by-passing freeway arches. To the east of the fields it comes around to us close on the other side. We hear the traffic as a low, constant hum. It's getting a little cooler. I call to him and as I do I decide I'll wait until I know what my tears are before I burden him with them. Perhaps we'll walk to services the back way to the town hall, down over the field and the hill.

We've been so close for so long that it is only in flashes that I see him aging, and I have one of these as he comes toward me. How gray he is now! There are wrinkles around his eyes. It must be the same with me, although I don't really see it. In another twenty years, if we are lucky, we will both be old. I ask him about his day.

BETTE PESETSKY was born in Wisconsin in 1932. An alumna of the Iowa Writers' Workshop, she has published two novels, *Author From a Savage People* (1983) and *Digs* (1984). Her first volume of short stories, *Stories Up To a Point* (1981) has been described as a series of dispirited reports from shellshocked women on the state of human relations, but because of its flashes of hilarious pessimism it is, against all the odds, an enjoyable book. The novelist and critic Francine Du Plessix Gray has recommended this collection with unqualified praise. "I have been more moved, impressed, captivated, by this work of Bette Pesetsky," she wrote, "than by any other new collection of short fiction I've read in recent years. Her very personal, tragicomic vision of women's lives; the startling, telegraphic irony of her prose; her deftly compressed, dislocated handling of space and time; her faultless dialogue; her gift for communicating the nomadic quality of America—these are only a few of the aspects of Bette Pesetsky's enormous talent, which is all the more exhilarating because this is her first publication."

Bette Pesetsky

A WALKER'S MANUAL

Whenever possible, I walk to my destination. In order to do this, I must live at the very center of my activities. I am not referring to walking as chore or as exercise but rather as function, which, like breathing or drinking, cannot be stopped. By constant walking, I have learned to use my hips and to extend the length of my stride. Although I seem to be a fast walker to those who move no more than from taxi to building, I wear no speedometer and neither run nor jog. When it rains, I ride, and I would never think of carrying heavy things in my arms. In other words, I am not an obsessive walker, just a very good one.

I feel sorry for those who do not walk and thus see the world only from start to finish. Once, I joined a walking club and rambled in the countryside. But the other walkers made too much of it. They spoke of measured distances and of time, and when they walked, it was a formal activity. They wagered on endurance.

My only concession to scheduling is to map out my daily rounds. It is inefficient to do otherwise. On the back of my kitchen door I have pinned a map with a red dot to represent my apartment house. Cross-streets for forty blocks in any direction are indicated. In ink, I have noted all the places where I might stop. Stores, theaters, homes of friends—a useful navigational scheme.

While walking, you have truly a chance to see. That is the pleasure of walking. The fifteenth-century monk Hegastus, who set himself walking as a penance, was horrified to discover how much he enjoyed the physical movement, how stimulating was the passing scene, men in fields, children at play. He prayed for guidance as his

soles wore thin. He sent back letters intended for a pam-
phlet on the torment of walking. At last he bought shoes
made by a poor craftsman. Calluses and bunions appeared.
In bleeding pain and joy, he returned to the monastery.

My paternal grandmother, an Eastern European lady in
whose custody I was often left, feared the intricacies of
buses and subways. If you missed your stop on the subway, God knew where you would land. Once, holding
tight to my hand, she took me on a subway. We were
going in search of a freshly killed chicken in a store that
might or might not be mythical. We missed our station,
and when we ventured up the stairs to the street, it was to
stand in an area of warehouses. As my grandmother muttered a prayer for our salvation, a car stopped across the
street, and two men got out. One shot the other. The dead
man fell face down. This is what happens when you don't
know where you're going.

My daughter Danielle does not walk, although she has
hiked the Appalachian Trail and marched down into the
Grand Canyon. She was the first in her group to have
black patent slippers with T-straps. You cannot walk in
such shoes. For children, it is best to buy brown leather
oxfords, snub-nosed with a well-sewn welt. Christina of
Sweden, in her romantic journey through New England,
gave up pinching slippers for moccasins made of calfskin.
A yielding shoe is the first necessity. A moccasin with
padded sole provided Christina of Sweden with the perfect
footwear to move through the forest and along unpaved
streets.

Walking leads to many pleasures. One afternoon in the
suburbs, Georgette ran from her house and stood in the
road wringing her hands. She offered me fifty dollars a
week for life if I would never speak of the car that pulled
into her driveway every afternoon at three. Of course, I
took the money.

When you walk down a street, you look in windows,
even into the windows of apartments or private residences
if the blinds are up or the drapes are open. It was a
miniature Queen Anne desk in the window of an antiques

store that caught my attention, and I stopped. It was then that I saw them walking across the street. I had never seen her before.

She was young already, as I knew, early twenties, I'd say, slender and small and not unpretty. Her head just reached his shoulder. They weren't holding hands, but their arms swung together in an intimate rhythm. Occasionally their fingers clasped and unclasped. She wore a plaid coat and a small red tam. Rigidly, I faced the store window, grateful that the street was wide. I followed their disgusting progress in the reflections of glass. She walked at a pace presumably not naturally hers—this, I surmised, to keep up with him. Two short steps and then a little skip. She was what Danielle would call smart, stylish. She looked okay to me too.

I started forward, foolishly quickening my step until I felt the beat of my heart. It was inevitable that I should at some time or other see my former husband. No matter what else changes, habits remain—the same bakery, tailor, dimestore. Charmel, in his account of walking through England, speaks of meeting the same person first down one twist of the road and then again far away on another. Charmel, as best I can recall, does not mention his opinion of the people he thus encountered. My former husband, whom I have not seen for five years, a period long enough for wariness to dissolve, is not, however, someone I hold in high regard. We last met in the lawyer's office, divvying up the spoils.

I forced myself to complete my chores. I stopped in at the cleaners, where they were altering a skirt for me. Midcalf with a single pleat in the front. Too much material in a garment causes it to flap about the knees. It is tiring and interferes with movement. Slacks, of course, are perfect. They permit the stride unfettered. But skirts are once again in fashion and, being single, so must be I.

I carry paper bags in one hand and the box with the skirt in the other. Nigel said that the best time he had was strolling through Paris carrying nothing and buying nothing, a single key and two coins in his pocket.

*   *   *

The search for the perfect boot is difficult. It must protect the foot from the cold, yet remain light and supple. The boots that I already own are unsatisfactory. First of all, there is the question of appearance; those boots are thick and unshapely, suitable for suburban snowbanks. Friends tell me of a mail-order bootmaker in Maine, fearsomely expensive. I take the measurements that his advertisement requests and attach these to a cardboard tracing of my feet. The boots, ordered late, do not arrive until early December. When I open the package, the things within tremble. The leather softened with neat's-foot oil glows and glistens with life. I am transformed. The dreariness of winter is lifted.

I go forth again, my stride never better than it is. It is past two in the afternoon, and I am almost late for my two-twenty class in antiques. The school is twelve blocks away. After class, I stop in the midtown library for the books that I have reserved on dolls. In his heuristic account *Winter Walks*, LeGere says that in the wind one must remove one's head-covering and permit the hair to blow freely. The pleasure will make the cold as nothing. As I unfastened my scarf, they emerged from a restaurant hardly more than a cold breath away. He holds her arm as he escorts her to the edge of the curb. Then he turns up his collar against the weather and steps into the street to signal for a cab. She waits on the sidewalk, secure and confident. One thing he never had with me was trouble getting a taxi.

I was paralyzed. Nothing could have made my legs move past them. A taxi did a pas de deux through the traffic and slid to the curb. He opened the door and stood back for her to enter. She wore high boots made for curb-to-building travel. His hand touched her arm. I take care of you, the gesture said.

Following Danielle's advice, I have my hair cut. It will be a while before I can adjust. Gusts no longer whip stray strands across my forehead as I walk. I have the giddy sensation of false Ménière's disease. As a child, I read an interview with the ingenue Sally Martin. She said that after her hair was bobbed she walked through the streets with the first liberty she had known in years.

Jake, a friend from college days, is giving a party at his Long Island estate. The waterfront paths permit one to walk for two unobstructed miles. I planned to go. Mr. Stanley would be my escort. I'd met him at an auction, where he bought a small wooden train and a doll I didn't want. Afterwards, we talked. I found him amusing and companionable enough. I bought a silver-gray chiffon dress, the merest froth of a garment, dips and panels and triangular sleeves. There are occasions, perhaps once or twice in your life, when you look extremely right, and the narcissistic impulse races forward. I caught glimpses of myself in every reflective object.

So I walked with Mr. Stanley through the summer night. Mr. Stanley was chilled. We returned to the house. As we sipped champagne in the second-floor ballroom, I saw them enter the hall. I was truly startled. Jake must know her. That must be it. I turned away, wondering if I dared suggest to my escort that we tour the grounds again. Her hair, as long as Danielle's, swung free. She wore silk pajamas with the color, the cut, the swagger of youth.

I decided that she looked unutterably out of place.

My attention turned to my foot. It hurt. It was the silver sandal, a concession to the dress. The next morning I could barely hobble. I went to my podiatrist. "Stay off your feet," he said.

I have decided to have all my footwear made by hand. I begin to think about the last, about the instep, about interior construction and ventilation. These feet of mine must serve me till the end. On both sides of my family the women lived well into their eighties. The daughter of the King of Seville practically walked to her funeral.

I am walking down the west side of the street to avoid the direct heat of the sun. I see them waiting across the way for the light to change.

I have placed the key to my apartment on a chain around my neck and I have wrapped in tissue three one-dollar bills tucked into the single pocket of my cotton skirt. I have abandoned all synthetic materials for the summer. Pure cotton absorbs perspiration and keeps the body cool. Unfortunately, I am sometimes recognized by residents and shopkeepers on certain streets. But I do not break my stride. I pretend to be winding my watch. Or I clutch my jaw in imaginary pain. People, the eighteenth-century philosopher Langer writes, do not understand an activity that is beyond their understanding.

PENELOPE LIVELY was born in Cairo, Egypt, in 1933 and spent her childhood there, coming to England in the last year of the war. She read Modern History at St. Anne's College, Oxford. Her novels, which include *Treasures of Time, Nothing Missing but the Samovar, The Road to Lichfield, According to Mark, The Ghost of Thomas Kempe, A Stitch in Time,* and *Perfect Happiness*, have received numerous awards: the Whitbread Award, the Carnegie Medal, the Arts Council National Book Award, the Southern Arts Literature Prize, and nominations for the Booker Prize. She has reviewed books regularly for *Encounter, The Literary Review,* and *The London Times.* Her short stories, which have appeared in *Vogue, Cosmopolitan, Encounter,* and *Quarto,* have recently been collected in a volume entitled *Corruption,* from which the story that follows is taken. Relatively unknown in America, in England Penelope Lively is ranked with Doris Lessing and Margaret Drabble as one of the best British fiction writers of our day. That her solid reputation is amply justified a reading of one of her few novels to be published in America, *Perfect Happiness,* bears out. "Although about pain," wrote Andrew Sinclair in *The London Times,* "it is a pleasure to read, so wise it is on the depth of feeling and abiding of love." So understated an accolade offers only the smallest suggestion of the intense beauty and perfect grace of Mrs. Lively's fiction. She lives in Oxfordshire and London with her husband and two children.

Penelope Lively

GROW OLD ALONG WITH ME, THE BEST IS YET TO BE

"Oh, *I* don't know . . .." said Sarah. "Decisions, decisions. I hate them. I mean, one of the things that bothers me is—would I stop being *me*? Would I change. If we did."

She wore dungarees in pale turquoise, and a white T-shirt. She drove the Fiat hunched forward over the steering-wheel. Her face was engulfed by large reflecting sun-glasses across which flew hedges, trees, a passing car. "It's rather gorgeous round here, isn't it? Half-asleep, as though nothing happens in a hundred years."

Tony said, "We both might. It's a significant step in a relationship—that's the point of it, I suppose."

"And the point of waiting. Thinking about it. Not rushing."

"Not that we have."

"Quite. Shall we stop and eat soon?"

"Yes—when there's a reasonable pub."

Gloucestershire unreeled at either side: dark green, straw-coloured, unpopulated. Trees drooped in the fields; a village was still and silent except for a lorry throbbing outside a shop. High summer gripped the landscape; birds twitched from hedge to hedge.

"Half the time," said Sarah, "it doesn't crop up. One sort of puts it out of one's mind—there are too many other things to think of. And then it begins to nag. We've got to either do it or not do it."

"We've been not doing it for three years, darling."

"I know, I know. But all the same, it looms."

"We are actually," he said, "better off, from a tax

point of view, unmarried. Since your rise. We went into that in the winter—remember?''

''What about this—Free House, Bar Snacks. How much better off, exactly?''

''Oh, lord, I don't know. Hundreds, anyway.''

She turned the car into the pub yard. ''It's a point, then. Ma keeps saying, what happens if there's a baby? And I say well that would of course put a different complexion on things but *until* we are absolutely free to choose. The trouble is that dear ma thinks I'm on the shelf at twenty-six. I keep saying, there aren't shelves now.''

The woman behind the bar watched them come in, a good-looking young couple, in the pink of health, not short of money, the kind of people who know their way around. She served them lagers and chicken salad, and noted Sarah's neat figure, not an ounce in the wrong place, which induced vague discontent. I'm dieting, she thought, as from Monday I am, I swear to God. She observed also Tony's tanned forearms, below the rolled sleeves of an indefinably modish shirt, like blokes in colour supp. ads. Thirtyish, nice voice. He didn't look at her, pocketing the change, turning away with the plates. She watched them settle in the corner by the window, sitting close, talking. In love, presumably, lucky so-and-so's.

''Tax is certainly a point,'' said Sarah. ''Getting dependent on each other is another. Look at Tom and Alison. But one still feels that eventually we're going to have to make some kind of decision. You can have my pickled onion.''

''Lots of people don't. Decide, I mean. Look at Blake and Susan.''

''I don't want to look at Blake and Susan. Blake's forty-two, did you know that? And anyway he's *been* married. Oh, isn't it all difficult? We decided no baby, barring accidents, at least not yet, and that was one decision. Thank God for the pill, I suppose. I mean, imagine when they just *happened*.''

''They still do sometimes. Look at Maggie.''

''Oh, Maggie meant to, for goodness sake. That baby was no accident. It was psychological.''

They ate, for a while, in silence. At the bar middle-aged men, locals, sporadically conversed, out of kilter like clocks ticking at different speeds. The woman wiped glasses. A commercial traveller came in and ordered a steak and kidney with chips. On the wall, hand-written posters advertised a Bring and Buy, a Darby and Joan Outing. Tony stacked their empty plates. "Not exactly the hub of the universe, this."

"It's rather sweet. Laurie Lee country. I used to adore that book—what's-it-called?—we did it for O-levels. Sex in the hedges and all that. O.K.—I'll find the loo and we'll get moving. Where are we, by the way, I've lost track?"

When she came back he had the map book open on his knee. "Let's have a look, there might be something to go and see. Oh, goodness, there is—we're not far from Deerhurst. Oh, we must see Deerhurst. You know—Saxon church, very special."

"Right you are. Do we have Pevsner?"

"On the back shelf of the car. What luck—I never realised Deerhurst was hereabouts."

"Aren't you a clever girl?" he said, patting her knee. "Knowing about Saxon churches."

The woman behind the bar, watching them, thought, yes, that's how it is when you're like that. Can't keep your hands off each other. Ah well. "How's the back, John?" she said. "That stuff I told you about do any good?" The young couple were getting up now, slinging sweaters about their shoulders, leaving without a backwards glance. People passing through, going off into other lives. Young intense lives. "What? Oh, thanks very much—I'll have a lager and lime. Cheers, John."

"Drive or navigate?" said Sarah, in the car park. "You're better with the map than I am, and it's all side roads to this church. I'll tell you one thing—if we do get married it's not going to be any flipping church business. That's what ma's got her eye on, you realise."

"There'd have to be some sort of do."

"We could have it at the flat. Cheaper. The do, I mean.

And registry office. But it's all a bit academic, until we actually decide something. Do I go left or right?''

Signposts fingered toward slothful hinterlands. Cars glittered between the hedges, sparks of colour in a world of green and fawn. On the edge of the village, washing-lines held up stiff shapes of clothes, slumping pink and yellow sheets, a rank of nappies. A man scraped around young cabbages with a hoe.

"Corfu," said Tony, "was livelier."

"I thought we agreed never again a package holiday. Anyway, it's the new car this year instead."

"This is our fourth holiday together, Sarah."

"Cor . . . Hey—you're not directing me. That sign said Deerhurst."

"Sorry. My mind was on other things. Incidentally, what started us off on this marriage discussion? Today, I mean."

"I can't remember. Oh yes I can—it was you talking about this aunt of yours. Will you have to go to the wedding, by the way?"

"I hope not. I'd be the only person there under fifty, I should imagine. No—hearty good wishes over the phone and that kind of thing."

"It's nice for her," said Sarah charitably. "At that age. If a bit kind of fake, if you see what I mean."

"Yes. But for that generation there wouldn't be any alternative."

They nodded, sombrely.

"Here we are," said Sarah. "And this must be where you leave cars. Good—there's no one else there, I hate looking at churches when there's anyone else. Where's Pevsner? We're going to do this place properly—it's supposed to be important."

They advanced into the churchyard. The church, squatting amid yews, seemed almost derisive in its antiquity, tethered to something dark and incomprehensible, uncaring, too far away to be understood. Its stone was blurred, its shapes strange and unlovely. Gravestones drowned in grass. An aeroplane, unseen, rumbled across the milky sky.

" '. . . tall narrow nave of the C8,' " Tony read. "Seven hundred and something. Jesus! That makes you think, doesn't it?"

"There's this famous sculpture thing over the door. An animal head. That's it, I suppose. Goodness, isn't it all sinister?"

They stood in silence. "Things that are so incredibly old," Sarah went on, "just leave you feeling respectful. I mean, that they're there at all."

They went into the church. Tony took a few steps down the nave. "Yes. I know what you mean. Even more so inside. All this stone standing for so long"—he gestured at piers, crossing arch, narrow uncompromising windows. "Read Pevsner," instructed Sarah. "I like to understand what I'm looking at." They toured the building, side by side, heads cocked from book to architectural feature, understanding.

The church door, which they had closed behind them, burst open. The sound made them both jump. Turning, they saw a man who stood framed in the gush of light from without: a tall man in tweed jacket and baggy-kneed trousers, an odd prophetic-looking figure with a mane of white hair, like a more robust version of the aged Bertrand Russell. A memorable person, who stood for a moment staring wildly round the church, at Sarah and Tony for one dismissive instant, and who then strode down the aisle searching, apparently, the pillars, and then back to the entrance and out, slamming the door.

"The vicar?" said Tony, after a moment.

"No. Frankly. That was no vicar. Funny to storm out like that, though. This place *vaut le detour*, as *Michelin* says."

"P'raps he's seen it already."

"Presumably." Sarah turned back to Pevsner. "Apparently there's this other carving outside, round at the back, we'd better go and find it. We've done the rest, I think."

She led the way out of the church and round the side, through the long grass and the leaning grave-stones. And came, thus, upon them first.

In the angle of a buttress, up against the wall of the

church. The man, the white-haired tall man, his back now turned. Turned because he was locked in an embrace, a succulent sexual embrace (the sound, just, of mouths—the impression of loins pushed together) with a woman little of whom could be seen as, eyes averted, Sarah scurried past, followed a few paces behind by Tony. Both of them at once seeing, and quickly looking away. Seeing of the man his tweed back and his mane of yellow-white hair and of the woman—well, little except an impression of blue denim skirt and plimsolls. And more white hair: crisp curly grey-white hair.

They achieved the back of the church and stood peering up at the wall.

"I can't see this sculpture," said Sarah (voice firm, ordinary, not lowered, rather loud indeed). "It's supposed to be a Virgin—ah, that must be it. Right up just under the window there."

When they came back past the buttress the couple were gone. The churchyard was quite empty. The whole place, which had briefly rocked, had sunk back into its lethargy. That crackling startling charge of passion had dissipated into the stagnant air of the summer afternoon. It was three o'clock, and felt as if it forever would be. Somewhere beyond the hedge a tractor ground across a field.

"Let's go," said Sarah brightly. "I think I've had Deerhurst."

The car was no longer alone. Two others, now, were parked alongside. Sarah whipped the key into the lock and opened the door. She plumped down into the driving-seat. "You know what? That was an assignation we stumbled into."

"So it would seem."

"Where are they now, do you imagine?"

Tony shrugged.

Sarah started the engine. She said with sudden violence, "You know, it was a bit revolting. They were seventy if they were a day."

Tony nodded. Embarrassment filled the car.

FAY WELDON was born in England in 1933 and raised in New Zealand. She received an M.A. in economics and psychology before turning to the writing of novels, film scripts, and plays. Her novels include *Puffball*, *Praxis*, *Female Friends*, *Down Among the Women*, *The Life and Loves of a She-Devil*, and the recent *Letters to Alice*. *The Life and Loves of a She-Devil* is a hilarious, outrageous and devastating unmasking of the faces of romantic and married love. Reading it explains why Miss Weldon is considered one of England's wittiest and wickedest novelists. The story that follows here, "Alopecia," which was included in the English collection *The Best of Winter: 25 Years of the Best of Winter's Tales*, shows Miss Weldon zeroing in on feminism in its fake and authentic guises; it resounds with the merciless satiric honesty for which her fiction has been widely acclaimed in England and America. Anita Brookner in the London *Times*, *Literary Supplement* has called her "one of the most astute and distinctive women writing fiction today." Miss Weldon lives in London with her husband and four children.

Fay Weldon

ALOPECIA

It's 1972.

"Fiddlesticks," says Maureen. Everyone else says "crap" or "balls," but Maureen's current gear, being Victorian sprigged muslin, demands an appropriate vocabulary. "Fiddlesticks. If Erica says her bald patches are anything to do with Brian, she's lying. It's alopecia."

"I wonder which would be worse," murmurs Ruthie in her soft voice, "to have a husband who tears your hair out in the night, or to have alopecia."

Ruthie wears a black fringed satin dress exactly half a century old, through which, alas, Ruthie's ribs show even more prominently than her breasts. Ruthie's little girl Poppy (at three too old for playgroup, too young for school) wears a long white (well, yellowish) cotton shift which contrasts nicely with her mother's dusty black.

"At least the husband might improve, with effort," says Alison, "unlike alopecia. You wake up one morning with a single bald patch and a month or so later there you are, completely bald. Nothing anyone can do about it." Alison, plump mother of three, sensibly wears a flowered Laura Ashley dress which hides her bulges.

"It might be quite interesting," remarks Maureen. "The egg-head approach. One would have to forgo the past, of course, and go all space-age, which would hardly be in keeping with the mood of the times."

"You are the mood of the times, Maureen," murmurs Ruthie, as expected. Ruthie's simple adulation of Maureen is both gratifying and embarrassing, everyone agrees.

Everyone agrees, on the other hand, that Erica Bisham of the bald patches is a stupid, if ladylike, bitch.

Maureen, Ruthie and Alison are working in Maureen's premises off the Kings Road. Here Maureen, as befits the glamour of her station, the initiator of Mauromania, meets the media, expresses opinions, answers the phone, dictates to secretaries (male), selects and matches fabrics, approves designs and makes, in general, multitudinous decisions—although not, perhaps, as multitudinous as the ones she was accustomed to make in the middle and late sixties, when the world was young and rich and wild. Maureen is forty but you'd never think it. She wears a large hat by day (and, one imagines, night) which shades her anxious face and guards her still pretty complexion. Maureen leads a rich life. Maureen once had her pubic hair dyed green to match her fingernails—or so her husband Kim announced to a waiting (well, such were the days) world: she divorced him not long after, having lost his baby at five months. The head of the foetus, rumour had it, emerged green, and her National Health Service GP refused to treat her any more, and she had to go private after all—she with her Marxist convictions.

That was 1968. If the state's going to tumble, let it tumble. The sooner the better. Drop out, everyone! Mauromania magnifique! And off goes Maureen's husband Kim with Maureen's *au pair*—a broad-hipped, big-bosomed girl, good breeding material, with an ordinary coarse and curly bush, if somewhat reddish.

Still, it had been a good marriage as marriages go. And as marriages go, it went. Or so Maureen remarked to the press, on her way home (six beds, six baths, four recep., American kitchen, patio, South Ken) from the divorce courts. Maureen cried a little in the taxi, when she'd left her public well behind, partly from shock and grief, mostly from confusion that beloved Kim, Kim, who so despised the nuclear family, who had so often said that he and she ought to get divorced in order to have a true and unfettered relationship, that Maureen's Kim should have speeded up Maureen's divorce in order to marry Maureen's *au pair* girl before the baby arrived. Kim and Maureen had been married for fifteen years. Kim had been Kevin from Liverpool before seeing the light or at any rate the guru. Mau-

reen had always been just Maureen from Hoxton, east
London: remained so through the birth, rise and triumph of
Mauromania. It was her charm. Local girl makes good.

Maureen has experience of life: she knows by now it is
wise to watch what people do, not listen to what they say.
Well, it's something to have learned. Ruthie and Alison,
her (nominal) partners from the beginning, each her junior
by some ten years, listen to Maureen with respect and
diffidence.

And should they not? After the green pubic hair episode, after the *au pair* and divorce incident, Maureen
marries a swinging professor of philosophy, a miracle of
charm and intelligence who appears on TV, a catch indeed. Maureen's knowledge of life and ideas is considerable: it must be: lying next to a man all night, every night,
wouldn't you absorb something from him? Sop up some
knowledge, some information, some wisdom?

Someone, somewhere, surely, must know everything?
God help us if they don't.

Maureen and the professor have a son. He's dyslexic—
the professor tries to teach him English at two, Latin at
three, and Greek at four—and now, away at a special
boarding-school, is doing well on the sports field and
happy. She and the professor are divorced. He lives in the
South Ken home, for reasons known only to lawyers. All
Maureen wants now (she says, from her penthouse) is
another chance: someone familiar, trustworthy, ordinary.
A suburban house, a family, privacy, obscurity. To run
Mauromania from a distance: delegating: dusting, only
pausing to rake in the money.

Mauromania magnifique!

"Mind you," says Maureen now, matching up purple
feathers with emerald satin to great effect, "if I was Brian
I'd certainly beat Erica to death. Fancy having to listen to
that whining voice night after night. The only trouble is
he's become too much of a gentleman. He'll never have
the courage to do it. Turned his back on his origins, and
all that. It doesn't do."

Maureen has known Brian since the old days in Hoxton.
They were evacuees together: shared the same bomb shelter

on their return from Starvation Hall in Ipswich—a boys'
public school considered unsafe for the gentry's children
but all right for the East Enders'. (The cooking staff nobly
stayed on; but, distressingly, the boys, it seems, had been
living on less than rations for generations, hence Starvation Hall.)

"It's all Erica's fantasy," says Ruthie, knowledgeably.
"A kind of dreadful sexual fantasy. She *wants* him to beat
her up so she trots around London saying he does. Poor
Brian. It comes from marrying into the English upper
classes, old style. She must be nearly fifty. She has this
kind of battered-looking face."

Her voice trails away. There is a slight pause in the
conversation.

"Um," says Alison.

"That's drink," says Maureen, decisively. "Poor bloody
Brian. What a ball-breaker to have married." Brian was
Maureen's childhood sweetheart. What a romantic, pla-
tonic idyll! She nearly married him once, twice, three
times. Once in the very early days, before Kim, before
anyone, when Brian was selling books from a barrow in
Hoxton market. Once again, after Kim and before the
professor, by which time Brian was taking expensive photographs of the trendy and successful—only then Erica
turned up in Brian's bed, long-legged, disdainful, beautiful, with a model's precise and organised face, and the
fluty tones of the girl who'd bought her school uniform at
Harrods, and that was the end of that. Not that Brian had
ever exactly proposed to Maureen; not that they'd ever
even been to bed together: they just knew each other and
each other's bed partners so well that each knew what the
other was thinking, feeling, hoping. Both from Hoxton,
east London: Brian, Maureen; and a host of others, too.
What was there, you might ask, about that particular acre
of the East End which over a period of a few years gave
birth to such a crop of remarkable children, such a flare-up
of human creativity in terms of writing, painting, designing,
entertaining? Changing the world? One might almost think
God had chosen it for an experiment in intensive talent-
breeding. Mauromania, God-sent.

And then there was another time in the late sixties, when there was a short break between Brian and Erica— Erica had a hysterectomy against Brian's wishes; but during those two weeks of opportunity Maureen, her business flourishing, her designs world-famous, Mauromania a label for even trendy young queens (royal, that is) to boast, rich beyond counting—during those two special weeks of all weeks Maureen fell head over heels classically in love with Pedro: no, not a fisherman, but as good as—Italian, young, open-shirted, sloe-eyed, a designer. And Pedro, it later transpired, was using Maureen as a means to laying all the models, both male and female (Maureen had gone into menswear). Maureen was the last to know, and by the time she did Brian was in Erica's arms (or whatever) again. A sorry episode. Maureen spent six months at a health farm, on a diet of grapes and brown rice. At the end of that time Mauromania Man had collapsed, her business manager had jumped out of a tenth-floor window, and an employee's irate mother was bringing a criminal suit against Maureen personally for running a brothel. It was all quite irrational. If the employee, a runaway girl of, it turned out, only thirteen, but looking twenty, and an excellent seamstress, had contracted gonorrhea whilst in her employ, was that Maureen's fault? The judge, sensibly, decided it wasn't, and that the entire collapse of British respectability could not fairly be laid at Maureen's door. Legal costs came to more than £12,000: the country house and stables had to be sold at a knock-down price. That was disaster year.

And who was there during that time to hold Maureen's hand? No one. Everyone, it seemed, had troubles enough of their own. And all the time, Maureen's poor heart bled for Pedro, of the ridiculous name and the sloe eyes, long departed, laughing, streptococci surging in his wake. And of all the old friends and allies only Ruthie and Alison lingered on, two familiar faces in a sea of changing ones, getting younger every day, and hungrier year by year not for fun, fashion, and excitement, but for money, promotion, security, and acknowledgement.

The staff even went on strike once, walking up and

down outside the workshop with placards announcing hours and wages, backed by Maoists, women's liberationists and trade unionists, all vying for their trumpery allegiance, puffing up a tiny news story into a colossal media joke, not even bothering to get Maureen's side of the story—absenteeism, drug addiction, shoddy workmanship, falling markets, constricting profits.

But Ruthie gave birth to Poppy, unexpectedly, in the black and gold ladies' rest-room (customers only—just as well it wasn't in the staff toilets where the plaster was flaking and the old wall-cisterns came down on your head if you pulled the chain) and that cheered everyone up. Business perked up, staff calmed down as unemployment rose. Poppy, born of Mauromania, was everyone's favourite, everyone's mascot. Her father, only seventeen, was doing two years inside, framed by the police for dealing in pot. He did not have too bad a time—he got three A-levels and university entrance inside, which he would never have got outside, but it meant poor little Poppy had to do without a father's care and Ruthie had to cope on her own. Ruthie of the ribs.

Alison, meanwhile, somewhat apologetically, had married Hugo, a rather straight and respectable actor who believed in women's rights; they had three children and lived in a cosy house with a garden in Muswell Hill: Alison even belonged to the PTA! Hugo was frequently without work, but Hugo and Alison managed, between them, to keep going and even happy. Hugo thinks Alison should ask for a rise, but Alison doesn't like to. That's the trouble about working for a friend and being only a nominal partner.

"Don't let's talk about Erica Bisham any more," says Maureen now. "It's too draggy a subject." So they don't.

But one midnight a couple of weeks later, when Maureen, Ruthie and Alison are working late to meet an order—as is their frequent custom these days (and one most unnerving to Hugo, Alison's husband)—there comes a tap on the door. It's Erica, of course. Who else would tap, in such an ingratiating fashion? Others cry "Hi!" or "Peace!" and enter. Erica, smiling nervously and crookedly; her yellow hair eccentric in the extreme; bushy in places, sparse in others. Couldn't she wear a wig? She is wearing a Marks & Spencer nightie which not even Ruthie would think of wearing, in the house or out of it. It is bloodstained down the back. (Menstruation is not yet so fashionable as to be thus demonstrable, though it can be talked about at length.) A strong smell of what? alcohol, or is it nail-varnish? hangs about her. Drinking again. (Alison's husband, Hugo, in a long period of unemployment, once veered on to the edge of alcoholism but fortunately veered off again, and the smell of nail-varnish, acetone, gave a warning sign of an agitated, overworked liver, unable to cope with acetaldehyde, the highly toxic product of alcohol metabolism.)

"Could I sit down?" says Erica. "He's locked me out. Am I speaking oddly? I think I've lost a tooth. I'm hurting under my ribs and I feel sick."

They stare at her—this drunk, dishevelled, trouble-making woman.

"He," says Maureen finally. "Who's he?"

"Brian."

"You're going to get into trouble, Erica," says Ruthie, though more kindly than Maureen, "if you go round saying dreadful things about poor Brian."

"I wouldn't have come here if there was anywhere else," says Erica.

"You must have friends," observes Maureen, as if to say, Don't count us amongst them if you have.

"No," Erica sounds desolate. "He has his friends at work. I don't seem to have any."

"I wonder why," says Maureen under her breath; and then, "I'll get you a taxi home, Erica. You're in no state to be out."

"I'm not drunk, if that's what you think."

"Who ever is," sighs Ruthie, sewing relentlessly on. Four more blouses by one o'clock. Then, thank God, bed.

Little Poppy has passed out on a pile of orange ostrich feathers. She looks fantastic.

"If Brian does beat you up," says Alison, who has seen

her father beat her mother on many a Saturday night, "why don't you go to the police?"

"I did once, and they told me to go home and behave myself."

"Or leave him?" Alison's mother left Alison's father.

"Where would I go? How would I live? The children? I'm not well." Erica sways. Alison puts a chair beneath her. Erica sits, legs planted wide apart, head down. A few drops of blood fall on the floor. From Erica's mouth, or elsewhere? Maureen doesn't see, doesn't care. Maureen's on the phone, calling radio cabs who do not reply.

"I try not to provoke him, but I never know what's going to set him off," mumbles Erica. "Tonight it was Tampax. He said only whores wore Tampax. He tore it out and kicked me. Look."

Erica pulls up her nightie (Erica's wearing no knickers) and exposes her private parts in a most shameful, shameless fashion. The inner thighs are blue and mottled, but then, dear God, she's nearly fifty.

What does one look like, thigh-wise, nearing fifty? Maureen's the nearest to knowing, and she's not saying. As for Ruthie, she hopes she'll never get there. Fifty!

"The woman's mad," mutters Maureen. "Perhaps I'd better call the loony wagon, not a taxi?"

"Thank God Poppy's asleep." Poor Ruthie seems in a state of shock.

"You can come home with me, Erica," says Alison. "God knows what Hugo will say. He hates matrimonial upsets. He says if you get in between, they both start hitting you."

Erica gurgles, a kind of mirthless laugh. From behind her, mysteriously, a child steps out. She is eight, stocky, plain and pale, dressed in boring Ladybird pyjamas.

"Mummy?"

Erica's head whips up; the blood on Erica's lip is wiped away by the back of Erica's hand. Erica straightens her back. Erica smiles. Erica's voice is completely normal, ladylike.

"Hallo darling. How did you get here?"

"I followed you. Daddy was too angry."

"He'll be better soon, Libby," says Erica brightly. "He always is."

"We're not going home? Please don't let's go home. I don't want to see Daddy."

"Bitch," mutters Maureen, "she's even turned his own child against him. Poor bloody Brian. There's nothing at all the matter with her. Look at her now."

For Erica is on her feet, smoothing Libby's hair, murmuring, laughing.

"Poor bloody Erica," observes Alison. It is the first time she has ever defied Maureen, let alone challenged her wisdom. And rising with as much dignity as her plump frame and flounced cotton will allow, Alison takes Erica and Libby home and installs them for the night in the spare room of the cosy house in Muswell Hill.

Hugo isn't any too pleased. "Your smart sick friends," he says. And, "I'd beat a woman like that to death myself, any day." And, "Dragging that poor child into it: it's appalling." He's nice to Libby, though, and rings up Brian to say she's safe and sound, and looks after her while Alison takes Erica round to the doctor. The doctor sends Erica round to the hospital, and the hospital admits her for tests and treatment.

"Why bother?" enquires Hugo. "Everyone knows she's mad."

In the evening, Brian comes all the way to Muswell Hill in his Ferrari to pick up Libby. He's an attractive man: intelligent and perspicacious, fatherly and gentle. Just right, it occurs to Alison, for Maureen.

"I'm so sorry about all this," he says. "I love my wife dearly but she has her problems. There's a dark side to her nature—you've no idea. A deep inner violence—which of course manifests itself in this kind of behaviour. She's deeply psychophrenic. I'm so afraid for the child."

"The hospital did admit her," murmurs Alison. "And not to the psychiatric ward, but the surgical."

"That will be her hysterectomy scar again," says Brian. "Any slight tussle—she goes quite wild, and I have to restrain her for her own safety—and it opens up. It's symptomatic of her inner sickness, I'm afraid. She even says herself it opens to let the build-up of wickedness out. What I can't forgive is the way she drags poor little Libby into things. She's turning the child against me. God knows what I'm going to do. Well, at least I can bury myself in work. I hear you're an actor, Hugo.''

Hugo offers Brian a drink, and Brian offers (well, more or less) Hugo a part in a new rock musical going on in the West End. Alison goes to visit Erica in hospital.

"Erica has some liver damage, but it's not irreversible: she'll be feeling nauseous for a couple of months, that's all. She's lost a back tooth and she's had a couple of stitches put in her vagina,'' says Alison to Maureen and Ruthie next day. The blouse order never got completed—re-orders now look dubious. But if staff haven't the loyalty to work unpaid overtime any more, what else can be expected? The partners (nominal) can't do everything.

"Who said so?'' enquires Maureen, sceptically. "The hospital or Erica?''

"Well,'' Alison is obliged to admit, "Erica.''

"You are an innocent, Alison.'' Maureen sounds quite cross. "Erica can't open her poor sick mouth without uttering a lie. It's her hysterectomy scar opened up again, that's all. No wonder. She's a nymphomaniac: she doesn't leave Brian alone month in, month out. She has the soul of a whore. Poor man. He's so upset by it all. Who wouldn't be?''

Brian takes Maureen out to lunch. In the evening, Alison goes to visit Erica in hospital, but Erica has gone. Sister says, oh yes, her husband came to fetch her. They hadn't wanted to let her go so soon but Mr. Bisham seemed such a sensible, loving man, they thought he could look after his wife perfectly well, and it's always nicer at home, isn't it? Was it *the* Brian Bisham? Yes, she'd thought so. Poor Mrs. Bisham—what a dreadful world we live in, when a respectable married woman can't even walk the streets without being brutally attacked, sexually assaulted by strangers.

It's 1973.

Winter. A chill wind blowing, a colder one still to come. A three-day week imposed by an insane government. Strikes, power-cuts, black-outs. Maureen, Ruthie and Alison work by candlelight. All three wear fun-furs—old stock, unsaleable. Poppy is staying with Ruthie's mother, as she usually is these days. Poppy has been developing a squint, and the doctor says she has to wear glasses with one blanked-out lens for at least eighteen months. Ruthie, honestly, can't bear to see her daughter thus. Ruthie's mother, of a prosaic nature, a lady who buys her clothes at C & A Outsize, doesn't seem to mind.

"If oil prices go up," says Maureen gloomily, "what's going to happen to the price of synthetics? What's going to happen to Mauromania, come to that?"

"Go up the market," says Alison, "the rich are always with us."

Maureen says nothing. Maureen is bad-tempered, these days. She is having some kind of painful trouble with her teeth, which she seems less well able to cope with than she can the trouble with staff (overpaid), raw materials (unavailable), delivery dates (impossible), distribution (unchancy), costs (soaring), profits (falling), re-investment (non-existent). And the snow has ruined the penthouse roof and it has to be replaced, at the cost of many thousands. Men friends come and go: they seem to get younger and less feeling. Sometimes Maureen feels they treat her as a joke. They ask her about the sixties as if it were a different age: of Mauromania as if it were something as dead as the dodo—but it's still surely a label which counts for something, brings in foreign currency, ought really to bring her some recognition. The Beatles got the MBE; why not Maureen of Mauromania? Throw-away clothes for throw-away people?

"Ruthie," says Maureen. "You're getting careless. You've put the pocket on upside-down, and it's going for copying. That's going to hold up the whole batch. Oh, what the hell. Let it go through."

"Do you ever hear anything of Erica Bisham?" Ruthie asks Alison, more to annoy Maureen than because she wants to know. "Is she still wandering round in the middle of the night?"

"Hugo does a lot of work for Brian, these days," says Alison carefully. "But he never mentions Erica."

"Poor Brian. What a fate. A wife with alopecia! I expect she's bald as a coot by now. As good a revenge as any, I dare say."

"It was nothing to do with alopecia," says Alison. "Brian just tore out chunks of her hair, nightly." Alison's own marriage isn't going so well. Hugo's got the lead in one of Brian's long runs in the West End. Show business consumes his thoughts and ambitions. The ingenue lead is in love with Hugo and says so, on TV quiz games and in the Sunday supplements. She's under age. Alison feels old, bored and boring.

"These days I'd believe anything," says Ruthie. "She must provoke him dreadfully."

"I don't know what you've got against Brian, Alison," says Maureen. "Perhaps you just don't like men. In which case you're not much good in a fashion house. Ruthie, that's another pocket upside-down."

"I feel sick," says Ruthie. Ruthie's pregnant again. Ruthie's husband was out of prison and with her for exactly two weeks; then he flew off to Istanbul to smuggle marijuana back into the country. He was caught. Now he languishes in a Turkish jail. "What's to become of us?"

"We must develop a sense of sisterhood," says Alison, "that's all."

It's 1974.

Alison's doorbell rings at three in the morning. It is election night, and Alison is watching the results on television. Hugo (presumably) is watching them somewhere else, with the ingenue lead—now above the age of consent, which spoils the pleasure somewhat. It is Erica and Libby. Erica's nose is broken. Libby, at ten, is now in charge. Both are in their night-clothes. Alison pays off the taxi-driver, who won't take a tip. "What a world," he says.

"I couldn't think where else to come," says Libby. "Where he wouldn't follow her. I wrote down this address last time I was here. I thought it might come in useful, sometime."

It is the end of Alison's marriage, and the end of Alison's job. Hugo, whose future career largely depends on Brian's good will, says, you have Erica in the house or you have me. Alison says, I'll have Erica. "Lesbian, dyke," says Hugo, bitterly. "Don't think you'll keep the children, you won't."

Maureen says, "That was the first and last time Brian ever hit her. He told me so. She lurched towards him on purpose. She *wanted* her nose broken; idiot Alison, don't you understand? Erica nags and provokes. She calls him dreadful, insulting, injuring things in public. She flays him with words. She says he's impotent: an artistic failure. I've heard her. Everyone has. When finally he lashes out, she's delighted. Her last husband beat hell out of her. She's a born victim."

Alison takes Erica to a free solicitor, who—surprise, surprise—is efficient and who collects evidence and affidavits from doctors and hospitals all over London, has a restraining order issued against Brian, gets Libby and Erica back into the matrimonial home, and starts and completes divorce proceedings and gets handsome alimony. It all takes six weeks, at the end of which time Erica's face has altogether lost its battered look.

Alison turns up at work the morning after the alimony details are known and has the door shut in her face. Mauromania. The lettering is flaking. The door needs re-painting.

Hugo sells the house over Alison's head. By this time she and the children are living in a two-room flat.

Bad times.

"You're a very destructive person," says Maureen to Alison in the letter officially terminating her appointment. "Brian never did you any harm, and you've ruined his life, you've interfered in a marriage in a really wicked way. You've encouraged Brian's wife to break up his perfectly good marriage, and turned Brian's child against him, and not content with that you've crippled Brian financially. Erica would never have been so vindictive if she hadn't had you egging her on. It was you who made her go to law, and once things get into lawyers' hands they escalate, as who better than I should know? The law has nothing to do with natural justice, idiot Alison. Hugo is very concerned for you and thinks you should have mental treatment. As for me, I am really upset. I expected friendship and loyalty from you, Alison; I trained you and employed you, and saw you through good times and bad. I may say, too, that your notion of Mauromania becoming an exclusive fashion house, which I followed through for a time, was all but disastrous, and symptomatic of your general bad judgement. After all, this is the people's age, the sixties, the seventies, the eighties, right through to the new century. Brian is coming in with me in the new world Mauromania.''

Mauromania, meretricious!

A month or so later, Brian and Maureen are married. It's a terrific wedding, somewhat marred by the death of Ruthie—killed, with her new baby, in the Paris air crash, on her way home from Istanbul, where she'd been trying to get her young husband released from prison. She'd failed. But then, if she'd succeeded, he'd have been killed too, and he was too young to die. Little Poppy was at the memorial service, in a sensible trouser-suit from C & A, bought for her by Gran, without her glasses, both enormous eyes apparently now functioning well. She didn't remember Alison, who was standing next to her, crying softly. Soft beds of orange feathers, far away, another world.

Alison wasn't asked to the wedding, which in any case clashed with the mass funeral of the air-crash victims. Just as well. What would she have worn?

It's 1975.

It's summer, long and hot. Alison walks past Mauromania. Alison has remarried. She is happy. She didn't know that such ordinary everyday kindness could exist and endure. Alison is wearing, like everyone else, jeans and a T-shirt. A new ordinariness, a common sense, a serio-cheerfulness infuses the times. Female breasts swing free, libertarian by day, erotic by night, costing nobody anything, or at most a little modesty. No profit there.

Mauromania is derelict, boarded up. A barrow outside is piled with old stock, sale-priced. Coloured tights, fun-furs, feathers, slinky dresses. Passers-by pick over the stuff, occasionally buy, mostly look, and giggle, and mourn, and remember.

Alison, watching, sees Maureen coming down the steps. Maureen is rather nastily dressed in a bright yellow silk shift. Maureen's hair seems strange, bushy in parts, sparse in others. Maureeen has abandoned her hat. Maureen bends over the barrow, and Alison can see the bald patches on her scalp.

"Alopecia," says Alison, out loud. Maureen looks up. Maureen's face seems somehow worn and battered, and old and haunted beyond its years. Maureen stares at Alison, recognising, and Maureen's face takes on an expression of half-apology, half-entreaty. Maureen wants to speak.

But Alison only smiles brightly and lightly and walks on.

"I'm afraid poor Maureen has alopecia, on top of everything else," she says to anyone who happens to enquire after that sad, forgotten figure, who once had everything—except, perhaps, a sense of sisterhood.

ELLEN GILCHRIST was born in 1935 and raised on a Mississippi plantation in Issaquena County, near Greenville. During World War II her father, as an Army engineer, moved his family in and out of small towns in Indiana, Illinois, and Missouri. (The wartime atmosphere of small town life in the American Midwest is palpable in the story that follows here.) At 14, Miss Gilchrist wrote a column for a Kentucky newspaper, "Chit and Chat About This and That," which died when at 19 she dropped out of school, ran off to the North Carolina mountains, married, had three children and divorced. In 1966 she enrolled at Millsaps College in Jackson, Mississippi, where she studied creative writing with Eudora Welty. Her first collection of stories, *In the Land of Dreamy Dreams*, was published in 1981 by the University of Arkansas Press, an event still noted in those lists of authors made famous by university press books. Her first novel, *The Annunciation*, came out in 1983. Except to a small following, hers was an unknown talent until her second collection *Victory Over Japan*—the title story follows—was published in 1984 and won the American Book Award in fiction. Writing in *The New York Times Book Review*, the novelist Beverly Lowry praised Gilchrist's nerve and generosity and especially her heroines, New South hellions with a dark and crackling sense of humor such as Tennessee Williams and Lillian Hellman never conjured. "Reynolds Price has written about [such] women," writes Miss Lowry, "as does Alice Adams, but Ellen Gilchrist's racy females probably take the cake." Miss Gilchrist currently lives in the Ozarks, in the small college town of Fayetteville, Arkansas, which in recent years has become something of a writers' colony.

Ellen Gilchrist

VICTORY OVER JAPAN

When I was in the third grade I knew a boy who had to have fourteen shots in the stomach as the result of a squirrel bite. Every day at two o'clock they would come to get him. A hush would fall on the room. We would all look down at our desks while he left the room between Mr. Harmon and his mother. Mr. Harmon was the principal. That's how important Billy Monday's tragedy was.

Mr. Harmon came along in case Billy threw a fit. Every day we waited to see if he would throw a fit but he never did. He just put his books away and left the room with his head hanging down on his chest and Mr. Harmon and his mother guiding him along between them like a boat.

"Would you go with them like that?" I asked Letitia at recess. Letitia was my best friend. Usually we played girls chase the boys at recess or pushed each other on the swings or hung upside down on the monkey bars so Joe Franke and Bobby Saxacorn could see our underpants but Billy's shots had even taken the fun out of recess. Now we sat around on the fire escape and talked about rabies instead.

"Why don't they put him to sleep first?" Letitia said. "I'd make them put me to sleep."

"They can't," I said. "They can't put you to sleep unless they operate."

"My father could," she said. "He owns the hospital. He could put me to sleep." She was always saying things like that but I let her be my best friend anyway.

"They couldn't give them to me," I said. "I'd run away to Florida and be a beachcomber."

"Then you'd get rabies," Letitia said. "You'd be foaming at the mouth."

"I'd take a chance. You don't always get it." We moved closer together, caught up in the horror of it. I was thinking about the Livingstons' bulldog. I'd had some close calls with it lately.

"It was a pet," Letitia said. "His brother was keeping it for a pet."

It was noon recess. Billy Monday was sitting on a bench by the swings. Just sitting there. Not talking to anybody. Waiting for two o'clock, a small washed-out-looking boy that nobody paid any attention to until he got bit. He never talked to anybody. He could hardly even read. When Mrs. Jansma asked him to read his head would fall all the way over to the side of his neck. Then he would read a few sentences with her having to tell him half the words. No one would ever have picked him out to be the center of a rabies tragedy. He was more the type to fall in a well or get sucked down the drain at the swimming pool.

Fourteen days. Fourteen shots. It was spring when it happened and the schoolroom windows were open all day long and every afternoon after Billy left we had milk from little waxy cartons and Mrs. Jansma would read us chapters from a wonderful book about some children in England that had a bed that took them places at night. There we were, eating graham crackers and listening to stories while Billy was strapped to the table in Doctor Finley's office waiting for his shot.

"I can't stand to think about it," Letitia said. "It makes me so sick I could puke."

"I'm going over there and talk to him right now," I said. "I'm going to interview him for the paper." I had been the only one in the third grade to get anything in the Horace Mann paper. I got in with a story about how Mr. Harmon was shell-shocked in the First World War. I was on the lookout for another story that good.

I got up, smoothed down my skirt, walked over to the bench where Billy was sitting and held out a vial of cinnamon toothpicks. "You want one," I said. "Go ahead. She won't care." It was against the rules to bring cinnamon toothpicks to Horace Mann. They were afraid someone would swallow one.

"I don't think so," he said. "I don't need any."

"Go on," I said. "They're really good. They've been soaking all week."

"I don't want any," he said.

"You want me to push you on the swings?"

"I don't know," he said. "I don't think so."

"If it was my brother's squirrel, I'd kill it," I said. "I'd cut its head off."

"It got away," he said. "It's gone."

"What's it like when they give them to you?" I said. "Does it hurt very much?"

"I don't know," he said. "I don't look." His head was starting to slip down onto his chest. He was rolling up like a ball.

"I know how to hypnotize people," I said. "You want me to hypnotize you so you can't feel it?"

"I don't know," he said. He had pulled his legs up on the bench. Now his chin was so far down into his chest I could barely hear him talk. Part of me wanted to give him a shove and see if he would roll. I touched him on the shoulder instead. I could feel his little bones beneath his shirt. I could smell his washed-out rusty smell. His head went all the way down under his knees. Over his shoulder I saw Mrs. Jansma headed our way.

"Rhoda," she called out. "I need you to clean off the blackboards before we go back in. Will you be a sweet girl and do that for me?"

"I wasn't doing anything but talking to him," I said. She was beside us now and had gathered him into her wide sleeves. He was starting to cry, making little strangled noises like a goat.

"Well, my goodness, that was nice of you to try to cheer Billy up. Now go see about those blackboards for me, will you?"

I went on in and cleaned off the blackboards and beat the erasers together out the window, watching the chalk dust settle into the bricks. Down below I could see Mrs. Jansma still holding on to Billy. He was hanging on to her like a spider but it looked like he had quit crying.

That afternoon a lady from the PTA came to talk to us about the paper drive. "One more time," she was saying. "We've licked the Krauts. Now all we have left is the Japs. Who's going to help?" she shouted.

"I am," I shouted back. I was the first one on my feet.

"Who do you want for a partner?" she said.

"Billy Monday," I said, pointing at him. He looked up at me as though I had asked him to swim the English Channel, then his head slid down on the desk.

"All right," Mrs. Jansma said. "Rhoda Manning and Billy Monday. Team number one. To cover Washington and Sycamore from Calvin Boulevard to Conner Street. Who else?"

"Bobby and me," Joe Franke called out. He was wearing his coonskin cap, even though it was as hot as summer. How I loved him! "We want downtown," he shouted. "We want Dirkson Street to the river."

"Done," Mrs. Jansma said. JoEllen Scaggs was writing it all down on the blackboard. By the time Billy's mother and Mr. Harmon came to get him the paper drive was all arranged.

"See you tomorrow," I called out as Billy left the room. "Don't forget. Don't be late."

When I got home that afternoon I told my mother I had volunteered to let Billy be my partner. She was so proud of me she made me some cookies even though I was supposed to be on a diet. I took the cookies and a pillow and climbed up into my treehouse to read a book. I was getting to be more like my mother every day. My mother was a saint. She fed hoboes and played the organ at early communion even if she was sick and gave away her ration stamps to anyone that needed them. She had only had one pair of new shoes the whole war.

I was getting more like her every day. I was the only one in the third grade that would have picked Billy Monday to help with a paper drive. He probably couldn't even pick up a stack of papers. He probably couldn't even help pull the wagon.

I bet this is the happiest day of her life, I was thinking. I was lying in my treehouse watching her. She was sitting on the back steps putting liquid hose on her legs. She was waiting for the Episcopal minister to come by for a drink. He'd been coming by a lot since my daddy was overseas. That was just like my mother. To be best friends with a minister.

"She picked out a boy that's been sick to help her on the paper drive," I heard her tell him later. "I think it helped a lot to get her to lose weight. It was smart of you to see that was the problem."

"There isn't anything I wouldn't do for you, Ariane," he said. "You say the word and I'll be here to do it."

I got a few more cookies and went back up into the treehouse to finish my book. I could read all kinds of books. I could read Book-of-the-Month Club books. The one I was reading now was called *Cakes and Ale*. It wasn't coming along too well.

I settled down with my back against the tree, turning the pages, looking for the good parts. Inside the house my mother was bragging on me. Above my head a golden sun beat down out of a blue sky. All around the silver maple leaves moved in the breeze. I went back to my book. "She put her arms around my neck and pressed her lips against mine. I forgot my wrath. I only thought of her beauty and her enveloping kindness.

" 'You must take me as I am, you know,' she whispered.

" 'All right,' I said."

Saturday was not going to be a good day for a paper drive. The sky was gray and overcast. By the time we lined up on the Horace Mann playground with our wagons a light rain was falling.

"Our boys are fighting in rain and snow and whatever the heavens send," Mr. Harmon was saying. He was standing on the bleachers wearing an old baseball shirt and a cap. I had never seen him in anything but his gray suit. He looked more shell-shocked than ever in his cap.

"They're working over there. We're working over here. The Germans are defeated. Only the Japs left to go. There're canvas tarps from Gentilly's Hardware, so take one to cover your papers. All right now. One grade at a time. And remember, Mrs. Winchester's third grade is still ahead by seventy-eight pounds. So you're going to have to go some to beat that. Get to your stations now. Get ready, get set, go. Everybody working together . . ."

Billy and I started off. I was pulling the wagon, he was walking along beside me. I had meant to wait awhile before I started interviewing him but I started right in.

"Are you going to have to leave to go get it?" I said.

"Go get what?"

"You know. Your shot."

"I got it this morning. I already had it."

"Where do they put it in?"

"I don't know," he said. "I don't look."

"Well, you can feel it, can't you?" I said. "Like, do they stick in in your navel or what?"

"It's higher than that."

"How long does it take? To get it."

"I don't know," he said. "Till they get through."

"Well, at least you aren't going to get rabies. At least you won't be foaming at the mouth. I guess you're glad about that." I had stopped in front of a house and was looking up the path to the door. We had come to the end of Sycamore, where our territory began.

"Are you going to be the one to ask them?" he said.

"Sure," I said. "You want to come to the door with me?"

"I'll wait," he said. "I'll just wait."

We filled the wagon by the second block. We took that load back to the school and started out again. On the second trip we hit an attic with bundles of the *Kansas City Star* tied up with string. It took us all afternoon to haul that. Mrs. Jansma said she'd never seen anyone as lucky on a paper drive as Billy and I. Our whole class was having a good day. It looked like we might beat every-body, even the sixth grade.

"Let's go out one more time," Mrs. Jansma said. "One more trip before dark. Be sure and hit all the houses you missed."

Billy and I started back down Sycamore. It was growing dark. I untied my Brownie Scout sweater from around my waist and put it on and pulled the sleeves down over my wrists. "Let's try that brick house on the corner," I said. "They might be home by now." It was an old house set back on a high lawn. It looked like a house where old people lived. I had noticed old people were the ones who saved things. "Come on," I said. "You go to the door with me. I'm tired of doing it by myself."

He came along behind me and we walked up to the door and rang the bell. No one answered for a long time although I could hear footsteps and saw someone pass by a window. I rang the bell again.

A man came to the door. A thin man about my father's age.

"We're collecting papers for Horace Mann School," I said. "For the war effort."

"You got any papers we can have?" Billy said. It was the first time he had spoken to anyone but me all day. "For the war," he added.

"There're some things in the basement if you want to go down there and get them," the man said. He turned a light on in the hall and we followed him into a high-ceilinged foyer with a set of winding stairs going up to another floor. It smelled musty, like my grandmother's house in Clarksville. Billy was right beside me, sticking as close as a burr. We followed the man through the kitchen and down a flight of stairs to the basement.

"You can have whatever you find down here," he said. "There're papers and magazines in that corner. Take whatever you can carry."

There was a large stack of magazines. Magazines were the best thing you could find. They weighed three times as much as newspapers.

"Come on," I said to Billy. "Let's fill the wagon. This

will put us over the top for sure." I picked up a bundle
and started up the stairs. I went in and out several times
carrying as many as I could at a time. On the third trip
Billy met me at the foot of the stairs. "Rhoda," he said.
"Come here. Come look at this."

He took me to an old table in a corner of the basement.
It was a walnut table with grapes carved on the side and
feet like lion's feet. He laid one of the magazines down on
the table and opened it. It was a photograph of a naked
little girl, a girl smaller than I was. He turned the page.
Two naked boys were standing together with their legs
twined. He kept turning the pages. It was all the same.
Naked children on every page. I had never seen a naked
boy. Much less a photograph of one. Billy looked up at
me. He turned another page. Five naked little girls were
grouped together around a fountain.

"Let's get out of here," I said. "Come on. I'm getting
out of here." I headed for the stairs with him right behind
me. We didn't even close the basement door. We didn't
even stop to say thank you.

The magazines we had collected were in bundles. About
a block from the house we stopped on a corner, breathless
from running. "Let's see if there's any more," I said. We
tore open a bundle. The first magazine had pictures of
naked grown people on every page.

"What are we going to do?" he said.

"We're going to throw them away," I answered, and
started throwing them into the nandina bushes by the
Hancock's vacant lot. We threw them into the nandina
bushes and into the ditch that runs into Mills Creek. We
threw the last ones into a culvert and then we took our
wagon and got on out of there. At the corner of Sycamore
and Wesley we went our separate ways.

"Well, at least you'll have something to think about
tomorrow when you get your shot," I said.

"I guess so," he replied.

"Look here, Billy. I don't want you to tell anyone about
those magazines. You understand?"

"I won't." His head was going down again.

"I mean it, Billy."

He raised his head and looked at me as if he had just remembered something he was thinking about. "I won't," he said. "Are you really going to write about me in the paper?"

"Of course I am. I said I was, didn't I? I'm going to do it tonight."

I walked on home. Past the corner where the Scout hikes met. Down the alley where I found the card shuffler and the Japanese fan. Past the yard where the violets grew. I was thinking about the boys with their legs twined. They looked like earthworms, all naked like that. They looked like something might fly down and eat them. It made me sick to think about it and I stopped by Mrs. Alford's and picked a few iris to take home to my mother.

Billy finished getting his shots. And I wrote the article and of course they put it on page one. BE ON THE LOOKOUT FOR MAD SQUIRREL, the headline read. By Rhoda Katherine Manning. Grade 3.

We didn't even know it was mean, the person it bit said. That person is in the third grade of our school. His name is William Monday. On April 23 he had his last shot. Mrs. Jansma's class had a cake and gave him a pencil set. Billy Monday is all right now and things are back to normal.

I think it should be against the law to keep dangerous pets or dogs where they can get out and get people. If you see a dog or squirrel acting funny go in the house and stay there.

I never got around to telling my mother about those magazines. I kept meaning to but there never seemed to be anywhere to start. One day in August I tried to tell her. I had been to the swimming pool and I thought I saw the man from the brick house drive by in a car. I was pretty sure it was him. As he turned the corner he looked at me. *He looked right at my face.* I stood very still, my heart pounding inside my chest, my hands as cold and wet as a frog, the smell of swimming pool chlorine rising from my skin. What if he found out where I lived? What if he followed me home and killed me to keep me from telling on him? I was terrified. At any moment the car might return. He might grab me and put me in the car and take me off and kill me. I threw my bathing suit and towel down on the sidewalk and started running. I ran down Linden Street and turned into the alley behind Calvin Boulevard, running as fast as I could. I ran down the alley and into my yard and up my steps and into my house looking for my mother to tell her about it.

She was in the living room, with Father Kenniman and Mr. and Mrs. DuVal. They lived across the street and had a gold star in their window. Warrene, our cook, was there. And Connie Barksdale, our cousin who was visiting from the Delta. Her husband had been killed on Corregidor and she would come up and stay with my mother whenever she couldn't take it anymore. They were all in the living room gathered around the radio.

"Momma," I said. "I saw this man that gave me some magazines . . ."

"Be quiet, Rhoda," she said. "We're listening to the news. Something's happened. We think maybe we've won the war." There were tears in her eyes. She gave me a little hug, then turned back to the radio. It was a wonderful radio with a magic eye that glowed in the dark. At night when we had blackouts Dudley and I would get into bed with my mother and we would listen to it together, the magic eye glowing in the dark like an emerald.

Now the radio was bringing important news to Seymour, Indiana. Strange, confused, hush-hush news that said we had a bomb bigger than any bomb ever made and we had already dropped it on Japan and half of Japan was sinking into the sea. Now the Japs had to surrender. Now they couldn't come to Indiana and stick bamboo up our fingernails. Now it would all be over and my father would come home.

The grown people kept on listening to the radio, getting up every now and then to get drinks or fix each other sandwiches. Dudley was sitting beside my mother in a white shirt acting like he was twenty years old. He always did that when company came. No one was paying any attention to me.

Finally I went upstairs and lay down on the bed to think things over. My father was coming home. I didn't know how to feel about that. He was always yelling at someone when he was home. He was always yelling at my mother to make me mind.

"What do you mean, you can't catch her," I could hear him yelling. "Hit her with a broom. Hit her with a table. Hit her with a chair. But, for God's sake, Ariane, don't let her talk to you that way."

Well, maybe it would take a while for him to get home. First they had to finish off Japan. First they had to sink the other half into the sea. I curled up in my soft old eiderdown comforter. I was feeling great. We had dropped the biggest bomb in the world on Japan and there were plenty more where that one came from.

I fell asleep in the hot sweaty silkiness of the comforter. I was dreaming I was at the wheel of an airplane carrying the bomb to Japan. Hit 'em, I was yelling. Hit 'em with a mountain. Hit 'em with a table. Hit 'em with a chair. Off we go into the wild blue yonder, climbing high into the sky. I dropped one on the brick house where the bad man lived, then took off for Japan. Down we dive, spouting a flame from under. Off with one hell of a roar. We live in flame. Buckle down in flame. For nothing can stop the Army Air Corps. Hit 'em with a table, I was yelling. Hit 'em with a broom. Hit 'em with a bomb. Hit 'em with a chair.

SALLIE BINGHAM was born in Louisville, Kentucky, in 1937. She graduated from Radcliffe in 1958. A year later her first novel, *After Such Knowledge*, a story of undergraduate life and sexual initiation at Radcliffe and Harvard, was published to intensely admiring reviews. Her collections of short stories are *The Touching Hand* (1967) and *The Way It Is Now* (1972), from which the following story about a young mother's terror in the face of her own child abuse is taken. Reviewing this collection, the novelist and critic Diane Johnson wrote that "Miss Bingham is very good at capturing the beleaguered hysteria of the mothers of small children, the ironic detachment of men. These stories are not recommended for men." Indeed, Miss Bingham has the courage to take a very close and painful look at what goes wrong between men and women: All of her stories are centered on sensitive women and complex family tensions. With supreme artistry and sympathy, Miss Bingham makes her readers feel the urgency of her female characters' search for compassion and an emotional integrity which is often elusive. (Often her male characters are engaged not in a search but in finding their sensitive women difficult.) In the face of such detachment, Sallie Bingham makes her women's desire for emotional strength and truth feel like a matter of life and death.

Sallie Bingham

FEAR

Turning the knob so slowly it seemed to glide, greased, under her palm, Jean finally opened the baby's door. It was early morning, the pink lambs and blue horses on the curtains just becoming visible; the crib, under its canopy, was still a pit of shadows, and Jean saw the brown bear, the snake, and the cat lined up at the rail, on guard.

She took a step toward the crib and stopped. The baby's smell, made of milk and powder and the soap she used in the washing machine, stood in front of her like a screen. She drew several breaths, trying to believe that since he smelled the same, nothing could be wrong. There had been so much crying the evening before, so much panic and screaming that she thought her observations might have been crazed.

Hearing him stir, she bent down. His eyes were open; he lay on his back, his hands out, and looked up at her as though he had always expected her to be there. "Hello, little duck," she said and reached in to pick him up. His body felt changed to her, limp, yielding; fat as a sack, she thought. Holding him tightly in her arms, she remembered how he had clung to her neck after she had punished him. "I'm sorry, I'm so sorry," she had sobbed, and he had repeated, "Orry."

Then she put him down. As his feet touched the floor, he began to whimper. Turning, he tried to clutch her knees as his legs splayed out. She moved back and he slid to the floor where he sat, whimpering and looking up at her. "You can do it," she whispered cheerily, and picked him up and set him again on his feet. He gave a cry and leaned against her hands. She tried to push him away but he clung, crumpling at the same time at the knees. They're not working, she thought. The legs are still not working. She picked him up and rocked him in her arms.

He stopped crying immediately. "Here's the little kitty," she said, taking the animal out of the crib. As the baby seized the toy, she closed her eyes and buried her mouth in his cheek. It seemed to her that she ought to put him down again, to make sure, but she knew she would not be able to bear his crying. That was what had caused it, in the beginning—his crying. He would start over something so trivial—the cat had been misplaced, in this case—and his crying would wind on and on, endlessly on and on, growing into small shrieks that pierced her head. She had looked frantically for the cat and then, giving up, she had walked the baby up and down, trying to console him. It seemed to her that the crying would never stop. She was trapped inside the sound; the hour of the day and the day of the week drifted away and she was trapped, helplessly, inside the sound of a baby's screams. She had picked him up once more to try to comfort him but instead she had plunged him down onto the floor, plunging him again and again until his cries turned into hysterical screams. Then she had sat beside him on the floor, dazed, gasping for breath, and gone at last to open a window.

Coming back, she had seen him trying to get up.

Now, as she held him in her arms, she knew she had never really hoped, not even in the night when she had felt quite calm, lying against her husband's back. She had never really hoped. As soon as she had seen him trying to get up, she had known that she had hurt him in some terrible way. Her life had shriveled as she watched him, wallowing. She had never loved anyone as she had loved him, since she had felt his first tentative flutter inside her womb. She had been guiltily aware that she loved him more than she could ever love her husband, who was critical at times, and never really hers. But she had never hurt her husband, except glancingly, she had never even scratched the surface of all the offensive strangers she had known, she had hardly ruffled her parents' composure although she had hated them for years, and she had allowed people to disturb and wound her without even frowning. It was the baby she had hurt.

Still carrying him in her arms, she walked into the kitchen. Maria, the housekeeper, was standing at the sink, filling the percolator with water. She glanced at Jean, her eyes glassy and aglow. Jean stopped abruptly. The woman had no way of knowing, had been out of the apartment when it happened. Jean went to the high chair and propped the baby inside its arms; he was still as limp as string. She had to take his hands from her shoulder finger by finger, but this time, he did not cry. He looked at her with his round flat eyes which she had never been able to penetrate; his happy eyes, like buttons. He had always been a happy baby and she had known it was at least partly because she mothered him well, flying to satisfy his demands, giving up her sleep and her freedom too willingly and gladly, as though they had never meant anything at all.

"Will you give him his breakfast, please, Maria? It's so early, I'm going back to bed."

In the hall, she thought, I will wake up John and tell him what happened, and he will tell me what to do.

She opened the bedroom door and the cold breeze from the window lapped against her ankles. Her husband, darkly bundled, lay in the middle of the bed. She stood with the doorknob in her hand, squeezing and turning it. It seemed to her that he must hear the sound and wake up, but he did not stir. She could not see his face, and she wished he would turn over so that she could at least see his eyes, which were generally kind. But he did not move. She had looked at him the evening before, intending to tell him, even imagining a scene with some tears but final comfort; looking at him, she had felt something fearful and cringing rise up inside her, authoritative, too, as though it possessed the final wisdom: do not tell him. No, never tell him. It was as though she had taken a lover, a foul black passion, and must guard with all her strength against the relief of revelation. John had remarked that she was looking pale.

She went out of the bedroom and closed the door. In the kitchen, Maria was talking to the baby. Jean listened to her soft, pattering voice. Borne along on the sound, she went to the front door and opened it. Maria will take care of him, she thought; he will be all right as long as he is with her. She rang the bell for the elevator. The morning paper was lying on the floor, crumpled, a fallen bird; she picked it up and laid it neatly on the bench.

In the elevator, she realized that she was not dressed and looked down at her short housecoat. It would pass; only her slippers gave her away. She took them off and put them in her pocket.

Outside, she felt the gritty pavement under her feet and was frightened. Dog filth and the litter from an overturned garbage pail lay along her way; smoking pyramids of dog filth, torn streamers of paper stained with hamburger blood. She placed each foot heavily, wondering how long it would be before she felt something wet. Crossing the street, she went into the park.

The smoky morning sky lay along the tops of the trees; looking up, she saw the sun burning a hole the size of a penny. The trampled grass, shaggy as an old dog's coat, was lifting a blade at a time. She remembered spreading the plaid wool shawl here for the baby and herding him in from the edges; his white shoes had been as clean when they went as they had been at the start. Walking a little farther, she reached a point where one path led into the interior. The path she always took with the baby stretched along the edge of the street. The other, inside path was rutted from tree roots, and the only bench she could see had lost one of its legs. She had never hesitated before: the choice had been made for her by the sight of the baby's white bonnet, nodding like a peony inside the carriage hood. Now she took the broken path.

It was very early; she had passed one man with a dog, but otherwise the park was empty. Empty, but edged with sounds and odd half-animate rustlings; she saw a squirrel move down a tree trunk with small crippled feet. She stopped to look back, wondering what the animal expected. His tail was as thin as an old feather. His eyes, however, were shining, and she hurried on, remembering the crib animals at the rail. She thought she heard the squirrel coming after her, on light crippled feet, and turned to shout and wave him away. A small man, muffled in a coat, passed her quickly, his breeze fanning her cheek.

She was so startled she sat down on the broken bench. Above the tops of the trees, the apartment buildings raised their crenelated towers; she looked the other way and saw the little man, hurrying on his small feet, turn the corner and disappear. Awkwardly, she pushed herself up off the bench and followed.

She was out of her territory at once; the plaid shawl had never been spread on these grassy places. She was astonished by the thickness of growth—weeds, mosses, trees; the park, abandoned, had grown up like the back fields of a lost farm. Purple nettles, their heads as big as apples, stood at the edge of the path. The sidewalk, cracked and cracked again by shadows, ran in semicircles down into a little valley where a dry fountain lay half full of leaves.

At the edge of the pool, she stopped. A marble cupid, its flesh green with mold, raised an amputated elbow toward her. Its eyes were marked in the center by straight slits, like a cat's. Jean stood still and waited. Under her feet, the warm sidewalk grew cool and she imagined the green mold starting there and spreading around her like a shallow pool. The sounds of the city, sifted through the leaves, were as remote as summer thunder. She stood until her thighs began to ache, and then she sat down quickly on the lip of the pool.

She knew that she was being watched from the trees, and she sat carefully, her short robe drawn over her knees. Staring into the leaf-filled pool, she showed the back of her neck, bare and white, between her hair and the edge of her collar. As he watched from the shadow, he would catch the glint of white skin. Waiting, she began slowly to freeze, until she knew that soon she would be unable to lift her hand. She moved her head slightly, adjusting it for the last time, and saw that the cupid had a chain of beer-can tops around his neck.

As she waited, a blade of sunlight stretched slowly across the pavement, approaching her feet. After a long time, its point touched her toes, and she saw that she was shod in filth; only her insteps were still white. Revolted, she stood up. She had always hated dirt, any form of dirt, but public dirt collected from the feet of other people was intolerable. As she started purposefully back, she saw the trees, coalesced against her, shrouding the small black hole where the path ran toward the street.

Suddenly, she was afraid. Wishing could make anything happen, might already have set the disaster on its course. She stood prepared to defend herself and examined the ranks of trees. If he was watching, he must see that she was ready, her bare neck hidden now, her fists gripped. She remembered that he had been very small and thought that her assurance alone might quell him. But the wish, the terrible self-fulfilling wish for pain and mutilation still hung in the air above her like a beacon. She knew that he would see it and understand that her defenses were only temporary. Panting, she began to walk slowly toward the entrance.

Sweat ran down the insides of her arms, thick as honey. Her own smell, rank as the weeds', tortured her with its implications; animals, in danger, give off a hot rich stench. Moving carefully, on lead feet, she began to believe that if she could reach the trees, she would be safe. It occurred to her to run, but remotely, dreamily. She kept repeating, doggedly, that she did not want anything to happen, although she knew that her doubt would flash through as her bare neck had flashed, inviting the blow.

Shadows fell over her as heavily; she had reached the trees. She panted. The trees were around her now and she could no longer feel the weight of his eyes. He would be moving closer, in order to keep her in view. Lifting her knees, she began at last to run, jogging clumsily, her breasts jerking. Her body inside the housecoat was as loose and thick as jelly, and she imagined her stomach dropping to her knees. Perhaps if he saw that she had borne a child, he would spare her. At that she began to run more quickly.

Dashing, her flesh quickening, she left the shade of the trees. Below the embankment, a bus stopped and passed on. She could see the faces of the passengers at their windows, and she wanted to call and hold her hands out to them. Running down the slope, she nearly collided with a large woman leading a brace of hounds. The woman muttered and scowled as Jean stared at her. Jean crossed the street, skipping through a stream of cars, and heard their wild cries remotely. Her own building shone in a special patch of sun. She rushed in and flung herself into the open elevator.

As soon as she opened the door of the apartment, she knew that she was too late. The smell of frying bacon still hung in the air, but the baby's dishes were heaped in the sink and his bib was lying like a fallen flag on the floor. She went from room to room, looking carefully, but she knew they had already gone.

Sinking down on the kitchen floor, she fixed her eyes on the linoleum. The history of the apartment, replacing her life, streamed around her, and she wondered if anyone else out of the dozens who had lived there had ever crouched down on the kitchen floor. She remembered picking out the tiles, with much effort and indecision; she remembered her satisfaction as they were laid down. Now the bright blue was melting into the old tiles beneath it and the floor was turning mud-colored again. She had imagined when they had first moved in that she would make a life consciously chosen in every detail, and she had put her hand on her stomach to feel the baby's light kick, sure that this was the first great choice and that the rest would follow. There had been a clear connection between the daisies she had arranged and her passion for her husband, between the pablum she had prepared and her love for the baby that had gradually grown and engulfed all the rest.

I loved him too much, she thought, and that is why they have taken him away.

Time passed: she heard the big electric clock draw its hand through several numbers. She did not dare to raise her eyes from the floor, and the back of her neck and her knees began to ache. She thought that if they found her like that, kneeling, they might forgive her. When she heard the front door open, however, she sprang to her feet, and screamed because of the cramped pain in her knees.

"Jean?" her husband called.

She ran down the dark hall which lengthened in front of her, a tunnel with their faces at the end. The baby, wrapped in a blanket, lay in the crook of Maria's arm; when he saw his mother's face, he began to cry, reaching out for her with both hands. Still too far away to touch him, she held out her arms, and her husband took the child and placed him in her hands. She did not dare to move him closer; she held him out at the ends of her arms, which trembled under his weight.

John pressed the baby against her chest, and she saw Maria's face, dark, without any smile. She turned to look at her husband. His hands, at her back and the baby's back, held them clamped together, but he was looking away. "He's all right, isn't he?" she asked softly.

"It was just a bruise, wasn't it?" Neither of them answered. "Then what was it?" she asked, her voice rising.

"The doctor couldn't find anything wrong," John said finally. "He examined him, but he couldn't find anything wrong."

"But he couldn't walk! This morning—" She stopped herself.

Maria lifted the baby out of her arms and set him on the floor. He stumbled forward, his hands stretched toward the gleaming doorknob.

Jean sobbed.

"It's all right now," John said, touching her arm.

"But what happened?"

John looked away. The gap of their silent understanding widened between them; Jean knew they would never speak of what she had done.

The baby had reached the doorknob and was patting it with his hand.

ANITA DESAI was born in Mussoorie, India, in 1937. Her father was Bengali, her mother German, and she was educated in Delhi. She is married, the mother of four children, and lives in Bombay. She is the author of several novels including *Cry, The Peacock, Bye-bye Blackbird, Where Shall We Go This Summer, Fire on the Mountain* (for which she won the Royal Society of Literature's Winifred Holtby Memorial Prize and the 1978 National Academy of Letters Award), and *Clear Light of Day*, a nominee for the Booker Prize in 1980. Each of the eleven stories in her first volume of short stories, *Games at Twilight* (called "sensitive, delicate and successful" by one London critic, and "absolutely first-rate" by another), is an exquisite miniature capturing the unique atmosphere of India and conveying a sense of what it is like to live in that confusing country. The collection's title story that follows here evokes brilliantly the white-hot heat of a summer afternoon in India. But finally this story has at its center something much larger than a sense of place. What it brings to life with absolute authority is the child Ravi's first experience of his own mortality, his sense of his own small, brief place in a vast and difficult universe. Anita Desai has been called in *The New Yorker* "one of the most gifted of contemporary Indian writers." Upon reading "Games At Twilight" the reader immediately knows why.

Anita Desai

GAMES AT TWILIGHT

It was still too hot to play outdoors. They had had their tea, they had been washed and had their hair brushed, and after the long day of confinement in the house that was not cool but at least a protection from the sun, the children strained to get out. Their faces were red and bloated with the effort, but their mother would not open the door, everything was still curtained and shuttered in a way that stifled the children, made them feel that their lungs were stuffed with cotton wool and their noses with dust and if they didn't burst out into the light and see the sun and feel the air, they would choke.

"Please, ma, please," they begged. "We'll play in the veranda and porch—we won't go a step out of the porch."

"You will, I know you will, and then—"

"No—we won't, we won't," they wailed so horrendously that she actually let down the bolt of the front door so that they burst out like seeds from a crackling, over-ripe pod into the veranda, with such wild, maniacal yells that she retreated to her bath and the shower of talcum powder and the fresh sari that were to help her face the summer evening.

They faced the afternoon. It was too hot. Too bright. The white walls of the veranda glared stridently in the sun. The bougainvillea hung about it, purple and magenta, in livid balloons. The garden outside was like a tray made of beaten brass, flattened out on the red gravel and the stony soil in all shades of metal—aluminium, tin, copper and brass. No life stirred at this arid time of day—the birds still drooped, like dead fruit, in the papery tents of the trees; some squirrels lay limp on the wet earth under the garden tap. The outdoor dog lay stretched as if dead on the veranda mat, his paws and ears and tail all reaching out like dying travellers in search of water. He rolled his eyes at the children—two white marbles rolling in the purple sockets, begging for sympathy—and attempted to lift his tail in a wag but could not. It only twitched and lay still.

Then, perhaps roused by the shrieks of the children, a band of parrots suddenly fell out of the eucalyptus tree, tumbled frantically in the still, sizzling air, then sorted themselves out into battle formation and streaked away across the white sky.

The children, too, felt released. They too began tumbling, shoving, pushing against each other, frantic to start. Start what? Start their business. The business of the children's day which is—play.

"Let's play hide-and-seek."

"Who'll be It?"

"You be It."

"Why should I? You be—"

"You're the eldest—"

"That doesn't mean—"

The shoves became harder. Some kicked out. The motherly Mira intervened. She pulled the boys roughly apart. There was a tearing sound of cloth but it was lost in the heavy panting and angry grumbling and no one paid attention to the small sleeve hanging loosely off a shoulder.

"Make a circle, make a circle!" she shouted, firmly pulling and pushing till a kind of vague circle was formed. "Now clap!" she roared and, clapping, they all chanted in melancholy unison: "Dip, dip, dip—my blue ship—" and every now and then one or the other saw he was safe by the way his hands fell at the crucial moment—palm on palm, or back of hand on palm—and dropped out of the circle with a yell and a jump of relief and jubilation.

Raghu was It. He started to protest, to cry "You cheated—Mira cheated—Anu cheated—" but it was too late, the others had all already streaked away. There was no one to hear when he called out, "Only in the veranda—the porch—Ma said—Ma *said* to stay in the porch!" No one had stopped to listen, all he saw were their brown legs flashing through the dusty shrubs, scrambling up brick walls, leaping over compost heaps and hedges, and then the porch stood empty in the purple shade of the bougainvillea and the garden was as empty as before; even the limp squirrels had whisked away, leaving everything gleaming, brassy and bare.

Only small Manu suddenly reappeared, as if he had dropped out of an invisible cloud or from a bird's claws, and stood for a moment in the centre of the yellow lawn, chewing his finger and near to tears as he heard Raghu shouting, with his head pressed against the veranda wall, "Eighty-three, eighty-five, eighty-nine, ninety . . ." and then made off in a panic, half of him wanting to fly north, the other half counselling south. Raghu turned just in time to see the flash of his white shorts and the uncertain skittering of his red sandals, and charged after him with such a blood-curdling yell that Manu stumbled over the hosepipe, fell into its rubber coils and lay there weeping, "I won't be It—you have to find them all—all—All!"

"I know I have to, idiot," Raghu said, superciliously kicking him with his toe. "You're dead," he said with satisfaction, licking the beads of perspiration off his upper lip, and then stalked off in search of worthier prey, whistling spiritedly so that the hiders should hear and tremble.

Ravi heard the whistling and picked his nose in a panic, trying to find comfort by burrowing the finger deep-deep into that soft tunnel. He felt himself too exposed, sitting on an upturned flower pot behind the garage. Where could he burrow? He could run around the garage if he heard Raghu come—around and around and around—but he hadn't much faith in his short legs when matched against Raghu's long, hefty, hairy footballer legs. Ravi had a frightening glimpse of them as Raghu combed the hedge of crotons and hibiscus, trampling delicate ferns underfoot as he did so. Ravi looked about him desperately, swallowing a small ball of snot in his fear.

The garage was locked with a great heavy lock to which the driver had the key in his room, hanging from a nail on

the wall under his work-shirt. Ravi had peeped in and seen
him still sprawling on his string-cot in his vest and striped
underpants, the hair on his chest and the hair in his nose
shaking with the vibrations of his phlegm-obstructed snores.
Ravi had wished he were tall enough, big enough to reach
the key on the nail, but it was impossible, beyond his
reach for years to come. He had sidled away and sat
dejectedly on the flower pot. That at least was cut to his
own size.

But next to the garage was another shed with a big green
door. Also locked. No one even knew who had the key to
the lock. That shed wasn't opened more than once a year
when Ma turned out all the old broken bits of furniture and
rolls of matting and leaking buckets, and the white ant
hills were broken and swept away and Flit sprayed into the
spider webs and rat holes so that the whole operation was
like the looting of a poor, ruined and conquered city. The
green leaves of the door sagged. They were nearly off their
rusty hinges. The hinges were large and made a small gap
between the door and the walls—only just large enough for
rats, dogs and, possibly, Ravi to slip through.

Ravi had never cared to enter such a dark and depress-
ing mortuary of defunct household goods seething with such
unspeakable and alarming animal life but, as Raghu's
whistling grew angrier and sharper and his crashing and
storming in the hedge wilder, Ravi suddenly slipped off
the flower pot and through the crack and was gone. He
chuckled aloud with astonishment at his own temerity so
that Raghu came out of the hedge, stood silent with his
hands on his hips, listening, and finally shouted ''I heard
you! I'm coming! *Got* you—'' and came charging round
the garage only to find the upturned flower pot, the yellow
dust, the crawling of white ants in a mud-hill against the
closed shed door—nothing. Snarling, he bent to pick up a
stick and went off, whacking it against the garage and shed
walls as if to beat out his prey.

Ravi shook, then shivered with delight, with self-congratu-
lation. Also with fear. It was dark, spooky in the shed. It
had a muffled smell, as of graves. Ravi had once got
locked into the linen cupboard and sat there weeping for

half an hour before he was rescued. But at least that had been a familiar place, and even smelt pleasantly of starch, laundry and, reassuringly, of his mother. But the shed smelt of rats, ant hills, dust and spider webs. Also of less definable, less recognizable horrors. And it was dark. Except for the white-hot cracks along the door, there was no light. The roof was very low. Although Ravi was small, he felt as if he could reach up and touch it with his finger tips. But he didn't stretch. He hunched himself into a ball so as not to bump into anything, touch or feel anything. What might there not be to touch him and feel him as he stood there, trying to see in the dark? Something cold, or slimy—like a snake. Snakes! He leapt up as Raghu whacked the wall with his stick—then, quickly realizing what it was, felt almost relieved to hear Raghu, hear his stick. It made him feel protected.

But Raghu soon moved away. There wasn't a sound once his footsteps had gone around the garage and disappeared. Ravi stood frozen inside the shed. Then he shivered all over. Something had tickled the back of his neck. It took him a while to pick up the courage to lift his hand and explore. It was an insect—perhaps a spider—exploring *him*. He squashed it and wondered how many more creatures were watching him, waiting to reach out and touch him, the stranger.

There was nothing now. After standing in that position—his hand still on his neck, feeling the wet splodge of the squashed spider gradually dry—for minutes, hours, his legs began to tremble with the effort, the inaction. By now he could see enough in the dark to make out the large solid shapes of old wardrobes, broken buckets and bedsteads piled on top of each other around him. He recognized an old bathtub—patches of enamel glimmered at him and at last he lowered himself onto its edge.

He contemplated slipping out of the shed and into the fray. He wondered if it would not be better to be captured by Raghu and be returned to the milling crowd as long as he could be in the sun, the light, the free spaces of the garden and the familiarity of his brothers, sisters and cousins. It would be evening soon. Their games would become legitimate. The parents would sit out on the lawn on cane basket chairs and watch them as they tore around the garden or gathered in knots to share a loot of mulberries or black, teeth-splitting *jamun* from the garden trees. The gardener would fix the hosepipe to the water tap and water would fall lavishly through the air to the ground, soaking the dry yellow grass and the red gravel and arousing the sweet, the intoxicating scent of water on dry earth—that loveliest scent in the world. Ravi sniffed for a whiff of it. He half-rose from the bathtub, then heard the despairing scream of one of the girls as Raghu bore down upon her. There was the sound of a crash, and of rolling about in the bushes, the shrubs, then screams and accusing sobs of, "I touched the den—" "You did not—" "I did—" "You liar, you did *not*" and then a fading away and silence again.

Ravi sat back on the harsh edge of the tub, deciding to hold out a bit longer. What fun if they were all found and caught—he alone left unconquered! He had never known that sensation. Nothing more wonderful had ever happened to him than being taken out by an uncle and bought a whole slab of chocolate all to himself, or being flung into the soda-man's pony cart and driven up to the gate by the friendly driver with the red beard and pointed ears. To defeat Raghu—that hirsute, hoarse-voiced football champion—and to be the winner in a circle of older, bigger, luckier children—that would be thrilling beyond imagination. He hugged his knees together and smiled to himself almost shyly at the thought of so much victory, such laurels.

There he sat smiling, knocking his heels against the bathtub, now and then getting up and going to the door to put his ear to the broad crack and listening for sounds of the game, the pursuer and the pursued, and then returning to his seat with the dogged determination of the true winner, a breaker of records, a champion.

It grew darker in the shed as the light at the door grew softer, fuzzier, turned to a kind of crumbling yellow pollen that turned to yellow fur, blue fur, grey fur. Evening. Twilight. The sound of water gushing, falling. The scent of earth receiving water, slaking its thirst in great gulps and releasing that green scent of freshness, coolness. Through the crack Ravi saw the long purple shadows of the shed and the garage lying still across the yard. Beyond that, the white walls of the house. The bougainvillea had lost its lividity, hung in dark bundles that quaked and twittered and seethed with masses of homing sparrows. The lawn was shut off from his view. Could he hear the children's voices? It seemed to him that he could. It seemed to him that he could hear them chanting, singing, laughing. But what about the game? What had happened? Could it be over? How could it when he was still not found?

It then occurred to him that he could have slipped out long ago, dashed across the yard to the veranda and touched the "den". It was necessary to do that to win. He had forgotten. He had only remembered the part of hiding and trying to elude the seeker. He had done that so success-fully, his success had occupied him so wholly that he had quite forgotten that success had to be clinched by that final dash to victory and the ringing cry of "Den!"

With a whimper he burst through the crack, fell on his knees, got up and stumbled on stiff, benumbed legs across the shadowy yard, crying heartily by the time he reached the veranda so that when he flung himself at the white pillar and bawled, "Den! Den! Den!" his voice broke with rage and pity at the disgrace of it all and he felt himself flooded with tears and misery.

Out on the lawn, the children stopped chanting. They all turned to stare at him in amazement. Their faces were pale and triangular in the dusk. The trees and bushes around them stood inky and sepulchral, spilling long shadows across them. They stared, wondering at his reappearance, his passion, his wild animal howling. Their mother rose from her basket chair and came towards him, worried, annoyed, saying, "Stop it, stop it, Ravi. Don't be a baby. Have you hurt yourself?" Seeing him attended to, the children went back to clasping their hands and chanting "The grass is green, the rose is red. . . ."

But Ravi would not let them. He tore himself out of his

mother's grasp and pounded across the lawn into their midst, charging at them with his head lowered so that they scattered in surprise. "I won, I won, I won," he bawled, shaking his head so that the big tears flew. "Raghu didn't find me. I won, I won—"

It took them a minute to grasp what he was saying, even who he was. They had quite forgotten him. Raghu had found all the others long ago. There had been a fight about who was to be It next. It had been so fierce that their mother had emerged from her bath and made them change to another game. Then they had played another and another. Broken mulberries from the tree and eaten them. Helped the driver wash the car when their father returned from work. Helped the gardener water the beds till he roared at them and swore he would complain to their parents. The parents had come out, taken up their positions on the cane chairs. They had begun to play again, sing and chant. All this time no one had remembered Ravi. Having disappeared from the scene, he had disappeared from their minds. Clean.

"Don't be a fool," Raghu said roughly, pushing him aside, and even Mira said, "Stop howling, Ravi. If you want to play, you can stand at the end of the line," and she put him there very firmly.

The game proceeded. Two pairs of arms reached up and met in an arc. The children trooped under it again and again in a lugubrious circle, ducking their heads and intoning

"The grass is green,
The rose is red;
Remember me
When I am dead, dead, dead, dead . . ."

And the arc of thin arms trembled in the twilight, and the heads were bowed so sadly, and their feet tramped to that melancholy refrain so mournfully, so helplessly, that Ravi could not bear it. He would not follow them, he would not be included in this funereal game. He had wanted victory and triumph—not a funeral. But he had been forgotten, left out and he would not join them now. The ignominy of being forgotten—how could he face it? He felt his heart go heavy and ache inside him unbearably. He lay down full length on the damp grass, crushing his face into it, no longer crying, silenced by a terrible sense of his insignificance.

TONI CADE BAMBARA was born in New York City in 1939. She was educated at Queens College of the City University of New York, the University of Florence, and New York University. She has been a social worker at the New York State Department of Welfare, an instructor of English in the SEEK Program at City College, and writer-in-residence at Spelman College in Atlanta, Georgia. Her writing has been included in Addison Gayle's *Black Expressions: Essays By and About Black Americans in the Creative Arts, Black and White in American Culture,* and *Backgrounds to Black American Literature.* She is the editor of the collection *The Black Woman* (1970) and has contributed to *Tales and Stories for Black Folks.* Her two volumes of short stories are *Gorilla, My Love* (1971), from which the following story is taken, and *The Sea Birds Are Still Alive* (1977). In her stories Toni Cade Bambara has been said to express the Black Style, a style at once ineffable and immediately recognizable, with a keener ear and a surer touch than any other writer of our time. "She sows in her wake understanding and humanity," wrote one reviewer in the *Washington Post.* "*Gorilla, My Love* is filled with both love and respect."

Toni Cade Bambara

MY MAN BOVANNE

Blind people got a hummin jones if you notice. Which is understandable completely once you been around one and notice what no eyes will force you into to see people, and you get past the first time, which seems to come out of nowhere, and it's like you in church again with fat-chest ladies and old gents gruntin a hum low in the throat to whatever the preacher be saying. Shakey Bee bottom lip all swole up with Sweet Peach and me explainin how come the sweet potato bread was a dollar-quarter this time stead of dollar regular and he say uh hunh he understand, then he break into this *thizzin* kind of hum which is quiet, but fiercesome just the same, if you ain't ready for it. Which I wasn't. But I got used to it and the onliest time I had to say somethin bout it was when he was playin checkers on the stoop one time and he commenst to hummin quite churchy seem to me. So I says, "Look here Shakey Bee, I can't beat you and Jesus too." He stop.

So that's how come I asked My Man Bovanne to dance. He ain't my man mind you, just a nice ole gent from the block that we all know cause he fixes things and the kids like him. Or used to fore Black Power got hold their minds and mess em around till they can't be civil to ole folks. So we at this benefit for my niece's cousin who's runnin for somethin with this Black party somethin or other behind her. And I press up close to dance with Bovanne who blind and I'm hummin and he hummin, chest to chest like talkin. Not jammin my breasts into the man. Wasn't bout tits. Was bout vibrations. And he dug it and asked me what color dress I had on and how my hair was fixed and how I was doin without a man, not nosy but nice-like, and who was at this affair and was the canapés dainty-stingy or healthy enough to get hold of proper. Comfy and cheery is what I'm tryin to get across. Touch talkin like the heel of the hand on the tambourine or on a drum.

But right away Joe Lee come up on us and frown for dancin so close to the man. My own son who knows what kind of warm I am about; and don't grown men call me long distance and in the middle of the night for a little Mama comfort? But he frown. Which ain't right since Bovanne can't see and defend himself. Just a nice old man who fixes toasters and busted irons and bicycles and things and changes the lock on my door when my men friends get messy. Nice man. Which is not why they invited him. Grass roots you see. Me and Sister Taylor and the woman who does heads at Mamies and the man from the barber shop, we all there on account of we grass roots. And I ain't never been souther than Brooklyn Battery and no more country than the window box on my fire escape. And just yesterday my kids tellin me to take them countrified rags off my head and be cool. And now can't get Black enough to suit em. So everybody passin sayin My Man Bovanne. Big deal, keep steppin and don't even stop a minute to get the man a drink or one of them cute sandwiches or tell him what's goin on. And him standin there with a smile ready case someone do speak he want to be ready. So that's how come I pull him on the dance floor and we dance squeezin past the tables and chairs and all them coats and people standin round up in each other face talkin bout this and that but got no use for this blind man who mostly fixed skates and skooters for all these folks when they was just kids. So I'm pressed up close and we touch talkin with the hum. And here come my daughter cuttin her eye at me like she do when she tell me about my "apolitical" self like I got hoof and mouf disease and there ain't no hope at all. And I don't pay her no mind and just look up in Bovanne shadow face and tell him his stomach like a drum and he laugh. Laugh real loud. And here come my youngest, Task, with a tap on my elbow like he the third grade monitor and I'm cuttin up on the line to assembly.

"I was just talkin on the drums," I explained when they hauled me into the kitchen. I figured drums was my best defense. They can get ready for drums what with all this heritage business. And Bovanne stomach just like that drum Task give me when he come back from Africa. You just touch it and it hum thizzm, thizzm. So I stuck to the drum story. "Just drummin that's all."

"Mama, what are you talkin about?"

"She had too much to drink," say Elo to Task cause she don't hardly say nuthin to me direct no more since that ugly argument about my wigs.

"Look here Mama," say Task, the gentle one. "We just tryin to pull your coat. You were makin a spectacle of yourself out there dancing like that."

"Dancin like what?"

Task run a hand over his left ear like his father for the world and his father before that.

"Like a bitch in heat," say Elo.

"Well uhh, I was goin to say like one of them sex-starved ladies gettin on in years and not too discriminating. Know what I mean?"

I don't answer cause I'll cry. Terrible thing when your own children talk to you like that. Pullin me out the party and hustlin me into some stranger's kitchen in the back of a bar just like the damn police. And ain't like I'm old. I can still wear me some sleeveless dresses without the meat hangin off my arm. And I keep up with some thangs through my kids. Who ain't kids no more. To hear them tell it. So I don't say nuthin.

"Dancin with that tom," say Elo to Joe Lee, who leanin on the folks' freezer. "His feet can smell a cracker a mile away and go into their shuffle number post haste. And them eyes. He could be a little considerate and put on some shades. Who wants to look into them blown-out fuses that—"

"Is this what they call the generation gap?" I say.

"Generation gap," spits Elo, like I suggested castor oil and fricassee possum in the milk-shakes or somethin. "That's a white concept for a white phenomenon. There's no generation gap among Black people. We are a col—"

"Yeh, well never mind," says Joe Lee. "The point is Mama . . . well, it's pride. You embarrass yourself and us too dancin like that."

"I wasn't shame." Then nobody say nuthin. Them standin there in they pretty clothes with drinks in they hands and gangin up on me, and me in the third-degree chair and nary a olive to my name. Felt just like the police got hold to me.

"First of all," Task say, holdin up his hand and tickin off the offenses, "the dress. Now that dress is too short, Mama, and too low-cut for a woman your age. And Tamu's going to make a speech tonight to kick off the campaign and will be introducin you and expecting you to organize the council of elders—"

"Me? Didn nobody ask me nuthin. You mean Nisi? She change her name?"

"Well, Norton was supposed to tell you about it. Nisi wants to introduce you and then encourage the older folks to form a Council of the Elders to act as an advisory—"

"And you going to be standing there with your boobs out and that wig on your head and that hem up to your ass. And people'll say, 'Ain't that the horny bitch that was grindin with the blind dude?' "

"Elo, be cool a minute," say Task, gettin to the next finger. "And then there's the drinkin. Mama, you know you can't drink cause next thing you know you be laughin loud and carryin on," and he grab another finger for the loudness. "And then there's the dancin. You been tattooed on the man for four records straight and slow draggin even on the fast numbers. How you think that look for a woman your age?"

"What's my age?"

"What?"

"I'm axin you all a simple question. You keep talkin bout what's proper for a woman my age. How old am I anyhow?" And Joe Lee slams his eyes shut and squinches up his face to figure. And Task run a hand over his ear and stare into his glass like the ice cubes goin calculate for him. And Elo just starin at the top of my head like she goin rip the wig off any minute now.

"Is your hair braided up under that thing? If so, why don't you take it off? You always did do a neat cornroll."

"Uh huh," cause I'm thinkin how she couldn't undo her hair fast enough talking bout cornroll so countrified. None of which was the subject. "How old, I say?"

"Sixtee-one or—"

"You a damn lie Joe Lee Peoples."

"And that's another thing," say Task on the fingers.

"You know what you all can kiss," I say, gettin up and brushin the wrinkles out my lap.

"Oh Mama," Elo say, puttin a hand on my shoulder like she hasn't done since she left home and the hand landin light and not sure it supposed to be there. Which hurt me to my heart. Cause this was the child in our happiness fore Mr. Peoples die. And I carried that child strapped to my chest till she was nearly two. We was close is what I'm tryin to tell you. Cause it was more me in the child than the others. And even after Task it was the girlchild I covered in the night and wept over for no reason at all less it was she was a chub-chub like me and not very pretty, but a warm child. And how did things get to this, that she can't put a sure hand on me and say Mama we love you and care about you and you entitled to enjoy yourself cause you a good woman?

"And then there's Reverend Trent," say Task, glancin from left to right like they hatchin a plot and just now lettin me in on it. "You were suppose to be talking with him tonight, Mama, about giving us his basement for campaign headquarters and—"

"Didn nobody tell me nuthin. If grass roots mean you kept in the dark I can't use it. I really can't. And Reven Trent a fool anyway the way he tore into the widow man up there on Edgecomb cause he wouldn't take in three of them foster children and the woman not even comfy in the ground yet and the man's mind messed up and—"

"Look here," say Task. "What we need is a family conference so we can get all this stuff cleared up and laid out on the table. In the meantime I think we better get back into the other room and tend to business. And in the meantime, Mama, see if you can't get to Reverend Trent and—''

"You want me to belly rub with the Reven, that it?''

"Oh damn,'' Elo say and go through the swingin door.

"We'll talk about all this at dinner. How's tomorrow night, Joe Lee?'' While Joe Lee being self-important I'm wonderin who's doin the cookin and how come no body ax me if I'm free and do I get a corsage and things like that. Then Joe nod that it's O.K. and he go through the swingin door and just a little hubbub come through from the other room. Then Task smile his smile, lookin just like his daddy and he leave. And it just me in this stranger's kitchen, which was a mess I wouldn't never let my kitchen look like. Poison you just to look at the pots. Then the door swing the other way and it's My Man Bovanne standin there sayin Miss Hazel but lookin at the deep fry and then at the steam table, and most surprised when I come up on him from the other direction and take him on out of there. Pass the folks pushin up towards the stage where Nisi and some other people settin and ready to talk, and folks gettin to the last of the sandwiches and the booze fore they settle down in one spot and listen serious. And I'm thinkin bout tellin Bovanne what a lovely long dress Nisi got on and the earrings and her hair piled up in a cone and the people bout to hear how we all gettin screwed and gotta form our own party and everybody there listenin and lookin. But instead I just haul the man on out of there, and Joe Lee and his wife look at me like I'm terrible, but they ain't said boo to the man yet. Cause he blind and old and don't nobody there need him since they grown up and don't need they skates fixed no more.

"Where we goin, Miss Hazel?'' Him knowin all the time.

"First we gonna buy you some dark sunglasses. Then you comin with me to the supermarket so I can pick up tomorrow's dinner, which is goin to be a grand thing proper and you invited. Then we goin to my house.''

"That be fine. I surely would like to rest my feet.'' Bein cute, but you got to let men play out they little show, blind nor not. So he chat on bout how tired he is and how he appreciate me takin him in hand this way. And I'm thinkin I'll have him change the lock on my door first thing. Then I'll give the man a nice warm bath with jasmine leaves in the water and a little Epsom salt on the sponge to do his back. And then a good rubdown with rose water and olive oil. Then a cup of lemon tea with a taste in it. And a little talcum, some of that fancy stuff Nisi mother sent over last Christmas. And then a massage, a good face massage round the forehead which is the worryin part. Cause you gots to take care of the older folks. And let them know they still needed to run the mimeo machine and keep the spark plugs clean and fix the mailboxes for folks who might help us get the breakfast program goin, and the school for the little kids and the campaign and all. Cause old folks is the nation. That what Nisi was sayin and I mean to do my part.

"I imagine you are a very pretty woman, Miss Hazel."

"I surely am," I say just like the hussy my daughter always say I was.

BOBBIE ANN MASON was born in 1940 and raised on a farm near Mayfield, Kentucky. She received her B.A. from the University of Kentucky, her M.A. from SUNY Binghamton, and her Ph.D from the University of Connecticut. She has taught English and Journalism at Mansfield State College in Pennsylvania where she now lives with her husband. Since 1980 she has been a regular contributor to *The New Yorker*. Her fiction has also appeared in *The Atlantic*, *Redbook*, *Vanity Fair*, *North American Review*, and *Virginia Quarterly Review*. She is the author of two nonfiction books, *Nabokov's Garden* and *The Girl Sleuth*, and the novel *In Country*. Her first collection of short stories, *Shiloh and Other Stories*, was the winner of The Ernest Hemingway Award for the most distinguished first-published work of fiction of 1982. In addition, it was a nominee for the National Book Critic's Circle Award for Fiction, The American Book Award for Fiction and The PEN Faulkner Award. The collection's title story, "Shiloh," which follows here, begins: "Leroy Moffitt's wife, Norma Jean, is working on her pectorals." As one reviewer observed, it is a story whose second line is guaranteed to be read. Writing in the San Francisco *Examiner-Chronicle*, Alice Adams has praised Bobbie Ann Mason's gentle regard for her small-town characters' feelings, in particular the women of her fictional population. "Although hardly radical feminists, even the youngest of them, they are strong and alert and observant likable women; their stance is one of amusement (generally) rather than of worry. When one young woman announces to her (deaf) grandfather, 'Times are different now, Pappy. We're just as good as the men,' her (almost-estranged) husband finds it necessary to explain, 'She gets that from television.' ''

Bobbie Ann Mason

SHILOH

Leroy Moffitt's wife, Norma Jean, is working on her pectorals. She lifts three-pound dumbbells to warm up, then progresses to a twenty-pound barbell. Standing with her legs apart, she reminds Leroy of Wonder Woman.

"I'd give anything if I could just get these muscles to where they're real hard," says Norma Jean. "Feel this arm. It's not as hard as the other one."

"That's 'cause you're right-handed," says Leroy, dodging as she swings the barbell in an arc.

"Do you think so?"

"Sure."

Leroy is a truckdriver. He injured his leg in a highway accident four months ago, and his physical therapy, which involved weights and a pulley, prompted Norma Jean to try building herself up. Now she is attending a body-building class. Leroy has been collecting temporary disability since his tractor-trailer jackknifed in Missouri, badly twisting his left leg in its socket. He has a steel pin in his hip. He will probably not be able to drive his rig again. It sits in the backyard, like a gigantic bird that has flown home to roost. Leroy has been home in Kentucky for three months, and his leg is almost healed, but the accident frightened him and he does not want to drive any more long hauls. He is not sure what to do next. In the meantime, he makes things from craft kits. He started by building a miniature log cabin from notched Popsicle sticks. He varnished it and placed it on the TV set, where it remains. It reminds him of a rustic Nativity scene. Then he tried string art (sailing ships on black velvet), a macramé owl kit, a snap-together B-17 Flying Fortress, and a lamp made out

117

of a model truck, with a light fixture screwed in the top of the cab. At first the kits were diversions, something to kill time, but now he is thinking about building a full-scale log house from a kit. It would be considerably cheaper than building a regular house, and besides, Leroy has grown to appreciate how things are put together. He has begun to realize that in all the years he was on the road he never took time to examine anything. He was always flying past scenery.

"They won't let you build a log cabin in any of the new subdivisions," Norma Jean tells him.

"They will if I tell them it's for you," he says, teasing her. Ever since they were married, he has promised Norma Jean he would build her a new home one day. They have always rented, and the house they live in is small and nondescript. It does not even feel like a home, Leroy realizes now.

Norma Jean works at the Rexall drugstore, and she has acquired an amazing amount of information about cosmetics. When she explains to Leroy the three stages of complexion care, involving creams, toners, and moisturizers, he thinks happily of other petroleum products—axle grease, diesel fuel. This is a connection between him and Norma Jean. Since he has been home, he has felt unusually tender about his wife and guilty over his long absences. But he can't tell what she feels about him. Norma Jean has never complained about his traveling; she has never made hurt remarks, like calling his truck a "widow-maker." He is reasonably certain she has been faithful to him, but he wishes she would celebrate his permanent homecoming more happily. Norma Jean is often startled to find Leroy at home, and he thinks she seems a little disappointed about it. Perhaps he reminds her too much of the early days of their marriage, before he went on the road. They had a child who died as an infant, years ago. They never speak about their memories of Randy, which have almost faded, but now that Leroy is home all the time, they sometimes feel awkward around each other, and Leroy wonders if one of them should mention the child. He has the feeling that they are waking up out of a dream together—that they must create a new marriage, start afresh. They are lucky they are still married. Leroy has read that for most people losing a child destroys the marriage—or else he heard this on *Donahue*. He can't always remember where he learns things anymore.

At Christmas, Leroy bought an electric organ for Norma Jean. She used to play the piano when she was in high school. "It don't leave you," she told him once. "It's like riding a bicycle."

The new instrument had so many keys and buttons that she was bewildered by it at first. She touched the keys tentatively, pushed some buttons, then pecked out "Chopsticks." It came out in an amplified fox-trot rhythm, with marimba sounds.

"It's an orchestra!" she cried.

The organ had a pecan-look finish and eighteen preset chords, with optional flute, violin, trumpet, clarinet, and banjo accompaniments. Norma Jean mastered the organ almost immediately. At first she played Christmas songs. Then she bought *The Sixties Songbook* and learned every tune in it, adding variations to each with the rows of brightly colored buttons.

"I didn't like these old songs back then," she said. "But I have this crazy feeling I missed something."

"You didn't miss a thing," said Leroy.

Leroy likes to lie on the couch and smoke a joint and listen to Norma Jean play "Can't Take My Eyes Off You" and "I'll Be Back." He is back again. After fifteen years on the road, he is finally settling down with the woman he loves. She is still pretty. Her skin is flawless. Her frosted curls resemble pencil trimmings.

Now that Leroy has come home to stay, he notices how much the town has changed. Subdivisions are spreading across western Kentucky like an oil slick. The sign at the edge of town says "Pop: 11,500"—only seven hundred more than it said twenty years before. Leroy can't figure out who is living in all the new houses. The farmers who used to gather around the courthouse square on Saturday afternoons to play checkers and spit tobacco juice have gone. It has been years since Leroy has thought about the farmers, and they have disappeared without his noticing.

Leroy meets a kid named Stevie Hamilton in the parking lot at the new shopping center. While they pretend to be strangers meeting over a stalled car, Stevie tosses an ounce of marijuana under the front seat of Leroy's car. Stevie is wearing orange jogging shoes and a T-shirt that says CHAT-TAHOOCHEE SUPER-RAT. His father is a prominent doctor who lives in one of the expensive subdivisions in a new white-columned brick house that looks like a funeral parlor. In the phone book under his name there is a separate number, with the listing "Teenagers."

"Where do you get this stuff?" asks Leroy. "From your pappy?"

"That's for me to know and you to find out," Stevie says. He is slit-eyed and skinny.

"What else you got?"

"What you interested in?"

"Nothing special. Just wondered."

Leroy used to take speed on the road. Now he has to go slowly. He needs to be mellow. He leans back against the car and says, "I'm aiming to build me a log house, soon as I get time. My wife, though, I don't think she likes the idea."

"Well, let me know when you want me again," Stevie says. He has a cigarette in his cupped palm, as though sheltering it from the wind. He takes a long drag, then stomps it on the asphalt and slouches away.

Stevie's father was two years ahead of Leroy in high school. Leroy is thirty-four. He married Norma Jean when they were both eighteen, and their child Randy was born a few months later, but he died at the age of four months and three days. He would be about Stevie's age now. Norma Jean and Leroy were at the drive-in, watching a double feature (*Dr. Strangelove* and *Lover Come Back*), and the baby was sleeping in the back seat. When the first movie ended, the baby was dead. It was the sudden infant death syndrome. Leroy remembers handing Randy to a nurse at the emergency room, as though he were offering her a large doll as a present. A dead baby feels like a sack of flour. "It just happens sometimes," said the doctor, in what Leroy always recalls as a nonchalant tone. Leroy can hardly remember the child anymore, but he still sees vividly a scene from *Dr. Strangelove* in which the President of the United States was talking in a folksy voice on the hot line to the Soviet premier about the bomber accidentally headed toward Russia. He was in the War Room, and the world map was lit up. Leroy remembers Norma Jean standing catatonically beside him in the hospital and himself thinking: Who is this strange girl? He had forgotten who she was. Now scientists are saying that crib death is caused by a virus. Nobody knows anything, Leroy thinks. The answers are always changing.

When Leroy gets home from the shopping center, Norma Jean's mother, Mabel Beasley, is there. Until this year, Leroy has not realized how much time she spends with Norma Jean. When she visits, she inspects the closets and then the plants, informing Norma Jean when a plant is droopy or yellow. Mabel calls the plants "flowers," although there are never any blooms. She always notices if Norma Jean's laundry is piling up. Mabel is a short, overweight woman whose tight, brown-dyed curls look more like a wig than the actual wig she sometimes wears. Today she has brought Norma Jean an off-white dust ruffle she made for the bed; Mabel works in a custom-upholstery shop.

"This is the tenth one I made this year," Mabel says. "I got started and couldn't stop."

"It's real pretty," says Norma Jean.

"Now we can hide things under the bed," says Leroy, who gets along with his mother-in-law primarily by joking with her. Mabel has never really forgiven him for disgracing her by getting Norma Jean pregnant. When the baby died, she said that fate was mocking her.

"What's that thing?" Mabel says to Leroy in a loud voice, pointing to a tangle of yarn on a piece of canvas.

Leroy holds it up for Mabel to see. "It's my needlepoint," he explains. "This is a *Star Trek* pillow cover."

"That's what a woman would do," says Mabel. "Great day in the morning!"

"All the big football players on TV do it," he says.

"Why, Leroy, you're always trying to fool me. I don't believe you for one minute. You don't know what to do with yourself—that's the whole trouble. Sewing!"

"I'm aiming to build us a log house," says Leroy. "Soon as my plans come."

"Like *heck* you are," says Norma Jean. She takes Leroy's needlepoint and shoves it into a drawer. "You have to find a job first. Nobody can afford to build now anyway."

Mabel straightens her girdle and says, "I still think before you get tied down y'all ought to take a little run to Shiloh."

"One of these days, Mama," Norma Jean says impatiently.

Mabel is talking about Shiloh, Tennessee. For the past few years, she has been urging Leroy and Norma Jean to visit the Civil War battleground there. Mabel went there on her honeymoon—the only real trip she ever took. Her husband died of a perforated ulcer when Norma Jean was ten, but Mabel, who was accepted into the United Daughters of the Confederacy in 1975, is still preoccupied with going back to Shiloh.

"I've been to kingdom come and back in that truck out yonder," Leroy says to Mabel, "but we never yet set foot in that battleground. Ain't that something? How did I miss it?"

"It's not even that far," Mabel says.

After Mabel leaves, Norma Jean reads to Leroy from a list she has made. "Things you could do," she announces. "You could get a job as a guard at Union Carbide, where they'd let you set on a stool. You could get on at the lumberyard. You could do a little carpenter work, if you want to build so bad. You could—"

"I can't do something where I'd have to stand up all day."

"You ought to try standing up all day behind a cosmetics counter. It's amazing that I have strong feet, coming from two parents that never had strong feet at all." At the moment Norma Jean is holding on to the kitchen counter, raising her knees one at a time as she talks. She is wearing two-pound ankle weights.

"Don't worry," says Leroy. "I'll do something."

"You could truck calves to slaughter for somebody. You wouldn't have to drive any big old truck for that."

"I'm going to build you this house," says Leroy. "I want to make you a real home."

"I don't want to live in any log cabin."

"It's not a cabin. It's a house."

"I don't care. It looks like a cabin."

"You and me together could lift those logs. It's just like lifting weights."

Norma Jean doesn't answer. Under her breath, she is counting. Now she is marching through the kitchen. She is doing goose steps.

Before his accident, when Leroy came home he used to stay in the house with Norma Jean, watching TV in bed and playing cards. She would cook fried chicken, picnic ham, chocolate pie—all his favorites. Now he is home alone much of the time. In the mornings, Norma Jean disappears, leaving a cooling place in the bed. She eats a cereal called Body Buddies, and she leaves the bowl on the table, with the soggy tan balls floating in a milk puddle. He sees things about Norma Jean that he never realized before. When she chops onions, she stares off into a corner, as if she can't bear to look. She puts on her house slippers almost precisely at nine o'clock every evening and nudges her jogging shoes under the couch. She saves bread heels for the birds. Leroy watches the birds at the feeder. He notices the peculiar way goldfinches fly past the window. They close their wings, then fall, then spread their wings to catch and lift themselves. He wonders if they close their eyes when they fall. Norma Jean closes her eyes when they are in bed. She wants the lights turned out. Even then, he is sure she closes her eyes.

He goes for long drives around town. He tends to drive a car rather carelessly. Power steering and an automatic shift make a car feel so small and inconsequential that his body is hardly involved in the driving process. His injured leg stretches out comfortably. Once or twice he has almost hit something, but even the prospect of an accident seems minor in a car. He cruises the new subdivisions, feeling like a criminal rehearsing for a robbery. Norma Jean is probably right about a log house being inappropriate here in the new subdivisions. All the houses look grand and complicated. They depress him.

One day when Leroy comes home from a drive he finds Norma Jean in tears. She is in the kitchen making a potato and mushroom-soup casserole, with grated-cheese topping. She is crying because her mother caught her smoking.

"I didn't hear her coming. I was standing here puffing away pretty as you please," Norma Jean says, wiping her eyes.

"I knew it would happen sooner or later," says Leroy, putting his arm around her.

"She don't know the meaning of the word 'knock,' " says Norma Jean. "It's a wonder she hadn't caught me years ago."

"Think of it this way," Leroy says. "What if she caught me with a joint?"

"You better not let her!" Norma Jean shrieks. "I'm warning you, Leroy Moffitt!"

"I'm just kidding. Here, play me a tune. That'll help you relax."

Norma Jean puts the casserole in the oven and sets the timer. Then she plays a ragtime tune, with horns and banjo, as Leroy lights up a joint and lies on the couch, laughing to himself about Mabel's catching him at it. He thinks of Stevie Hamilton—a doctor's son pushing grass. Everything is funny. The whole town seems crazy and small. He is reminded of Virgil Mathis, a boastful policeman Leroy used to shoot pool with. Virgil recently led a drug bust in a back room at a bowling alley, where he seized ten thousand dollars' worth of marijuana. The newspaper had a picture of him holding up the bags of grass and grinning widely. Right now, Leroy can imagine Virgil breaking down the door and arresting him with a lungful of smoke. Virgil would probably have been alerted to the scene because of all the racket Norma Jean is making. Now she sounds like a hard-rock band. Norma Jean is terrific. When she switches to a Latin-rhythm version of "Sunshine Superman," Leroy hums along. Norma Jean's foot goes up and down, up and down.

"Well, what do you think?" Leroy says, when Norma Jean pauses to search through her music.

"What do I think about what?"

His mind has gone blank. Then he says, "I'll sell my rig and build us a house." That wasn't what he wanted to say. He wanted to know what she thought—what she *really* thought—about them.

"Don't start in on that again," says Norma Jean. She begins playing "Who'll Be the Next in Line?"

Leroy used to tell hitchhikers his whole life story—about his travels, his hometown, the baby. He would end with a question: "Well, what do you think?" It was just a rhetorical question. In time, he had the feeling that he'd been telling the same story over and over to the same hitchhikers. He quit talking to hitchhikers when he realized how his voice sounded—whining and self-pitying, like some teenage-tragedy song. Now Leroy has the sudden impulse to tell Norma Jean about himself, as if he had just met her. They have known each other so long they have forgotten a lot about each other. They could become reacquainted. But when the oven timer goes off and she runs to the kitchen, he forgets why he wants to do this.

The next day, Mabel drops by. It is Saturday and Norma Jean is cleaning. Leroy is studying the plans of his log house, which have finally come in the mail. He has them spread out on the table—big sheets of stiff blue paper, with diagrams and numbers printed in white. While Norma Jean runs the vacuum, Mabel drinks coffee. She sets her coffee cup on a blueprint.

"I'm just waiting for time to pass," she says to Leroy, drumming her fingers on the table.

As soon as Norma Jean switches off the vacuum, Mabel says in a loud voice, "Did you hear about the datsun dog that killed the baby?"

Norma Jean says, "The word is 'dachshund.' "

"They put the dog on trial. It chewed the baby's legs

off. The mother was in the next room all the time." She raises her voice. "They thought it was neglect."

Norma Jean is holding her ears. Leroy manages to open the refrigerator and get some Diet Pepsi to offer Mabel. Mabel still has some coffee and she waves away the Pepsi.

"Datsuns are like that," Mabel says. "They're jealous dogs. They'll tear a place to pieces if you don't keep an eye on them."

"You better watch out what you're saying, Mabel," says Leroy.

"Well, facts is facts."

Leroy looks out the window at his rig. It is like a huge piece of furniture gathering dust in the backyard. Pretty soon it will be an antique. He hears the vacuum cleaner. Norma Jean seems to be cleaning the living room rug again.

Later, she says to Leroy, "She just said that about the baby because she caught me smoking. She's trying to pay me back."

"What are you talking about?" Leroy says, nervously shuffling blueprints.

"You know good and well," Norma Jean says. She is sitting in a kitchen chair with her feet up and her arms wrapped around her knees. She looks small and helpless. She says, "The very idea, her bringing up a subject like that! Saying it was neglect."

"She didn't mean that," Leroy says.

"She might not have *thought* she meant it. She always says things like that. You don't know how she goes on."

"But she didn't really mean it. She was just talking."

Leroy opens a king-sized bottle of beer and pours it into two glasses, dividing it carefully. He hands a glass to Norma Jean and she takes it from him mechanically. For a long time, they sit by the kitchen window watching the birds at the feeder.

Something is happening. Norma Jean is going to night school. She has graduated from her six-week body-building course and now she is taking an adult-education course in composition at Paducah Community College. She spends her evenings outlining paragraphs.

"First you have a topic sentence," she explains to Leroy. "Then you divide it up. Your secondary topic has to be connected to your primary topic."

To Leroy, this sounds intimidating. "I never was any good in English," he says.

"It makes a lot of sense."

"What are you doing this for, anyhow?"

She shrugs. "It's something to do." She stands up and lifts her dumbbells a few times.

"Driving a rig, nobody cared about my English."

"I'm not criticizing your English."

Norma Jean used to say, "If I lose ten minutes' sleep, I just drag all day." Now she stays up late, writing compositions. She got a B on her first paper—a how-to theme on soup-based casseroles. Recently Norma Jean has been cooking unusual foods—tacos, lasagna, Bombay chicken. She doesn't play the organ anymore, though her second paper was called "Why Music Is Important to Me." She sits at the kitchen table, concentrating on her outlines, while Leroy plays with his log house plans, practicing with a set of Lincoln Logs. The thought of getting a truckload of notched, numbered logs scares him, and he wants to be prepared. As he and Norma Jean work together at the kitchen table, Leroy has the hopeful thought that they are sharing something, but he knows he is a fool to think this. Norma Jean is miles away. He knows he is going to lose her. Like Mabel, he is just waiting for time to pass.

One day, Mabel is there before Norma Jean gets home from work, and Leroy finds himself confiding in her. Mabel, he realizes, must know Norma Jean better than he does.

"I don't know what's got into that girl," Mabel says. "She used to go to bed with the chickens. Now you say she's up all hours. Plus her a-smoking. I like to died."

"I want to make her this beautiful home," Leroy says, indicating the Lincoln Logs. "I don't think she even wants it. Maybe she was happier with me gone."

"She don't know what to make of you, coming home like this."

"Is that it?"

Mable takes the roof off his Lincoln Log cabin. "You couldn't get *me* in a log cabin," she says. "I was raised in one. It's no picnic, let me tell you."

"They're different now," says Leroy.

"I tell you what," Mabel says, smiling oddly at Leroy.

"What?"

"Take her on down to Shiloh. Y'all need to get out together, stir a little. Her brain's all balled up over them books."

Leroy can see traces of Norma Jean's features in her mother's face. Mabel's worn face has the texture of crinkled cotton, but suddenly she looks pretty. It occurs to Leroy that Mabel has been hinting all along that she wants them to take her with them to Shiloh.

"Let's all go to Shiloh," he says. "You and me and her. Come Sunday."

Mabel throws up her hands in protest. "Oh, no, not me. Young folks want to be by theirselves."

When Norma Jean comes in with groceries, Leroy says excitedly, "Your mama here's been dying to go to Shiloh for thirty-five years. It's about time we went, don't you think?"

"I'm not going to butt in on anybody's second honeymoon," Mabel says.

"Who's going on a honeymoon, for Christ's sake?" Norma Jean says loudly.

"I never raised no daughter of mine to talk that-a-way," Mabel says.

"You ain't seen nothing yet," says Norma Jean. She starts putting away boxes and cans, slamming cabinet doors.

"There's a log cabin at Shiloh," Mabel says. "It was there during the battle. There's bullet holes in it."

"When are you going to *shut up* about Shiloh, Mama?" asks Norma Jean.

"I always thought Shiloh was the prettiest place, so full of history," Mabel goes on. "I just hoped y'all could see it once before I die, so you could tell me about it." Later, she whispers to Leroy, "You do what I said. A little change is what she needs."

*   *   *

"Your name means 'the king,' " Norma Jean says to
Leroy that evening. He is trying to get her to go to Shiloh,
and she is reading a book about another century.

"Well, I reckon I ought to be right proud."

"I guess so."

"Am I still king around here?"

Norma Jean flexes her biceps and feels them for hard-
ness. "I'm not fooling around with anybody, if that's what
you mean," she says.

"Would you tell me if you were?"

"I don't know."

"What does *your* name mean?"

"It was Marilyn Monroe's real name."

"No kidding!"

"Norma comes from the Normans. They were invad-
ers," she says. She closes her book and looks hard at
Leroy. "I'll go to Shiloh with you if you'll stop staring at
me."

On Sunday, Norma Jean packs a picnic and they go to
Shiloh. To Leroy's relief, Mabel says she does not want to
come with them. Norma Jean drives, and Leroy, sitting
beside her, feels like some boring hitchhiker she has picked
up. He tries some conversation, but she answers him in
monosyllables. At Shiloh, she drives aimlessly through the
park, past bluffs and trails and steep ravines. Shiloh is an
immense place, and Leroy cannot see it as a battleground.
It is not what he expected. He thought it would look like a
golf course. Monuments are everywhere, showing through
the thick clusters of trees. Norma Jean passes the log cabin
Mabel mentioned. It is surrounded by tourists looking for
bullet holes.

"That's not the kind of log house I've got in mind,"
says Leroy apologetically.

"I know *that*."

"This is a pretty place. Your mama was right."

"It's O.K.," says Norma Jean. "Well, we've seen it. I
hope she's satisfied."

They burst out laughing together.

At the park museum, a movie on Shiloh is shown every half hour, but they decide that they don't want to see it. They buy a souvenir Confederate flag for Mabel, and then they find a picnic spot near the cemetery. Norma Jean has brought a picnic cooler, with pimiento sandwiches, soft drinks, and Yodels. Leroy eats a sandwich and then smokes a joint, hiding it behind the picnic cooler. Norma Jean has quit smoking altogether. She is picking cake crumbs from the cellophane wrapper, like a fussy bird.

Leroy says, "So the boys in gray ended up in Corinth. The Union soldiers zapped 'em finally. April 7, 1862."

They both know that he doesn't know any history. He is just talking about some of the historical plaques they have read. He feels awkward, like a boy on a date with an older girl. They are still just making conversation.

"Corinth is where Mama eloped to," says Norma Jean.

They sit in silence and stare at the cemetery for the Union dead and, beyond, at a tall cluster of trees. Campers are parked nearby, bumper to bumper, and small children in bright clothing are cavorting and squealing. Norma Jean wads up the cake wrapper and squeezes it tightly in her hand. Without looking at Leroy, she says, "I want to leave you."

Leroy takes a bottle of Coke out of the cooler and flips off the cap. He holds the bottle poised near his mouth but cannot remember to take a drink. Finally he says. "No, you don't."

"Yes, I do."

"I won't let you."

"You can't stop me."

"Don't do me that way."

Leroy knows Norma Jean will have her own way. "Didn't I promise to be home from now on?" he says.

"In some ways, a woman prefers a man who wanders," says Norma Jean. "That sounds crazy, I know."

"You're not crazy."

Leroy remembers to drink from his Coke. Then he says, "Yes, you *are* crazy. You and me could start all over again. Right back at the beginning."

"We *have* started all over again," says Norma Jean. "And this is how it turned out."

"What did I do wrong?"

"Nothing."

"Is this one of those women's lib things?" Leroy asks.

"Don't be funny."

The cemetery, a green slope dotted with white markers, looks like a subdivision site. Leroy is trying to comprehend that his marriage is breaking up, but for some reason he is wondering about white slabs in a graveyard.

"Everything was fine till Mama caught me smoking," says Norma Jean, standing up. "That set something off."

"What are you talking about?"

"She won't leave me alone—*you* won't leave me alone." Norma Jean seems to be crying, but she is looking away from him. "I feel eighteen again. I can't face that all over again." She starts walking away. "No, it *wasn't* fine. I don't know what I'm saying. Forget it."

Leroy takes a lungful of smoke and closes his eyes as Norma Jean's words sink in. He tries to focus on the fact that thirty-five hundred soldiers died on the grounds around him. He can only think of that war as a board game with plastic soldiers. Leroy almost smiles, as he compares the Confederates' daring attack on the Union camps and Virgil Mathis's raid on the bowling alley. General Grant, drunk and furious, shoved the Southerners back to Corinth, where Mabel and Jet Beasley were married years later, when Mabel was still thin and good-looking. The next day, Mabel and Jet visited the battleground, and then Norma Jean was born, and then she married Leroy and they had a baby, which they lost, and now Leroy and Norma Jean are here at the same battleground. Leroy knows he is leaving out a lot. He is leaving out the insides of history. History was always just names and dates to him. It occurs to him that building a house out of logs is similarly empty—too simple. And the real inner workings of a marriage, like most of history, have escaped him. Now he sees that building a log house is the dumbest idea he could have had. It was clumsy of him to think Norma Jean would want a log house. It was a crazy idea. He'll have to think of something else, quickly. He will wad the blueprints into tight balls and fling them into the lake. Then he'll get moving again. He opens his eyes. Norma Jean has moved away and is walking through the cemetery, following a serpentine brick path.

Leroy gets up to follow his wife, but his good leg is asleep and his bad leg still hurts him. Norma Jean is far away, walking rapidly toward the bluff by the river, and he tries to hobble toward her. Some children run past him, screaming noisily. Norma Jean has reached the bluff, and she is looking out over the Tennessee River. Now she turns toward Leroy and waves her arms. Is she beckoning to him? She seems to be doing an exercise for her chest muscles. The sky is unusually pale—the color of the dust ruffle Mabel made for their bed.

ANNE TYLER was born in Minneapolis in 1941, spent her childhood in a Utopian community in North Carolina, and was educated at Duke University and Columbia. She is married to an Iranian psychiatrist, has two children, and lives in Baltimore, the scene of some of her fiction, which is often set in small Southern towns. Her first novels— *If Morning Ever Comes* (1965), *The Tin Can Tree* (1966), and *A Slipping Down Life* (1970)—published before she was 30, deal with families and the sufferings they endure through death and the sad isolation of one member from another. Family life, which John Updike has called her favorite theme, is also the focus of later novels: *The Clock Winder* (1973), *Celestial Navigation* (1975), *Searching for Caleb* (1976), *Earthly Possessions* (1977), *Morgan's Passing* (1980), and *Dinner at the Homesick Restaurant* (1982) in which, according to John Updike's enthusiastic review in *The New Yorker*, Anne Tyler has arrived at a new level of power. Other critics reviewed with similar praise her latest novel, *The Accidental Tourist* (1985). Miss Tyler's short stories have appeared in *Seventeen*, *Antioch Review*, *Critic*, and *Southern Review*. The story that follows here was included in *The Editor's Choice*, a collection of the best short fiction of 1984 as selected by America's top magazine editors. Of the writing life, she has said to one interviewer, "Mostly it's lies, writing novels. You set out to tell an untrue story and you try to make it believable, even to yourself. Which calls for details; any good lie does." She says she writes "because I want more than one life."

Anne Tyler

TEENAGE WASTELAND

He used to have very blond hair—almost white—cut shorter than other children's so that on his crown a little cowlick always stood up to catch the light. But this was when he was small. As he grew older, his hair grew darker, and he wore it longer—past his collar even. It hung in lank, taffy-colored ropes around his face, which was still an endearing face, fine-featured, the eyes an unusual aqua blue. But his cheeks, of course, were no longer round, and a sharp new Adam's apple jogged in his throat when he talked.

In October, they called from the private school he attended to request a conference with his parents. Daisy went alone; her husband was at work. Clutching her purse, she sat on the principal's couch and learned that Donny was noisy, lazy, and disruptive; always fooling around with his friends, and he wouldn't respond in class.

In the past, before her children were born, Daisy had been a fourth-grade teacher. It shamed her now to sit before this principal as a parent, a delinquent parent, a parent who struck Mr. Lanham, no doubt, as unseeing or uncaring. "It isn't that we're not concerned," she said. "Both of us are. And we've done what we could, whatever we could think of. We don't let him watch TV on school nights. We don't let him talk on the phone till he's finished his homework. But he tells us he doesn't *have* any homework or he did it all in study hall. How are we to know what to believe?"

From early October through November, at Mr. Lanham's suggestion, Daisy checked Donny's assignments every day. She sat next to him as he worked, trying to be encouraging, sagging inwardly as she saw the poor quality of everything he did—the sloppy mistakes in math, the illogical leaps in his English themes, the history questions left blank if they required any research.

Daisy was often late starting supper, and she couldn't give as much attention to Donny's younger sister. "You'll never guess what happened at . . ." Amanda would begin, and Daisy would have to tell her, "Not now, honey."

By the time her husband, Matt, came home, she'd be snappish. She would recite the day's hardships—the fuzzy instructions in English, the botched history map, the morass of unsolvable algebra equations. Matt would look surprised and confused, and Daisy would gradually wind down. There was no way, really, to convey how exhausting all this was.

In December, the school called again. This time, they wanted Matt to come as well. She and Matt had to sit on Mr. Lanham's couch like two bad children and listen to the news: Donny had improved only slightly, raising a D in history to a C, and a C in algebra to a B-minus. What was worse, he had developed new problems. He had cut classes on at least three occasions. Smoked in the furnace room. Helped Sonny Barnett break into a freshman's locker. And last week, during athletics, he and three friends had been seen off the school grounds; when they returned, the coach had smelled beer on their breath.

Daisy and Matt sat silent, shocked. Matt rubbed his forehead with his fingertips. Imagine, Daisy thought, how they must look to Mr. Lanham: an overweight housewife in a cotton dress and a too-tall, too-thin insurance agent in a baggy, frayed suit. Failures, both of them—the kind of people who are always hurrying to catch up, missing the point of things that everyone else grasps at once. She wished she'd worn nylons instead of knee socks.

It was arranged that Donny would visit a psychologist for testing. Mr Lanham knew just the person. He would set this boy straight, he said.

When they stood to leave, Daisy held her stomach in and gave Mr. Lanham a firm, responsible handshake.

Donny said the psychologist was a jackass and the tests

were really dumb; but he kept all three of his appointments, and when it was time for the follow-up conference with the psychologist and both parents, Donny combed his hair and seemed unusually sober and subdued. The psychologist said Donny had no serious emotional problems. He was merely going through a difficult period in his life. He required some academic help and a better sense of self-worth. For this reason, he was suggesting a man named Calvin Beadle, a tutor with considerable psychological training.

In the car going home, Donny said he'd be damned if he'd let them drag him to some stupid fairy tutor. His father told him to watch his language in front of his mother.

That night, Daisy lay awake pondering the term "self-worth." She had always been free with her praise. She had always told Donny he had talent, was smart, was good with his hands. She had made a big to-do over every little gift he gave her. In fact, maybe she had gone too far, although, Lord knows, she had meant every word. Was that his trouble?

She remembered when Amanda was born. Donny had acted lost and bewildered. Daisy had been alert to that, of course, but still, a new baby keeps you so busy. Had she really done all she could have? She longed—she ached—for a time machine. Given one more chance, she'd do it perfectly—hug him more, praise him more, or perhaps praise him less. Oh, who can say . . .

The tutor told Donny to call him Cal. All his kids did, he said. Daisy thought for a second that he meant his own children, then realized her mistake. He seemed too young, anyhow, to be a family man. He wore a heavy brown handlebar mustache. His hair was as long and stringy as Donny's, and his jeans as faded. Wire-rimmed spectacles slid down his nose. He lounged in a canvas director's chair with his fingers laced across his chest, and he casually, amiably questioned Donny, who sat upright and glaring in an armchair.

"So they're getting on your back at school," said Cal. "Making a big deal about anything you do wrong."

"Right," said Donny.

"Any idea why that would be?"

"Oh, well, you know, stuff like homework and all," Donny said.

"You don't do your homework?"

"Oh, well, I might do it sometimes but not just exactly like they want it." Donny sat forward and said, "It's like a prison there, you know? You've got to go to every class, you can never step off the school grounds."

"You cut classes sometimes?"

"Sometimes," Donny said, with a glance at his parents.

Cal didn't seem perturbed. "Well," he said, "I'll tell you what. Let's you and me try working together three nights a week. Think you could handle that? We'll see if we can show that school of yours a thing or two. Give it a month; then if you don't like it, we'll stop. If *I* don't like it, we'll stop. I mean, sometimes people just don't get along, right? What do you say to that?"

"Okay," Donny said. He seemed pleased.

"Make it seven o'clock till eight, Monday, Wednesday, and Friday," Cal told Matt and Daisy. They nodded. Cal shambled to his feet, gave them a little salute, and showed them to the door.

This was where he lived as well as worked, evidently. The interview had taken place in the dining room, which had been transformed into a kind of office. Passing the living room, Daisy winced at the rock music she had been hearing, without registering it, ever since she had entered the house. She looked in and saw a boy about Donny's age lying on a sofa with a book. Another boy and a girl were playing Ping-Pong in front of the fireplace. "You have several here together?" Daisy asked Cal.

"Oh, sometimes they stay on after their sessions, just to rap. They're a pretty sociable group, all in all. Plenty of goof-offs like young Donny here."

He cuffed Donny's shoulder playfully. Donny flushed and grinned.

Climbing into the car, Daisy asked Donny, "Well? What did you think?"

But Donny had returned to his old evasive self. He

jerked his chin toward the garage. "Look," he said. "He's got a basketball net."

Now on Mondays, Wednesdays, and Fridays, they had supper early—the instant Matt came home. Sometimes, they had to leave before they were really finished. Amanda would still be eating her dessert. "Bye, honey. Sorry," Daisy would tell her.

Cal's first bill sent a flutter of panic through Daisy's chest, but it was worth it, of course. Just look at Donny's face when they picked him up: alight and full of interest. The principal telephoned Daisy to tell her how Donny had improved. "Of course, it hasn't shown up in his grades yet, but several of the teachers have noticed how his attitude's changed. Yes, sir, I think we're onto something here."

At home, Donny didn't act much different. He still seemed to have a low opinion of his parents. But Daisy supposed that was unavoidable—part of being fifteen. He said his parents were too "controlling"—a word that made Daisy give him a sudden look. He said they acted like wardens. On weekends, they enforced a curfew. And any time he went to a party, they always telephoned first to see if adults would be supervising. "For God's sake!" he said. "Don't you trust me?"

"It isn't a matter of trust, honey . . ." But there was no explaining to him.

His tutor called one afternoon. "I get the sense," he said, "that this kid's feeling . . . underestimated, you know? Like you folks expect the worst of him. I'm thinking we ought to give him more rope."

"But see, he's still so suggestible," Daisy said. "When his friends suggest some mischief—smoking or drinking or such—why, he just finds it hard not to go along with them."

"Mrs. Coble," the tutor said, "I think this kid is hurting. You know? Here's a serious, sensitive kid, telling you he'd like to take on some grown-up challenges, and you're giving him the message that he can't be trusted. Don't you understand how that hurts?"

"Oh," said Daisy.

"It undermines his self-esteem—don't you realize that?"

"Well, I guess you're right," said Daisy. She saw Donny suddenly from a whole new angle: his pathetically poor posture, that slouch so forlorn that his shoulders seemed about to meet his chin . . . oh, wasn't it awful being young? She'd had a miserable adolescence herself and had always sworn no child of hers would ever be that unhappy.

They let Donny stay out later, they didn't call ahead to see if the parties were supervised, and they were careful not to grill him about his evening. The tutor had set down so many rules! They were not allowed any questions at all about any aspect of school, nor were they to speak with his teachers. If a teacher had some complaint, she should phone Cal. Only one teacher disobeyed—the history teacher, Miss Evans. She called one morning in February. "I'm a little concerned about Donny, Mrs. Coble."

"Oh, I'm sorry, Miss Evans, but Donny's tutor handles these things now . . ."

"I always deal directly with the parents. You are the parent," Miss Evans said, speaking very slowly and distinctly. "Now, here is the problem. Back when you were helping Donny with his homework, his grades rose from a D to a C, but now they've slipped back, and they're closer to an F."

"They are?"

"I think you should start overseeing his homework again."

"But Donny's tutor says . . ."

"It's nice that Donny has a tutor, but you should still be in charge of his homework. With you, he learned it. Then he passed his tests. With the tutor, well, it seems the tutor is more of a crutch. 'Donny,' I say, 'a quiz is coming up on Friday. Hadn't you better be listening instead of talking?' 'That's okay, Miss Evans,' he says. 'I have a tutor now.' Like a talisman! I really think you ought to take over, Mrs. Coble."

"I see," said Daisy. "Well, I'll think about that. Thank you for calling."

Hanging up, she felt a rush of anger at Donny. A

talisman! For a talisman, she'd given up all luxuries, all that time with her daughter, her evenings at home!

She dialed Cal's number. He sounded muzzy. "I'm sorry if I woke you," she told him, "but Donny's history teacher just called. She says he isn't doing well."

"She should have dealt with me."

"She wants me to start supervising his homework again. His grades are slipping."

"Yes," said the tutor, "but you and I both know there's more to it than mere grades, don't we? I care about the *whole* child—his happiness, his self-esteem. The grades will come. Just give them time."

When she hung up, it was Miss Evans she was angry at. What a narrow woman!

It was Cal this, Cal that, Cal says this, Cal and I did that. Cal lent Donny an album by the Who. He took Donny and two other pupils to a rock concert. In March, when Donny began to talk endlessly on the phone with a girl named Miriam, Cal even let Miriam come to one of the tutoring sessions. Daisy was touched that Cal would grow so involved in Donny's life, but she was also a little hurt, because she had offered to have Miriam to dinner and Donny had refused. Now he asked them to drive her to Cal's house without a qualm.

This Miriam was an unappealing girl with blurry lipstick and masses of rough red hair. She wore a short, bulky jacket that would not have been out of place on a motorcycle. During the trip to Cal's she was silent, but coming back, she was more talkative. "What a neat guy, and what a house! All those kids hanging out, like a club. And the stereo playing rock . . . gosh, he's not like a grown-up at all! Married and divorced and everything, but you'd think he was our own age."

"Mr. Beadle was married?" Daisy asked.

"Yeah, to this really controlling lady. She didn't understand him a bit."

"No, I guess not," Daisy said.

Spring came, and the students who hung around at Cal's drifted out to the basketball net above the garage. Sometimes, when Daisy and Matt arrived to pick up Donny, they'd find him there with the others—spiky and excited, jittering on his toes beneath the backboard. It was staying light much longer now, and the neighboring fence cast narrow bars across the bright grass. Loud music would be spilling from Cal's windows. Once it was the Who, which Daisy recognized from the time that Donny had borrowed the album. *"Teenage Wasteland,"* she said aloud, identifying the song, and Matt gave a short, dry laugh. "It certainly is," he said. He'd misunderstood; he thought she was commenting on the scene spread before them. In fact, she might have been. The players looked like hoodlums, even her son. Why, one of Cal's students had recently been knifed in a tavern. One had been shipped off to boarding school in midterm; two had been withdrawn by their parents. On the other hand, Donny had mentioned someone who'd been studying with Cal for five years. "Five years!" said Daisy. "Doesn't anyone ever stop needing him?"

Donny looked at her. Lately, whatever she said about Cal was read as criticism. "You're just feeling competitive," he said. "And controlling."

She bit her lip and said no more.

In April, the principal called to tell her that Donny had been expelled. There had been a locker check, and in Donny's locker they found five cans of beer and half a pack of cigarettes. With Donny's previous record, this offense meant expulsion.

Daisy gripped the receiver tightly and said, "Well, where is he now?"

"We've sent him home," said Mr. Lanham. "He's packed up all his belongings, and he's coming home on foot."

Daisy wondered what she would say to him. She felt him looming closer and closer, bringing this brand-new situation that no one had prepared her to handle. What other place would take him? Could they enter him in public school? What were the rules? She stood at the living room window, waiting for him to show up. Gradually, she realized that he was taking too long. She checked the clock. She stared up the street again.

When an hour had passed, she phoned the school. Mr. Lanham's secretary answered and told her in a grave, sympathetic voice that yes, Donny Coble had most definitely gone home. Daisy called her husband. He was out of the office. She went back to the window and thought awhile, and then she called Donny's tutor.

"Donny's been expelled from school," she said, "and now I don't know where he's gone. I wonder if you've heard from him?"

There was a long silence. "Donny's with me, Mrs. Coble," he finally said.

"With you? How'd he get there?"

"He hailed a cab, and I paid the driver."

"Could I speak to him, please?"

There was another silence. "Maybe it'd be better if we had a conference," Cal said.

"I don't *want* a conference. I've been standing at the window picturing him dead or kidnapped or something, and now you tell me you want a—"

"Donny is very, very upset. Understandably so," said Cal. "Believe me, Mrs. Coble, this is not what it seems. Have you asked Donny's side of the story?"

"Well, of course not, how could I? He went running off to you instead."

"Because he didn't feel he'd be listened to."

"But I haven't even—"

"Why don't you come out and talk? The three of us," said Cal, "will try to get this thing in perspective."

"Well, all right," Daisy said. But she wasn't as reluctant as she sounded. Already, she felt soothed by the calm way Cal was taking this.

Cal answered the doorbell at once. He said, "Hi, there," and led her into the dining room. Donny sat slumped in a chair, chewing the knuckle of one thumb. "Hello, Donny," Daisy said. He flicked his eyes in her direction.

"Sit here, Mrs. Coble," said Cal, placing her opposite Donny. He himself remained standing, restlessly pacing. "So," he said.

Daisy stole a look at Donny. His lips were swollen, as if he'd been crying.

"You know," Cal told Daisy, "I kind of expected something like this. That's a very punitive school you've got him in—you realize that. And any half-decent lawyer will tell you they've violated his civil rights. Locker checks! Where's their search warrant?"

"But if the rule is—" Daisy said.

"Well, anyhow, let him tell you his side."

She looked at Donny. He said, "It wasn't my fault. I promise."

"They said your locker was full of beer."

"It was a put-up job! See, there's this guy that doesn't like me. He put all these beers in my locker and started a rumor going, so Mr. Lanham ordered a locker check."

"What was the boy's name?" Daisy asked.

"Huh?"

"Mrs. Coble, take my word, the situation is not so unusual," Cal said. "You can't imagine how vindictive kids can be sometimes."

"What was the boy's *name*," said Daisy, "so that I can ask Mr. Lanham if that's who suggested he run a locker check."

"You don't believe me," Donny said.

"And how'd this boy get your combination in the first place?"

"Frankly," said Cal, "I wouldn't be surprised to learn the school was in on it. Any kid that marches to a different drummer, why, they'd just love an excuse to get rid of him. The school is where I lay the blame."

"Doesn't *Donny* ever get blamed?"

"Now, Mrs. Coble, you heard what he—"

"Forget it," Donny told Cal. "You can see she doesn't trust me."

Daisy drew in a breath to say that of course she trusted him—a reflex. But she knew that bold-faced, wide-eyed look of Donny's. He had worn that look when he was small, denying some petty misdeed with the evidence plain as day all around him. Still, it was hard for her to accuse him outright. She temporized and said, "The only thing I'm sure of is that they've kicked you out of school, and now I don't know what we're going to do."

"We'll fight it," said Cal.

"We can't. Even you must see we can't."

"I could apply to Brantly," Donny said.

Cal stopped his pacing to beam down at him. "Brantly! Yes. They're really onto where a kid is coming from, at Brantly. Why, *I* could get you into Brantly. I work with a lot of their students."

Daisy had never heard of Brantly, but already she didn't like it. And she didn't like Cal's smile, which struck her now as feverish and avid—a smile of hunger.

On the fifteenth of April, they entered Donny in a public school, and they stopped his tutoring sessions. Donny fought both decisions bitterly. Cal, surprisingly enough, did not object. He admitted he'd made no headway with Donny and said it was because Donny was emotionally disturbed.

Donny went to his new school every morning, plodding off alone with his head down. He did his assignments, and he earned average grades, but he gathered no friends, joined no clubs. There was something exhausted and defeated about him.

The first week in June, during final exams, Donny vanished. He simply didn't come home one afternoon, and no one at school remembered seeing him. The police were reassuring, and for the first few days, they worked hard. They combed Donny's sad, messy room for clues; they visited Miriam and Cal. But then they started talking about the number of kids who ran away every year. Hundreds, just in this city. "He'll show up, if he wants to," they said. "If he doesn't, he won't."

Evidently, Donny didn't want to.

It's been three months now and still no word. Matt and Daisy still look for him in every crowd of awkward, heartbreaking teenage boys. Every time the phone rings, they imagine it might be Donny. Both parents have aged. Donny's sister seems to be staying away from home as much as possible.

At night, Daisy lies awake and goes over Donny's life. She is trying to figure out what went wrong, where they made their first mistake. Often, she finds herself blaming

Cal, although she knows he didn't begin it. Then at other times she excuses him, for without him, Donny might have left earlier. Who really knows? In the end, she can only sigh and search for a cooler spot on the pillow. As she falls asleep, she occasionally glimpses something in the corner of her vision. It's something fleet and round, a ball—a basketball. It flies up, it sinks through the hoop, descends, lands in a yard littered with last year's leaves and striped with bars of sunlight as white as bones, bleached and parched and cleanly picked.

ELLEN WILBUR was born in Montclair, New Jersey, in 1943. She attended Bennington College and Wesleyan University and began publishing short stories in the early seventies in *Ploughshares*, *The Virginia Quarterly Review*, *Shenandoah*, and *The Georgia Review*. Her first collection of stories, *Wind and Birds and Human Voices*, was published in 1984 (NAL's Plume edition, 1985). It was highly praised by other first-rate writers of fiction such as George Garrett, Andre Dubus, Gail Godwin, Rosellen Brown, and Richard Yates, who said that all the stories are told in "a fresh, pure, original voice that deserves to be widely and gratefully heard." Eudora Welty called the stories "at once tender and unsparing; skilled, sensitive, daring in their reach, they are clearly the work of a born writer." In this editor's opinion, Eudora Welty and Ellen Wilbur have more in common than their initials. The art of both women is quickened with a profound and loving wisdom.

Ellen Wilbur

FAITH

I was christened Faith Marie after my mother's favorite sister who died of Hodgkin's disease the week before her eighteenth birthday, and whose memory has been preserved with stories of her courage and kindness that always inspired me as a girl. "The good die young," my mother used to sigh whenever she mentioned Auntie Fay, and the saying always worried me. I wanted to be good. It was the one success I could imagine. While I was young, I tried to be as good as I could be, and for as long as my father lived, I gave him little trouble. I was his pride, my mother used to say. If he hadn't died of a stroke in his sleep that Sunday afternoon ten years ago, my life would never have taken the turn it did.

Were mother and father alive today, I know we'd be living just the same as always. We'd be rising at six and retiring at eleven seven days a week. Father would be winning at checkers, gin rummy, and hearts, and mother and I would still be trying to beat him. On Thursday nights we'd eat out at one of the same three restaurants we always went to, and father would be manager of Compton Bank and Trust, where he hardly missed a day for thirty years. Wherever he went, he'd be making a grand impression with the profound conviction of his voice and the power of his penetrating eyes, which could see right into a man. And all the anger in him, which he rarely expressed, would still be stored at the back of his eyes or in the edge of his voice, so that even when he laughed you'd know he wasn't relaxed. He never was relaxed, no matter how he tried. I know I'd be dressed like a proper school girl, conservative and neat in cotton or wool dresses, never pants, my long hair pinned at the sides and rippling down my back or tied up in a braid for church or holidays or dinners out, but never short and boyish the way I wear it now. I'd be odorless and immaculate as ever, without an inkling of a body. And people would still be saying what a graceful girl I was. The way I moved was more like floating. The way I'd walk across our lawn, carrying a frosted glass of mother's minted tea out to the hammock where father read his evening paper in the summer before dinner. Sipping his drink and surveying the mowed yard and trimmed bushes and ever blooming flowers (which were my mother's work), he'd tousle my hair and sigh, "Now this is the life," as if he nearly believed it. Listening to him, I know I'd be as pale as ever, with the face of a girl who lives as much in books as in the world. And I'd feel as far removed from father and that yard as if each page of history or poetry I'd ever read were another mile I'd walked away from home, and each word I learned another door that closed behind me. Though I'd know, no matter what I read, that my mind would never countermand my conscience or overrule my heart. Looking at me, my father's eyes would turn as warm as ever, the way they only seemed to do when he looked at me. Not even at my mother, whose whole mind and heart had been amended, geared to please him, would he ever look that way, without a trace of anger or suspicion. But when he looked at me I'd see the love he never put in words and the faith that I'd never disappoint him. I hoped I never would. To keep the peace, his, my mother's and my own, was such a need I had that had they lived I'm sure the three of us would have passed from Christmas to Christmas, through the dips and peaks of every year, like a ship that's traveling the same circle where the view is always familiar.

I remember one Sunday Father and I were walking home from church all finely dressed and fit to impress whomever we passed. We crossed the green at the center of town and were approached by a pretty girl no more than twenty, who was singing at the top of her voice. She smiled at us as she went by, leaving a strong soprano trill in our ears. I wasn't surprised when Father turned to look at her, outraged. "Now that's the kind of bitch I'd like to see run out of town," he said. I knew he'd say the same to Mother or me if we ever crossed or disappointed him. Because he couldn't tolerate the slightest deviation from his rules. He loved me with all of his heart on the condition that I please him.

Poor Mother couldn't live without Father. He'd been the center of her life for thirty years. Unlike Father, whose beliefs were sacred to him, she had no strong opinions of her own. When he died, she wept with fear as much as grief, as if his death had been a shattering explosion that left our house and town in ruins. She sat all day in his easy chair and couldn't be moved, as if all of her habits as well as her heart were permanently broken. My words and tears never touched her, and it was only two months after Father was gone that she was laid beside him. She was buried in June, the week before our high school graduation.

Compton people who wouldn't speak to me today were concerned and kind when Mother died. There were several families that offered me a home. But I was eighteen, old enough to be on my own, and more at ease in the drawing rooms of novels than I'd ever be in any Compton house. Today there are many in town who believe it was a great mistake, letting me live alone. But I was adamant about it, and I appeared to be as responsible and as mature as any valedictorian of her class is expected to be.

I was as shaken by my parents' death as if the colors of the world had all been changed. Having adjusted myself to my father's wishes for so many years, I had no other inclination. After he was gone, I continued to live exactly as he would have liked me to. If anything, I was more careful than before not to hurt him, as if in death his feelings had become more sensitive than ever and the burden of his happiness was entirely left to me. After Mother's death and the end of school, I took the first available job in town, at Compton library. I was grateful that the work suited me, because I would have taken any job to keep me busy.

Our town of Compton is a tourist town. For three months out of every year the population triples, and Decatur Street is a slow parade of bodies and cars that doesn't end for ninety days. At the end of June, the summer people come. In their enormous yachts and their flashy cars, they arrive. Every year it is a relief to see them come and then a relief to see them go. They are so different from us.

Compton people are short on words. Even in private with their closest kin, the talk is sparse, and actions have more meaning. Whenever Father was troubled, Mother made him a squash pie or one of his other favorites to indicate her sympathy or support. She never asked him to explain. If a man in Compton is well-liked, he'll never have to buy himself a drink at the taverns. By the little favors, by the number of nods he receives on the street, or by the way he is ignored as much as if he were dead, he'll know exactly what his measure is with people. And by the silences, by whether there is comfort or communion in the long pauses between sentences, he'll know exactly how close he is to an acquaintance. I've always known that Compton people were unique. Our women never chattered the way the summer women do, as if there were no end to what they'd say. I've seen the summer people's children awed and muted by the grave reserve and the repressed emotion of a Compton child. And I've seen the staring fascination of all Compton with the open manner of the summer people, who wander through the streets at noon, baring their wrinkled thighs, their cleavage and their bulges to the sun for everyone to see—a people whose feelings flash across their faces as obvious and naked as if they had no secrets. As a child, I used to wander down to watch them at the docks. They seemed as alien and entertaining as a circus troupe. At five o'clock, from boat to boat, there was the sound of ice and glasses, the smell of tonic water, shaving lotion, lipstick and perfume. For evening the women dressed in shocking pink and turquoise, colors bright enough to make a Compton woman blush. There was always laughter interwoven with their conversation, and the liquor made the laughter louder and the talk still freer until the people were leaning into each other's faces or falling into embraces with little cries of "darling" or "my dear." And as I watched them, the gaiety, the confidence, and the warmth of these people always inspired me with affection and yearning for the closeness and the freedom that they knew. It wasn't till I was older I realized that all of their words and embraces brought them no closer to each other than Compton people are—that the distances between them were just as painful and exactly as vast, in spite of the happy illusion they created.

The summer Mother died, I walked to work through the crowds to the rhythm of the cash registers, which never stopped ringing till ten o'clock at night in the restaurants and gift shops all along Decatur Street. And all summer the library, which is a busy place in winter, was nearly empty. I sat at the front desk in the still, dark room, listening to the commotion of cars and voices in the streets. And through the windows I could tell the weather in the patch of sky above the heavy laden elms whose leaves were never still, but trembled, bobbed, and shuddered to every slightest nuance of the air. And seemed to capture and proclaim the whole vitality of every day more truly and completely than any self-afflicted soul could ever hope to render it. I have no other memory of that summer, which disappeared as quickly as it came. But the end of every Compton summer is the same. Even the most greedy merchants are frazzled and fatigued by the daily noise and the rising exuberance of the tourists passing down the coast to home. By then, the beaches and the streets are strewn with cans and papers, as if the town had been a carnival or a zoo, and Compton is glad to see the last of the crowd, whose refuse is only further evidence of the corruption of their pleasure-happy souls.

My first winter alone there were many nights when I cried myself to sleep. I missed my mother's quiet presence in the house and the smells that always rose from the warm, little kitchen where she baked or washed or sat across from me on winter afternoons when I came in from school. Even for a Compton woman she was more than usually quiet, so shy that she had no friends. She went to church on Sunday but the rest of the week she hardly left the yard. My father shopped for all of our food to save her the pain of going out in public. If she'd had her way, she'd never have eaten out with us on Thursday nights. But father insisted on it. ''She needs the change,'' he used to say.

I don't remember Mother ever raising her voice to me in anger. All discipline was left to father. She didn't often kiss or hug me either. But she used to brush my hair one hundred strokes a night, and I remember the gentle touch of her hands. There were times when her shyness made her seem as self-effacing as a nun, and times when I thought I must be living with a saint, the way she read her Bible daily and seemed to have no selfish desires or worldly needs. She dressed in greys and browns, and her dresses hung loose on her bony frame. Though her face was usually serious if not sad, I always believed she was happy in her life with Father and me. She couldn't do enough for us, particularly Father. About her past I only knew that she was born of alcoholic parents who were now both dead, that she'd worshipped her sister, Faith, and that she never corresponded with her other sister, Mary, who lived in California and was also alcoholic. Most often Mother didn't like to reminisce. If I asked her a question she didn't like, she didn't answer it. There were some weeks when she spoke so little that if she hadn't read aloud to me, I hardly would have heard her voice. It was her reading aloud at night that I missed the most after she was gone. It was a habit we kept from before I could read to myself, when to hear her speak page after page was a luxury as soothing and as riveting as any mystery unravelling itself to revelation. It was through the sound of her voice speaking someone else's words that I knew my mother best.

That first winter I cried many nights with all the fear and passion of the child I was and would ever have remained had I been given a choice. And, with a child's love, I saw the images of my father and mother rise up in the dark above my bed as clear and painfully defined as the impression they had left upon my heart. I cried also for the simplicity of my old life. The simple life of a child who wants to please. For I recognized myself among the spinster women of our town, of whom there are many. Women who never leave the houses of their stern fathers and their silent, sacrificing mothers, houses of a kind so prevalent in Compton. Daughters with all of the rebellion driven out of them at an early age, all of the rudeness skimmed away, severely lashed and molded by the father's anger and the mother's fear of all the changing values in the sinful world. Many of our Compton spinsters are sensitive, high strung. You can see they were the children who avoided pain, preferred endearments and affection. They rarely gossip the way the married women do. To their mothers and their fathers they are faithful and devoted to the end, loyal to the present and the past, forgetful of the future. So much I see about them now that I didn't know when I counted myself one of them.

I had one friend from childhood, Mary Everly, who was studying to be a nurse in a city fifty miles away. Though she sometimes wrote to me, she never came home, finding Compton a "stifling" place. I was close to no one else in town. A few months after Mother died, the invitations to supper and the concerned calls from neighbors stopped. Like my mother, I was shy. I had no skill at small talk and was relieved to be left in peace. But I analyzed myself the way a lonely person wonders why he is not loved. And I studied my life until I was as far removed from it as if I had been carved and lifted out of Compton and left to hover like a stranger over everything familiar.

Two times I went to visit Father Ardley in his blue-walled office at the vestry, and twice the touch of his thumb on my forehead, where he signed the cross, brought me to tears. I was drawn to the love of the church. I had an unexamined faith in God, but a fear that His demands would be crushing, were I to take them to heart. It was an irrational fear I tried to explain to Father Ardley, whose eyes were as cold as a winter sky while his voice was like the sun warming it. "You are still in mourning, Faith," he said to me. "Such a loss as you've suffered can't be gotten over quickly. You must pray to God and keep yourself busy, child," he said, though I had never been idle in my life, not ever, then or now.

For seven years I was as busy as I could be. My conscience kept me well supplied with tasks, and there is no end to what a person ought to do. I worked at the library. I lived in my father's house. I baked for the church bazaars. I visited Father Ardley. The summer people came and left as regularly as the tides. I had as many warm acquaintances as ever, and I had no close friends. I still wrote letters to Mary Everly, who was now a nurse, married, and living in Cincinnati with her second baby on the way. Though the memory of my parents' love sustained me, and my father's wishes continued to guide me, time diluted their power to comfort me. Some mornings, walking through the sunny streets to work, the thought of death would take me by surprise, and I knew that mine would mean no more to anyone in town than the sudden disappearance of a picket fence on Elm Street or a missing bed of flowers in Gilbey Park.

I never went out with men. Not that I wasn't attractive. My father used to tell me I was pretty, and Mrs. Beggin at the library said I was a "lovely looking girl" and she couldn't see why I wasn't married yet. But Compton men knew different. Something they saw behind my shyness frightened them away. Something my mother and father had never seen. For beneath it all I wasn't a normal Compton woman, not typical no matter how I tried to be. Whether it was the influence of the summer people or the hours I had escaped in books, I was always "different" as far as Compton men could see, and they were just as strange to me.

It was the eighth summer after mother's death that I met Billy Tober. I was just twenty-six. William Tober IV, his family had named him. He was a summer boy, four years younger than I, a college student, though his eyes were the shallow blue of a flier's or a sailor's. I noticed him before he ever noticed me. I'd always see him with a different girl with the same smile on his lips. He began to come to the library many afternoons. He liked poetry and novels, and he'd ask me for suggestions. I was surprised when he began to appear at the end of the day to walk me home. It wasn't long before we began to meet in the evenings too.

I wish I could say that I remember Billy well, and I wish that I could describe him clearly. But I can't remem-

ber much that he ever said and barely how he looked. I
only remember the effect he had upon me. As if I knew
how it would end, I never invited him to my house, and
I'd only allow him to walk me halfway home, which made
him laugh at first. In the evening, I'd meet him at Gilbey
Park, which is just outside the center of Compton. It is a
pretty hill of bushes, trees, and flowers which overlooks
the harbor. On a hidden bench we sat and sipped the wine
that Billy always brought. Though I'd never tasted liquor
or sat and talked with a young man, I was completely at
ease. The wine and the dusky out-of-doors loosened my
tongue until my hidden thoughts rose up as urgently as if
my life depended on telling them. It often surprised me
what I said, because whenever I was with Billy I was a
different woman, so unlike my usual self I'm sure no one
in Compton would have recognized me. It was as natural
as breathing, the way I'd change into a giddy girl whenever I was with him. "Where did you ever get such hair?"
he asked about the curls my mother never let me cut. After
that, it was my eyes he noticed. My neck was regal as a
queen's, he said. And there was pride as well as grace in
the way I walked. My hands, the smallness of my waist,
my legs, my voice he also praised. I couldn't hear enough.
For the month of July we saw each other every night. At
home, I'd often stare for an hour at the stranger in the
mirror, this woman with a body that a man desired.

Whatever it is that attracts a man to a woman I've too
little experience to know. But I believe that for Billy every
woman was a challenge. He was as restless and driven a
person as I've known. Obsession with a woman must have
soothed him. He used to tell me that he loved me, but I'm
sure that if he'd heard the same from me, his feelings
would have died. If I'd loved him, I would have told him.
He begged me often enough to say it. But I never was able
to. "We're too different," I insisted. "I'm not myself
when I'm with you." But I gloried in the power he'd
given me. I was in love with his desire, which singled me
out from all the world and made the world a painless
kingdom where I ruled the more he wanted me. We met
most nights in August. We drove out to Haskall Beach to a

private place I knew. By then we hardly spoke, and there were times, with his breath hot on my face and his voice crying my name, I felt I'd be more comforted and serene if I were sitting there alone and free of all the yearning human arms can cause.

All those nights we spent together, I never took precautions. "Is it safe?" he asked me many times. But I ignored the question, as if it would have been the crowning sin if I'd been careful to prevent any meaning or possibility of love to come out of the fire of vanity and ignited pride which burned between us. Driving back to town, the silence in the car was so oppressive that it taunted us.

The day that Billy left, I felt relieved, and in the weeks that followed, I didn't miss him once, which surprised me. We wrote no letters to each other. Life went back to normal, and the longer he was gone the more I began to hope I'd never see him again.

When Doctor Filser told me I was pregnant, I could see he was surprised the way all Compton would be. I saw the way he looked at me with new, appraising eyes, and I burned to think of all the other eyes that would be privy to scenes of Billy and me on Haskall Beach. For I knew they'd piece it all together down to every detail.

When I told Father Ardley the news, I aimed the words and threw them at him one by one like darts. But his tone was not what I expected. He wasn't angry with me. "I suppose it was that summer boy you were seeing," he sighed, and he knew enough not to suggest the marriage he'd have insisted upon had Billy Tober been a Compton boy. Instead, he gave me the name of Brighton Adoption Agency.

For all of the nine months I carried the child as if it were a sin beyond forgiveness and there was no forgetting or ignoring it. I felt my father's wrath in every room of the house, and I never visited his or my mother's grave, knowing the affront it would be. As if they'd died again, I felt bereft. I was sure they wanted no part of me now and that I could never turn to them again.

Compton people were not so harsh. As much as they disapproved, they also pitied me. No one tried to deprive me of my job. Though there were some who would no longer speak to me, there were more whose pity moved them to be kinder than before. My humiliation was enough for them and lesson enough for their children. When they saw that my cross was sufficiently heavy, they approved. Even now, times when my heart is light and I'm tempted to laugh in public, I check myself. I know I'll always be on good behavior in Compton, and the more abject I appear, the better off I'll be.

It is ten o'clock, the last day of May, a Saturday, and all of the windows in the house are open for the first time this season. There is a cold breeze coming off the harbor, running through the rooms in currents that break against the walls and boil the curtains halfway to the ceiling. Every year it is the same, the day of opening the windows. The sea wind scours every corner of the house until its heavy atmosphere is broken. All of the memories which hang in odors are borne away until the rooms are only rooms and this woman, dreaming at a littered kitchen table, is as relieved as if she'd just received communion, left all of her habits at the altar rail, and returned to her pew with no identity but her joy.

It is so quiet. The baby is asleep upstairs under a pink quilt. When he wakes, he will have roses in his cheeks. He is so blond, his hair is nearly white. He bears no likeness to my family, and yet the night he was born I knew he was mine as surely as these arms or thoughts belong to me. After the pain of labor, as if I had been delivered of all shame, I asked to see the child. When I saw two waving arms, a tiny head, my heart rose up, amazed. And when they put him in my arms, it was love I held, all warmly wrapped, alive.

So many tired-looking mothers you see in Compton. They hardly seem to care how they appear. Wearing shabby clothes, herding their little broods across the streets, worried and snapping orders at them. But a Compton woman never shows her deepest feelings to the world. When Paul was first at home, I used to kiss his little face at least a hundred times a day. Who but an infant or God could stand so much affection? And all of those kisses were just the beginning of love, the first expression of my newly seeded heart which bloomed, expanded, and flowered with every kiss.

At five o'clock I'd pick the baby up from Mrs. Warren who cared for him the hours I worked. We'd ride home on a crowded bus of Compton women in their fifties, carefully dressed, who rested their heavy bodies behind a row of shopping bags. When they saw the child, their eyes grew soft and bright. "What a love," they'd say, all smiles, and they'd ask his name or age and touch the corner of his blanket so gingerly, with reverence, as if they had forgotten all of the strain, the distraction, the heavy weight of care which had exalted them and only remembered how close they once had come to perfect love. I could see them in their kitchens years ago, bathing their babies in the little plastic tubs that Compton mothers use. I could imagine them, once so shy and bending to the will of the town, their fathers, and their husbands, becoming fierce and stubborn, demanding so much satisfaction, comfort, and such happiness for their little ones as they had never dreamed of for themselves.

By now I ought to have the kitchen clean, the wash brought in and folded, and the vegetables picked and washed. It is so rare I sit and dream that when I do the memories come fast and heavy as an avalanche. I've known some cynics who remember only pain and ugliness, as if the way a man remembers corresponds with what he hopes. When Paul was born, it changed my past as well as the future. Now, when I look back, I see beauty. The older the memory, the more beautiful it has become. Even moments of great pain or disappointment have been transformed, given an importance and a dignity they never had at the time, as if whatever happens and wherever I have failed may one day be redeemed in the far future. I pray it will be so.

LAURIE COLWIN was born in 1944 and grew up in Chicago and Philadelphia. She is the author of four novels: *Shine On*, *Bright and Dangerous Object*, *Happy All the Time*, *Family Happiness*, and *Another Marvelous Thing*. Her short stories appear regularly in many magazines, including *The New Yorker*, *Redbook*, *Playboy*, and *Cosmopolitan*, and they have been included in the 1976 *O. Henry Prize Stories* and the *Best American Short Stories of 1983*, edited by Anne Tyler and Shannon Ravenel. She has published two collections of short stories, *Passion and Affect* and *The Lone Pilgrim*. The title story of the latter volume appears here. Many of Laurie Colwin's stories concern the absurd and comic situations of urban adulthood and all of them have been highly praised for their insight, their generous good humor, and their spirited tone of abiding optimism. "Mozartian" is the critical word used to describe the pleasing and delicate elegance of her style. Her approach to character has been called fertile: she delights in the quirks and inconsistencies of life, believing that open-ended life and emotional vitality are exciting and synonymous layers within that lovely realm called possibility. Miss Colwin lives in New York City with her husband and daughter.

Laurie Colwin

THE LONE PILGRIM

I have been the house pet to several families: friendly, cheerful, good with children, and, most important, I have an acute sensitivity to the individual rhythms of family life. I blend in perfectly, without losing myself. A good houseguest is like an entertainer: Judy Garland, Alfred Hitchcock, Noel Coward. You know what a specific public wants—in my case, groups of two, with children.

For example, Paul and Vera Martin and their children, Ben and Violet. Paul and Vera are lawyers. Paul spends rainy Sundays fishing, and although Vera is a good cook, she is not fond of cleaning fish, so Paul's grandfather's knife is entrusted to me. I do the neat job of a surgeon. Vera, who likes precision, was so impressed by my initial performance that she allowed me into her kitchen, and we have been cooking together ever since. I knew by instinct where she would keep her pots, her baking dishes, her mixing bowls, her silverware. If you are interested in people, their domestic arrangements are of interest, too. That's the sort of student of human conduct I am.

In Maine, I visit Christopher and Jean Goodison and their little son Jean Luc. The Goodisons are haphazard housekeepers, but I have their routine down pat. Their baby and I get along famously. We have a few moments together: a hailstorm he observed from my lap; a lesson in crawling; an afternoon with a kitten. The best way with babies, I have come to know, is quietude. Never approach first. Be casual. Pay minimal tactile attention, and never try to make them love you. You can sit on the same sofa with a child and do nothing more than clutch its little foot from time to time, and before long you will have that child on your lap.

The Goodisons will leave Jean Luc with me when they go shopping, although ordinarily—with ordinary mortals, that is—they are very protective of their son. When they return, I surprise them with a Lady Baltimore cake. Alone in their house, I admire their Shaker table, the fancy-back spoons I find mixed in with their spatulas, the dried-flower arrangements in their lusterware pitchers.

And there are others: the Hartwells in Boston, who live in a Spartan apartment decorated with city-planning charts. The rigorous Mazzinas, who take me camping. The Jerricks, who dress for dinner and bring you a breakfast tray on Sunday morning: coffee, toast, and a small vase with a single flower in it. My friends admire my charm, my sagacity, my propriety, and my positive talent for fitting in with the daily life of others while holding my own.

The adhesive tape on my mailbox reads "P. Rice." Paula Rice, that is, known to all as Polly. I am the charming girl illustrator. I did the pictures for *Hector the Hero, The Pig Who Said Pneu, Fish with Feathers, Snow White and Rose Red,* and *The I Don't Care Papers*—all children's books. Five feet four, reddish hair, brown eyes, long legs. At college, I studied medieval French literature, but kept a sketchbook with me at all times. During the summers, I studied calligraphy, papermaking, and book-binding, and worked as an apprentice at the Lafayette Press, printers of fine editions. I make a living illustrating children's books, but to please myself I do etchings and ink drawings, which I often present to friends on special occasions—marriages, anniversaries, birthdays.

On the side, I am a perfect houseguest. I have the temperament for it. Being a designer teaches you the habit of neatness, and an appreciation for a sense of order not your own. Being a houseguest allows you to fantasize with no one crowding you. After all, you are but a guest, an adornment. Your object is to give pleasure to your hosts. Lolling around in other people's houses allows your mind to drift. Inspired by my surroundings, I indulge myself in this lazy, scene-setting kind of thought. For example: a big yellow moon; the kitchen of an old house in an academic community. On the window ledge a jar of homemade jam, a pot of chives, a cutting of grape ivy in a cracked mug. A big dog sleeps in front of the stove. If you open the window, you feel the crisp October air. An apple pie or a loaf of bread is in the oven, and the house is warm with the scent of it. You wonder if it is time to deal with the last pumpkin, or to pickle the basket of green tomatoes. In the study, your husband is drowsing over an elevating book, a university-press book in blue wrappers. You are wearing a corduroy skirt, a chic blouse, and a sweater of your husband's is tied around your shoulders. You are a woman contemplating seasonal change.

Or you go to the Martins on a rainy night. They occupy two floors of a Victorian brownstone, and as you contemplate the polished moldings and watch the rain through the leaded windows, you feel you are in England in the spring—in a little house in Devizes, say, or Bexhill-on-Sea. Your children have just been put to bed. You have finished reading a book on the life of Joseph Wright of Derby. There is a knock on the door. You start up. Your husband is away, and it is foggy outside. At the door is an old lover, someone who broke your heart, who is in England on business and has tracked you down.

Of course, the fact of the matter is that you live in a flat in New York. Your work is done at an oak drawing table, surrounded by pots of brushes and pens. In other people's houses your perspective widens. You contemplate the Martins' old Spode platter. You know the burn on their dining-room table—the only flaw in its walnut surface—is from Paul's cigar, placed there the night before Ben was born. These details feed the imagination.

Oh, domesticity! The wonder of dinner plates and cream pitchers. You know your friends by their ornaments. You want everything. If Mrs. A. has her mama's old jelly mold, you want one, too, and everything that goes with it—the family, the tradition, the years of having jelly molded in it. We domestic sensualists live in a state of longing, no matter how comfortable our own places are.

You cannot be a good houseguest and be married. Single, you carry only the uncluttered luggage of your own personality, selected and packed by only one pair of hands. Marriage is two-dimensional to the unmarried. No matter how close they get to a couple, they view the situation without any depth perception. If companionship is what you want, and you don't have it, any part of it looks good, including complaints, squabbles, misunderstandings. If only, you feel, you had someone close enough to misunderstand. Intimate enough to squabble with. Well known enough to complain about. Marriage is a condition, like neatness, or order. It is as safe as the wedding silver on the sideboard. To the unmarried, marriage is a sort of trapping, right down to the thin, unobtrusive gold bands.

That's romanticism for you. No one fantasizes about dreary afternoons, despair, unreasonableness, chaos, and boredom. Not the unmarried, that is—especially if they contemplate marriage from a perch of well-savored solitude. Solitude provides you the luxury of thinking about the closed, graceful shapes of other people's lives. My friends are steady, just like me. But, steady as I am, why am I so solitary? No matter how orderly, measured, and careful my arrangements are, they are only a distillation of me, not a fusion of myself and someone else. I have my domestic comforts, except that mine are only mine.

My life changed with the appearance into it of Gilbert Seigh. It was for Gilbert that I produced my best work: illustrations for *The Art of Courtly Love* and *The Poems of Marie de France*.

Gilbert's father, grandfather, and great-grandfather had been publishers of fine editions. After practicing law for five years, Gilbert took over the business when his father's eyesight began to fail. Gilbert was born into the business and was infected with it. His great-grandfather did editions of James Fenimore Cooper, Thackeray, and Mrs. Scott Courrier-Maynard, a now unknown poet of Connecticut. His grandfather went in for U.S. Grant's memoirs, Washington Irving, and speeches of American presidents. Gilbert's father did the poets of his day, edited and published a little magazine called *Lampfire*, and produced double-language volumes of Rimbaud, Rilke, and Christian Morgenstern. Gilbert goes in for the classics, for naturalist works, and for Melville. Three thousand dollars will get you the Seigh Press edition of "Billy Budd." Six will get you his two volumes of *Wild Flowers of the North American Continent*.

Gilbert does not look like a man of books. He looks like a young auto magnate: large, ruddy, and enthusiastic. His glasses fog over from sheer enjoyment. He has a hot temper and a big, loud laugh. I often picture him in his leather chair at his office, laughing and wiping his glasses on the vest of his woolly suit. I like to watch him go up against his master binder, a fiery Italian named Antonio Nello, fighting about the ornaments for a spine. This clash of hardheaded perfectionists brings forth stubborn shouting from Gilbert and operatic flights of invective from Antonio, after which the correct solution is reached.

Several months after I met Gilbert, I fell in love with him. I was sent to him by Paul Martin. Gilbert, at dinner with Paul and Vera, had said he was looking for an illustrator and couldn't find one whose work he liked. He had been to dozens of galleries, museums, and agents. He had looked through hundreds of illustrated books. Then Paul showed him a drawing I had done to celebrate the birth of Violet. It shows a homely little girl sitting in a field of lavender and purple flowers. Gilbert asked if the artist was still alive. It was the best thing he had seen since Arthur Rackham, he said. Vera produced copies of *Fish with Feathers* and *Snow White and Rose Red*. Thus the girl illustrator met Gilbert Seigh one rainy midmorning. He skimmed through my portfolio, and since there was nothing at stake, I felt free to dislike him. I felt he was cavalier with my work. I felt I had been set up by the Martins to meet an available man whose tastes were similar to my own. He closed the portfolio and began to hum happily, at which point I figured him for a moron.

" 'My heart is like a singing bird,' " he sang.

My reactions were coming thick and fast now. I thought he was arrogant, insolent, pretentious, and unattractively eccentric. I picked up the portfolio and tied its ribbons.

I said, "Thank you for seeing me," and began to leave.

"Oh, wait," he said. "I've put you off. I'm terribly sorry. You think I haven't paid proper attention to your work, but I already know your work. Vera showed me your books and the picture you did for Violet. I was behaving like a fool because it's so good. I'm too mono-minded to have told you. You're the illustrator I've been looking for. Please sit down."

I sat. I thought he was cuckoo. Then he described the project he had in mind: an edition of Andreas Capellanus' *The Art of Courtly Love*. I told him I had studied medieval literature. He glowed with delight, and wiped his glasses. He still seemed a little batty to me, but he certainly knew what beautiful books were all about.

That's how it began. I went home, finished my last assignment, and began doing my best work for Gilbert Seigh.

We worked elegantly together. It was a perfect match. He took me out to lunch often, and never so much as brushed my arm with his sleeve. It was said he had been keeping company with a lady lawyer, who had been more or less a fixture in his life since his divorce. So it was to Gilbert that I dedicated my heart. I brooded about him constantly. Being in love with him brought me all the things in life I counted on: a sense of longing, something to turn over and over in my mind, and that clear, slightly manic vision you get with unrequited love. Each line I drew was a dedication of sorts. Choosing type, browsing through books of paper samples, planning and designing, going over proofs with him, gave me an extreme sense of heady pleasure. If that wasn't love, what was?

Well, I'll tell you what was. I had suffered in love three years before, and it had not stopped haunting me. The man in question was an astronomer by the name of Jacob Bailey. Somewhere in the heavens is a galaxy named for him: the Bailey galaxy. It can only be seen through an observatory telescope—he showed it to me once at an observatory in Vermont. I will probably never see it again. I met Jacob in the line of work—the way I felt it was proper to meet those with whom you will have a profound connection. I was doing the drawings for a children's book on Kepler, and Jacob was checking the text and pictures for accuracy. It was love at once—hot, intense, brilliant, and doomed to fail. When it did, and we parted, it was with much puzzlement and despair. Jacob wanted a grand event—something you would never forget but not something to live with. I wanted something to live with. A love affair conducted with the same thrilling rev-up that starts a Grand Prix race usually runs its course and stops. When the Rice and Bailey show was over, I went into a form of mourning. I felt that being crossed in love had changed me, and it had, but my life stayed the same. I worked with what I felt was new depth, and carried Jacob around as a secret in my heart.

When you fall in love like that, it strikes like a disease, and you can understand why nineteenth-century poets felt they were either sick with love or dying of it. Divorced people sometimes remember the joys of married life as strains, but in a love affair just the reverse is true. Since marriages are final and love affairs are open-ended, you tend to think about what might have been instead of what was. So I recalled Jacob's gorgeous smile but not his cruel streak. I remembered the resemblance I thought he bore to an angel but not his frequent nastiness and its effect. But what difference does it make? I remembered. My life—my inner life—became a kind of reverie, and it would not have shocked me had I found that in some dreamlike state I had created a little shrine to Jacob Bailey: his photograph, my book on Kepler, a parking ticket from the Bronx Zoo, the little pearl earrings he gave me. The idea of committed, settled love is as remote to a romantic as lunar soil.

Gilbert's taste in music is that of a tin-eared highbrow. He goes to the opera. He likes Mozart. He listens, abstractly, but music is just another taste to him, and not his primary taste by a long shot. To him it is a sort of cultivated white noise, like glasses tinkling in the background during an expensive meal at a restaurant. Well, I can hum along with the best of them, but my reactions are hardly cultivated. Music is not a taste to me but a craving— something I must have. If I find something I love to hear, I play it over and over again. Then I am able to sit on a bus and play a Brahms quartet in my mind from memory, or any of a million rock-and-roll songs I love. Music becomes foreground then, or landscape gardening. It alters or complements my mood. On windy nights, I like to go home, light a fire, and flip on a little Boccherini, to warm up. By the time I sit down to work, another mood overtakes me. My best drawing for *The Art of Courtly Love* was done listening to the Everly Brothers singing "Sleepless Nights." When that palled, I started on Jerry Lee Lewis singing "Another Place, Another Time." After a few hours of work, I like a good weep, to the Harp Quartet.

The thing about music is it's all your own. It puts you into a complex frame of mind without your even leaving the house. I can relive long moments with Jacob Bailey by playing what I listened to when he was around or what I wept to when he wasn't. It makes your past come back to you, and if you must pinpoint a moment in your life you can say, "That was when 'He's a Rebel,' by the Crystals, was a hit," or "right after the Dietrich Fischer-Dieskau concert." This kind of music worship is a form of privacy, and a great aid to highly emotional people who live in a hermetic state—a door key to the past, an inspiration.

Gilbert and I worked on *Courtly Love* for a year, and after it was sent to the printer we began on the poems of Marie de France. The poems, since they are about love in vain, made me think of Jacob Bailey. I would break from work to stick my head out the window in an unsuccessful attempt to locate the Bailey galaxy. I worked accompanied by a record of country hymns. My favorite was called "The Lone Pilgrim." A man comes to the place where the Lone Pilgrim is buried, and hears someone calling to him. It is the Pilgrim, who tells his story. Away from home, far from his loved ones, he sickened and died. I played one stanza over and over again:

O tell my companion and children
  most dear
To weep not for me now I'm gone.
The same hand that led me
  through scenes most severe
Has kindly assisted me home.

Since I was thinking about Jacob Bailey anyway, this song made me long for him. I knew he was on an expedition in Greenland, all alone. I thought of the scenes most severe he might be passing through and the kind hand that might lead him home: mine.

These were days when I thought I saw him on the street. My heart jumped; I thought he had come back. But it never was Jacob. I wanted to go up to the man I thought was Jacob and shake him for not being, to shake him until he was. There were times when I could not believe our connection had been broken. That was love, wasn't it?

All this time, of course, I continued to be in love with Gilbert. What I thought might be a crush had turned into true affection. The year we spent working on *The Art of Courtly Love* had given me ample time to judge his character.

The worst you could say of him was that he was prone to fits of abstraction. In these states, when spoken to he took a long time to answer, and you felt he was being rude. When he was concentrating, papers littered his desk, causing his secretary to wonder if he was messy at home. At home he was messy when abstracted. His bed was unmade. Clothing piled up on his bed in the shape of an African termite nest. Mail, newspapers, books, and catalogues were scattered on his desk, his coffee table, in the kitchen.

But the result of his abstraction was perfection. Gilbert's books were more than handsome; they were noble. His energy was bountiful and steady, and he gave people the same attention to detail he gave to books. Gilbert got to know me, too. He knew when I was tired out, or when I had faded on a drawing and couldn't see what form it was

taking. He knew how to make me laugh, what sort of food
I liked. He learned to have a cup of hot tea waiting for me
at the end of a day, and he remembered things I told him.
When we first started working, I described to him a plate
that I had seen in an antique shop and that I wanted with
all my heart. This was by way of illustrating a point; we
were talking about impatience and the wisdom of holding
off from obtainable pleasure as a test of will. The day, one
year later, that *Courtly Love* went to press, the second
cousin to the plate I wanted was presented to me by
Gilbert: dark-blue Staffordshire, with flowers all around.

In short, he was just like me. When he was not abstracted, his quarters were immaculate, and arranged for
sheer domestic pleasure. He bought flowers when people
came to dinner. He liked to take a long time over a meal. I
in turn knew how to cheer him when he became cranky
and dispirited. I knew he loved rhubarb pie, so the first of
the season's rhubarb went to him. But best of all, we were
perfect workmates.

The night we saw the finished edition of *Courtly Love*,
we went out to dinner to celebrate and drank two bottles of
champagne. Gilbert walked me home, and on the way he
stopped and astonished me by taking me into his arms and
kissing me. I was giddy and drunk, but not so drunk as not
to know what my reactions were. He had never so much as
brushed my arm with his sleeve, and here we were locked
in an embrace on an empty street.

When he released me, I said, "Aren't you going to kiss
me again?"

"Sometimes if you work very closely with someone,
you get used to working, and don't know how to gauge
what they feel," Gilbert said.

In my apartment, he told me what he felt, and I told
him. Then we celebrated our first night together.

The solitary mind likes to reflect on the pain of past
love. If you are all alone, it gives you something to react
to, a sort of exercise to keep the muscles flexed.

I knew that Gilbert was falling in love with me. I
watched it happen. And Gilbert knew that I was falling in

love with him. We thought we had been fated for one another, but actually we were only getting used to good romantic luck. It is not so often that well-matched people meet. My being in love with Gilbert was accompanied by a sense of rightness I had never felt before, and we decided that we would marry within a year.

But when I worked alone in my apartment I was consumed with a desire to see Jacob Bailey. This desire was sharp as actual pain. I wasted many sheets of stationery beginning letters to him, which I tore up. When your heart's desire is right within your reach, what else is there to do but balk?

I pictured my oak desk secretary next to Gilbert's Chinese lamp, my books next to his, my clothing beside his in the closet. All my friends lived in pairs, except me. I had only fallen in love—love being what you one day wept over in private. What did you do with love that didn't end? That ceased to be sheer romance and moved on to something more serious?

You get used to a condition of longing. Live with it over time and it becomes part of your household—the cat you don't take much notice of that slinks up against you at mealtime or creeps onto the foot of your bed at night. You cannot fantasize being married if you are married. Married to Gilbert, what would I long for? I would not even be able to long for him.

Woe to those who get what they desire. Fulfillment leaves an empty space where your old self used to be, the self that pines and broods and reflects. You furnish a dream house in your imagination, but how startling and final when that dream house is your own address. What is left to you? Surrounded by what you wanted, you feel a sense of amputation. The feelings you were used to abiding with are useless. The conditions you established for your happiness are met. That youthful light-headed feeling whose sharp side is much like hunger is of no more use to you.

You long for someone to love. You find him. You pine for him. Suddenly, you discover you are loved in return. You marry. Before you do, you count up the days you spent in other people's kitchens, at dinner tables, putting other people's children to bed. You have basked in a sense of domesticity you have not created but enjoy. The Lone Pilgrim sits at the dinner parties of others, partakes, savors, and goes home in a taxi alone.

Those days were spent in quest—the quest to settle your own life, and now the search has ended. Your imagined happiness is yours. Therefore, you lose your old bearings. On the one side is your happiness and on the other is your past—the self you were used to, going through life alone, heir to your own experience. Once you commit yourself, everything changes and the rest of your life seems to you like a dark forest on the property you have recently acquired. It is yours, but still you are afraid to enter it, wondering what you might find: a little chapel, a stand of birches, wolves, snakes, the worst you can imagine, or the best. You take one timid step forward, but then you realize you are not alone. You take someone's hand—Gilbert Seigh's—and strain through the darkness to see ahead.

JOY WILLIAMS was born in Chelmsford, Massachusetts, in 1944. She was educated at Marietta College and the State University of Iowa and has received a number of academic and writing awards including membership in Phi Beta Kappa, a National Endowment for the Arts grant, a Wallace Stegner fellowship at Stanford University and a Guggenheim fellowship. She has published two novels, *State of Grace* and *The Changeling*. Her short fiction has been included in the 1966 *O. Henry Prize Stories*, in *Secret Lives of Our Time,* edited by Gordon Lish, and in *The Best American Short Stories of 1978,* edited by Theodore Solotaroff. Her volume of short stories, *Taking Care* (1982), was praised as a work of consistent percipience and wit. The title story, which follows, is the masterpiece of the collection, "a delicate treasure" in the words of the fiction writer and critic David Quammen, a triumphant and moving affirmation of human love as the ground of all true being.

Joy Williams

TAKING CARE

Jones, the preacher, has been in love all his life. He is baffled by this because as far as he can see, it has never helped anyone, even when they have acknowledged it, which is not often. Jones's love is much too apparent and arouses neglect. He is like an animal in a traveling show who, through some aberration, wears a vital organ outside the skin, awkward and unfortunate, something that shouldn't be seen, certainly something that shouldn't be watched working. Now he sits on a bed beside his wife in the self-care unit of a hospital fifteen miles from their home. She has been committed here for tests. She is so weak, so tired. There is something wrong with her blood. Her arms are covered with bruises where they have gone into the veins. Her hip, too, is blue and swollen where they have drawn out samples of bone marrow. All of this is frightening. The doctors are severe and wise, answering Jones's questions in a way that makes him feel hopelessly deaf. They have told him that there really is no such thing as a disease of the blood, for the blood is not a living tissue but a passive vehicle for the transportation of food, oxygen and waste. They have told him that abnormalities in the blood corpuscles, which his wife seems to have, must be regarded as symptoms of disease elsewhere in the body. They have shown him, upon request, slides and charts of normal and pathological blood cells which look to Jones like canapés. They speak (for he insists) of leukocytosis, myelocytes and megaloblasts. None of this takes into account the love he has for his wife! Jones sits beside her in this dim pleasant room, wearing a grey suit and his clerical collar, for when he leaves her he must visit other parishioners who are patients here. This part of the hospital is like a motel. One may wear one's regular clothes. The rooms have ice-buckets, rugs and colorful bedspreads. How he wishes that they were traveling and staying overnight, this night, in a motel. A nurse comes in with a tiny paper cup full of pills. There are three pills, or rather, capsules, and they are not for his wife but for her blood. The cup is the smallest of its type that Jones has ever seen. All perspective, all sense of time and scale seem abandoned in this hospital. For example, when Jones turns to kiss his wife's hair, he nicks the air instead.

Jones and his wife have one child, a daughter, who, in turn, has a single child, a girl, born one-half year ago. Jones's daughter has fallen in with the stars and is using the heavens, as Jones would be the first to admit, more than he ever has. It has, however, brought her only grief and confusion. She has left her husband and brought the baby to Jones. She has also given him her dog. She is going to Mexico where soon, in the mountains, she will have a nervous breakdown. Jones does not know this, but his daughter has seen it in the stars and is going out to meet it. Jones quickly agrees to care for both the baby and the dog, as this seems to be the only thing his daughter needs from him. The day of the baby's birth is secondary to the position of the planets and the terms of houses, quadrants and gradients. Her symbol is a bareback rider. To Jones, this is a graceful thought. It signifies audacity. It also means luck. Jones slips a twenty dollar bill in the pocket of his daughter's suitcase and drives her to the airport. The plane taxis down the runway and Jones waves, holding all their luck in his arms.

One afternoon, Jones had come home and found his wife sitting in the garden, weeping. She had been transplanting flowers, putting them in pots before the first frost came. There was dirt on her forehead and around her mouth. Her light clothes felt so heavy. Their weight made her body ache. Each breath was a stone she had to swallow. She cried and cried in the weak autumn sunshine. Jones could see the veins throbbing in her neck. "I'm dying," she said. "It's taking me months to die." But after he had brought her inside, she insisted that she felt better and made them both a cup of tea while Jones potted the rest of the plants and carried them down cellar. She lay on the sofa and Jones sat beside her. They talked quietly with one another. Indeed, they were almost whispering, as though they were in a public place surrounded by strangers instead of in their own house with no one present but themselves. "It's the season," Jones said. "In fall everything slows down, retreats. I'm feeling tired myself. We need iron. I'll go to the druggist right now and buy some iron tablets." His wife agreed. She wanted to go with him, for the ride. Together they ride, through the towns, for miles and miles, even into the next state. She does not want to stop driving. They buy sandwiches and milkshakes and eat in the car. Jones drives. They have to buy more gasoline. His wife sits close to him, her eyes closed, her head tipped back against the seat. He can see the veins beating on in her neck. Somewhere there is a dreadful sound, almost audible. "First I thought it was my imagination," his wife said. "I couldn't sleep. All night I would stay awake, dreaming. But it's not in my head. It's in my ears, my eyes. They ache. Everything. My tongue. My hair. The tips of my fingers are dead." Jones pressed her cold hand to his lips. He thinks of something mad and loving better than he—running out of control, deeply in the darkness of his wife. "Just don't make me go to the hospital," she pleaded. Of course she will go there. The moment has already occurred.

Jones is writing to his daughter. He received a brief letter from her this morning, telling him where she could be reached. The foreign postmark was so large that it almost obliterated Jones's address. She did not mention either her mother or the baby, which makes Jones feel peculiar. His life seems increate as his God's life, perhaps even imaginary. His daughter tells him about the town in which she lives. She does not plan to stay there long. She wants to travel. She will find out exactly what she wants to do and then she will come home again. The town is poor but interesting and there are many Americans there her own age. There is a zoo right on the beach. Almost all the towns, no matter how small, have little zoos. There are primarily eagles and hawks in the cages. And what can Jones reply to that? He writes *Every thing is fine here. We are burning wood from the old apple tree in the fire place and it smells wonderful. Has the baby had her full series of polio shots? Take care.* Jones uses this expression constantly, usually in totally unwarranted situations, as when he purchases pipe cleaners or drives through toll booths. Distracted, Jones writes off the edge of the paper and onto the blotter. He must begin again. He will mail this on the way to the hospital. They have been taking X-rays for three days now but the pictures are cloudy. They cannot read them. His wife is now in a real sickbed with high metal sides. He sits with her while she eats her dinner. She asks him to take her good nightgown home and wash it with a bar of Ivory. They won't let her do anything now, not even wash out a few things. *You must take care.*

Jones is driving down a country road. It is the first snowfall of the season and he wants to show it to the baby who rides beside him in a small cushioned car seat all her own. Her head is almost on a level with his and she looks earnestly at the landscape, sometimes smiling. They follow the road that winds tightly between fields and deep pine woods. Everything is white and clean. It has been snowing all afternoon and is doing so still, but very very lightly. Fat snowflakes fall solitary against the windshield. Sometimes the baby reaches out for them. Sometimes she gives a brief kick and cry of joy. They have done their errands. Jones has bought milk and groceries and two yellow roses which lie wrapped in tissue and newspaper in the trunk, in the cold. He must buy two on Saturday as the florist is closed on Sunday. He does not like to do this but there is no alternative. The roses do not keep well. Tonight he will give one to his wife. The other he will pack in sugar water and store in the refrigerator. He can only hope that the bud will remain tight until Sunday when he brings

it into the terrible heat of the hospital. The baby rocks
against the straps of her small carrier. Her lips are pursed
as she watches intently the fields, the grey stalks of crops
growing out of the snow, the trees. She is warmly dressed
and she wears a knitted orange cap. The cap is twenty-
three years old, the age of her mother. Jones found it just
the other day. It has faded almost to pink on one side. At
one time, it must have been stored in the sun. Jones,
driving, feels almost gay. The snow is so beautiful. Everything is white. Jones is an educated man. He has read
Melville, who says that white is the colorless all-color of
atheism from which we shrink. Jones does not believe this.
He sees a holiness in snow, a promise. He hopes that his
wife will know that it is snowing even though she is
separated from the window by a curtain. Jones sees something moving across the snow, a part of the snow itself,
running. Although he is going slowly, he takes his foot
completely off the accelerator. "Look, darling, a snow-
shoe rabbit." At the sound of his voice, the baby stretches
open her mouth and narrows her eyes in soundless glee.
The hare is splendid. So fast! It flows around invisible
obstructions, something out of a kind dream. It flies across
the ditch, its paws like paddles, faintly yellow, the color of
raw wood. "Look, sweet," cries Jones, "how big he is!"
But suddenly the hare is curved and falling, round as a
ball, its feet and head tucked closely against its body. It
strikes the road and skids upside down for several yards.
The car passes around it, avoids it. Jones brakes and stops,
amazed. He opens the door and trots back to the animal.
The baby twists about in her seat as well as she can and
peers after him. It is as though the animal had never been
alive at all. Its head is broken in several places. Jones
bends to touch its fur, but straightens again, not doing so.
A man emerges from the woods, swinging a shotgun. He
nods at Jones and picks the hare up by the ears. As he
walks away, the hare's legs rub across the ground. There
are small crystal stains on the snow. Jones returns to the
car. He wants to apologize but he does not know to whom
or for what. His life has been devoted to apologetics. It is
his profession. He is concerned with both justification and

remorse. He has always acted rightly, but nothing has ever come of it. He gets in the car, starts the engine. "Oh, sweet," he says to the baby. She smiles at him, exposing her tooth. At home that night, after the baby's supper, Jones reads a story to her. She is asleep, panting in her sleep, but Jones tells her the story of al-Boraq, the milk-white steed of Mohammed, who could stride out of the sight of mankind with a single step.

Jones sorts through a collection of records, none of which have been opened. They are still wrapped in cellophane. The jacket designs are subdued, epic. Names, instruments and orchestras are mentioned confidently. He would like to agree with their importance, for he knows that they have worth, but he is not familiar with the references. His daughter brought these records with her. They had been given to her by an older man, a professor she had been having an affair with. Naturally, this pains Jones. His daughter speaks about the men she has been involved with but no longer cares about. Where did these men come from? Where were they waiting and why have they gone? Jones remembers his daughter when she was a little girl, helping him rake leaves. What can he say? For years on April Fool's Day, she would take tobacco out of his humidor and fill it with corn flakes. Jones is full of remorse and astonishment. When he saw his daughter only a few weeks ago, she was thin and nervous. She had torn out almost all her eyebrows with her fingers from this nervousness. And her lashes. The roots of her eyes were white, like the bulbs of flowers. Her fingernails were crudely bitten, some bleeding below the quick. She was tough and remote, wanting only to go on a trip for which she had a ticket. What can he do? He seeks her in the face of the baby but she is not there. All is being both contin- ued and resumed, but the dream is different. The dream cannot be revived. Jones breaks into one of the albums, blows the dust from the needle, plays a record. Outside it is dark. The parsonage is remote and the only buildings nearby are barns. The river cannot be seen. The music is Bruckner's *Te Deum*. Very nice. Dedicated to God. He plays the other side. A woman, Kathleen Ferrier, is singing in German. Jones cannot understand the words but the music stuns him. *Kindertotenlieder.* It is devastating. In college he had studied only scientific German, the vocabulary of submarines, dirigibles and steam engines. Jones plays the record again and again, searching for his old grammar. At last he finds it. The wings of insects are between some of the pages. There are notes in pencil, written in his own young hand.

RENDER:

A. WAS THE TEACHER SATISFIED WITH YOU TODAY?

B. NO. HE WAS NOT. MY ESSAY WAS GOOD BUT IT WAS NOT COPIED WELL.

C. I AM SORRY YOU WERE NOT INDUSTRIOUS THIS TIME FOR YOU GENERALLY ARE.

These lessons are neither of life or death. Why was he instructed in them? In the hospital, his wife waits to be translated, no longer a woman, the woman whom he loves, but a situation. Her blood moves mysteriously as constellations. She is under scrutiny and attack and she has abandoned Jones. She is a swimmer waiting to get on with the drowning. Jones is on the shore. In Mexico, his daughter walks along the beach with two men. She is acting out a play that has become her life. Jones is on the mountaintop. The baby cries and Jones takes her from the crib to change her. The dog paws the door. Jones lets him out. He settles down with the baby and listens to the record. He still cannot make out many of the words. The baby wiggles restlessly on his lap. Her eyes are a foal's eyes, navy-blue. She has grown in a few weeks to expect everything from Jones. He props her on one edge of the couch and goes to her small toy box where he keeps a bear, a few rattles and balls. On the way, he opens the door and the dog immediately enters. His heavy coat is cold, fragrant with ice. He noses the baby and she squeals.

Oft denk'ich, sie sind nur ausgegangen
Bald werden sie wieder nach Hause gelangen

Jones selects a bright ball and pushes it gently in her direction.

It is Sunday morning and Jones is in the pulpit. The church is very old but the walls of the sanctuary have recently been painted a pale blue. In the cemetery adjoining, some of the graves are three hundred years old. It has become a historical landmark and no one has been buried there since World War I. There is a new place, not far away, which the families now use. Plots are marked not with stones but with small tablets, and immediately after any burial, workmen roll grassed sod over the new graves so that there is no blemish on the grounds, not even for a little while. Present for today's service are seventy-eight adults, eleven children and the junior choir. Jones counts them as the offertory is received. The church rolls say that there are three hundred fifty members but as far as Jones can see, everyone is here today. This is the day he baptizes the baby. He has made arrangements with one of the ladies to hold her and bring her up to the font at the end of the first hymn. The baby looks charming in a lacy white dress. Jones has combed her fine hair carefully, slicking it in a curl with water, but now it has dried and it sticks up awkwardly like the crest of a kingfisher. Jones bought the dress in Mammoth Mart, an enormous store which has a large metal elephant dressed in overalls dancing on the roof. He feels foolish at buying it there but he had gone to several stores and that is where he saw the prettiest dress. He blesses the baby with water from the silver bowl. He says, *We are saved not because we are worthy. We are saved because we are loved.* It is a brief ceremony. The baby, looking curiously at Jones, is taken out to the nursery. Jones begins his sermon. He can't remember when he wrote it, but here it is, typed, in front of him. *There is nothing wrong in what one does but there is something wrong in what one becomes.* He finds this questionable but goes on speaking. He has been preaching for thirty-four years. He is gaunt with belief. But his wife has a red cell count of only 2.3 millions. It is not enough! She is not getting enough oxygen! Jones is giving his sermon. Some-

where he has lost what he was looking for. He must have
known once, surely. The congregation sways, like the
wings of a ray in water. It is Sunday and for patients it is a
holiday. The doctors don't visit. There are no tests or
diagnoses. Jones would like to leave, to walk down the
aisle and out into the winter, where he would read his
words into the ground. Why can't he remember his life!
He finishes, sits down, stands up to present communion.
Tiny cubes of bread lie in a slumped pyramid. They are
offered and received. Jones takes his morsel, hacked earlier from a sliced enriched loaf with his own hand. It is so
dry, almost wicked. The very thought now sickens him.
He chews it over and over again, but it lies unconsumed,
like a muscle in his mouth.

Jones is waiting in the lobby for the results of his wife's
operation. Has there ever been a time before dread? He
would be grateful even to have dread back, but it has been
lost, for a long time, in rapid possibility, probability and
fact. The baby sits on his knees and plays with his tie. She
woke very early this morning for her orange juice and then
gravely, immediately, spit it all up. She seems fine now,
however, her fingers exploring Jones's tie. Whenever he
looks at her, she gives him a dazzling smile. He has spent
most of the day fiercely cleaning the house, changing the
bed-sheets and the pages of the many calendars that hang
in the rooms, things he should have done a week ago. He
has dusted and vacuumed and pressed all his shirts. He has
laundered all the baby's clothes, soft small sacks and
gowns and sleepers which froze in his hands the moment
he stepped outside. And now he is waiting and watching
his wristwatch. The tumor is precisely this size, they tell
him, the size of his clock's face.

Jones has the baby on his lap and he is feeding her. The
evening meal is lengthy and complex. First he must give
her vitamins, then, because she has a cold, a dropper of
liquid aspirin. This is followed by a bottle of milk, eight
ounces, and a portion of strained vegetables. He gives her
a rest now so that the food can settle. On his hip, she rides
through the rooms of the huge house as Jones turns lights

off and on. He comes back to the table and gives her a little more milk, a half jar of strained chicken and a few spoonfuls of dessert, usually cobbler, buckle or pudding. The baby enjoys all equally. She is good. She eats rapidly and neatly. Sometimes she grasps the spoon, turns it around and thrusts the wrong end into her mouth. Of course there is nothing that cannot be done incorrectly. Jones adores the baby. He sniffs her warm head. Her birth is a deep error, an abstraction. Born in wedlock but out of love. He puts her in the playpen and tends to the dog. He fills one dish with water and one with horsemeat. He rinses out the empty can before putting it in the wastebasket. The dog eats with great civility. He eats a little meat and then takes some water, then meat, then water. When the dog has finished, the dishes are as clean as though they'd been washed. Jones now thinks about his own dinner. He opens the refrigerator. The ladies of the church have brought brownies, venison, cheese and apple sauce. There are turkey pies, pork chops, steak, haddock and sausage patties. A brilliant light exposes all this food. There is so much of it. It must be used. A crust has formed around the punctures in a can of Pet. There is a clear bag of chicken livers stapled shut. There are large brown eggs in a bowl. Jones stares unhappily at the beads of moisture on cartons and bottles, at the pearls of fat on the cold cooked stew. He sits down. The room is full of lamps and cords. He thinks of his wife, her breathing body deranged in tubes, and begins to shake. All objects here are perplexed by such grief.

Now it is almost Christmas and Jones is walking down by the river, around an abandoned house. The dog wades heavily through the snow, biting it. There are petals of ice on the tree limbs and when Jones lingers under them, the baby puts out her hand and her mouth starts working because she would like to have it, the ice, the branch, everything. His wife will be coming home in a few days, in time for Christmas. Jones has already put up the tree and brought the ornaments down from the attic. He will not trim it until she comes home. He wants very much to make a fine occasion out of opening the boxes of old decorations. The two of them have always enjoyed this greatly in the past. Jones will doubtlessly drop and smash a bauble, for he does every year. He tramps through the snow with his small voyager. She dangles in a shoulder sling, her legs wedged around his hip. They regard the rotting house seriously. Once it was a doctor's home and offices but long before Jones's time, the doctor, who was very respected, had been driven away because a town girl accused him of fathering her child. The story goes that all the doctor said was, "Is that so?" This incensed the town and the girl's parents, who insisted that he take the child as soon as it was born. He did and he cared for the child very well even though his practice was ruined and no one had anything to do with him. A year later the girl told the truth—that the actual father was a young college boy whom she was now going to marry. They wanted the child back, and the doctor willingly returned the infant to them. Of course it is a very old, important story. Jones has always appreciated it, but now he is annoyed at the man's passivity. His wife's sickness has changed everything for Jones. He will continue to accept but he will no longer surrender. Surely things are different for Jones now.

For insurance purposes, Jones's wife is brought out to the car in a wheelchair. She is thin and beautiful. Jones is grateful and confused. He has a mad wish to tip the orderly. Have so many years really passed? Is this not his wife, his love, fresh from giving birth? Isn't everything about to begin? In Mexico, his daughter wanders disinterestedly through a jewelry shop where she picks up a small silver egg. It opens on a hinge and inside are two figures, a bride and groom. Jones puts the baby in his wife's arms. At first the baby is alarmed because she cannot remember this person very well and she reaches for Jones, whimpering. But soon she is soothed by his wife's soft voice and she falls asleep in her arms as they drive. Jones has readied everything carefully for his wife's homecoming. The house is clean and orderly. For days he has restricted himself to only one part of the house so that his clutter will be minimal. Jones helps his wife up the steps to the door. Together they enter the shining rooms.

ANN BEATTIE was born in Washington, D.C. in 1947. She was educated at American University and the University of Connecticut. She has been a visiting writer and lecturer at the University of Virginia, Charlottesville, and at Harvard. She is married to a psychiatrist and lives in Connecticut. A recipient of a Guggenheim fellowship (1978) and a frequent contributor to *The New Yorker*, her fiction has been included in many prize-winning collections of short stories. She is the author of three novels, *Chilly Scenes of Winter*, *Falling in Place*, and *Love Always*; and two volumes of short stories, *Distortions* and *Secrets and Surprises*. In both her long and short fiction, Ann Beattie tells the quirky stories of disaffected young people who felt defeated after the sixties and depressed in the seventies. The flat tone of nihilism, of a dead-end shopping-mall consumerism is easy to catch in these stories. What has escaped some readers and reviewers, however, is her freshly deadpan humor and her sympathy for her characters, which comes across as it always does in good fiction: in the writer's passion for the particulars of her characters' worlds. The suburban focus of her work as well as her exposure of the hollowness behind American plenty have contributed to her work being compared with that of John Cheever, J.D. Salinger, and John Updike. The latter, in turn, has compared her to Muriel Spark: "A flying saucer manifests itself as matter-of-factly in Miss Beattie's amazing story 'It's Just Another Day in Big Bear City, California' [which follows here] as an angel manifested itself in Mrs. Spark's amazing story 'The Seraph and the Zambesi' twenty-five years ago." Better than any other critic, John

Updike understands the temperament of Miss Beattie's fiction (which has also been compared to the photographs of Diane Arbus). "The accretion of plain lived moments, Miss Beattie has discovered, like Virginia Woolf and Nathalie Sarraute before her, is sentiment's very method; grain by grain the hours and days of fictional lives invest themselves with weight."

Ann Beattie

IT'S JUST ANOTHER DAY IN BIG BEAR CITY, CALIFORNIA

Spaceship, flying saucer, an hallucination . . . they don't know yet. They don't even notice it until it is almost over their car. Estelle, who has recently gone back to college, is studying Mortuary Science. Her husband, Alvin William "Big Bear" Benton, is so drunk from the party they have just left that he wouldn't notice if it were Estelle, risen from the passenger seat, up in the sky. Maybe that's where she'd like to be—floating in the sky. Or in the morgue with bodies. Big Bear Benton thinks she is completely nuts, and people who are nuts can do anything. *Will* do anything. Will go back to school after ten years and study Mortuary Science. It's enough to make him get drunk at parties. They used to ask his wife about the children at these parties, but now they ask, subtly, about the bodies. They are more interested in dead bodies than his two children. So is Estelle. He is not interested in anything, according to his wife, except going to parties and getting drunk.

Spaceship, flying saucer, an hallucination . . . Big Bear concentrates on the object and tells himself that he is just hallucinating. There is a pinpoint of light, actually a spot of light about the size of a tennis ball, dropping through space. Then it is the size of a football . . . he is trying to think it is a real object, no matter what it is doing up there . . . but maybe it's a flying saucer. Or a spaceship. He looks at Estelle, who is also drunk. She is staring at her hands, neatly folded on her lap. Those hands roam around in dead bodies the way coyotes roam around the desert— just for something to do. This is the first time he has ever been glad to concentrate on Mortuary Science. Like reading the stock pages in the bathroom.

"What is that?" Big Bear says, fighting to stay calm.

"Well, you know what it looks like," Estelle says. "It looks like a spaceship."

"Yeah, I know. But what is it really?"

Now that Estelle is becoming educated and urbane, he has become more childish. He is always asking questions.

"I don't know. It's a spaceship come to take us to Mars."

Big Bear begins to worry about the car being blown over. The car is a 1965 Peugeot, a real piece of crap that Big Bear would have gotten rid of long ago if it had not belonged to his wife's brother, who died in Viet Nam. His wife won't hear of getting rid of the car. She has some of her brother's underwear that she won't take out of the drawer. It's in Big Bear's drawer, in fact—not hers—and her reason for that is that it's men's underwear. But her brother's car is done for now, because the wind is going to blow it over and smash the roof.

"What's going on?" Big Bear yells to Estelle. It comes out a whisper. It occurs to Big Bear that this is some kind of joke. He would discuss with Estelle the possibility of the people at the party pulling a joke on them, but it's too noisy to converse. Through the windstorm he hears, "Earthlings! We are visitors from a friendly planet" and wets his pants.

Big Bear hears Estelle in the kitchen, memorizing: "The heart is a hollow muscular pump surrounded by the pericardium. . . ." Just by the tone of her voice, he understands that there is no hope for the human body. His two children, Sammy and David, stand around the kitchen eating cookies and listening to their mother. They like it better than talking to Big Bear, which makes him brood. His children are interested in intestines, the liver, bones, tissue, the optic nerve. It makes Big Bear sick just to think about it. If he could think of an excuse to stop giving Sammy and David an allowance, he would.

Big Bear tilts back his La-Z-Boy reclining chair and examines his feet, which block his view of the television.

*   *   *

Big Bear gives his wife a valentine, shyly. He thinks that the saleswoman might have been making a fool of him when she told him that the huge card with the quilted taffeta heart and embossed cupids would get across his message best. The card cost two dollars and fifty cents. The woman was young and had aviator glasses and an ironic smile. He prides himself in knowing women, but lately he doesn't trust any of them. Imagine Estelle enrolling in college, signing up for Mortuary Science. "Oh, this is lovely," she said when Big Bear gave her the valentine. He didn't want to mess it up in case there was something she could do with the card, so he just wrote his name on a little piece of paper and tucked it in the card. It falls out when Estelle opens it. He is standing right in front of her—she knows who it's from—why did he even put the piece of paper in? She picks it up. "Love, Bear," it says. "Oh, this is lovely," she says. Valentine's Day is not one of Big Bear's favorite occasions. He always feels like a fool. His wife did not give him a valentine. She forgot, she says. But she doesn't forget about the pericardium that surrounds that hollow muscular pump that no longer beats with love for him.

"Roll up your window," Big Bear says. Estelle is rolling down her window. She is rolling it down to throw her cigarette away. A spaceship has landed in front of their Peugeot and she is rolling down her window.

"Earthlings! Like you, we have ears, but they are very sensitive. We can hear what you are saying and do not want you to be afraid."

Big Bear stares. A round dome that seems to be made of something soft—foam rubber?—bobs slightly in front of them. The thing covers the whole road.

"We also read minds. There are three of us, and two of us speak English."

"Oh, holy shit!" Big Bear says. "Estelle?"

She has rolled the window down and is letting the smoke from another cigarette she just lit blow out of the car.

"We will leave our spaceship, Bill and Estelle. Please do not worry."

"God almighty," Big Bear says. "Roll it up, Estelle."

"What does it matter?" Estelle says. Big Bear reaches across her lap and rolls up the window. The car is still running, his foot is still on the brake. He thinks about trying to get around the spaceship. There is no way to get around it without driving into a marsh. Big Bear throws the car into reverse and starts backward, but when he does that a wind stops the car and slowly pulls it forward again.

"Please get out of your car," the voice says.

There is a man standing in the road. He has on a shirt and a pair of slacks. His face is red. He waves.

"Come on," Estelle says.

"Stay in the car, Estelle."

"We need pictures of both of you," the voice says.

Big Bear's pants are wet. He cringes. Estelle has left the car and is walking toward the red-faced man. He thinks about stepping on the gas and crushing her, running into her from behind, not letting her have her way.

"Estelle?" he says to the empty seat.

"Please get out," the voice says.

"I'm not getting out," Big Bear says.

"We must have pictures. There are twenty exposures on the roll."

"What do you need pictures for?"

"To take back, Bill. They sent us for pictures."

"What are they going to do with the pictures?"

"I don't know. I just take the pictures."

Big Bear rubs his hand over his face. "I will never drink again," he says. "Estelle?" he says.

"This is a random landing. We'll never see you again. We need twenty pictures, and we would like to be your friends before we leave. Please get out of the car."

Estelle is talking to the man. He rolls down his window and puts his head out. It smells damp. There is a lot of fog. The lights have been turned out on the spaceship, and it is hard to tell just how large it is. It looked huge in the sky over the car, but it doesn't look that big now. Just big enough to block the road. Big Bear puts the car in reverse again. Just as before, a stream of air draws him forward.

"We found you by accident. You'll do fine for the pictures, though. If you'll please get out."

Big Bear wants to go home and go to sleep. Big Bear wants to go home to throw away all his liquor. He wants his children. His children!

"What are you going to do to me?" he asks again.

"Take your picture," the man says.

Disgusted, Big Bear opens the door and gets out. He walks forward. The man shakes his hand and introduces himself as Bobby. Estelle smiles at him.

"You're drunk," Big Bear says to Estelle.

"That's okay," the man says. "If you two could stand by your car?"

Big Bear doesn't want to turn his back on the man.

"The other ones?" Big Bear asks.

"Donald is playing a game inside. He's tired of coming to Earth."

"What game?" Big Bear asks suspiciously, not sure why he's suspicious.

"Scrabble. He was worried about using the word 'toque.' That's a foreign word, isn't it?"

"Toe?"

"Toque."

"I'm drunk as a skunk," Big Bear says.

"Bear, you'll never make it."

"We'll make it."

"Why should you even try to make it?" Laura says. Laura is the wife of the man whose party Big Bear and Estelle have attended.

"Big Bear can make it!" Big Bear yells.

"You're a big oaf," Laura says, and walks away. That leaves her husband to get their coats.

"If we don't make it, I'll end up the same place I'd be working tomorrow anyway," Estelle says. Estelle is more drunk than Big Bear, and Big Bear is focusing on his feet to stay alert.

"What are you ashamed of?" Estelle asks Big Bear.

"Nothing. What are you talking about?" He fears that another one of her honesty sessions is coming on—a talk about how she wishes she had never married him or had children.

"You're staring at the floor, Bear. What's the matter with you?"

"He's drunk," their host says good-naturedly. Big Bear and Paul, their host, were in the service together. It was Paul's idea to keep calling him Big Bear when they got back to America. In Japan, a geisha came up with the name. Laura will have no part of it. She calls him Alvin. Big Bear holds Estelle's coat, happy to get away from the party.

The Peugeot is parked in Paul's driveway. Death. Death everywhere. Japan, Viet Nam, Mortuary Science.

"What's the matter with you, Bear?" Estelle asks. "You're not really too drunk to drive, are you?"

"Daddy! Did you know that there was a Big Bear City in California?"

"No."

"I found out in geography. My teacher said to ask if it was named for you."

"I've never met your teacher. How did she know I was called Big Bear?"

"I told her."

"Well, stop telling everybody. That's just a joke, you know."

"But that's what everybody calls you."

"Go watch TV or something."

"What are you two talking about?" Estelle calls from the kitchen.

"Geography," Big Bear answers.

"Mom, there's a place called Big Bear City in California."

"I don't want to hear any more about it," Big Bear says.

"What are you so grumpy about?" Estelle asks, standing in the kitchen doorway. "You're as grumpy as a bear."

"Oh, come off it. You two leave me alone."

"Why is that always what you want? Why can't anybody talk to you?" Estelle says.

"Leave me alone," Big Bear says, and tilts himself out of view in his La-Z-Boy reclining chair.

"I thought jumping rope with the intestine was a joke," Estelle says. "That's not what you're doing, is it? It's not really an intestine?"

"No, there are no cows on Mars, so we consider your milk a delicacy. We have alcohol. Juniper berries grow in profusion. It's really very pretty, all the bushes, in addition to the gin it produces."

"Are they coming out?" Big Bear asks, nodding toward the spaceship.

"We've been on so many missions that they just don't care any more."

"What do they come for, then?"

"There has to be a certain number aboard."

"What for?"

"I never asked. We keep busy, though."

"What do you do?"

"Well, Donald likes to play games. He got some jigsaw puzzles the last time we were here, and he never tires of that, particularly a round puzzle that's a pizza."

"He just plays games?"

"They drink milk if we stop for it. We have to stop in the woods, of course, and there usually aren't any stores. They loved Maine. There were stores in the middle of nowhere."

"We love Maine," Estelle says.

"It's awfully nice," the spaceman says.

"Are you going to take more pictures?" Big Bear asks.

"I'm just trying to think . . . where would be a good spot?"

"Can't we just stand by the car?"

"I think they'll want variety."

Estelle smiles. "Would you like me to take off my clothes?" she asks.

"She's kidding," Big Bear says.

"I thought we'd take those later," the spaceman says.

"We're not taking our clothes off," Big Bear says.

"I'll put you under a spell, Bill," the spaceman says.

"You can't put me under any spell."

"Please try not to be hostile. I personally have no interest in taking nude photographs."

"Then let's leave that crap out."

"I can't leave it out. They said to get some."

"Tell them it was foggy and it didn't turn out."

"I'll undress," Estelle says.

"Don't you think it's a little cold for nude posing?" Big Bear says.

"Yes," the spaceman says. "Maybe we should go to your place."

Sleep soundly, sweet ones. Don't wake up and want water, or you might see the spacemen in the kitchen. You don't like it when your brother plays with your special toys . . . how would you like it if a spaceman was tapping pegs through holes and squares through squares? You wouldn't like it. It's good you're a sound sleeper. One of the spacemen is in the bathroom. Imagine walking into the bathroom and seeing a spaceman urinating.

"I said I'm not too drunk to drive, and I'm not."

"You're no judge. Laura is probably right."

"Side with me. I'm your husband."

"In effect I *am* siding with you. If you had an accident . . ."

"Big Bear doesn't have accidents."

"Like John Wayne?"

"What are you taunting me for? You want to get home or don't you?"

"It might be better if I drove."

"It might be better, but you're not going to do it."

"All right. But drive slowly. There's so much fog."

"This piece of crap car isn't helping us any. The thing's so light, a wind would blow it over. When are you going to give up and let me turn it in for another one?"

"I thought flashy cars didn't matter to you."

"What did I say about flash? I just said a car—a decent car."

"This is a decent car. It was driven by my brother before he died in that horrible war."

"Where did you get his underwear from in the first place?"

"I don't want to talk about my brother."

"I don't want that underwear in my drawer. Where the hell did you get your brother's underwear?"

"Where do you think? From his drawer."

"Well, why did you take that, if it isn't prying?"

"It's not as though I just took that."

"What else did you take?"

"I took his things. I don't want to talk about my brother, Bear."

"What things? Tell me or I'm not going to pull out of the driveway, and Laura can wave and scowl all night."

"I took shirts and sweaters. Satisfied?"

The car pulls out of the driveway. Big Bear despises the car.

"Why haven't I ever seen them?"

"I put them away for the boys."

"They don't want your brother's stuff. By the time it fits them they wouldn't wear anything that unfashionable."

"I am not aware of radical style changes in men's sweaters."

"I want the underwear to go! You keep the shirts. I'll throw out the underwear."

"You keep your hands off my brother's things."

"You put it in my drawer and order me not to touch it. Why didn't you put it in your own damn drawer?"

"It makes me sad."

"Then get rid of it."

"Can't we please talk about something else? I thought you liked my brother."

"I didn't have anything against your brother, but I don't want his underwear in my drawer."

"If you keep driving this fast, you'll die before it can be removed."

"Don't change the subject. The subject is underwear.

You can keep it under your pillow if you want, but get it out of my drawer.''

"Yes, sir."

"I don't feel guilty," Big Bear says. "Nobody would put up with that.''

In front of their car something hovers in the sky, but it's too close to be a plane. It's shapeless, which is funny, because it's close enough to figure out a shape. A mound. A mound?

"What's that?" Big Bear asks.

"Maybe we should get the uncomfortable pictures over with, and then we could take a few more by the car, or over there.''

"Oh, cut it out," Big Bear says. "No nudie shots.''

"I'm a family man, too, Bill. I'd like to just simplify matters and get home to my family. Could you drop your pants?''

"No.''

Estelle is unbuttoning her coat.

"No," Big Bear says to her, and grabs her hand. She tries to get it away from him.

Estelle is shrugging her dress down, smiling at the spaceman.

The camera clicks.

"How old are your children?" she asks.

"That's enough!" Big Bear says. "Can we go home?"

"I'd like the others, and then you can go on your way.''

"It's too God damn cold," Big Bear says.

"Let's take them to our place, Bear. We could give them milk and they could take the other pictures.''

"That would be fine," the spaceman says.

"You're not invited," Big Bear says.

"I was just invited." The spaceman smiles politely. "I'll get the others.''

"I thought they had to stay with the ship.''

"I'm doing you a favor, Bill. Would you rather stay here longer?''

Big Bear shivers. What if Sammy and David drank the last of the milk.

*   *   *

The other spacemen are named Donald and Fred. There is something wrong with Fred; his wrists are bent funny, and his mouth wrinkles when he tries to smile, which is all of the time. "He's retarded," Donald says. Good God, Big Bear thinks. Won't Fred hear Donald?

"We've been stuck with him on the last seven missions," Donald says.

They are walking up Big Bear's front walk. They are inside the house. The babysitter has gone to sleep in the spare bedroom. She turned off all the lights. Big Bear can't see. Donald has a flashlight. He turns it on.

"Thanks," Big Bear says.

He heads for the light switch. Fred, it seems, is not only retarded, but violent. He struggles with Donald and wins. Fred has the flashlight. He pokes it into his mouth. His cheeks light up. No one tries to take the flashlight away from Fred. "I've had it up to here with him," Donald says, but no one tries to get the flashlight. Big Bear has located the light switch, so it's okay. Sort of okay. Fred's cheeks are orange.

"Did you know that this was called mooning in the sixties? College kids did it."

The spaceman snaps away. Estelle is making a fool of herself.

"What are you going to bring me, Daddy?" the spaceman's son asks.

"You're greedy."

"What are you going to bring me?"

"What do you want?"

"More goldfish."

"The damn things die. I bring them all the way back and they're dead in a week."

"I told you. That's because I need a real aquarium with a pump and a filter."

"It's too much trouble to bring the things back. Isn't there something else I could bring you?"

"No. I want that."

"I'll do it if I have time. You just can't buy goldfish everywhere."

"Go where you can get them."

"This is my mission, kid. Okay?"

"When are you going to take me with you?"

"When you grow up."

"I *am* grown up."

"Grownups don't want goldfish."

"How did it go in the morgue, Estelle?"

"Fine," Estelle says.

"Did you cut up dead bodies?"

Estelle comes into the living room. She can hardly wait to see if Big Bear is drunk. Estelle stares at Big Bear, who is reclining in his La-Z-Boy reclining chair. She sees that he is reclining because he is drunk.

"I thought you were going to Pete's party tonight."

"We were *both* going."

"That's what I said," Estelle says.

"But now we're *not* both going," Big Bear grins. "We're not going anywhere."

"I know!" Estelle cries. She doubles over, as though somebody just passed her a football.

"Jesus Christ," Big Bear says. "I didn't know you wanted to go to Pete's. I'm not so drunk we can't go. Stand up, for Christ's sake. What's the matter with you, Estelle?"

"I hate not to be the perfect host," Big Bear says to the spacemen. "But tomorrow is another day and . . ."

They seem not to have understood. If they smoked, Big Bear could empty the ashtrays.

"To be honest with you," Big Bear says, although none of the spacemen seem interested, "we've had a big night and it's about time for you to go."

"The disgusting thing," Donald says. "Blowing bubbles in his milk."

"We're all out of milk, now, Bobby. It's about time for you to go," Big Bear says.

"I hope he falls over and we can just leave him," Donald says.

Fred has thrown a glass of milk against the wall. The glass was soft plastic, so it just bounced. The sound wasn't loud enough to awaken Sammy and David. Estelle finds herself looking on the bright side of the spaceman's little *faux pas*.

At a gas station in Big Bear City, California, a little boy gets out of his mother's car to buy a soft drink.

Laura takes Big Bear's coat. She turns to look at Big Bear as he walks away. I hope he picks the hors d'oeuvres that have liver hidden inside them, she thinks.

"Mommy!" the little boy says. "I put the money in and nothing happened."

"Push the coin release."

"What's that?"

"Can I help?" the service attendant asks.

"That's all right," the little boy's mother says. "I'll take care of it." She goes to the machine and pushes the coin release lever. Nothing happens.

Lying in a field in Viet Nam, in the second before he dies, Estelle's brother wonders what will happen to his Peugeot. He wonders why he's thinking of his Peugeot instead of Estelle or his mother or father. Rather, he starts to wonder, but dies before the thought is fully formulated.

"Maybe I could get a picture of the two of you by the door. Could you get together and pretend that you're going grocery shopping?"

"We don't have to pretend we're going grocery shopping. We'll just stand by the door, as if we're going out."

"Pretend you're going grocery shopping," the spaceman says.

"We look the same way whether we're going to the P.T.A. meeting, or going to get groceries, or to visit her parents."

"Then, just stand by the door as though you were doing one of those things, please, Bill."

"Wake up, Estelle," Big Bear says. "Wake up. Come on, Estelle," Big Bear says. "This is the last picture. Are you going to wake up?"

"The machine doesn't work," the little boy's mother says to the service-station attendant. Just one more problem on grocery day in Big Bear City, California.

"You had quite a night," the babysitter says cheerfully. The babysitter and Sammy are awake. David is still sleeping. Big Bear envies David.

"I didn't know I left the milk bottle out," the babysitter says apologetically.

"Actually, we came home a while ago and some friends had milk."

The babysitter looks at the milk glasses. She also sees the one that has been thrown against the dining-room wall.

"Good-night," Big Bear says, and climbs the stairs. Since they did not smoke, Estelle will have no ashtrays to empty and will join him soon. Not that he really cares. He is so tired he'd sleep with the spacemen. Except Fred . . . Jesus, it sure is good they loaded him out of the house, Big Bear thinks. If I had irritated them, they might have left him. Big Bear is glad that he only has Sammy and David. If they had tried for a girl, like Estelle wanted, it might have been retarded.

Big Bear falls into bed, with visions of Fred. It rhymes: bed, Fred. Big Bear falls asleep.

There has been a spaceship sighting in Reno, Nevada, and that's where Estelle wants to go.

"Estelle, you heard them say that there are a lot of other spacemen. Any of them could have flown over Reno, Nevada."

"We haven't taken a trip in years. The boys should see some of the country."

"Aren't you going to summer school? What happened to your plans?"

"I don't want to talk about it."

"I paid a year's tuition. I'd like to have a talk about why you're quitting."

"Something disgusting happened."

"What?"

"I want to go to Reno," Estelle says. "Will you take me or won't you?"

"The spaceship won't still be there."

"There have been sightings all around Reno."

"We're going to take the boys to Reno and sit in a motel waiting to hear rumors of spaceships?"

"It's my birthday," Estelle says. "You have to please me on my birthday, and I want to take a trip."

"What do you mean, I have to please you on your birthday?"

"I suppose you don't have to be nice to me if you don't want to, Bear. Excuse my presumption."

"I already am nice to you. That night with the spacemen I let you act like a jackass. Anybody else would have straightened you out."

"How gallant of you not to criticize me in front of my friends."

"Friends? You met them once."

"Of course no one would want to be my friend," Estelle says. "Excuse me."

"I didn't say they weren't your friends. I did say that. I don't know. Let's forget this, okay?"

"Let's go to Reno, Nevada."

"Oh, leave me alone," Big Bear says.

Big Bear meant to avoid this card shop, but it's so convenient, and he doesn't have the time to look all around for another place to get Estelle's birthday card. The woman will probably not be there anyway.

The woman is there. She finds Big Bear as he stands browsing through the Relative Birthday group of cards. She asks if she can help him.

"No, thanks," Big Bear says.

"This is a nice one," the saleswoman says, taking a big pink card down.

Big Bear looks. There is a plastic window, in the shape of a heart, through which a blond lady is visible. "My Darling" it says across the top of the card.

"I don't like that one," Big Bear says.

"Then look at this one." She hands Big Bear a blue card with bluer velvet bluebirds on it. The bluebirds trail a ribbon that spells "Happy Birthday, Darling" as it unrolls.

"Okay," Big Bear says. "Fine."

The card costs one dollar and fifty cents. For a card! It takes the woman a long time to slip it carefully into the bag. It takes her a long time to count out his change. He is never going to come to this card shop again.

"Thank you, sir," the saleswoman says, with her usual ironic smile.

Big Bear holds the bag tightly and makes the mistake of crushing the velvet bird.

"You're wrecked. You going to work like that?"

"I couldn't work there if I wasn't wrecked."

"You should avoid getting wrecked sometime and try it."

"I don't want a job."

"Then that means I have to have one. So don't criticize me for getting wrecked."

"You're wrecked." The saleswoman's boyfriend laughs. He is also wrecked.

"Look at this one, look at this," Bobby says.

His friend's face turns red. "Put the things away," his friend says.

"Look, look, this one was Estelle's idea."

"I'm sure."

"No, I swear. She said this was a craze on campus in the sixties."

"*This* was something they did at college?"

"And look at this one. This is Bill pretending he's going to work. Look at it!"

"I've seen these things a dozen times already. Put those disgusting things away," his friend says.

"I'll put them away, but you've got to see the expression on her face in this one."

"I'm not likely to see her face in this series."

The spaceman's friend has just made a witty remark. Bobby appreciates it and starts laughing uncontrollably. He'd be doing that even if his friend weren't there, though. These pictures really kill him.

"Now the Air Force is even admitting that it's tied up with them," Big Bear says from his La-Z-Boy reclining chair.

"What do they say?"

"I just told you. All those sightings over Nebraska. The Air Force is coming out and admitting it."

"What do they *say*, Bear?"

"You love this subject, don't you? You love to talk about the spacemen."

"Who brought it up?" Estelle says.

"I did. I know you love the subject," Big Bear says.

"These bluebirds sing a happy tune. They say that you are mine . . ."

She is convulsed with laughter, that crazy, wiped-out laughter with no tears accompanying it. The eyes get wider and wider—wide enough to pour tears, but the laughter is all that comes.

"Why don't you stop memorizing the cards? Just take your shoes off and relax."

"It had velvet bluebirds on the front with a blue ribbon and a blue background, and it said 'These bluebirds sing . . .' "

"You're going to lose your job the first time you do a wiped-out thing like this with a customer."

"The bluebirds! The fucking bluebirds!"

"What the hell was that?"

"Probably hit ducks again. Remember the time we took off through a whole flock of them?" Bobby says.

"Disgusting," Donald says, but he is looking at Fred and not thinking about possible dead ducks.

*   *   *

"What are you mad at me for?" the little boy asks. "What did I do?"

"You didn't do anything. You got your soft drink. Drink it."

"You couldn't make the machine work either," the little boy says.

"It was broken," his mother says.

"Then what are you mad about?"

"I'm mad because you just add to the confusion. I want to get the groceries and go home and put them away. All right? Sit back and finish your drink."

It is just another day in Big Bear City, California.

MARY ROBISON was born in Washington, D.C. in 1949 and grew up in Ohio, the setting for her novel *Oh!* She is the mother of two children, was a Guggenheim Fellow in 1980, has taught at the University of Ohio and is currently Briggs-Copeland Lecturer in English at Harvard. Her short stories, which appear frequently in *The New Yorker* and *Esquire*, have been collected in two volumes: *Days* (1980) and *An Amateur's Guide To the Night* (1983). Reading the thirteen brilliant stories in the latter collection affords the experience one needs to appreciate the unanimous high praise Mary Robison has received from some of our most eminent reviewers and writers. (Selecting only one story to represent her in this collection was the most difficult choice made in the assembling of this anthology.) James Wolcott has written, "Mary Robison isn't afraid to light a few hotfoots, tweak a few noses. [Her] flair for brittle talk and catastrophe could result in a comic novel one wouldn't be ashamed to place on the shelf next to the best of Evelyn Waugh." Frances Taliaferro has said that "the temptation is to hear in Mrs. Robison and her colleagues the voice of a generation, the near nihilists in blue jeans who survived the heyday of the counterculture and now sit passively by while the iron enters their souls. Such identifications are convenient, . . . but Mrs. Robison's work will not fit cozily into 'the New York sensibility' or the pigeonholes of social history. At her best, [she] is both wise and entertaining, a technician with a sense of humor, a minimalist with a good eye for what can be salvaged from lives of quiet desperation." And finally, from Richard Yates: "Robison writes like an avenging angel, and I think she may be a genius."

Mary Robison

I AM TWENTY-ONE

I heard ringing, and I realized that what I had done was continued my answer to Essay Question I—"What effect did the discovery of the barrel vault have on the architecture of 13th century cathedrals?"—writing clockwise in the left, top, and right-hand margins of page one in my exam book. I had forgotten to move along to page two or to Essay Question II. The ringing was coming from in me—probably from overdoing it with diet pills or from the green tea all last night and from reading so much all the time.

I was doing C work in all courses but this one—"The Transition from Romanesque to Gothic." I needed to blast this course on its butt, and that was possible because for this course I knew it all. I needed only time and space to tell it. My study notes were 253 pencil sketches from slides we had seen and from plates in books at the Fine Arts Library and some were from our text. I had sixty-seven pages of lecture notes that I had copied over once for clarity. Everything Professor Williamson had said in class was recorded in my notes—practically even his throat clearings and asides about the weather. It got to the point where if he rambled, I thought, yeah, yeah, cut the commercial and get back to the program.

Some guy whose hair I could've ripped out was finished with his exam. He was actually handing it to the teaching assistant. How could he be *finished*, have given even a cursory treatment to the three questions? He was a quitter, a skimmer, I decided; a person who knew shit about detail.

I was having to stop now and then, really too often, to skin the tip of my pencil with the razor blade I had brought

along. I preferred a pencil because it couldn't dry up or
leak. But this was a Number 2 graphite and gushy-gummy
and I was writing the thing away. The eraser was just a
blackened nub. Why hadn't I brought a damn *box* of
pencils?

The teaching assistant was Clark—Clark Something or
Something Clark, I didn't know. He was baggy and sloppy,
but happy-looking. He had asked me out once for Cokes,
but I had brushed him off. That was maybe stupid because
he might've been in charge of grading exams.

I decided to ignore Essay Question II, pretend I hadn't
even seen it. I leaned hard into Question III, on church
decoration, windows, friezes, flora, fauna, bestiaries, the
iconography in general. I was quoting Honorius of Autun
when the class bell fired off.

I looked up. Most people were gone.

"Come on, everyone!" Clark called. "Please. Come on
now. Miss Bittle? Mr. Kenner, please. Miss Powers?"

"Go blow, Clark," I said right out loud. But I slapped
him my exam booklet and hurried out of Meverett, feeling
let down and apathetic all of a sudden, and my skin going
rubbery cold.

I biked home with a lot of trouble. I went on the side-
walks. I was scared that in the streets I'd get my ringing
confused with car warnings.

I was still ringing.

Last semester I had had a decorating idea for my apartment, this monastic idea of strict and sparse. I had stripped
the room down to a cot, a book table, one picture. The
plaster walls were a nothing oatmeal color, which was
okay. But not okay was that some earlier renter had gooped
orange—unbelievably—paint on the moldings and window
frames. So where I lived looked not like a scholar's den,
finally, but more like a bum's sleepover, like poverty.

My one picture up wasn't of a Blessed Virgin or a detail
from Amiens of the King of Judah holding a rod of the
Tree of Jesse. Instead, it was an eight-by-ten glossy of
Rudy and Leslie, my folks. Under the backing was written
Gold Coast, the first cool day. The photo had been shot

out on North Lake Shore Drive around 1964, I'd say, when I was three. Leslie, my mom, was huddled into Rudy, sharing his lined leather jacket. They appeared, for all the eye sparkle, like people in an engagement-ring ad. I kept the picture around because, oddly, putting away the *idea* of my folks would've been worse than losing the real them. In the photo, they at least *looked* familiar.

They had been secret artists. Rudy was a contractor for a living, Leslie a physical therapist. So they worked all their art urges out on me—on my school projects, for instance, which they hurled themselves into. One project "I did" for seventh grade that they helped me with was, I swear, good enough for a world's fair. It was a kind of three-dimensional diorama triptych of San Francisco Bay with both bridges—Oakland and Golden Gate—that may have even lit up or glowed in the dark. We had to borrow a neighbor's station wagon just to get the thing safely over to Dreiser Junior High—it lined up as long as an ironing board.

I got my bike tugged inside, left it leaning against the wall under the photograph. I clapped a kettle onto the midget stove in my kitchen part of the apartment, and paced, waiting for the water to heat. The pitch of the steam when it got going was only a quarter tone below the ringing in my head.

My folks were two and a half years gone.

I used to drive out to the site of their accident all the time—a willow tree on Route 987. The last time I went, the tree was still healing. The farmlands were a grim powdery blond in the white sun, and the earth was still ragged from winter. I sat there in my tiny Vega on the broken crumbly shoulder. The great tree and the land around—flat as a griddle for miles and miles—didn't seem as fitting as I had once thought, not such a poetic place for two good lives to have stopped.

I had my tea now and grieved about the exam. Leaving a whole essay question unanswered! How could I expect to get better than a C?

Just before my first sip of tea, my ringing shut off as

though somebody had punched a button, said, "Enough of that for her."

I decided it was time to try for sleep, but first I used a pen with a nylon point to tattoo a P on the back of my hand. This meant when I woke up I was to eat some protein—shrimp or eggs or a green something.

On the cot I tried, as a sleep trick, to remember my answer to Essay Question I—word for fucking word.

JEAN THOMPSON was born in Chicago in 1950. She was educated at the University of Illinois and Bowling Green State University. She is the author of the novel *My Wisdom* and two volumes of short stories, *Little Face* and *The Gasoline Wars*. In his review of the latter collection, Joe David Bellamy, the editor of *Fiction International*, called Jean Thompson as "sassy and hard-boiled a writer as Flannery O'Connor, and she knows some heartbreaking truths about the American Midwest that no one else has written about in quite the same way." Her short stories have appeared in *Ploughshares*, *Ascent*, the 1979 volume of *Best American Short Stories*, and the anthology *Matters of Life and Death*, edited by Tobias Wolff. A recent recipient of a Guggenheim fellowship, she has been on leave from her teaching position in the English department at the University of Illinois at Urbana-Champaign. The story that follows here, "Applause, Applause" is a masterly example of her ability to probe and extract those rare moments of recognition that most of us miss or take for granted; it also demonstrates Miss Thompson's powerful empathic imagination: the consciousness of her male protagonist in this story is as convincingly real as that of any of the female protagonists in this collection.

Jean Thompson

APPLAUSE, APPLAUSE

Poor Bernie, Ted thought, as rain thudded against the car like rotten fruit. Watching it stream and bubble on the windshield he promised himself not to complain about it lest Bernie's feelings be hurt. He was anxious to impress this on his wife. Poor Bernie, he said aloud. Things never work out the way he plans.

His wife nodded. Ted could see from her unsmiling, preoccupied face that it would be difficult to coax her into a conspiracy. In fact, she was probably blaming him for it: his friend, his weekend, therefore, his rain. Look, Ted said. He went to so much trouble setting this up. I'd hate to have him think we weren't enjoying it, whatever happens.

Lee, his wife, turned her chin toward him. He used to call her the Siennese Madonna because of that narrow face, long cheeks and haughty blue eyes. Easy to see her reduced to two-dimensional paint. She had never heard of Sienna. Now she said All right, I won't sulk. But I'll save the vivaciousness till later, OK?

He was a little hurt that she saw no need to be charming for him, but he said nothing. After all, she hadn't complained. He burrowed his hands in his pockets for warmth and looked out the smeared window.

The car was parked in a clearing of pebbled yellow clay. On all sides were dark sapping pine trees, impenetrable, suffocating. It made him a little dizzy to think of how limitless those trees were, how many square miles they covered. The clearing contained two gas pumps and a trading post that sold moccasins, orange pop, and insect repellant. If you turned your back on the building it was easy to believe the world contained only the pines and the implacable rain.

Poor Bernie. He wondered at what point the friends of one's youth acquire epithets. When do we begin to measure their achievements against their ambitions?

Ten years ago he and Bernie Doyle were in college. Ten years ago they sat in bars, Bernie's pipe smoke looped around their heads. Or perhaps on the broken-spined, cat-perfumed sofa that was always reincarnated in their succession of apartments. How they had talked: God, he had never talked that seriously, that openly, to a woman. Perhaps it was something one outgrew. Like the daydreams of the dusky, moody photographs that would appear on one's book jackets. The experimentation with names. Theodore Valentine? T. R. Valentine? T. Robert Valentine? The imaginary interviews. ("Valentine is a disarmingly candid, intensely personal man whose lean, somber features belie his formidable humor. The day I met him he wore an old black turtleneck, Levis and sandals, a singularly unpretentious yet becoming costume . . .")

Yes, he had admitted all these fantasies to Bernie, and Bernie admitted he shared them. How vulnerable they had been to each other, still were, he supposed. Behind the naive vanities, the daydreams, they had very badly wanted to be writers. Had wanted it without knowing at all what it was they wanted, their fervor making up for their ignorance. His older self was cooler, more noncommittal, for he had learned that to publicize your goals means running the risk of falling short of them.

Ten years of letters, of extravagant alcoholic phone calls. The continual measure they took of each other. Their vanished precocity, reluctantly cast aside at age twenty-five or so. Ten years which established Ted's increasingly self-conscious, increasingly offhand reports of publications, recognitions. Bernie had kept up for a few years, had even talked about getting a book together. After that he responded to Ted's letters with the same grave formula: he wasn't getting a lot done but he hoped to have more time soon. Ted was sure he'd given it up entirely. He knew how easy it was to let your discipline go slack. You had to drive yourself continually, not just to get the work done but to keep faith. Faith that what you were doing was worth the hideous effort you put into it. Easier, much easier, to let it go. The whole process of writing was a road as quirky and blind as the one they had driven this morning to the heart of the Adirondacks, this weekend, and the epithet, Poor Bernie.

Was he himself a success? He wasn't able to say that, not yet at least. Three years ago a national magazine printed a story. The smaller quarterlies published him with some regularity, paid him less frequently. His was one of the names an extremely well-read person might frown at and say Yes, I think I've heard of him. It was like being one of those Presidents no one can ever remember, Polk or Millard Fillmore. Of course you wanted more than that.

But he'd made progress. He hadn't given up. These were the important things. And he dreaded the inevitable discussions with Bernie when their younger incarnations would stand in judgment of them. How could he manage to be both tactful and truthful, feeling as he did that uncomfortable mixture of protectiveness and contempt. Yes, he admitted it, the slightest touch of contempt . . .

Is this them, Lee asked as an orange VW station wagon, its rain-slick paint lurid against the pines, slowed at the clearing. Ted squinted. Maybe . . . The car stopping. Yeah, I think so. The window on the passenger's side was rolled down and a woman's face bobbed and smiled at him. He had an impression of freckles, skin pink as soap. Paula? Ted grinned and pantomimed comprehension.

We're supposed to follow, he told Lee, and eased the car onto the road. Again the dripping trees closed over them. They were climbing now, trailing the VW along a tight spiral. It was impossible to see more than twenty yards ahead. At times they passed mailboxes, or shallow openings in the woods that indicated roads, but for the most part there was only the green-black forest, the thick pudding rain.

Where's that college he teaches at, asked Lee. Ted looked at her and tried to unravel the history of her thoughts for the last silent half-hour. She still wore her languid, neutral expression. The Madonna attends a required meeting of the Ladies' Auxiliary.

Sixty miles away. No, farther. Eighty. It was another thing he wondered about, Bernie's precarious instructor job. Four sections of composition. Abortion, Pro and Con. My First Date. Topic sentences. Footnotes.

And he married one of his students?

Ted nodded. It was hard for him to imagine Bernie as a figure of authority or some little girl regarding him with the reverence and hysteria of student crushes. But it had happened.

Lee pointed. The VW's bumper was winking at them and Ted slowed, ready to turn. Now it was scarcely a road they followed but a dirt lane. Milder, deciduous trees interlaced above them and screened the rain somewhat. They rocked along the muddy ruts for half a mile.

Then the sudden end of the lane, the cabin of dark brown shingles with Bernie already waving from the porch. Ted was out of the car almost before it had stopped, was shaking Bernie's hand and saying something like Son of a Gun, and grinning. Bernie said Valentine, you lout, and reached up to pound him on the back.

The women drifted after them. Hey, Paula, come shake hands with Ted. And this is Lee. Bernie, Paula. Ted found himself appraising Lee as she climbed the steps, took satisfaction in her length of leg, her severely beautiful face now softened with a smile. The four of them stood nodding at each other for a moment. Like two sets of dolls built to different scale, Ted thought, the Doyles so small, he and Lee an angular six inches taller. Furious exercise had kept Ted in shape, and he knew the faint line of sunburn under his eyes was becoming. He realized he was standing at attention, and cursed his vanity.

Bernie looked more than ever like a Swiss toymaker as imagined by Walt Disney. Small bones and white supple hands. His gray eyes unfocused behind rimless glasses. The ever-present pipe which, when inserted, drew his whole face into a preoccupied, constipated look. He had grown a dark manicured beard.

And Paula? He knew her to be at least twenty-four, but

she could have passed for sweet eighteen. Snub little nose. Smiling mouth like the squiggle painted on a china doll. Green eyes in that pink transparent skin. Yes, she would be something to take notice of in a stuffy classroom.

Even as he absorbed and ordered his impressions the group broke, Bernie pushing the front door open, Paula talking about food. He followed Bernie into a paneled room and the damp, bone-deep cold that would accompany the whole weekend first seized him. He heard Lee's lightly inflected voice keeping her promise: What a lovely fireplace. We can tell ghost stories around it.

You bet, said Bernie, and squatted before it, poking the grate. There's even dry wood on the porch.

Looking at him, Ted experienced the uneasy process of having to square his observations with his memories. As if this was not really Bernie until he conformed with Ted's image of him. How long had it been, three years? He began to be more sure of himself as he noted familiar mannerisms surfacing. Bernie's solemnity; he discussed firewood in the same tone another man might use for religion. The deftness of his hands wielding the fireplace tools. Ted imagined him shaping chunks of pine into cuckoo clocks, bears, and monkeys . . .

Now stop that, he warned himself. It was a writer's curse, this verbal embroidery. Never seeing anything as it was, always analyzing and reformulating it. Maybe the entire habit of observation, the thing he trained himself in, was just a nervous tic, a compulsion. He shook his head and joined Lee in her exploration of the cabin.

The main room was high-ceilinged, dark. In hot weather he imagined its shadows would bless the skin, but now the bare floors made his feet ache with cold. There were two bedrooms, one on each side of the main room. The furniture was a mixture of wicker and raw wood. In the rear were a trim new kitchen and bathroom. They stepped out the back door and Ted whistled.

Even in the rain the blue-gray bowl of the lake freshened his eyes. Its irregular shoreline formed bays, coves, little tongues of land, all furred with silent pine. He could not see the opposite shore. There was an island just where he might have wished for one, a mound of brush and rock. The air smelled clean and thin.

Lee spoke to Bernie, who had joined them. It's incredible. Just too lovely.

Bernie grinned, as if the lake were a treat he had prepared especially for them. And Ted felt all his discomfort drop away as he saw his friend's happiness, his desire to make them happy. God bless Bernie; he'd forget all this gloomy nonsense about artistic accomplishment. Are there many cabins up here, he asked.

Quite a few. But the lake is so big and the trees so thick we have a lot of privacy. He pointed with his pipe. There's the boathouse. And dock. No beach I'm afraid, it's all mud.

They stood in the shelter of the porch, rain hanging like lace from the gutters. Then Lee said Too cold out here for me, and they all went inside.

Paula was rummaging through groceries in the kitchen. Here, said Lee. Let me do something useful. A little cluster of polite words filled the air, Paula demurring, Lee insisting. Ted hoped that for once Lee would be graceful about helping in the kitchen, leave him and Bernie alone without getting sarcastic later about Man-Talk and Woman's Work. He tried to catch her eye but she was pulling her blonde hair into a knot and asking Paula about the mayonnaise.

Bernie offered him a beer and they drifted to the living room. Sitting down Ted had a moment of apprehension, like the beginning of a job interview. Bernie frowned and coaxed his pipe into life. How often had he used it as a prop; Ted knew his shyness. At last the bowl reddened. So tell me, Bernie said. How goes it with you?

Ted realized how much he'd rehearsed his answer: Not too bad. But I'll never be rich.

Bernie chuckled. Poor but honest.

Poor but poor. With Lee's job we get by. And I do some freelancing, write ad copy for a car dealer, that sort of thing. He shrugged. And how about you?

Ted was aware he had shifted too quickly, had seemed

to brush off Bernie's question in an attempt to be polite, reciprocal. Damn. He'd have to watch that.

Ah, Bernie said. The pastoral life of a college instructor. It's like being a country priest, really, with your life revolving around the feast days. Registration. Final exams. Department meetings on First Fridays.

You're getting tired of it?

It's a job, Ted. Like anything else it has its ups and downs. Actually I'm glad it's not excessively glamorous. This way I don't feel tied to it, committed. I can stay fluid, you know?

What would you do instead?

Sell hardware. Open a museum. I don't know. Paula wants to work as a photographer. She's pretty good. And I wouldn't mind getting back to the writing. It's been simmering in me for a long time.

That hint of justification. Ted felt the same prepared quality in Bernie's answer as in his own. He risked his question: Have you been able to get anything done?

Any writing, you mean? Dribs and drabs. I decided what I needed was to remove myself from pressure, you know? Work at my own pace without worrying about marketing a finished product. Of course I know that's not the way you go about it.

Yeah. It's out of the typewriter and into the mails.

You still work on a schedule?

Absolutely. Seems to be the only way I get anything done. Lee covers for me. I have tantrums if the phone rings.

You must really throw yourself into the thing.

The implied sympathy, the chance to speak of his frustrations with someone who would understand them, was a luxury. Jesus, he said. You spend hours wrestling with yourself, trying to keep your vision intact, your intensity undiminished. Sometimes I have to stick my head under the tap to get my wits back. And for what? You know what publishing is like these days. Paper costs going up all the time. Nothing gets printed unless it can be made into a movie. Everything is media. Crooked politicians sell their unwritten memoirs for thousands. I've got a great idea for a novel. It's about a giant shark who's possessed by a demon while swimming in the Bermuda Triangle. And the demon talks in CB lingo, see? There'll be recipes in the back.

Bernie laughed and Ted continued. Then the quarterlies, the places you expect to publish serious writing. They're falling all over themselves trying to be trendy, avant-garde. If you write in sentence fragments and leave plenty of blank space on the page, you're in. Pretentiousness disguised as trail-blazing. All the editors want to set themselves up as interpreters of a new movement. I hope they choke on their own jargon. Anti-meta-post-contemporary-surfictional literature. Balls.

He stopped for breath. I'm sorry, he said. Didn't mean to get carried away.

Not at all. It does me good to hear a tirade now and then. Reminds me of college, makes me feel ten years younger.

Still. He should not have spoken with such bitterness. It sounded like he was making excuses. Ted smiled, lightening his tone. The artist takes his lonely stand against the world.

As well he ought to. But really, Valentine, don't you get tired of beating your head against all that commercialism? Trying to compete with it? I mean, of course you do, but do you think it affects what you write?

Was it Bernie's solemnity that always made his questions sound so judgmental? Ted knew it was more than an issue of mannerisms. Bernie pondered things, thought them through; you respected his sincerity. Ted gave the only answer pride allowed: No, because the work can't exist in a vacuum. It has to get out there in the world, and reach people. Ted drained his beer and ventured to define the issue between them. You're saying it's better to be an Emily Dickinson, a violet by a mossy stone half-hidden to the eye, that sort of thing. Keep it in shoeboxes in the closet so you can remain uncorrupted.

Bernie turned his hands palms upward and managed to express dissent by spreading his white fingers. Just that it's possible to lose sight of what you set out to do. Even get too discouraged.

How quickly we've moved into position, Ted thought. Each of us defending our lives. He remembered his earlier resolution to speak tactfully, cushion any comparison between their accomplishments. And here was Bernie seeming to demand such comparison. How easy it would be to make some mention of his publications, play up some of the things he's muted in his letters, insist on Bernie's paying tribute to them. He even admitted to himself that beneath everything he'd wanted his success acknowledged. Like the high school loser who dreams of driving to the class reunion in a custom-made sports car. As if only those who knew your earlier weakness could verify your success.

But he would not indulge himself. Partly because, like his earlier outburst, it would threaten to say too much, and partly because he wanted this meeting to be without friction. Couldn't they rediscover their younger, untried selves? It was a kind of nostalgia. So he said I don't know, Bernie. You may be right. But the only way for me to accomplish anything is by competing with the market.

Bernie considered this, seemed to accept it as a final statement. He dumped his pipe into the fireplace. Ted noticed the beginning of a tonsure, a doorknob-sized patch of naked scalp. The sight enabled him to recapture all his tenderness. Shall we join the ladies, Bernie asked, rising.

They were sitting at the kitchen table with mugs of coffee. Well, Ted said, resting a hand on Lee's shoulder. I hope you haven't been bored. He meant it half as apology, half as warning: you'd better not be.

Au contraire, Lee answered. We've been trying to reconcile post-Hegelian dogma with Jamesian pragmatism. But she grinned.

And Paula said Actually, we were telling raunchy jokes. Give us ten more minutes.

He liked her. Her pinkness, plumpness. Like a neat little bird, all smooth lines and down. Her round good-humored chin. And Lee seemed to be doing all right with her.

I think it's quit raining, said Bernie. If you've got sturdy enough shoes we could take a hike.

It was still very wet under the trees. A careless tug at a branch might flip cold rainbow-edged drops down your back. And the sky was gray as concrete. But they enjoyed the silence, the soft sucking ground matted with last year's needles. They perched on a fallen tree at the lake's edge and chunked stones into the crisp water. Bernie explained it was too early, too cool for the black flies whose bites made bloody circles just beneath the skin.

How often do you get up here, Ted asked. Bernie told him about every other weekend when the weather was right. Ted launched into abundant, envious speech: They were lucky sons-of-bitches, did they know that back in Illinois there were only tame little man-made lakes, tidy parks, lines of Winnebagoes like an elephant graveyard, right Lee? As if complimenting this part of Bernie's life might restore some balance between them.

They walked back single file along the sunken trail. Ted was at the rear. Lee's blondeness looked whiter, milkier out here. Perhaps it was the heaviness of the dark green air, like the light just before a thunderstorm which plays up contrasts. Bernie and Paula's heads were the same shade of sleek brown, slipping in and out of his vision. It struck him that once again he was observing and being conscious of himself as an observer. It was a habit he'd fallen into, not necessarily a bad one. But he'd been working very hard at the writing lately (Lee had insisted on this vacation; he rather begrudged the time spent away from his desk) and this heightened self-awareness was a sign of strain. As if he couldn't really escape his work or the persona that went with it.

The Artist's impressions of a walk in the woods. The Artist's view on viewing. The Artist on Art. How do you get your ideas for stories, Mr. Valentine? Well, I simply exploit everything I come into contact with. One ended, of course, by losing all spontaneity. You saw people as characters, sunsets as an excuse for similes—

Bernie called a warning over his shoulder just as Ted felt a drop of rain slide down his nose. They quickened their pace to a trot as the rain fell, first in fat splatters that landed as heavily as frogs, then finer, harder. By the time they reached the porch their clothes were dark and dripping.

Fire, said Bernie. Coffee and hot baths, said Paula. The movement, the busyness, cheered them as much as the dry clothes. When at last they sat on each side of the stone fireplace, the odor of smoke working into their skins and hair, they all felt the same sense of shelter.

Damn, said Bernie. I wanted to take you fishing. But he looked comfortable, his pipe bobbing in his mouth.

Maybe tomorrow, said Paula. The rain had polished her skin, now the fire was warming it, bringing out different tints: apricot, cameo. She and Bernie made a peaceful, domestic couple. He could imagine them sitting like this, on either side of the fire, for the next thirty years. The retired Swiss toymaker and his wife.

But was Bernie happy? Did he feel, as Ted would have in his place, a sense of failure, of goals having shrunk. You never knew. Or, this visit would probably not allow him to learn. The time was too short to break down much of the politeness that passed between them as guest and host. Recapturing their former intimacy, that intensity, seemed as difficult as remembering what virginity had felt like. They should have left the wives behind, just come up here for a messy bachelor weekend of drinking and cards. This impulse moved him to ask if anyone wanted a whiskey.

They did. He passed glasses, leaned back into his chair.

Well, said Lee. It's too early to tell ghost stories.

Ted and I could talk about our misspent youth.

She wants something ghostly, Doyle, not ghastly.

Oh go ahead, Lee urged Bernie. Tell me something that can be used against him. She was at her most animated, perhaps from the first bite of the liquor. The Madonna is photographed for a Seagram's commercial. Go ahead, she repeated.

Tell her I was a football hero.

If you won't tell Paula about that indecent exposure thing.

Agreed. Ted gulped at his drink to induce the mood of nostalgia. One thing I'll always remember. You and me taking a bottle of strawberry wine up on the roof of the humanities building.

Did you really, said Paula.

We thought we were Bohemians, Bernie explained. Artistic, not ethnic.

We pretended it was absinthe.

A rooftop in Paris at the turn of the century.

I was James Joyce.

I was Oscar Wilde.

We were going to be paperback sensations.

We were full of shit.

I don't know, Ted objected. I mean, certainly we were naive. Who isn't at twenty? But you have to begin with wild idealism, dreams of glory. It's the raw fuel that gets you through the disappointments.

You mean the brute facts of editors, publishing.

Ted nodded. The manuscripts that come back stained with spaghetti sauce. The places that misspell your name. All the ambiguities of success. If we'd known what was actually involved in writing, we probably never would have attempted it.

When we leave here, Lee put in, we have to go to New York and talk with Ted's agent. You wouldn't believe the nastiness and wheeler-dealer stuff that goes on in that New York scene. It's like a court in Renaissance Italy. Intrigues within intrigues.

Bernie raised his eyebrows above the rim of his glasses. You have an agent now?

Yes. Since last November. He's trying to place the novel for me.

And you've finished the novel? Paula, do we have champagne? I've been hearing about this book for years.

Well, I've finished the draft. If it's accepted I'll no doubt have to do rewrites. Damn Lee for bringing up the agent; it would only make Bernie more aware of the gap between their achievements. He searched for some way to de-escalate things. You should be glad you've escaped all this messiness so far. Retained your youthful innocence.

The bottom log of the fire, which had been threatening to burn through, now collapsed. Red winking sparks flew up the black column of the chimney as the fire assumed a new pattern. Bernie squatted in front of it raking the embers into place. He spoke without turning around.

You know, I read that piece you had in—what was it—the one about the schizophrenic?

"The Lunatic." He sat up a little straighter in his chair, adopted the carefully pleasant expression with which he received criticism.

Ted was very happy with that piece, Lee informed everyone. And the magazine did a good production job. She beamed at him, sweetly proud of making a contribution to the discussion. He wished she hadn't spoken, had left him free to frame his reply after listening to Bernie. But she was only repeating what she'd heard him say.

That's it, "The Lunatic." I admire the language use, the control in the thing. The way you managed to milk images. But—

that terrible pause—

I felt there was a kind of slickness in the thing, almost glibness. I mean, you're talking about a man who's having a mental breakdown. And you treat that rather flippantly. Perhaps you intended it, but I wondered why.

There were a number of replies he could make. He settled for the most general: The story is something of a satire, Bernie. Think of all the literature that's dealt with madness. It's an extremely well-trodden path. You simply can't write about the subject straightforwardly anymore. People expect something new.

Bernie frowned and rubbed his jaw under the dense beard. Ted knew, watching him, that Bernie had thought his argument through. Had prepared it carefully, step by step, like he did everything.

I thought, Bernie continued, that your complaint against avant-garde fiction was its emphasis on form over content. Blank space on the page, tortured syntax, that sort of thing. The writing screaming for attention. Aren't you agreeing with them now? Saying, in effect, rather than exploring the individuality of this character or situation, I'll dress it up in a different package. Pretend not to take it seriously.

Both women were watching rather helplessly, as if they realized their little store of soothing words and social graces would be of no use. And the defense that came to Ted's mind (Nobody writes like Henry James anymore. Or, more crudely, Your aesthetic is outdated) sounded like a small boy's taunts. So he said I do take the character and situation seriously. That doesn't mean one can't experiment with form, depart from rigid storytelling conventions. Otherwise you wind up repeating what's already been done. Repeating yourself too.

Bernie shook his head. Again that gesture of judgment. I'm sorry, but I see it as a response to the market. The thing I was talking about earlier. You tailor the writing to what the editors are buying. Maybe unconsciously. You're certainly not writing about the giant sharks. But it's still a form of corruption.

And what, in particular, is being corrupted?

I hope I can put this right. It's like, that increased self-consciousness, that authorial presence that's always thrusting itself between the reader and the page—see, I'm telling this story, you're reading it, I'll try to amuse you, watch this—is rather paralyzing. What you're doing, a general you (a parenthetical smile), is making disclaimers for the piece, covering your tracks. I'll play this a little tongue-in-cheek so I won't be called to account for it.

You might as well dispute abstraction in painting, Bernie. Form can't be entirely neglected in favor of content. Otherwise we might still be seeing those Victorian pictures of blind children and noble hounds.

It runs the danger of shallowness, Ted.

Well, I suppose the only way to avoid the dangers is not to write anything at all.

He hadn't realized how angry he was until he heard himself speak. Damn the whiskey, damn his own thin-skinned hatred of criticism. He was too quick to take things as insults. Now, having said the one unforgivable thing, there was no retreat. The four of them sat without looking at each other. Bernie plunged into a fury of pipe-cleaning, tamping, lighting, as another man might have cracked his knuckles. The rain filled the silence, gusting against the windows and shrinking the warmth of the fire.

Finally Paula said I'm going to see what there is for dinner. Ted stood up as soon as she did, muttering about another drink. He paused in the kitchen only long enough to slosh the liquor in his glass. Paula opened the refrigerator and said Hm, fried chicken maybe? He said Fine and walked out the back door.

The rain had brought an early blue darkness. He could still make out the shoreline, the agitation of the lake as the rain pocked its surface. Far away on his left shone one point of light, a white feeble thing that he could not imagine indicated human companionship, laughter, warmth. Even though he stood under the ledge, moisture beaded his clothes like dew. He gave himself over completely to the melancholy of it all. The only consolation he could find was the thought that argument was a form of intimacy.

When he came back inside both women were busy in the kitchen. Can I peel potatoes or something, he asked. They sat him at the kitchen table with a bowl of strawberries to hull. A little boy hiding behind women. He didn't want to go back to the living room where he knew Bernie would be sitting. Lee and Paula seemed determined to speak of nothing more serious than gravy making. He watched Lee as she moved between stove and sink, a little surprised at her vivacity. As if she had formed some alliance without his being aware of it. Her hair had dried in soft waves with a hint of fuzziness; a looser style than she usually wore. Although she spoke to him occasionally, she did not meet his eye. It didn't seem that she was avoiding him; rather, she was busy, he was extraneous, incidental . . .

But he was projecting his injured feeling onto her, his gloom and self-pity. Snap out of it, he told himself. You're going to be here another thirty-six hours.

That realization must have been shared, must have been what got them through the evening. The act of sitting down to food together restored some tenuous rhythm. Afterward Paula suggested Monopoly. They let the bright cardboard, the little mock triumphs and defeats, absorb them. Ted thought how harmless all greed and competition were when reduced to this scale, then he berated himself for facile irony.

At midnight Bernie yawned and said I'm down to thirty dollars and Marvin Gardens. Somebody buy me out.

Who's ahead? Add it up, Paula suggested.

It turned out to be Ted, who felt hulking and foolish raking in his pile of paper money. Flimsy pastel trophies. He was duly congratulated. He did a parody of the young Lindbergh acknowledging cheers. Modestly tugging his forelock. The tycoon needs some rest, he said, and they all agreed.

Goodnight. Goodnight, and if you need extra blankets they're at the top of the closet. I'm sure we'll be fine. Bernie latched the door and said Maybe it'll clear up tomorrow.

It took Ted a moment to realize he was speaking of the rain.

He waited until everyone was settled before he used the bathroom. No use risking more sprightly greetings. When he got back Lee was in bed, her fair hair spilling from the rolled sheets like corn silk.

He wanted her to start talking first, but her eyes were squeezed shut against the bed-side lamp. Well, he said. Too neutral, inadequate.

Would you turn that light off?

He reached, produced darkness. She sighed and said Much better. He lay for a moment accustoming himself to the black stillness, the smell of the rough pine boards. The mattress was sparse, lopsided. It seemed to have absorbed the dank cold of the cabin. He burrowed into its thin center. Then the even sound of Lee's breathing told him she was falling asleep. Almost angry, he shook her shoulder.

What? She was more irritated than sleepy.

Don't fall asleep. I wanted to talk to you.

Go ahead.

He waited a moment to control himself. You're not making it very easy.

She twisted inside the sheets until she rested on one elbow, facing him. All right, I'll make it easy. What the hell were you arguing about? I hate it when you start talking like that. All that rhetoric. You take it so seriously. Was any of it worth snapping at him like that?

Of course I take it seriously. He was accusing me of shallowness. Corruption.

Oh boy. Lee drawled her sarcasm. And you couldn't forget your literary reflexes for one minute.

No. I guess I couldn't.

Her hand emerged from the darkness and gave his shoulder a series of small tentative pats. Poor Ted. Her voice was kinder. The pats continued, light but persistent, as if a moth were battering itself against him. He suppressed the impulse to brush it away.

Why poor Ted?

Because sometimes I think you don't enjoy what you're doing at all. The writing I mean. You get so upset.

Don't be silly.

I know. The Agony and the Ecstasy. She yawned. Well I hope you two make up. They're nice folks.

Her lips, seeming disembodied in the blind darkness, found his chin, his mouth. Good night.

Good night.

He waited until she was asleep or pretending to be asleep. He got up, put on his pants and sweater, and padded into the kitchen. Turned on the fluorescent light over the sink.

Her cruelest words spoken in her softest voice. Her revenge, thinking or unthinking, for all the times he'd shut himself away from her. He'd had his work to do. His sulks and tantrums. His insistence on the loftiness of his purpose, the promise of his future. His monstrous self-importance. The whole edifice threatened.

He didn't enjoy it.

Of course you were gratified at the high points. The little recognitions and deference. Of course you made a point of bemoaning the labor involved. Saying it drove you mad with frustration. That was expected. But enjoyment? Where was the enjoyment?

The pines still rattled in the wind. The rain was a dim silver fabric without seam or edge, unrolling from the sky.

He thought of walking into it, losing himself in all that fragrant blackness, in the thick gunmetal lake. Oh he was tired of his cleverness, his swollen sensitivity. Better to crouch under a rock in the rain and reduce yourself to nerve, skin, and muscle. But his self-consciousness would not allow this either. It told him it would be melodramatic, a petulant gesture. Bad form.

Something, some weight, passed over the floorboards behind him and he turned, his nostrils cocked. It was the ticklish perfume of pipe smoke that reached him first.

H'lo, he said, and Bernie's mouth curved around the polished wooden stem of his pipe. He managed to walk to where Ted was standing by the back door without seeming to advance in a straight line.

Foul weather, he said nodding. He too had resumed his clothes.

I'll say. They watched the faint movement of water on water. Then Bernie said Drink?

Sure.

While there was still tension perceptible in their cautious responses, in Bernie's stiff-wristed pouring of drinks, it seemed a formality. The simple fact of coming together like this was a promise of reconciliation. When Bernie was seated across from him, Ted began with the obvious. I'm sorry about tonight. I was way out of line.

I guess I provoked you, Ted. I'm jealous. I admit it.

And I am insecure and narcissistic.

Would it be too maudlin to wish we were kids again?

Ted shook his head. In some ways I think I'm still twenty. The prize student who's always fawning for approval, pats on the head.

You're too hard on yourself.

Yes. I am. He blinked at the checked tablecloth, trying to get his eyes to focus on its pattern.

And I'm not hard enough. Bernie smiled. Such confessions.

They're necessary. Who else can absolve us of our sordid pasts?

Now the room has the contours and atmosphere of all rooms in which people stay awake talking. The fluorescent light is grainy, staring. The clutter on the kitchen table—ketchup bottle, sagging butter dish, tin of Nestle's Quik, the rowdy crudded ashtray—the world is narrowed into these, a little universe that the eyes return to again and again. Now it begins, the sorting and testing of words. Remember that words are not symbols of other words. There are words which, when tinkered with, become honest representatives of the cresting blood, the fine living net of nerves. Define rain. Or even joy. It can be done.

AMY HEMPEL was born in Chicago in 1951 and moved to California, the setting of her stories, in her teens. She had, as she told one interviewer, "your basic nonlinear education" at four different colleges before taking a fiction workshop at Columbia three years ago with Gordon Lish, later her editor at Knopf, the publisher of her first volume of stories, *Reasons to Live* (1985). These stories, more than half of which had never been published before, have received a strong, enthusiastic, and thoughtful critical response. They deserve it, especially the story that follows here, one of the most tender and haunting pieces of fiction to be published in America since World War II. "The whole book is true," Amy Hempel has said. "I am really interested in resilience. There was a period in my life—my 20's were miserable—when every other day there was some horrible tragedy. Dr. Christiaan Barnard said, 'Suffering isn't ennobling, recovery is.' If I have a motto for this particular bunch of stories, that's what it is." Some of the stories are one-page vignettes. The novelist Sheila Ballantyne, writing in *The New York Times Book Review*, has discussed Miss Hempel's truncated style: "Minimalism has its uses, and can achieve surprisingly varied effects. At its worst, [it] is a kind of fraudulent tic that serves to hide a vacuum or defend against feeling. At its best it can force meaning to leap from the page. Amy Hempel has succeeded in revealing both the substance and intelligence beneath the surface of a spare, elliptical prose. This kind of minimalism has room for the largest themes."

There is the largest human charity at the heart of these stories and a courageous art. Amy Hempel lives in San Francisco and New York and is a contributing editor to *Vanity Fair*.

Amy Hempel

BEG, SL TOG, INC, CONT, REP

The mohair was scratchy, the stria too bulky, but the homespun tweed was right for a small frame. I bought slate-blue skeins softened with flecks of pink, and size-10 needles for a sweater that was warm but light. The pattern I chose was a two-tone V-neck with an optional six-stitch cable up the front. Pullovers mess the hair, but I did not want to buttonhole the first time out.

From a needlework book, I learned to cast on. In the test piece, I got the gauge and correct tension. Knit and purl came naturally, as though my fingers had been rubbed in spiderwebs at birth. The sliding of the needles was as rhythmic as water.

Learning to knit was the obvious thing. The separation of tangled threads, the working-together of raveled ends into something tangible and whole—this *mending* was as confounding as the groom who drives into a stop sign on the way to his wedding. Because symptoms mean just what they are. What about the woman whose empty hand won't close because she cannot grasp that her child is gone?

"Would you get me a Dr Pep, gal, and would you turn up the a-c?"

I put down my knitting. In the kitchen I found some sugar-free, and took it, with ice, to Dale Anne. It was August. Air-conditioning lifted her hair as she pressed the button on the Niagara bed. Dr. Diamond insisted she have it the last month. She was also renting a swivel TV table and a vibrating chaise—the Niagara adjustable home.

231

When the angle was right, she popped a Vitamin E and rubbed the oil where the stretch marks would be.

I could be doing this, too. But I had had the procedure instead. That was after the father had asked me, Was I sure? To his credit, he meant—sure that I *was*, not sure was it he. He said he had never made a girl pregnant before. He said that he had never even made a girl late.

I moved in with Dale Anne to help her near the end. Her husband is often away—in a clinic or in a lab. He studies the mind. He is not a doctor yet, but we call him one by way of encouragement.

I had picked up a hank of yarn and was winding it into a ball when the air-conditioner choked to a stop.

Dale Anne sighed. "I will *cook* in this robe. Would you get me that flowered top in the second drawer?"

While I looked for the top, Dale Anne twisted her hair and held it tight against her head. She took one of my double-pointed six-inch needles and wove it in and out of her hair, securing the twist against her scalp. With the hair off her face, she looked wholesome and very young—"the person you would most like to go camping with if you couldn't have sex," is how she put it.

I turned my back while Dale Anne changed. She was as modest as I was. If the house caught fire one night, we would both die struggling to hook brassieres beneath our gowns.

I went back to my chair, and as I did, a sensational cramp snapped me over until I was nearly on the floor.

"Easy, gal—what's the trouble?" Dale Anne started out of bed to come see.

I said it sometimes happens since the procedure, and Dale Anne said, "Let's not talk about that for at *least* ten years."

I could not think of what to say to that. But I didn't have to. The front door opened, earlier than it usually did. It was Dr. Diamond, home from the world of spooks and ghosts and loony bins and Ouija boards. I knew that a lack of concern for others was a hallmark of mental illness, so I straightened up and said, after he'd kissed his pregnant wife, "You look hot, Dr. Diamond. Can I get you a drink?"

I buy my materials at a place in the residential section. The owner's name is Ingrid. She is a large Norwegian woman who spells needles "kneedles." She wears sample knits she makes up for the class demonstrations. The vest she wore the day before will be hanging in the window.

There are always four or five women at Ingrid's round oak table, knitting through a stretch they would not risk alone.

Often I go there when I don't need a thing. In the small back room that is stacked high with pattern books, I can sift for hours. I scan the instructions abbreviated like musical notation: *K10, sl 1, K2 tog, psso, sl 1, K10 to end.* I feel I could *sing* these instructions. It is compression of language into code; your ability to decipher it makes you privy to the secrets shared by Ingrid and the women at the round oak table.

In the other room, Ingrid tells a customer she used to knit two hundred stitches a minute.

I scan the French and English catalogues, noting the longer length of coat. There is so much to absorb on each visit.

Mary had a little lamb, I am humming when I leave the shop. *Its feet were—its fleece was white as wool.*

Dale Anne wanted a nap, so Dr. Diamond and I went out for margaritas. At La Rondalla, the colored lights on the Virgin tell you every day is Christmas. The food arrives on manhole covers and mariachis fill the bar. Dr. Diamond said that in Guadalajara there is a mariachi college that turns out mariachis by the classful. But I could tell that these were not graduates of even mariachi high school.

I shooed the serenaders away, but Dr. Diamond said they meant well.

Dr. Diamond likes for people to mean well. He could be president of the Well-Meaning Club. He has had a buoyant feeling of fate since he learned Freud died the day he was born.

He was the person to talk to, all right, so I brought up the stomach pains I was having for no bodily reason that I could think of.

"You know how I think," he said. "What is it you can't stomach?"

I knew what he was asking.

"Have you thought about how you will feel when Dale Anne has the baby?" he asked.

With my eyes, I wove strands of tinsel over the Blessed Virgin. That was the great thing about knitting, I thought— everything was fiber, the world a world of natural resource.

"I thought I would burn that bridge when I come to it," I said, and when he didn't say anything to that, I said, "I guess I will think that there is a mother who *kept* hers."

"*One* of hers might be more accurate," Dr. Diamond said.

I arrived at the yarn shop as Ingrid turned over the *Closed* sign to *Open*. I had come to buy Shetland wool for a Fair Isle sweater. I felt nothing would engage my full attention more than a pattern of ancient Scottish symbols and alternate bands of delicate design. Every stitch in every color is related to the one above, below, and to either side.

I chose the natural colors of Shetland sheep—the chalky brown of the Moorit, the blackish brown of the black sheep, fawn, gray, and pinky beige from a mixture of Moorit and white. I held the wool to my nose, but Ingrid said it was fifty years since the women of Fair Isle dressed the yarn with fish oil.

She said the yarn came from Sheep Rock, the best pasture on Fair Isle. It is a ten-acre plot that is four hundred feet up a cliff, Ingrid said. "Think what a man has to go through to harvest the wool."

I was willing to feel an obligation to the yarn, and to the hardy Scots who supplied it. There was heritage there, and I could keep it alive with my hands.

*   *   *

Dale Anne patted capers into a mound of raw beef, and spread some onto toast. It was not a pretty sight. She offered some to me, and I said not a chance. I told her Johnny Carson is someone else who won't go near that. I said, "Johnny says he won't eat steak tartare because he has seen things hurt worse than that get better."

"Johnny was never pregnant," Dale Anne said.

When the contractions began, I left a message with the hospital and with Dr. Diamond's lab. I turned off the air-conditioner and called for a cab.

"Look at you," Dale Anne said.

I told her I couldn't help it. I get rational when I panic. The taxi came in minutes.

"Hold on," the driver said. "I know every bump in these roads, and I've never been able to miss one of them."

Dale Anne tried to squeeze my wrist, but her touch was weightless, as porous as wet silk.

"When this is over . . ." Dale Anne said.

When the baby was born, I did not go far. I sublet a place on the other side of town. I filled it with patterns and needles and yarn. It was what I did in the day. On a good day, I made a front and two sleeves. On a bad day, I ripped out stitches from neck to hem. For variety, I made socks. The best ones I made had beer steins on the sides, and the tops spilled over with white angora foam.

I did not like to work with sound in the room, not even the sound of a fan. Music slowed me down, and there was a great deal to do. I planned to knit myself a mailbox and a car, perhaps even a dog and a lead to walk him.

I blocked the finished pieces and folded them in drawers.

Dr. Diamond urged me to exercise. He called from time to time, looking in. He said exercise would set me straight, and why not have some fun with it? Why not, for example, tap-dancing lessons?

I told him it would be embarrassing because the rest of

the class would be doing it right. And with all the knitting, there wasn't time to dance.

Dale Anne did not look in. She had a pretty good reason not to.

The day I went to see her in the hospital, I stopped at the nursery first. I saw the baby lying face down. He wore yellow duck-print flannels. I saw that he was there—and then I went straight home.

That night the dreams began. A giant lizard ate people from the feet upwards, swallowing the argyles on the first bite, then drifting into obscurity like a ranger of forgotten death. I woke up remembering and, like a chameleon, assumed every shade of blame.

Asleep at night, I went to an elegant ball. In the center of the dance floor was a giant aquarium. Hundreds of goldfish swam inside. At a sign from the bandleader, the tank was overturned. Until someone tried to dance on the fish, the floor was aswirl with gold glory.

Dr. Diamond told a story about the young daughter of a friend. The little girl had found a frog in the yard. The frog appeared to be dead, so her parents let her prepare a burial site—a little hole surrounded by pebbles. But at the moment of the lowering, the frog, which had only been stunned, kicked its legs and came to.

"Kill him!" the girl had shrieked.

I began to take walks in the park. In the park, I saw a dog try to eat his own shadow, and another dog—I am sure of it—was herding a stand of elms. I stopped telling people how handsome their dogs were; too many times what they said was, "You want him?"

When the weather got nicer, I stayed home to sit for hours.

I had accidents. Then I had bigger ones. But the part that hurt was never the part that got hurt.

The dreams came back and back until they were just— again. I wished that things would stay out of sight the way they did in mountain lakes. In one that I know, the water is so cold, gas can't form to bring a corpse to the surface.

Although you would not want to think about the bottom of the lake, what you can say about it is—the dead stay down.

Around that time I talked to Dr. Diamond.

The point that he wanted to make was this: that conception was not like walking in front of traffic. No matter how badly timed, it was, he said, an affirmation of life.

"You have to believe me here," he said. "Do you see that this is true? Do you know this about yourself?"

"I do and I don't," I said.

"You do and you *do*," he said.

I remembered when another doctor made the news. A young retarded boy had found his father's gun, and while the family slept, he shot them all in bed. The police asked the boy what he had done. But the boy went mute. He told them nothing. Then they called in the doctor.

"We know *you* didn't do it," the doctor said to the boy, "but tell me, did the *gun* do it?"

And yes, the boy was eager to tell him just what that gun had done.

I wanted the same out, and Dr. Diamond wouldn't let me have it.

"Dr. Diamond," I said, "I am giving up."

"Now you are ready to begin," he said.

I thought of Andean alpaca because that was what I planned to work up next. The feel of that yarn was not the only wonder—there was also the name of it: Alpaquita Superfina.

Dr. Diamond was right.

I was ready to begin.

Beg, sl tog, inc, cont, rep.

Begin, slip together, increase, continue, repeat.

Dr. Diamond answered the door. He said Dale Anne had run to the store. He was leaving, too, flying to a conference back East. The baby was asleep, he said, I should make myself at home.

I left my bag of knitting in the hall and went into Dale Anne's kitchen. It had been a year. I could have looked in on the baby. Instead, I washed the dishes that were soaking in the sink. The scouring pad was steel wool waiting for knitting needles.

The kitchen was filled with specialized utensils. When Dale Anne couldn't sleep she watched TV, and that's where the stuff was advertised. She had a thing to core tomatoes—it was called a Tomato Shark—and a metal spaghetti wheel for measuring out spaghetti. She had plastic melon-ballers and a push-in device that turned ordinary cake into ladyfingers.

I found pasta primavera in the refrigerator. My fingers wanted to knit the cold linguini, laying precisely cabled strands across the oily red peppers and beans.

Dale Anne opened the door.

"*Look* out, gal," she said, and dropped a shopping bag on the counter.

I watched her unload ice cream, potato chips, carbonated drinks, and cake.

"It's been a long time since I walked into a market and expressed myself," she said.

She turned to toss me a carton of cigarettes.

"Wait for me in the bedroom," she said. "*West Side Story* is on."

I went in and looked at the color set. I heard the blender crushing ice in the kitchen. I adjusted the contrast, then Dale Anne handed me an enormous peach daiquiri. The goddamn thing had a tide factor.

Dale Anne left the room long enough to bring in the take-out chicken. She upended the bag on a plate and picked out a leg and a wing.

"I like my dinner in a bag and my life in a box," she said, nodding toward the TV.

We watched the end of the movie, then part of a lame detective program. Dale Anne said the show *owed* Nielsen four points, and reached for the *TV Guide*.

"Eleven-thirty," she read. "*The Texas Whiplash Massacre*: Unexpected stop signs were their weapon."

"Give me that," I said.

Dale Anne said there was supposed to be a comet. She said we could probably see it if we watched from the living room. Just to be sure, we pushed the couch up close to the window. With the lights off, we could see everything without it seeing us. Although both of us had quit, we smoked at either end of the couch.

"Save my place," Dale Anne said.

She had the baby in her arms when she came back in. I looked at the sleeping child and thought, Mercy, Land Sakes, Lordy Me. As though I had aged fifty years. For just a moment then I wanted nothing that I had and everything I did not.

"He told his first joke today," Dale Anne said.

"What do you mean he told a joke?" I said. "I didn't think they could talk."

"Well, he didn't really *tell* a joke—he poured his orange juice over his head, and when I started after him, he said, 'Raining?' "

" 'Raining?' That's what he said? The kid is a genius," I told Dale Anne. "What Art Linkletter could do with this kid."

Dale Anne laid him down in the middle of the couch, and we watched him or watched the sky.

"What a gyp," Dale Anne said at dawn.

There had not been a comet. But I did not feel cheated, or even tired. She walked me to the door.

The knitting bag was still in the hall.

"Open it later," I said. "It's a sweater for him."

But Dale Anne had to see it then.

She said the blue one matched his eyes and the camel one matched his hair. The red would make him glow, she said, and then she said, "Help me out."

Cables had become too easy; three more sweaters had pictures knitted in. They buttoned up the front. Dale Anne held up a parade of yellow ducks.

There were the Fair Isles, too—one in the pattern called Tree of Life, another in the pattern called Hearts.

It was an excess of sweaters—a kind of precaution, a rehearsal against disaster.

Dale Anne looked at the two sweaters still in the bag. "Are you really okay?" she said.

*   *   *

The worst of it is over now, and I can't say that I am glad. Lose that sense of loss—you have gone and lost something else. But the body moves toward health. The mind, too, in steps. One step at a time. Ask a mother who has just lost a child, How many children do you have? "Four," she will say, "—three," and years later, "Three," she will say, "—four."

It's the little steps that help. Weather, breakfast, crossing with the light—sometimes it is all the pleasure I can bear to sleep, and know that on a rack in the bath, damp wool is pinned to dry.

Dale Anne thinks she would like to learn to knit. She measures the baby's crib and I take her over to Ingrid's. Ingrid steers her away from the baby pastels, even though they are machine-washable. Use a pure wool, Ingrid says. Use wool in a grown-up shade. And don't boast of your achievements or you'll be making things for the neighborhood.

On Fair Isle there are only five women left who knit. There is not enough lichen left growing on the island for them to dye their yarn. But knitting machines can't produce their designs, and they keep on, these women, working the undyed colors of the sheep.

I wait for Dale Anne in the room with the patterns. The songs in these books are like lullabies to me.

K tog rem st. Knit together remaining stitches.

Cast off loosely.

JAYNE ANNE PHILLIPS was born in West Virginia in 1952. She was educated at West Virginia University and the University of Iowa, where she has been a Teaching-Writing Fellow at the Iowa Writers' Workshop. Three collections of her short stories have been published to date: *Sweethearts* and *Counting* (in limited editions) and *Black Tickets* (Delacorte/Seymour Lawrence, 1979) from which the following story is taken. Of *Black Tickets* Tillie Olsen wrote: "The unmistakable work of early genius trying her range, a dazzling virtuoso range that is distinctly her own. Jayne Anne Phillips is 'the real thing.' " She is also the recipient of the Sue Kaufman Prize from the American Academy of Arts and Letters, and a National Endowment for the Arts Fellowship in Fiction. Her first novel, *Machine Dreams* (1984), concerns the impact of the Vietnam War on a family of West Virginians. Nadine Gordimer's assessment of this novel is in the same key as Tillie Olsen's response to Phillips' short stories: "No number of books read or films seen," writes Miss Gordimer, "can deaden one to the intimate act of art by which this wonderful young writer has penetrated the definitive experience of her generation."

Jayne Anne Phillips

HOME

I'm afraid Walter Cronkite has had it, says Mom. Roger Mudd always does the news now—how would you like to have a name like that? Walter used to do the conventions and a football game now and then. I mean he would sort of appear, on the sidelines. Didn't he? But you never see him anymore. Lord. Something is going on.

Mom, I say. Maybe he's just resting. He must have made a lot of money by now. Maybe he's tired of talking about elections and mine disasters and the collapse of the franc. Maybe he's in love with a young girl.

He's not the type, says my mother. You can tell *that* much. No, she says, I'm afraid it's cancer.

My mother has her suspicions. She ponders. I have been home with her for two months. I ran out of money and I wasn't in love, so I have come home to my mother. She is an educational administrator. All winter long after work she watches television and knits afghans.

Come home, she said. Save money.

I can't possibly do it, I said. Jesus, I'm twenty-three years old.

Don't be silly, she said. And don't use profanity.

She arranged a job for me in the school system. All day, I tutor children in remedial reading. Sometimes I am so discouraged that I lie on the couch all evening and watch television with her. The shows are all alike. Their laugh tracks are conspicuously similar; I think I recognize a repetition of certain professional laughters. This laughter marks off the half hours.

Finally I make a rule: I won't watch television at night. I will watch only the news, which ends at 7:30. Then I will go to my room and do God knows what. But I feel sad that she sits there alone, knitting by the lamp. She seldom looks up.

Why don't you ever read anything? I ask.

I do, she says. I read books in my field. I read all day at work, writing those damn proposals. When I come home I want to relax.

Then let's go to the movies.

I don't want to go to the movies. Why should I pay money to be upset or frightened?

But feeling something can teach you. Don't you want to learn anything?

I'm learning all the time, she says.

She keeps knitting. She folds yarn the color of cream, the color of snow. She works it with her long blue needles, piercing, returning, winding. Yarn cascades from her hands in long panels. A pattern appears and disappears. She stops and counts; so many stitches across, so many down. Yes, she is on the right track.

Occasionally I offer to buy my mother a subscription to something mildly informative: *Ms., Rolling Stone, Scientific American*.

I don't want to read that stuff, she says. Just save your money. Did you hear Cronkite last night? Everyone's going to need all they can get.

Often, I need to look at my mother's old photographs. I see her sitting in knee-high grass with a white gardenia in her hair. I see her dressed up as the groom in a mock wedding at a sorority party, her black hair pulled back tight. I see her formally posed in her cadet nurse's uniform. The photographer has painted her lashes too lushly, too long; but her deep red mouth is correct.

The war ended too soon. She didn't finish her training. She came home to nurse only her mother and to meet my father at a dance. She married him in two weeks. It took twenty years to divorce him.

When we traveled to a neighboring town to buy my high school clothes, my mother and I would pass a certain road that turned off the highway and wound to a place I never saw.

There it is, my mother would say. The road to Wonder Bar. That's where I met my Waterloo. I walked in and he said, 'There she is. I'm going to marry that girl.' Ha. He sure saw me coming.

Well, I asked, Why did you marry him?

He was older, she said. He had a job and a car. And Mother was so sick.

My mother doesn't forget her mother.

Never one bedsore, she says. I turned her every fifteen minutes. I kept her skin soft and kept her clean, even to the end.

I imagine my mother at twenty-three; her black hair, her dark eyes, her olive skin and that red lipstick. She is growing lines of tension in her mouth. Her teeth press into her lower lip as she lifts the woman in the bed. The woman weighs no more than a child. She has a smell. My mother fights it continually; bathing her, changing her sheets, carrying her to the bathroom so the smell can be contained and flushed away. My mother will try to protect them both. At night she sleeps in the room on a cot. She struggles awake feeling something press down on her and suck her breath: the smell. When my grandmother can no longer move, my mother fights it alone.

I did all I could, she sighs. And I was glad to do it. I'm glad I don't have to feel guilty.

No one has to feel guilty, I tell her.

And why not? says my mother. There's nothing wrong with guilt. If you are guilty, you should feel guilty.

My mother has often told me that I will be sorry when she is gone.

I think. And read alone at night in my room. I read those books I never read, the old classics, and detective stories. I can get them in the library here. There is only one bookstore; it sells mostly newspapers and *True Confessions* oracles. At Kroger's by the checkout counter I buy a few paperbacks, best sellers, but they are usually bad.

The television drones on downstairs.

I wonder about Walter Cronkite.

When was the last time I saw him? It's true his face was pouchy, his hair thinning. Perhaps he is only cutting it shorter. But he had that look about the eyes—

He was there when they stepped on the moon. He forgot he was on the air and he shouted, 'There . . . there . . . now—We have Contact!' Contact. For those who tuned in late, for the periodic watchers, he repeated: 'One small step . . .'

I was in high school and he was there with the body count. But he said it in such a way that you knew he wanted the war to end. He looked directly at you and said the numbers quietly. Shame, yes, but sorrowful patience, as if all things had passed before his eyes. And he understood that here at home, as well as in starving India, we would pass our next lives as meager cows.

My mother gets *Reader's Digest*. I come home from work, have a cup of coffee, and read it. I keep it beside my bed. I read it when I am too tired to read anything else. I read about Joe's kidney and Humor in Uniform. Always, there are human interest stories in which someone survives an ordeal of primal terror. Tonight it is Grizzly! Two teen-agers camping in the mountains are attacked by a bear. Sharon is dragged over a mile, unconscious. She is a good student loved by her parents, an honest girl loved by her boyfriend. Perhaps she is not a virgin; but in her heart, she is virginal. And she lies now in the furred arms of a beast. The grizzly drags her quietly, quietly. He will care for her all the days of his life . . . Sharon, his rose.

But alas. Already, rescuers have organized. Mercifully, her boyfriend is not among them. He is sleeping en route to the nearest hospital; his broken legs have excused him. In a few days, Sharon will bring him his food on a tray. She is spared. She is not demure. He gazes on her face, untouched but for a long thin scar near her mouth. Sharon says she remembers nothing of the bear. She only knows the tent was ripped open, that its heavy canvas fell across her face.

I turn out my light when I know my mother is sleeping.

By then my eyes hurt and the streets of the town are deserted.

My father comes to me in a dream. He kneels beside me, touches my mouth. He turns my face gently toward him.

Let me see, he says. Let me see it.

He is looking for a scar, a sign. He wears only a towel around his waist. He presses himself against my thigh, pretending solicitude. But I know what he is doing; I turn my head in repulsion and stiffen. He smells of a sour musk and his forearms are black with hair. I think to myself, It's been years since he's had an erection—

Finally he stands. Cover yourself, I tell him.

I can't, he says, I'm hard.

On Saturdays I go to the Veterans of Foreign Wars rummage sales. They are held in the drafty basement of a church, rows of collapsible tables piled with objects. Sometimes I think I recognize the possessions of old friends: a class ring, yearbooks, football sweaters with our high school insignia. Would this one have fit Jason?

He used to spread it on the seat of the car on winter nights when we parked by country churches and graveyards. There seemed to be no ground, just water, a rolling, turning, building to a dull pain between my legs.

What's wrong? he said, What is it?

Jason, I can't . . . This pain—

It's only because you're afraid. If you'd let me go ahead—

I'm not afraid of you, I'd do anything for you. But Jason, why does it hurt like this?

We would try. But I couldn't. We made love with our hands. Our bodies were white. Out the window of the car, snow rose up in mounds across the fields. Afterward, he looked at me peacefully, sadly.

I held him and whispered, Soon, soon . . . we'll go away to school.

His sweater. He wore it that night we drove back from the football awards banquet. Jason made All-State but he hated football.

I hate it, he said. So what? he said, that I'm out there puking in the heat? Screaming 'Kill' at a sandbag?

I held his award in my lap, a gold man frozen in midleap. Don't play in college, I said. Refuse the money.

He was driving very slowly.

I can't see, he said, I can't see the edges of the road . . . Tell me if I start to fall off.

Jason, what do you mean?

He insisted I roll down the window and watch the edge. The banks of the road were gradual, sloping off into brush and trees on either side. White lines at the edge glowed up in dips and turns.

We're going to crash, he said.

No, Jason. You've driven this road before. We won't crash.

We're crashing, I know it, he said. Tell me, tell me I'm OK—

Here on the rummage sale table, there are three football sweaters. I see they are all too small to have belonged to Jason. So I buy an old soundtrack, *The Sound of Music*. Air, Austrian mountains. And an old robe to wear in the mornings. It upsets my mother to see me naked; she looks at me so curiously, as though she didn't recognize my body.

I pay for my purchases at the cash register. Behind the desk I glimpse stacks of *Reader's Digests*. The Ladies Auxiliary turns them inside out, stiffens and shellacs them. They make wastebaskets out of them.

I give my mother the record. She is pleased. She hugs me.

Oh, she says, I used to love the musicals. They made me happy. Then she stops and looks at me.

Didn't you do this? she says. Didn't you do this in high school?

Do what?

Your class, she says. You did *The Sound of Music*.

Yes, I guess we did.

What a joke. I was the beautiful countess meant to marry Captain von Trapp before innocent Maria stole his heart. Jason was a threatening Nazi colonel with a bit part. He should have sung the lead but sports practices interfered with rehearsals. Tall, blond, aged in makeup under the lights, he encouraged sympathy for the bad guys and overshadowed the star. He appeared just often enough to make the play ridiculous.

My mother sits in the blue chair my father used for years.

Come quick, she says. Look—

She points to the television. Flickerings of Senate chambers, men in conservative suits. A commentator drones on about tax rebates.

There, says my mother. Hubert Humphrey. Look at him.

It's true. Humphrey is different, changed from his former toady self to a dessicated old man, not unlike the discarded shell of a locust. Now he rasps into the microphone about the people of these great states.

Old Hubert's had it, says my mother. He's a death mask.

That's what he gets for sucking blood for thirty years.

No, she says. No, he's got it too. Look at him! Cancer. Oh.

For God's sake, will you think of something else for once?

I don't know what you mean, she says. She goes on knitting.

All Hubert needs, I tell her, is a good roll in the hay.

You think that's what everyone needs.

Everyone does need it.

They do not. People aren't dogs. I seem to manage perfectly well without it, don't I?

No, I wouldn't say that you do.

Well, I do. I know your mumbo jumbo about sexuality. Sex is for those who are married, and I wouldn't marry again if it was the Lord himself.

Now she is silent. I know what's coming.

Your attitude will make you miserable, she says. One man after another. I just want you to be happy.

I do my best.

That's right, she says. Be sarcastic.

I refuse to answer. I think about my growing bank account. Graduate school, maybe in California. Hawaii. Somewhere beautiful and warm. I will wear few clothes and my skin will feel the air.

What about Jason, says my mother. I was thinking of him the other day.

Our telepathy always frightens me. Telepathy and beyond. Before her hysterectomy, our periods often came on the same day.

If he hadn't had that nervous breakdown, she says softly, do you suppose—

No, I don't suppose.

I wasn't surprised that it happened. When his brother was killed, that was hard. But Jason was so self-centered. You're lucky the two of you split up. He thought everyone was out to get him. Still, poor thing.

Silence. Then she refers in low tones to the few months Jason and I lived together before he was hospitalized.

You shouldn't have done what you did when you went off to college. He lost respect for you.

It wasn't respect for me he lost—He lost his fucking mind if you remember—

I realize I'm shouting. And shaking. What is happening to me?

My mother stares.

We'll not discuss it, she says.

She gets up. I hear her in the bathroom. Water running into the tub. Hydrotherapy. I close my eyes and listen. Soon, this weekend. I'll get a ride to the university a few hours away and look up an old lover. I'm lucky. They always want to sleep with me. For old time's sake.

I turn down the sound of the television and watch its silent pictures. Jason's brother was a musician; he taught Jason to play the pedal steel. A sergeant in uniform delivered the message two weeks before the State Play-Off games. Jason appeared at my mother's kitchen door with the telegram. He looked at me, opened his mouth, backed off wordless in the dark. I pretend I hear his pedal steel; its sweet country whine might make me cry. And I recognize this silent movie—I've seen it four times. Gregory Peck and his submarine crew escape fallout in Australia, but not for long. The cloud is coming. And so they run rampant in auto races and love affairs. But in the end, they close the hatch and put out to sea. They want to go home to die.

Sweetheart? my mother calls from the bathroom. Could you bring me a towel?

Her voice is quavering slightly. She is sorry. But I never know what part of it she is sorry about. I get a towel from the linen closet and open the door of the steamy bathroom. My mother stands in the tub, dripping, shivering a little. She is so small and thin; she is smaller than I. She has two long scars on her belly, operations of the womb, and one breast is misshapen, sunken, indented near the nipple.

I put the towel around her shoulders and my eyes smart. She looks at her breast.

Not too pretty is it, she says. He took out too much when he removed that lump—

Mom, it doesn't look so bad.

I dry her back, her beautiful back which is firm and unblemished. Beautiful, her skin. Again, I feel the pain in my eyes.

But you should have sued the bastard, I tell her. He didn't give a shit about your body.

We have an awkward moment with the towel when I realize I can't touch her any longer. The towel slips down and she catches it as one end dips into the water.

Sweetheart, she says. I know your beliefs are different than mine. But have patience with me. You'll just be here a few more months. And I'll always stand behind you. We'll get along.

She has clutched the towel to her chest. She is so fragile, standing there, naked, with her small shoulders. Suddenly I am horribly frightened.

Sure, I say, I know we will.

I let myself out of the room.

Sunday my mother goes to church alone. Daniel calls me from D.C. He's been living with a lover in Oregon.

Now he is back East; she will join him in a few weeks. He is happy, he says. I tell him I'm glad he's found someone who appreciates him.

Come on now, he says. You weren't that bad.

I love Daniel, his white and feminine hands, his thick chestnut hair, his intelligence. And he loves me, though I don't know why. The last few weeks we were together I lay beside him like a piece of wood. I couldn't bear his touch; the moisture his penis left on my hips as he rolled against me. I was cold, cold. I huddled in blankets away from him.

I'm sorry, I said. Daniel, I'm sorry please—what's wrong with me? Tell me you love me anyway . . .

Yes, he said, of course I do. I always will. I do.

Daniel says he has no car, but he will come by bus. Is there a place for him to stay?

Oh yes, I say. There's a guest room. Bring some Trojans. I'm a hermit with no use for birth control. Daniel, you don't know what it's like here.

I don't care what it's like. I want to see you.

Yes, I say. Daniel, hurry.

When he arrives the next weekend, we sit around the table with my mother and discuss medicine. Daniel was a medic in Vietnam. He smiles at my mother. She is charmed though she has reservations; I see them in her face. But she enjoys having someone else in the house, a presence; a male. Daniel's laughter is low and modulated. He talks softly, smoothly: a dignified radio announcer, an accomplished anchorman.

But when I lived with him, he threw dishes against the wall. And jerked in his sleep, mumbling. And ran out of the house with his hands across his eyes.

After we first made love, he smiled and pulled gently away from me. He put on his shirt and went to the bathroom. I followed and stepped into the shower with him. He faced me, composed, friendly, and frozen. He stood as though guarding something behind him.

Daniel, turn around. I'll soap your back.

I already did.

Then move, I'll stand in the water with you.

He stepped carefully around me.

Daniel, what's wrong? Why won't you turn around?

Why should I?

I'd never seen him with his shirt off. He'd never gone swimming with us, only wading, alone, down Point Reyes Beach. He wore long-sleeved shirts all summer in the California heat.

Daniel, I said, you've been my best friend for months. We could have talked about it.

He stepped backwards, awkwardly, out of the tub and put his shirt on.

I was loading them on copters, he told me. The last one was dead anyway; he was already dead. But I went after him, dragged him in the wind of the blades. Shrapnel and napalm caught my arms, my back. Until I fell, I thought it was the other man's blood in my hands.

They removed most of the shrapnel, did skin grafts for the burns. In three years since, Daniel made love five times; always in the dark. In San Francisco he must take off his shirt for a doctor; tumors have grown in his scars. They bleed through his shirt, round rust-colored spots.

Face-to-face in bed, I tell him I can feel the scars with my fingers. They are small knots on his skin. Not large, not ugly. But he can't let me, he can't let anyone, look: he says he feels wild, like raging, and then he vomits. But maybe, after they remove the tumors—Each time they operate, they reduce the scars.

We spend hours at the veterans' hospital waiting for appointments. Finally they schedule the operation. I watch the black-ringed wall clock, the amputees gliding by in chairs that tick on the linoleum floor. Daniel's doctors curse about lack of supplies; they bandage him with gauze and layers of Band-Aids. But it is all right. I buy some real bandages. Every night I cleanse his back with a sponge and change them.

In my mother's house, Daniel seems different. He has shaved his beard and his face is too young for him. I can only grip his hands.

I show him the house, the antiques, the photographs on

the walls. I tell him none of the objects move; they are all cemented in place. Now the bedrooms, my room.

This is it, I say. This is where I kept my Villager sweaters when I was seventeen, and my dried corsages. My cups from the Tastee Freeze labeled with dates and boys' names.

The room is large, blue. Baseboards and wood trim are painted a spotless white. Ruffled curtains, ruffled bedspread. The bed itself is so high one must climb into it. Daniel looks at the walls, their perfect blue and white.

It's a piece of candy, he says.

Yes, I say, hugging him, wanting him.

What about your mother?

She's gone to meet friends for dinner. I don't think she believes what she says, she's only being my mother. It's all right.

We take off our clothes and press close together. But something is wrong. We keep trying. Daniel stays soft in my hands. His mouth is nervous; he seems to gasp at my lips.

He says his lover's name. He says they aren't seeing other people.

But I'm not other people. And I want you to be happy with her.

I know. She knew . . . I'd want to see you.

Then what?

This room, he says. This house. I can't breathe in here.

I tell him we have tomorrow. He'll relax. And it is so good just to see him, a person from my life.

So we only hold each other, rocking.

Later, Daniel asks about my father.

I don't see him, I say. He told me to choose.

Choose what?

Between them.

My father. When he lived in this house, he stayed in the dark with his cigarette. He sat in his blue chair with the lights and television off, smoking. He made little money; he said he was self-employed. He was sick. He grew dizzy when he looked up suddenly. He slept in the basement. All night he sat reading in the bathroom. I'd hear him walking up and down the dark steps at night. I lay in the dark and listened. I believed he would strangle my mother, then walk upstairs and strangle me. I believed we were guilty; we had done something terrible to him.

Daniel wants me to talk.

How could she live with him, I ask. She came home from work and got supper. He ate it, got up and left to sit in his chair. He watched the news. We were always sitting there, looking at his dirty plates. And I wouldn't help her. She should wash them, not me. She should make the money we lived on. I didn't want her house and his ghost with its cigarette burning in the dark like a sore. I didn't want to be guilty. So she did it. She sent me to college; she paid for my safe escape.

Daniel and I go to the Rainbow, a bar and grill on Main Street. We hold hands, play country songs on the jukebox, drink a lot of salted beer. We talk to the barmaid and kiss in the overstuffed booth. Twinkle lights blink on and off above us. I wore my burgundy stretch pants in here when I was twelve. A senior pinched me, then moved his hand slowly across my thigh, mystified, as though erasing the pain.

What about tonight? Daniel asks. Would your mother go out with us? A movie? A bar? He sees me in her, he likes her. He wants to know her.

Then we will have to watch television.

We pop popcorn and watch the late movies. My mother stays up with us, mixing whiskey sours and laughing. She gets a high color in her cheeks and the light in her eyes glimmers up. She is slipping, slipping back and she is beautiful, oh, in her ankle socks, her red mouth and her armor of young girl's common sense. She has a beautiful laughter. She and Daniel end by mock arm wrestling; he pretends defeat and goes upstairs to bed.

My mother hears his door close. He's nice, she says. You've known some nice people, haven't you?

I want to make her back down.

Yes, he's nice, I say. And don't you think he respects

me? Don't you think he truly cares for me, even though we've slept together?

He seems to, I don't know. But if you give them that, it costs them nothing to be friends with you.

Why should it cost? The only cost is what you give, and you can tell if someone is giving it back.

How? How can you tell? By going to bed with every man you take a fancy to?

I wish I took a fancy oftener, I tell her. I wish I wanted more. I can be good to a man, but I'm afraid—I can't be physical, not really . . .

You shouldn't.

I should. I want to, for myself as well. I don't think— I've ever had an orgasm.

What? she says, Never? Haven't you felt a sort of building up, and then a dropping off . . . a conclusion? like something's over?

No, I don't think so.

You probably have, she assures me. It's not necessarily an explosion. You were just thinking too hard, you think too much.

But she pauses.

Maybe I don't remember right, she says. It's been years, and in the last years of the marriage I would have died if your father had touched me. But before, I know I felt something. That's partly why I haven't . . . since . . . what if I started wanting it again? Then it would be hell.

But you have to try to get what you want—

No, she says. Not if what you want would ruin everything. And now, anyway. Who would want me?

I stand at Daniel's door. The fear is back; it has followed me upstairs from the dead dark bottom of the house. My hands are shaking. I'm whispering . . . Daniel, don't leave me here.

I go to my room to wait. I must wait all night, or something will come in my sleep. I feel its hands on me now, dragging, pulling. I watch the lit face of the clock: three, four, five. At seven I go to Daniel. He sleeps with his pillow in his arms. The high bed creaks as I get in. Please now, yes . . . he is hard. He always woke with erections . . . inside me he feels good, real, and I tell him no, stop, wait . . . I hold the rubber, stretch its rim away from skin so it smooths on without hurting and fills with him . . . now again, here, yes but quiet, be quiet . . . oh Daniel . . . the bed is making noise . . . yes, no, but be careful, she . . . We move and turn and I forget about the sounds. We push against each other hard, he is almost there and I am almost with him and just when it is over I think I hear my mother in the room directly under us—But I am half dreaming. I move to get out of bed and Daniel holds me. No, he says, stay.

We sleep and wake to hear the front door slam.

Daniel looks at me.

There's nothing to be done, I say. She's gone to church.

He looks at the clock. I'm going to miss that bus, he says. We put our clothes on fast and Daniel moves to dispose of the rubber—how? the toilet, no, the wastebasket— He drops it in, bends over, retrieves it. Finally he wraps it in a Kleenex and puts it in his pocket. Jesus, he swears. He looks at me and grins. When I start laughing, my eyes are wet.

I take Daniel to the bus station and watch him out of sight. I come back and strip the bed, bundle the sheets in my arms. This pressure in my chest . . . I have to clutch the sheets tight, tighter—

A door clicks shut. I go downstairs to my mother. She refuses to speak or let me near her. She stands by the sink and holds her small square purse with both hands. The fear comes. I hug myself, press my hands against my arms to stop shaking. My mother runs hot water, soap, takes dishes from the drainer. She immerses them, pushes them down, rubbing with a rag in a circular motion.

Those dishes are clean, I tell her. I washed them last night.

She keeps washing. Hot water clouds her glasses, the window in front of us, our faces. We all disappear in steam. I watch the dishes bob and sink. My mother begins to sob. I move close to her and hold her. She smells as she used to smell when I was a child and slept with her.

I heard you, I heard it, she says. Here, in my own house. Please, how much can you expect me to take? I don't know what to do about anything . . .

She looks into the water, keeps looking. And we stand here just like this.

LORRIE MOORE was born in Glens Falls, New York, in 1957. She received a B.A. from St. Lawrence University and an M.F.A. from Cornell. In 1976 she was awarded first prize in the *Seventeen* magazine short-story contest, and in 1983 a Granville Hicks Memorial Fellowship at Yaddo. Her short stories have appeared in *Mss, Epoch, Storyquarterly,* and *Cosmopolitan*. Many of the stories in her first collection, *Self-Help,* improvise on the idea of a self-help manual: "How to Become a Writer" (which follows here), "How to Be an Other Woman" and "The Kid's Guide to Divorce." The novelist Hilma Wolitzer called all the stories "surprising, moving and absolutely delightful." Alison Lurie found them "wry, poetic, [the] stories of love and loss make me want to laugh and cry at the same time." Writing in *Vanity Fair,* the critic James Wolcott, describing Lorrie Moore as a "nervy, still-maturing writer, sharp, flicking, on-target," placed her firmly within the exciting contemporary tradition of new American fiction: "[She] is part of that remarkable constellation of promising young women writers which includes Jayne Anne Phillips, Mary Robison, Amy Hempel, Susan Minot, Linda Svendsen, T. Gertler, and, though she's a bit older than the others, Bobbie Ann Mason—a post-napalm, post-barricades group that has retreated from apocalypse now and quietly pitched its tent in the living room, where the TV is always on and the rustle of a cellophane bag fills the snack bowl with greasy chips." Much has been said about Miss Moore's incredible sense of humor. The story "What Is Seized," however, from *Self-help,* captures the terrible sadness of a daughter's heartbroken affection for her dead mother: Lorrie Moore's eye for mischief and both cruel and funny absurdities also penetrates most profoundly the tragic failures of love.

Lorrie Moore

HOW TO BECOME A WRITER

First, try to be something, anything, else. A movie star/astronaut. A movie star/missionary. A movie star/kindergarten teacher. President of the World. Fail miserably. It is best if you fail at an early age—say, fourteen. Early, critical disillusionment is necessary so that at fifteen you can write long haiku sequences about thwarted desire. It is a pond, a cherry blossom, a wind brushing against sparrow wing leaving for mountain. Count the syllables. Show it to your mom. She is tough and practical. She has a son in Vietnam and a husband who may be having an affair. She believes in wearing brown because it hides spots. She'll look briefly at your writing, then back up at you with a face blank as a donut. She'll say: "How about emptying the dishwasher?" Look away. Shove the forks in the fork drawer. Accidentally break one of the freebie gas station glasses. This is the required pain and suffering. This is only for starters.

In your high school English class look only at Mr. Killian's face. Decide faces are important. Write a villanelle about pores. Struggle. Write a sonnet. Count the syllables: nine, ten, eleven, thirteen. Decide to experiment with fiction. Here you don't have to count syllables. Write a short story about an elderly man and woman who accidentally shoot each other in the head, the result of an inexplicable malfunction of a shotgun which appears mysteriously in their living room one night. Give it to Mr. Killian as your final project. When you get it back, he has written on it: "Some of your images are quite nice, but you have no sense of plot." When you are home, in the privacy of your own room, faintly scrawl in pencil beneath his black-inked comments: "Plots are for dead people, pore-face."

Take all the babysitting jobs you can get. You are great with kids. They love you. You tell them stories about old people who die idiot deaths. You sing them songs like "Blue Bells of Scotland," which is their favorite. And when they are in their pajamas and have finally stopped pinching each other, when they are fast asleep, you read every sex manual in the house, and wonder how on earth anyone could ever do those things with someone they truly loved. Fall asleep in a chair reading Mr. McMurphy's *Playboy*. When the McMurphys come home, they will tap you on the shoulder, look at the magazine in your lap, and grin. You will want to die. They will ask you if Tracey took her medicine all right. Explain, yes, she did, that you promised her a story if she would take it like a big girl and that seemed to work out just fine. "Oh, marvelous," they will exclaim.

Try to smile proudly.

Apply to college as a child psychology major.

As a child psychology major, you have some electives. You've always liked birds. Sign up for something called "The Ornithological Field Trip." It meets Tuesdays and Thursdays at two. When you arrive at Room 134 on the first day of class, everyone is sitting around a seminar table talking about metaphors. You've heard of these. After a short, excruciating while, raise your hand and say diffidently, "Excuse me, isn't this Bird-watching One-oh-one?" The class stops and turns to look at you. They seem to all have one face—giant and blank as a vandalized clock. Someone with a beard booms out, "No, this is Creative Writing." Say: "Oh—right," as if perhaps you knew all along. Look down at your schedule. Wonder how the hell you ended up here. The computer, apparently, has made an error. You start to get up to leave and then don't. The lines at the registrar this week are huge. Perhaps you should stick with this mistake. Perhaps your creative writing isn't all that bad. Perhaps it is fate. Perhaps this is what your dad meant when he said, "It's the age of computers, Francie, it's the age of computers."

Decide that you like college life. In your dorm you meet many nice people. Some are smarter than you. And some, you notice, are dumber than you. You will continue, unfortunately, to view the world in exactly these terms for the rest of your life.

The assignment this week in creative writing is to narrate a violent happening. Turn in a story about driving with your Uncle Gordon and another one about two old people who are accidentally electrocuted when they go to turn on a badly wired desk lamp. The teacher will hand them back to you with comments: "Much of your writing is smooth and energetic. You have, however, a ludicrous notion of plot." Write another story about a man and a woman who, in the very first paragraph, have their lower torsos accidentally blitzed away by dynamite. In the second paragraph, with the insurance money, they buy a frozen yogurt stand together. There are six more paragraphs. You read the whole thing out loud in class. No one likes it. They say your sense of plot is outrageous and incompetent. After class someone asks you if you are crazy.

Decide that perhaps you should stick to comedies. Start dating someone who is funny, someone who has what in high school you called a "really great sense of humor" and what now your creative writing class calls "self-contempt giving rise to comic form." Write down all of his jokes, but don't tell him you are doing this. Make up anagrams of his old girlfriend's name and name all of your socially handicapped characters with them. Tell him his old girlfriend is in all of your stories and then watch how funny he can be, see what a really great sense of humor he can have.

Your child psychology advisor tells you you are neglecting courses in your major. What you spend the most time on should be what you're majoring in. Say yes, you understand.

In creative writing seminars over the next two years, everyone continues to smoke cigarettes and ask the same things: ''But does it work?'' ''Why should we care about this character?'' ''Have you earned this cliché?'' These seem like important questions.

On days when it is your turn, you look at the class hopefully as they scour your mimeographs for a plot. They look back up at you, drag deeply, and then smile in a sweet sort of way.

You spend too much time slouched and demoralized. Your boyfriend suggests bicycling. Your roommate suggests a new boyfriend. You are said to be self-mutilating and losing weight, but you continue writing. The only happiness you have is writing something new, in the middle of the night, armpits damp, heart pounding, something no one has yet seen. You have only those brief, fragile, untested moments of exhilaration when you know: you are a genius. Understand what you must do. Switch majors. The kids in your nursery project will be disappointed, but you have a calling, an urge, a delusion, an unfortunate habit. You have, as your mother would say, fallen in with a bad crowd.

Why write? Where does writing come from? These are questions to ask yourself. They are like: Where does dust come from? Or: Why is there war? Or: If there's a God, then why is my brother now a cripple?

These are questions that you keep in your wallet, like calling cards. These are questions, your creative writing teacher says, that are good to address in your journals but rarely in your fiction.

The writing professor this fall is stressing the Power of the Imagination. Which means he doesn't want long descriptive stories about your camping trip last July. He wants you to start in a realistic context but then to alter it. Like recombinant DNA. He wants you to let your imagination sail, to let it grow big-bellied in the wind. This is a quote from Shakespeare.

Tell your roommate your great idea, your great exercise of imaginative power: a transformation of Melville to contemporary life. It will be about monomania and the fish-eat-fish world of life insurance in Rochester, New York. The first line will be "Call me Fishmeal," and it will feature a menopausal suburban husband named Richard, who because he is so depressed all the time is called "Mopey Dick" by his witty wife Elaine. Say to your roommate: "Mopey Dick, get it?" Your roommate looks at you, her face blank as a large Kleenex. She comes up to you, like a buddy, and puts an arm around your burdened shoulders. "Listen, Francie," she says, slow as speech therapy. "Let's go out and get a big beer."

The seminar doesn't like this one either. You suspect they are beginning to feel sorry for you. They say: "You have to think about what is happening. Where is the story here?"

The next semester the writing professor is obsessed with writing from personal experience. You must write from what you know, from what has happened to you. He wants deaths, he wants camping trips. Think about what has happened to you. In three years there have been three things: you lost your virginity; your parents got divorced; and your brother came home from a forest ten miles from the Cambodian border with only half a thigh, a permanent smirk nestled into one corner of his mouth.

About the first you write: "It created a new space, which hurt and cried in a voice that wasn't mine, 'I'm not the same anymore, but I'll be okay.' "

About the second you write an elaborate story of an old married couple who stumble upon an unknown land mine in their kitchen and accidentally blow themselves up. You call it: "For Better or for Liverwurst."

About the last you write nothing. There are no words for this. Your typewriter hums. You can find no words.

*　　*　　*

At undergraduate cocktail parties, people say, "Oh, you write? What do you write about?" Your roommate, who has consumed too much wine, too little cheese, and no crackers at all, blurts: "Oh, my god, she always writes about her dumb boyfriend."

Later on in life you will learn that writers are merely open, helpless texts with no real understanding of what they have written and therefore must half-believe anything and everything that is said of them. You, however, have not yet reached this stage of literary criticism. You stiffen and say, "I do not," the same way you said it when someone in the fourth grade accused you of really liking oboe lessons and your parents really weren't just making you take them.

Insist you are not very interested in any one subject at all, that you are interested in the music of language, that you are interested in—in—syllables, because they are the atoms of poetry, the cells of the mind, the breath of the soul. Begin to feel woozy. Stare into your plastic wine cup.

"Syllables?" you will hear someone ask, voice trailing off, as they glide slowly toward the reassuring white of the dip.

Begin to wonder what you do write about. Or if you have anything to say. Or if there even is such a thing as a thing to say. Limit these thoughts to no more than ten minutes a day; like sit-ups, they can make you thin.

You will read somewhere that all writing has to do with one's genitals. Don't dwell on this. It will make you nervous.

Your mother will come visit you. She will look at the circles under your eyes and hand you a brown book with a brown briefcase on the cover. It is entitled: *How to Become a Business Executive*. She has also brought the *Names for Baby* encyclopedia you asked for; one of your characters, the aging clown–school teacher, needs a new name. Your mother will shake her head and say: "Francie, Francie, remember when you were going to be a child psychology major?''

Say: "Mom, I like to write."

She'll say: "Sure you like to write. Of course. Sure you like to write."

Write a story about a confused music student and title it: "Schubert Was the One with the Glasses, Right?" It's not a big hit, although your roommate likes the part where the two violinists accidentally blow themselves up in a recital room. "I went out with a violinist once," she says, snapping her gum.

Thank god you are taking other courses. You can find sanctuary in nineteenth-century ontological snags and invertebrate courting rituals. Certain globular mollusks have what is called "Sex by the Arm." The male octopus, for instance, loses the end of one arm when placing it inside the female body during intercourse. Marine biologists call it "Seven Heaven." Be glad you know these things. Be glad you are not just a writer. Apply to law school.

From here on in, many things can happen. But the main one will be this: you decide not to go to law school after all, and, instead, you spend a good, big chunk of your adult life telling people how you decided not to go to law school after all. Somehow you end up writing again. Perhaps you go to graduate school. Perhaps you work odd jobs and take writing courses at night. Perhaps you are working on a novel and writing down all the clever remarks and intimate personal confessions you hear during the day. Perhaps you are losing your pals, your acquaintances, your balance.

You have broken up with your boyfriend. You now go out with men who, instead of whispering "I love you," shout: "Do it to me, baby." This is good for your writing.

Sooner or later you have a finished manuscript more or less. People look at it in a vaguely troubled sort of way and say, "I'll bet becoming a writer was always a fantasy of yours, wasn't it?" Your lips dry to salt. Say that of all the fantasies possible in the world, you can't imagine being a writer even making the top twenty. Tell them you were going to be a child psychology major. "I bet," they always sigh, "you'd be great with kids." Scowl fiercely. Tell them you're a walking blade.

Quit classes. Quit jobs. Cash in old savings bonds. Now you have time like warts on your hands. Slowly copy all of your friends' addresses into a new address book.

Vacuum. Chew cough drops. Keep a folder full of fragments.

> *An eyelid darkening sideways.*
> *World as conspiracy.*
> *Possible plot? A woman gets on a bus.*
> *Suppose you threw a love affair and nobody came.*

At home drink a lot of coffee. At Howard Johnson's order the cole slaw. Consider how it looks like the soggy confetti of a map: where you've been, where you're going— "You Are Here," says the red star on the back of the menu.

Occasionally a date with a face blank as a sheet of paper asks you whether writers often become discouraged. Say that sometimes they do and sometimes they do. Say it's a lot like having polio.

"Interesting," smiles your date, and then he looks down at his arm hairs and starts to smooth them, all, always, in the same direction.

A Selected Bibliography

TONI CADE BAMBARA

Gorilla, My Love (1971); *The Sea Birds Are Still Alive* (1977).

ANN BEATTIE
Distortions (1974); *Chilly Scenes of Winter* (1976); *Secrets and Surprises* (1979); *Falling In Place* (1980); *Love Always* (1985).

SALLIE BINGHAM

After Such Knowledge (1959); *The Touching Hand* (1967); *The Way It Is Now* (1972).

LAURIE COLWIN

Passion and Affect (1974); *Shine On Bright and Dangerous Object* (1975); *Happy All The Time* (1978); *The Lone Pilgrim* (1981).

ANITA DESAI

Cry The Peacock (1963); *Voices In The City* (1965); *Bye-Bye Blackbird* (1968); *Where Shall We Go This Summer* (1975); *Fire On The Mountain* (1977); *Games At Twilight* (1978); *Clear Light Of Day* (1980); *In Custody* (1985).

ELLEN GILCHRIST

In The Land Of Dreamy Dreams (1981); *The Annunciation* (1983); *Victory Over Japan* (1984).

JOANNE GREENBERG, pseudonym Hannah Green

The King's Persons (1963); *I Never Promised You A Rose Garden* (1964); *The Monday Voices* (1965); *Summering* (1966); *In This Sign* (1970); *Rites of Passage* (1972); *Founder's Praise* (1976); *High Crimes & Misdemeanors* (1980); *A Season of Delight* (1981); *The Far Side of Victory* (1983).

AMY HEMPEL

Reasons To Live (1985).

ELLA LEFFLAND

Mrs. Munck (1970); *Love Out Of Season* (1974); *Rumors of Peace* (1979); *Last Courtesies & Other Stories* (1980).

PENELOPE LIVELY

The Road To Lichfield (1977); *Nothing Missing But The Samovar* (1978); *Treasures Of Time* (1979); *Judgement Day* (1980); *Next To Nature, Art* (1982); *Perfect Happiness* (1983); *Corruption* (1984).

BOBBIE ANN MASON

Shiloh And Other Stories (1982); *In Country* (1985).

LORRIE MOORE

Self-Help (1985).

CYNTHIA OZICK

Trust (1966); *The Pagan Rabbi and Other Stories* (1971); *Bloodshed* (1976); *Levitation* (1982); *The Cannibal Galaxy* (1983); *Art & Ardor* (1983).

BETTE PESETSKY

Stories Up To A Point (1982); *Author From A Savage People* (1983); *Digs* (1984).

JAYNE ANNE PHILLIPS

Black Tickets (1979); *Machine Dreams* (1984).

MARY ROBISON

Days (1979); *Oh* (1981); *An Amateur's Guide To The Night* (1983).

JEAN THOMPSON

The Gasoline Wars (1979); *My Wisdom* (1982); *Little Face* (1983).

ANNE TYLER

If Morning Ever Comes (1965); *The Tin Can Tree* (1966); *A Slipping Down Life* (1970); *The Clock Winder* (1973); *Celestial Navigation* (1975); *Searching For Caleb* (1976); *Earthly Possessions* (1977); *Morgan's Passing* (1980); *Dinner At The Homesick Restaurant* (1982); *The Accidental Tourist* (1985).

FAY WELDON

The Fat Woman's Joke (1967), republished as *And The Wife Ran Away* (1968); *Down Among The Women* (1971); *Words of Advice*, one-act play, (1974); *Female Friends* (1975); *Remember Me* (1976); *Praxis* (1979); *Puffball* (1980); *Watching Me, Watching You* (1981); *The President's Child* (1982); *The Life and Loves Of A She-Devil* (1983); *Letters To Alice* (1985).

ELLEN WILBUR

Wind and Birds and Human Voices (1984).

JOY WILLIAMS

State of Grace (1973); *The Changeling* (1978); *Taking Care* (1982).